THE WAYFARERS WAR

BOOK THREE - THE SUNSTONE SAGA

NICOLIN ODEL

CONTENTS

TRIGGER WARNINGS

This story include scenes of.

- Abuse

- Alcohol

- Animal death

- Attempted rape

- Blood

- Bones

- Death

- Drugs

- Gore

- Kidnapping

- Murder

- Miscarriage

- Profanity

- Pregnancy

- Slavery

- Sexual Content

- Violence

- War

Chapter One

RYK

It was a world of sapphire skies and floating islands. Levitating iceberg-shaped land masses dotted the horizon, and the islands were riddled with colorful crystalline forests.

Captivated, Hata Vasara stared at the scene in amazement. Then the pain tore at her shoulder where the four-armed man, Hear-fan Skaad, had seared a hole through it. Nearly the diameter of a finger. She touched it tenderly, said finger fitting nearly perfectly. *No blood.* The spell had cauterized the wound. Hata had fled from the Skaad Lân. Retreated from Hear-fan Skaad. She doubted that he'd been killed when she collapsed the mountain and caused it to crush through the Gate around him. Hata looked back at the similar Gate she had fled through. She stood on a minor island with only her and the ominous archway. *I ran from that man pretending to be a god. Feigning to be the almighty Primus, the creator.* Hata shook her head. *He is powerful. He could come after me at any second.* She cautiously walked to the edge and peeked over the side to see white clouds and sparkling seas thousands of feet below. No landmass, only the sea stretching for miles on end. *Teras's thunder. Where am I?* A wave of dizziness quivered through her.

Hata found a thick chain spiked into the earth near the island's edge. The chain stretched across the abyss toward another floating landmass nearly a hundred feet away. Broken black iron panels clung to the chain at intervals. *This used to be a bridge.* She imagined there used to be two such chains across the void, set with the flat pieces of iron. She knelt, grasped the chain, and tried to shake it, the links nearly as big as her hand. It swayed a bit but did not come loose. *I can't do this. I don't have the strength to carry myself across.* Agony burnt in her shoulder.

A ghastly howl echoed from the gateway behind her. She turned, and three of the Skaad hounds leaped through the portal. They lifted their heads at the sight of her and snarled, hackles raised. Their black matted fur was dust-covered. *From destroying my home...Oitilla.* Their jagged joint bones protruded unnaturally from their forelegs.

They dashed toward her.

Hata dropped her spear, slapped her hands together, and then raised them to the sky, palms upward. She *created* the piercing stalagmites directly beneath two of the hounds. The spikes erupted from the floating earth, crystal-flecked veins throughout. The two hounds were skewered, screaming, black blood gushing down the columns.

The last hound was fast, nearly upon her.

Hata created another column of the earth at her feet as the hound leaped at her. She soared away from the beast's snapping jaws and landed painfully with a *thud* a dozen feet away. A tingling sense pulled Hata's focus to the steel tip of the spear that lay discarded near the hound.

The hound turned and snarled, circling, readying to renew its attack.

Hata clung to the metal of the spear in her mind. She took control of the weapon, which zipped into the air, spinning rapidly as its slingshot orbited around her. She released it as it hissed through the air toward the hound.

The beast screamed as it took it in the side, causing the hound and spear to be carried a few feet before thudding into the ground, skewering it. The hound shrieked and gnashed at the shaft, jutting from its side as it was pinned to the ground.

Hata Vasara, the Sunstone, strode over, grasped the shaft, and called upon the earth to swallow the beast. She pulled the weapon free as the hound's shrieks became muffled as the soil engulfed it. Then there was silence.

Suddenly, a cacophony of howls and drawn-out wailing echoed through the gateway.

Enough of this. Hata shaped a foothold of the earth beneath her feet and raised it into the air. She floated skyward. Instead of making for the island directly across from her, Hata floated upward toward one of the hundreds of massive islands above her. She looked down just in time to see a horde of screeching *Children of Skaad* pour through the Gateway like a black wave.

Hata studied the islands. Most were covered in crystal trees and glimmering rock formations. She noticed small animals darting around the forest floor. *A food source, perhaps,* she pondered, her stomach growling. She continued, kneeling on her little cone of earth, hands grasping tight to the edges. The pain in her shoulder threatened to make her pass out. *By Teras's mountain, I need to set down and rest.* Then she saw movement in the distance. Some sort of *crate* moving by its own volition from one island to the next. She squinted and realized the thing was connected to two thick cords with gears churning above the cart.

A dark shape hissed past her ear, and a repetitive *thumping* sound grew in the wind. Then, another projectile thudded into the earth right between her knees, where she knelt. *An arrow?* She leaned over and wheeled her platform about. Another strange crate with two blurred spinning blades atop it thundered toward her. A figure stood on its forefront, leveling a crossbow at her.

Hata lifted her hands, shaking her head to indicate she meant no harm.

The figure continued aiming at her but held its fire. The flying contraption circled about her. She saw another figure in a divot, huddled in front of the one, leveling the weapon at her. They wore hard round helmets and thick round pains of dark glass on their eyes while covering their faces with outlandishly painted pieces of cloth. They circled once more. Hata stayed still, hands held up. The one figure lowered the crossbow and pointed toward the island that the crate on the rope was slowly plodding along toward.

Hata nodded in answer and leaned in that direction. As she approached, she realized extravagant structures were also among this island's crystal trees. Towers of multi-colored minerals reached up toward her as they descended. It was the largest of all the islands around them. Farms built on step-like plateaus skirted the buildings of grainy wood, glimmering metal, vivid stone, and crystal.

Hata heard a faint shout and looked over to the craft escorting her. The figure was waving and pointing down to a flat area near the edge of the island city. She nodded again and soon landed on the smooth stone area. Flecks of crystal could be seen in the rock at her feet.

The *thumping* aircraft landed nearby. The back end of it had a deafening, rumbling box with colorful crystal gems repeatedly blinking with light, causing steaming puffs of azure and crimson. The sound halted. The whirling blades of the flying thing puttered to a stop, and the two short people climbed a small ladder down the side and tramped toward her. They looked just over four feet tall, but their bodies were broad-shouldered and sturdy. They wore pieces of cloth painted with teeth or wings over the lower halves of their faces and tight round helms upon their heads with black glass covering their eyes.

One of them grumbled at her in a language she could not understand.

Hata raised her hands and scrunched her face as she answered in Auru, "Sorry, I don't speak that language."

They bickered back and forth for a minute. One pulled down their face covering to reveal a short, curly black beard. He smacked his counterpart, then returned to Hata and spoke in a different language.

Yet again, she did not understand and stood there blankly.

The other little man threw his arms up in desperation.

The man speaking to her lifted the helm from his head and held it under his arm. His face was strong with high cheekbones, his curly beard connecting to his short, black hair. His dark brown tone not dissimilar to the Tal'tulu people back home. His sparky green eyes examined her for a long while, his counterpart pacing back and forth behind him. Finally, he sighed and muttered, "Does the old dweller folk dialect ring a bell?"

"Vouri." Hata exclaimed in her native tongue. "You speak Vouri?"

"Cracked crystals," he shouted, then did a little dance and slapped his thigh.

The other little man stomped up, removing his own coverings and helm. Hata saw a similar man, but his beard was stubble with a sheen of red. His skin was of a lighter complexion through the whiskers on his chin and upper lip. His deep brown eyes sparkled as he smacked the first man on the back with a resounding *thud*. "I told you to try that first, you damned propeller face."

"Nay, you did not, Rorik Windbeard. Completely mine own idea, it was."

"Zep off, Bryn, I spotted her first." The short man stopped and looked up at Hata, who towered over them. "By the pillars of Luminar, she near reaches the sky this lass." Rorik chuckled and grinned mischievously. "This *Sky-lass*."

"Bryn Sparkheart, at your service, madam Sky-lass." The black-bearded man bowed with a mighty flourish.

"Hata Vasara, at yours, good sirs." Hata curtsied elegantly, then winced in pain.

"By the bright beard. You're wounded." Bryn began fiddling in a belt full of pouches. "Come here, I've got just the thing for that." He pulled out a tiny green gem cut flat like a coin. From another pouch, he smothered some greasy ointment over the jade-colored rock, then moved to press it against her wound.

"What is that?" Hata asked as she knelt so he could reach her.

"Malachite," Bryn mumbled as he stuck it over the small hole, the ointment causing it to stick to her. "It does wonders to boost the body's healing capabilities."

The itching pain began to cool instantly. Hata smiled in relief. "Thank you."

"Now, where are you coming from, and what is your business in the Ryk Lân?" Rorik asked, tilting his head questionably.

"I fled from the Skaad Lân."

Rorik and Bryn sucked in curse-like breaths simultaneously.

"Skaad. Those feckin' monsters came to the Ryk Lân nearly a century ago, but we drove them off," Bryn grumbled. "You came through the Wayfarers Gate then?"

"Wayfarers? If that's what it is called, then yes, I did," Hata answered unsurely.

"The damned Iban'mael Wayfarers were the ones who created the feckin' thing," Bryn grumbled.

"Did the bastards follow you then?" Rorik asked, his pale face darkening.

Hata nodded.

"Feckin' hells," Bryn cursed. "Well, we'd best tell her royal majesty pronto, you hear, Rorik?"

Rorik was staring at Hata, his eyes wide with wonder. "By Luminar's light. Wait, a bright bearded minute, how did you survive the other side? And, for that matter, how are you flying on that little piece of dirt there?"

"Well," Hata said, smiling reservedly. "I can tell you, but shall we do it on the way? The *Children of Skaad* poured out of the Gate shortly after me."

"That is what they are named? *Children*? Luminar's light." Bryn spat onto the ground. "Quickly then. Let's be off."

They ushered Hata off the smooth stone platform toward the city of glowing crystal spires. Hata filled them in on who she was, how she acquired her powers, and everything she had learned from her short conversation with Hear-fan Skaad.

CHAPTER TWO

SHADOW

"What are you doing here?" Naurr Andiges asked in surprise as Saudett trudged through the muck toward him. The burly Tulu man tilted his head, swatting at the massive flies that buzzed around him and his workmen, who were digging a trench through the swamp of the Moreas Lân. The channel was to run water toward the Wayfarers Gate back into the Earste Lân. The oasis valley of Hasiera and its nomadic people were in dire need of it.

"Simon sent me," Saudett mumbled, exhausted from trekking aimlessly through the swamplands while avoiding massive spiders, ants, and other creatures along the way. *Not to mention blood loss.* Eventually, she had come to the river, which led back to the village of Rawa, where her husband, Simon Meridio, was battling against the foul beasts of the Daanav. She had been in that battle...recklessly. *I fought while carrying our son in my womb, and now he is gone. I've lost him, and it's all my fault.* She suddenly felt nauseous, like her stomach wanted to jump out of her throat.

"Alone?" Naurr questioned curiously.

"Not alone," someone whispered from behind her.

Saudett spun about to see Darkclaw Marah, the Volkinn, crouched low, panting, bandages wrapping their torso and back. Fur peeked through the wraps as blood seeped through them.

"Marah. Why—" Saudett started but caught herself as Naurr strode up. *I cannot let him know I ran away. I ran away because Simon told me time and time again to stop fighting, and I didn't listen.*

Darkclaw Marah studied Saudett, sniffing the air deeply before speaking. "Lady, I have escorted you safely as the First Otsoa commanded."

"By the Primus, you two look near death." Naurr sighed. "Let's get you back to the Gate, then."

"Much appreciated, Naurr." Saudett nodded as Naurr offered an arm for support. She took it as he waved at one of the other workmen to offer Marah the same assistance, but the Volkinn growled and shook their head stubbornly.

"Suit yourself then," Naurr muttered. "Skrull's unholy balls. I need a raise."

Saudett smiled weakly at the jest. "I promise you will get it. You have been beyond loyal to Simon over the past few months."

"There was talk about going into a partnership once we have saved the Lân and all that." Naurr shook his head dejectedly. "Yet, there seems no end in sight with these fell beasts on the loose."

"I agree with you on that front," Saudett whispered. *I wish we were home with our son in Dagad. Just Simon and me with our baby, living in peace. Our baby...oh gods, I killed him.* Her heart twisted in her chest at the thought of Simon looking at her with such disgust when he discovered the truth. Tears trickled down her cheeks, but she kept quiet as they continued through the muck.

The workmen were half done with the river divergence project. They followed the large trench around massive tree trunks and through mud-slicken earth. Groundwater was already filling the base of the channel, even before the connection was made to the broad river back the way they had come. The nomads of Hasiera moved in both directions, carrying waterskins or buckets to bring back through the Wayfarers Gate to the valley. These were the few who hadn't gone to battle for the freedom of the Kadal lizard people.

Finally, Saudett caught sight of the Wayfarers Gate through the canopy-covered marsh's fog. Its white glowing surface was a bright contrast to the dreary swamp. Tents had been erected around the Gate, and people bustled about. A massive cauldron bubbled above a fire in front of one of the tents. The smell made Saudett's mouth water. *Thank Hettra, I haven't eaten anything in days.*

Darkclaw Marah's stomach groaned loudly from behind her.

"You two look to be right famished," Naurr said with a chuckle. Ushering them toward the cauldron. "Grab a bowl and take some rest in one of the tents. Keeps the damn flies at bay."

"My thanks again, Naurr." Saudett weakly put her thumb to her lips.

"Of course, ma'am." He smiled warmly, spooning a bowl of steaming curry out of the pot and handing it to her. Then, he did the same for Marah and himself. With a sigh, he took his bowl and turned to leave. "Best I get back to work then, eh?" He waved and quickly disappeared into the mists once more.

They ate enthusiastically from the aromatic curried meat and vegetable bowls.

Saudett filled another bowl to bring with her into the tent, but exhaustion suddenly washed over her as she stumbled toward it.

Marah followed her in, grimacing with pain as they lowered themselves to a seat beside Saudett.

Before Saudett could spoon another mouthful of the curried stew, Marah confronted her.

"The pup is lost, then?" Marah whispered hoarsely.

"Yes." Saudett blurted, bursting into tears, trying desperately to hold her lips together and keep the words inside. But they spilled out of her. "I killed him. I killed our son, Marah."

Darkclaw Marah immediately set down their food bowl and wrapped their arms around Saudett. "I am sorry, Lady Saudett. Had I been by your side—"

"No." Saudett buried her face into the coarse fur of Marah's shoulder. "No, you *did* protect me. I would be dead had you not stood in the path of the hound's needles."

Marah groaned in discomfort. The Volkinn's fur-covered body was still wrapped in linen bandages. "Lady, why did you flee? After the battle, I went looking for you as soon as possible. I followed your scent and set out on the hunt for you. I did not even tell the Lord First that you fled."

"That is for the better." Saudett stifled a sob. "Simon is why I fled. I could not imagine how much he would hate me for this."

"Is he such a lowly man?"

That caught Saudett by surprise. *Is Simon such a lowly man? Would he honestly despise me for losing our child?* Yet the thought of even telling him caused her gut to twist and her heart to quicken anxiously. *No, I can't do it.* She said nothing in answer to Marah's question and simply leaned against the Volkinn warrior.

"Eat now. Get some rest," Marah suggested as they put their hands on Saudett's shoulders and looked into her eyes. Marah's canine golden eyes were mesmerising and comforting.

"Thank you for following me, Marah."

Marah downed the remaining contents of their bowl, yawned, and stretched contently. They lay down, beckoning Saudett into their arms.

Saudett finished her food and curled up into Darkclaw Marah's warm fur, facing the Volkinn's chest. Saudett stirred as she remembered what Marah's lips tasted like, but soon exhaustion took them both into darkness.

"Saudett," Simon Meridio called out over the aftermath of the battle. So many bodies were burnt and mutilated. *My people.* The nomads of Hasiera were still scattered in the scorched swamplands. The low, mucky flatland below the treetop town of Rawa, the village in the world of the Moreas Lân, and home to the lizard-like people, the Kadal. Puddles of obsidian muck were all that remained of the enemy forces. They were called the Children of Skaad, or so said the flying humanoid named Trije-fan Skaad.

"Saudett!" Simon shouted again.

"Lady Builder." One of the nomads near him took up the cry.

"Hassssssst," a squat lizard-folk hissed out in unity.

One by one, the people around him took up his call to find her. And one by one, they examined and gathered the bodies together. She was not among them. *Where is that woman? Where did you go? I need you now.* Simon's hand went to his belt where he once kept the magic-infused bone dagger made of the very bone of Gaelin Yesnala. The Iban'mael Wayfarer. *The Skrull-damned bastard betrayed me and took the blade for himself.* That blade had granted Simon unfathomable knowledge and elemental power. *Now, I am nothing but a lowly architect once again.* He shrugged. *It's probably for the best. Now I can leave all this behind and go home to Dagad. That is...as soon as I find my wife.*

Saudett's eyes shot open as an explosion reverberated through the air. Darkclaw Marah jolted upright beside her within the canvas tent. They both scrambled outside. A hole had been torn open in the tree canopy above, the leaves and branches sizzling with violet smoking energy. Grey skies leak dim light into the clearing before the Gate. A hooded man stood in a small crater before the Wayfarers Gate, the same violet smoke flowing across his body...*across his wings.* His clothes were in tatters, and he looked wounded. He placed his hands on the green-black marble of the gateway.

"Halt. Stop what you are doing," a nearby Hasieran warrior shouted, leveling his spear at the newcomer.

The winged man ignored him.

The nomadic warrior rushed forward with his glinting spear tip leveled.

The hooded man lashed out with one of his bat-like wings. Black-violet smoke burst from the attack as the Hasieran spear warrior was hurled through the air, his body crackling and burning with violet energy.

Saudett hesitated, putting her hand to her stomach where her child had once been. *I have no weapon. I don't want to die.*

The roiling, cloudy portal of the Wayfarers Gate began to change. Its white mists bubbled and foamed into a crimson haze.

Darkclaw Marah sprang forward, their muscles pulsing, teeth bared, and clawed fingers taut.

Saudett followed more slowly, cautiously.

The winged man stepped through the portal.

"Marah. No," Saudett cried out as Darkclaw Marah disappeared through the clouded surface after him. *Fucks.* Saudett sprinted, kicking up the dead warrior's spear into her hands and plunging through the portal. The next thing she knew, something slammed into her, and she landed with a splash in knee-deep water. Darkclaw Marah lay limp nearby. The smell of the Volkinn's burnt fur filled Saudett's nostrils. *No...Marah.* She saw the rise and fall of their chest. *Thank Hettra, they're still alive.*

"What, do tell, is this then?" a low, sultry voice tickled her ears. "You brought me gifts, my son?"

Saudett ground her teeth through the pain and came to her knees. A man dressed in white. *No, not a man.*

Four arms gestured welcomingly as the Iban'mael spoke to the winged man who stood behind her at the Wayfarers Gate. "I have never seen such a beast." The Iban'mael crouched low next to Darkclaw Marah.

"Quickly, Father, help me close this Gate. One of your predecessors is on my trail."

"A Wayfarer?"

"Yes. Yes. I've been fighting him and fleeing across the Moreas Lân for nearly a day."

"Why not kill him?" the grey skinned Iban'mael asked incredulously as he moved to the Gate.

The winged man snorted as both men placed their hands against the towering Gateway, ten times the size of the one in the Moreas Lân.

Saudett finally took in her surroundings. The water rippled out across a velvety twilight star-ridden sky. Six massive versions of the Wayfarers Gates were arranged in a circle. Other than that, there was nothing but the two strange beings. The cloudy red portal suddenly dissipated into nothing, and she could look through and see the water stretching far beyond it.

The two men turned back to her.

"Where are we?" Saudett dared to ask, her voice hoarse.

"Welcome, *human*," the man in majestic white clothing said calmly, smiling at her warmly. "I am Hear-fan Skaad." He put a hand on the shoulder of the winged man. "This is my third son, Trije-fan Skaad." He opened his lower two arms and gestured about them, spinning elegantly around. "And this is my domain, the Skaad Lân."

Saudett's gaze went back and forth between Hear-fan and Trije-fan. The father had a friendly air about him. *He does not seem ill-intent.* She could barely make out the face of the son under his low hood. She felt around in the water for her spear. It was gone. *We are trapped here. Perhaps I could surprise them with a spear to the gut if I had it, but then what? Take one down to have the other burn me alive with that strange violet-black fire.* As she stood there facing the two formidable beings, she felt the weight of her own insignificance. Despite her best efforts, she knew she was no match for their power and prowess. The realization dawned on her that she was completely out of her depth, and a ripple of apprehension washed over her, like the very waters she stood in.

Finally, she breathed deeply and asked, "What will you do with us?"

"Treat you both as honored guests, for that is certain," Hear-fan said, still smiling, his black teeth glistening. He beckoned to her as he strode past to the center of the circle of gates. Saudett watched Trije-fan Skaad lift Darkclaw Marah from the water with little effort and take the Volkinn to stand beside his father.

Saudett painfully stood and cautiously limped toward them. As she came before them, the ground suddenly shook, and the sound of metal creaking and groaning surrounded her. Then they were sinking. Sinking into the earth. Water spilled off what she now realized was a rust-covered metal platform. They descended into *darkness*.

CHAPTER THREE

DUPLICITY

Simon listened to his right-hand man, Naurr Andiges, apologize repeatedly.

"Boss, I should have stayed by her side," Naurr said, clutching his head in dismay. "I felt that something was strangely off with her. She came back alone with that Volkinn panting at her heels."

Simon turned to an older woman, a nomad of Hasiera. "You say you saw Darkclaw Marah, and my wife Saudett chase the winged man through the portal? And then the portal vanished?"

"Aye indeed, Lord First. Darkclaw was damned near the demon's neck when they both plunged into that crimson fog. The lady grabbed up a spear and followed them right in. She did indeed."

Why did Saudett come back here alone? Or not alone, but with Marah. Simon closed his eyes wearily. *The Wayfarers Gate has gone inert. I have lost my magic to rectify that. We are stranded here in the Moreas Lân, and Hasiera will soon dry up. Where in Skrull's damned name did that bastard Gaelin get to?* The frustration peaked as he cursed out at no one in particular. "I just need a minute to fucking think."

Naurr bowed his head where he was seated on a rotting stump.

The old woman backed away, then turned and hurried off.

"Naurr, my good man." Simon stood and touched the man's shoulder. "You had nothing to do with my wife's actions. She chased the bastard into the Gate of her own free will." Simon crouched in front of Naurr. "Once I get this Gate pointed back to home, it is time you took the men and headed there. I'll send you through the same Gate we sent Kiana Ahmadi and the others. The Aurulan Gate is far closer to Dagad. The Hasieran can finish this damned trench themselves."

"You are speaking the truth?" Naurr asked as he looked up into Simon's eyes.

"Of course, my good man," Simon said with a smile. "I would have joined you had my dear wife not run off alone. I was ready to be done with this shit and return to Dagad. Join the fatherhood assembly like yourself now that our little girl is on the way."

"Ha. So, you finally went and did it. No more fooling about with others in your spare time, then?" Naurr chuckled slightly. "Fair warning, prepare to never sleep again there, boss."

"Oh, gods, we did, and I don't know about the former." Simon laughed. "As to the latter, so have I heard are the woes of parenthood."

"Honest to Qav, I could not do what my dear Cenna does. She handles my young Noa day and night, the damned rowdy rascal he is."

"By Hettra's bouncing bosoms, my good man, I should apologize. You have been away from your family for far too long as it is."

"You'll still be honoring our deal?" Naurr asked questionably as he arched a brow. "To go into partnership?"

"Indeed, I will." Simon nodded. "Whenever I return, that is. I will write a bank note to give to the Court of Freemen when you return to Dagad. You will have access to all my funds until my return."

"Primus's blessing to you." Naurr put his thumb to his lips in thanks.

There was a sudden commotion as Gaelin Yesnala slowly descended through the hole that Trije-fan Skaad had burnt through the tree cover.

Skrull-damned piece of pissing warts on a fat fucking cock, you son-of-a – Simon raged internally as he sighted the Iban'mael sorcerer and stomped toward where Gaelin had landed before the Wayfarers Gate.

Gaelin landed lightly on his feet and began to inspect the Gate, ignoring everyone around him.

"Oi!" Simon shouted as he approached. "You fucking bastard."

Gaelin did not turn about and continued his studies, resting a hand on the black marble of the archway.

"You murdered our people in that blood bath back there..."

"Ah yes," Gaelin muttered to himself. "The foul creature retreated to the Skaad Lân. I should have known."

"I'm talking to you, Gaelin Yesnala." Simon was right up behind the Iban'mael now, reaching out to grab him by the shoulder and spin him about. But as he was about to touch him, Gaelin turned about abruptly.

"No, Simon Meridio, not *our* people. They're barely even *your* people."

"By the Primus. These people died because you could not control your lust for vengeance against the Daanav. You burnt a score of them alive."

"Yet I took out three times as many of those despicable abominations in the process," Gaelin said dully.

"Couldn't finish their leader, though, could you?!" Simon screamed, spittle splashing at Gaelin. "The flying one. Even with my dagger, you damned fucking thief."

"*Your* dagger?" Gaelin tilted his head curiously, one of four hands appearing with a handkerchief and wiping away Simon's spit. "What dagger?" The Iban'mael shrugged with all four arms.

Simon blinked, and his mouth hung open. Gaelin's arm, once torn off and used to create the magic-infused dagger, was as good as new.

Gaelin grinned wickedly, his blackened teeth gleaming. "Indeed, Simon, my power is returned to me. I am back at full strength. Honestly, I do not think I have any further need for you. *Strangung.*"

Simon snapped his jaw shut as Gaelin's double-fisted punch slammed into his chest, sending him soaring. *Lind...*Simon thought unconsciously as he crashed into the trunk of a thick swampland tree. The magical barrier was dim and shattered upon impact, but it protected him from most of the force.

"Good luck returning to the Earste Lân without *my* power," Gaelin called as he touched the archway, and a swirling navy haze appeared. The Iban'mael Wayfarer did not look back as he stepped through the portal. A moment later, the cobalt cloud dissipated into nothing.

Simon gasped for air as his chest burnt with agony. *A couple ribs broken, I think.* Again, without thinking, his hand fell on his chest, and he muttered, "*Gehae.*" A soft yellow light from his hand caused the pain to recede, and he heard his ribs crack back together. As he lay there, he looked at his hand in realization. *I still have the magic.* He jumped to his feet. "I still have it!" he shouted as the Hasieran gathered around him.

"First Otsoa, the Wayfarer has betrayed us. What are we to do?" one warrior asked nervously.

Gebod. Simon's voice became abnormally loud and echoed throughout the crowd. "Fear not, Hasiera. I will take us home. We will diverge the river through the Wayfarers Gate, and Hasiera will be alive again."

The crowd's anxious fidgeting erupted into a cheer.

Ah, to be whole again. Simon clenched his fist. The jagged white scars on his left arm tingled with energy. He strode to the gateway and rested that hand upon it. Simon brought the image of the valley of Hasiera to his mind. "*Sefa,*" he uttered the spell. The white mist exploded to life as the portal again coupled to the Earste Lân. *Take that, you smug bastard. If I see you again, Gaelin Yesnala, one of us will not survive the encounter.* Simon smirked haughtily, flexing his hand repeatedly. He looked at all the hopeful eyes watching him and puffed up his chest as he presided over them. "Now. Let us get the Skrull-forsaken trench finished so we can go home."

He watched proudly as his people returned to work, digging and carrying water through the Wayfarers Gate as if nothing had disrupted their day. There was an itch at the back of Simon's mind. *I feel like I'm forgetting something.* He shrugged and returned to supervise the proceedings.

CHAPTER FOUR

SOLITUDE

Saudett bit her tongue in terror. They had been descending for an eternity. But as they sunk, Saudett gazed upon massive caverns, alight with azure burning torches and hordes of Daanav gnashing and howling, pushing toward the edge of the abyss. All striving, it seemed, to catch a glimpse of the Iban'mael man in white, Hear-fan Skaad. In some caverns, strange hunch-backed beings worked metals with violet-fired smithies. Worse even were the tunnels disappearing into darkness, screams and shrieks echoing out of the black beyond. She saw two of the lumbering hulks come out of one such tunnel and toss the body of a mutilated hound over the edge. The hound's body was cut and stitched with an extra limb jutting from its back.

What in Skrull's name are they doing in there? Saudett trembled at the thought.

"Fancy my art?" Hear-fan Skaad enquired frankly.

"Art?" Saudett gulped.

"Oh indeed, all my children are pieces of majestic art, my creations." He grinned wickedly. "Though some have my true blood in their veins." He placed his hand on Trije-fan Skaad's back. "Along with some simple...*enhancements.*"

Saudett shuddered again.

Hear-fan's eyes fell on Marah, still in Trije-fan's arms.

I can't imagine what he will do to the Volkinn. They are unique people, and this sick bastard seems like he will be overly inquisitive.

"Ah, here we are," Hear-fan said as the platform groaned to a halt. A corridor stretched before them, lit with warm white lights on the ceiling. Beautiful marble tiles of whites, greys, and blues lined the floor and walls. They strode leisurely through the hallway until they came to a larger room. The white and silver trimmed walls and ceiling curved in an almost unnatural shape upward, coming to a focus on a massive hanging candelabrum. Yet instead of candles, the crystals themselves gave off twinkling light from the clear and azure gemstones. Below the chandelier were four oversized armchairs with soft tan cushions, the chairs curving fantastically. A fireplace crackled before the chairs, and an intricately woven rug, with the same curving designs of black and white, silvers and blues. It spread out under an elegant low table fashioned from a gnarly stump topped with clear crystal. Paintings decorated the walls, and plants in large clay pots brought vibrant greens and colors to the chamber. A massive curving blackwood shelf was full of scrolls and tomes on one side of the room with a ladder attached.

Hear-fan plopped down in one of the chairs and waved his son away. "See to its wounds, then return to me with a full report of your time in the Moreas Lân."

Trije-fan Skaad moved to what looked like more marble wall, but it was jutting strangely outward. The wall slid open upon his approach and closed as he and Darkclaw Marah vanished beyond it.

"You will care for their wounds?" Saudett asked, unsure of his intent for the Volkinn.

"Of course, you are my guests. Speaking of wounds." He stood and strode over to her, his eyes moving across her body, *inspecting* her. "You are not faring well. Your legs are covered in dried blood."

Fucks. Hettra, help me. He's right. There was an ever-present pain in her lower abdomen. *But should I trust this man?*

"Let me help you, human. I can make the pain disappear."

Reluctantly, Saudett nodded.

"*Scua gehae,*" he whispered, his hand lit with violet and yellow warmth. He placed it gently on her stomach.

Immediately, the constant throbbing faded away.

He smiled and promptly returned to his seat.

"Thank you," she murmured.

"Anything for my honored guests. Sit now, human. We have much to discuss." He snapped his fingers, and another seemingly hidden door glided open, and two humanoid people strode in carrying trays of tea and a sliced loaf of grainy bread. Slender in their simple beige robes that moved strangely as they walked, as if their knees were slightly ajar. Their facial features were pale, almost with a blue tinge, and were sharp and beautiful. White hair tied back in buns. As one of them smiled at Saudett, she noticed the small, sharp teeth behind her lips. As the servant placed the tray gently on the glass tabletop, Saudett finally saw the wings on the servant's back. They were tightly wrapped in bonds and chains, making them deformed and stunted. The wings looked similar to Trije-fan Skaad's wings, but his were muscular and well-built.

Hear-fan smiled warmly as he took a crystal teacup that one of the servants had just poured into. Then he blew on it softly and took a small sip. "Ah yes, Grot Lân khing root. Excellent, it truly opens one's sinuses. It was once very complicated to acquire."

Saudett hesitated to drink. "And now it is not so difficult?"

"Now that the Grot Lân is mine, along with its people." He waved at the servants who stood silently near the wall.

"Do you conquer all Lâns you happen across?" she asked further, eyeing the cup. *It does smell delicious, and the bread is steaming. Fresh from the oven. Skrull's balls. Am I hungry?* Her stomach grumbled.

"Please eat, hum—" He stopped abruptly. "I'm terribly sorry. How rude of me. I didn't get your name."

"Saudett Meridio."

"Now, my esteemed guest, Lady Saudett." Hear-fan nodded at the provisions before her as he took a slice of the warm bread and bit into it. "You have nothing to fear. Please eat and drink."

Reluctantly, Saudett did so. *By the Primus.* The tea was soothing with a hint of spice. The bread melted in her mouth. She took her time eating and pondering this strange man. *He is one of Gaelin's people, and he is leading this conquest. Gaelin said the Iban'mael was peaceful and worshiped knowledge above all else.* After swallowing a second slice of the bread, she finally mumbled, "You didn't answer my question."

"Of course, we do not conquer all Lâns. The Grot Lân, for example, surrendered to my rule peacefully. All they must do is deliver the odd tribute of servants and offerings. For the most part, I leave them to their own devices."

"Under the threat of annihilation?"

He shrugged his four arms nonchalantly.

"What about my home, the Earste Lân?"

"You can blame the sycophantic Wayfarer, Gaelin Yesnala, for that." Hear-fan Skaad snorted contemptuously. "His presence in the Earste Lân has directly led to the resistance by your people, especially those he'd aided in awakening their inert magical senses."

"Did you not destroy the Iban'mael's Lân? What was it called?"

"It was the Hiel Lân."

Saudett gently let the cup rest on the transparent tabletop, then rubbed at her temples. "There is so much history that's a mystery between you and these Wayfarers, the Iban'mael. Are you not one yourself?"

"Very astute," he chuckled, holding up his lower two arms. "Indeed, I am Iban'mael. And I did indeed have my children destroy the Hiel Lân."

"Why?"

"They sent me here, to this forsaken Lân. I was a Wayfarer. They sent me here knowing there was nothing. For millennia, I wondered about the waters above. There were only the migrating creatures wading in massive hordes across the surface. That and the odd patches of pole-like trees with jagged leaves. But those wandering creatures were my first children, which I claimed unto myself." He leaned over and touched Saudett's hand gently, his inverted eyes looking deeply into her own.

An image formed in her mind. Thousands of the Daanav hulks moaning and wailing as they walked endlessly through the rippling waters with starry skies stretching far above.

By Hettra's mercy, it is eerily beautiful yet downright terrifying.

Suddenly, in the vision, Hear-fan Skaad swooped in from above, eyes bulging and mouthwatering. She *felt* his hunger as he picked one of the hulks off, tearing into it and eating its flesh. Black blood sprayed across him and dripped from his mouth.

The other hulks continued moaning...wailing...and walking.

Saudett sucked in a breath and found herself seated before the man once again in the comfortable sitting-room. A wave of nausea swelled through her.

"I apologize, that was a bit much, but you needed to know. I was stranded here, starving and alone."

It must have been hell. Saudett poured herself another cup of tea to push down the dizziness. After settling her stomach, she said, "I can't imagine the agony of spending hundreds of years in hunger and solitude."

He stared blankly past her for a long moment, then seemed to snap back to the present. "True agony. With all my heart, I vowed vengeance upon my so-called brethren."

Saudett could not help but empathize with the man. *Thousands of years alone.* She felt suddenly exhausted.

As if reading her mind, he said, "Your room is ready. Please retire and get some rest. I will send for you in the morning." Hear-fan stood, and one of the servants hurried over to them. "See our guest to her quarters." He turned back to Saudett and held out a hand.

Slowly, she reached out and placed her own in his.

He bent and gently kissed her atop it. "Sweet dreams, my Lady Saudett."

At that moment, Trije-fan Skaad returned.

The servant offered her arm to Saudett and led her away through one of the nearly hidden doors into an equally beautiful corridor. Not long after entering the hall, they turned at an intersection. After another few minutes, a door slid open on one side of the hallway. The servant guided her into a two-chambered room with the same marbled floors and walls.

A massive fur rug covered nearly the entirety of the first chamber. It looked to be the skin of an enormous beast. It stretched under an elegant serpentine, carved, four-post wooden bed with transparent azure silk-like curtains. Another fireplace crackled warmly. The smoke looked like it was being sucked into a hole above it. Two of the same oversized cushioned chairs sat before the hearth.

Saudett strolled to the other chamber, separated by a wall of hanging glass beads and stones. A massive steaming bath dipped into the floor. The room was dim, with warm glowing gems set into the walls. *By Hettra's sagging tits, I desperately need a bath.*

The servant hissed something in a strange language behind her.

Saudett turned to see the woman before yet another hidden door opened into a chamber full of elegant clothing. She joined the servant and inspected the luxurious silk gowns and blouses. *Skrull, take me. I don't even remember the last time I wore a skirt.*

The servant hissed something else and then hurried off.

Saudett could not resist the tempting bath and removed her tattered, soiled clothing. She stepped into the perfectly heated waters. She submerged herself in it, feeling the warmth across every inch of her skin. She surfaced and found a wonderful-smelling soap on a dish beside many scrubbing apparatuses, from a sponge-like rock to a horsehair brush. *At least, I pray it's horsehair...*

She took her time cleaning every Skrull-damned inch of her body. The coarse stone and brush exfoliated and felt incredible against her skin. It had been weeks since she had found time to clean her soiled, sweaty, and blood-covered body. When she came to her bloodstained legs, she rubbed so vigorously it hurt. *This is the blood of my baby. My child I will never meet.*

"Fucking hells, it's all my fault. I should have died in your place." Saudett wept, tears splashing into the water as she continued scrubbing even after the blood was long gone. The skin of her thighs began to redden and peel. She flung the brush away in fury as she crawled to the edge of the bath and lay her head on her arms along the tiled lip. She couldn't keep her burning eyes open for another minute.

CHAPTER FIVE

STORMFALL

Hata stared in awe at the crystalline keep with a massive spiraling tower looming skyward. Crafted of glittering stone, polished metal, and wood with a grain that gave off a faint humming glow, the fortress floated on its own separate island above the large one below it where the sprawling city resided. Many flying contraptions circled the skies above the keep, like the one that Bryn and Rorik had flown. Hoists of massive chains pulled and clanged, lifting people up and down from the keep to the city. One of the large hoists carried supplies such as oversized caskets of ale or wine, baskets, and food crates.

The short, stout people of the kingdom were a raucous bunch, always shouting heartily back and forth to one another. Some had stopped to stare at Hata as Rorik and Bryn led her through the city streets. Some called out, and her two guides would laugh and shout back at the caller. The roads were paved in glittering stone slabs. The buildings themselves were usually built around one of the massive crystal-like trees, the trunk jutting out of the center roof of each homestead. Everything around her seemed to have that same magical glow.

"What do you call this place?" Hata asked as they strode through. "And sorry if this is rude, what are your people called?"

"This is the city of Aerion," Bryn said with a grin, gesturing with both hands around him. "And we are the Himin-dvergar."

"It is beautiful," Hata answered in awe. "Your people, the Himin-dvergar, are truly remarkable to have built all this."

"Aye, it is indeed," Rorik answered. "Let's hope we can keep it that way. If what you tell us of these Children of Skaad is accurate, they have never before sent such a force against us. Pray to Luminar that we will be ready."

Hata's chest tightened anxiously. *I brought the Children here and have now put more lives at risk. Teras protect them.*

Finally, they stepped onto one of the lifts and ascended to the Queen's palace.

"Welcome to the Keep of Crystalia," Bryn said, his broad chest puffed up with pride.

A semi-circular flat area lay before a massive portcullis, walls of stone, and majestically crafted metal designs stretched impossibly high above them. The crystal veins snaked through the surface of the walls. Huge ballista could be seen peaking over the walls at every angle. The platforms that lifted people to and from the keep housed metal beams and pullies connected with rumbling apparatuses. The strange creations had red and blue crystals jutting out from the sides, flashing with light as glowing steam puffed out of the ends of the contraptions.

It looks like a bigger version of the one in their flying cart. Hata nodded toward the noisy device and asked curiously, "What are these things?"

"The crystal engines?" Bryn lifted a brow. "You don't have these things where you come from?"

"Nothing like it."

"By the bright beard. Well then, let me just tell you a little about 'em, as it is my specialty." Bryn laughed and grinned enthusiastically as he proceeded under the massive portcullis. "The crystals of our islands are a potent fuel, or *magic* as you called that earth-moving ability of yours. We have studied it for a long time and have only begun utilizing it in the last few decades. The crystals are connected to the machines we have built with gears, cylinders, pistons, rotor hubs, crystal injectors, radiators, and—"

"Luminar's light, man." Rorik smacked the back of Bryn's head. "We don't need the schematics. Look at the Sky-lass. She can't follow a thing you're saying."

Thank you, Rorik, Hata thought. *I have no idea what any of those words mean.* She smiled sheepishly and shrugged. "Sorry, Bryn, it is a little much for me, but I can tell that you are very passionate about it."

"Tinkering with trinkets ain't a lick of fun," Rorik scolded playfully, then nudged Bryn as he continued, "Now, piloting a rotor-wing is where life's excitement truly is."

"Zep off, Rorik Windbeard." Bryn rebuked. "You'd fall from the sky in a heartbeat if I didn't keep your portly arse in its seat."

Hata gasped.

Rorik blushed and exclaimed, "Portly." He moved his hips to the side so his bottom stuck out as he looked over his shoulder to inspect himself. "By Luminar's bright beard, you really think it's portly?"

"Ahem," Bryn coughed, clearing his throat as he mumbled, "I mean—uhm..." He trailed off as his face flushed with color. His grumbles continued nearly imperceptibly, "By all the gears and gaskets..."

Are they lovers? Hata pondered and couldn't help but smile at their antics.

They entered a sprawling courtyard with fountains and gardens of crystalline bushes and low-growing trees in droves of diverse colors. A massive tower stood at the center of the keep. Turrets on the main outer wall were connected to the tower by bridges overhead. A handful of guards dressed in heavy white and sapphire metal armor, with large cobalt crystal gems embedded in the chest pieces, stood on guard. As the trio entered the courtyard, the soldiers formed a line and crossed their massive two-handed axes across the path.

"State your business, Bryn Sparkheart. What is it this time—" One of the guards started but stopped as his gaze came to rest on Hata. "By Luminar's luminous light. What is that?"

"Finn Sunstrider. We must see the Queen now, don't you see?" Bryn urged as he gestured to Hata. "She calls herself a *human*. She hails from the Earste Lân and brings fell news of Skaad."

"Skaad," Finn blurted in astonishment. "Cracked crystals. What news is it?"

"Invasion, it seems."

"By the hammer and tongs, Sparkheart. Why didn't you say so sooner?" The guardsman chided as he ushered them through, leading the way. "To the Queen. Quick as a crystal elf now."

"I *was* trying to say sooner, you son-of-a sinewy skulled arse," Bryn muttered as they followed.

Rorik leaned over to Hata and whispered under his breath, "Isn't Bryn such an endearing little bloke?"

"He is adorable," Hata agreed, smiling. "Are you two not...uhm, together?"

Rorik blushed vibrantly once again. "Luminar's light. No. We work together. Bryn and I, we can't possibly..." This time, Rorik trailed off, mumbling about unprofessionalism. "By the wind in his thick, curly whiskers, it's strictly a professional working relationship."

Yet they are oh so alike. It is so lovely to be in pleasant company for once. Hata had spent months enslaved and abused by Ebras Corb, the Alpha Passeriform of the Council of the Aerie of Aurulan. Imprisoned in his secluded *Convent Enclosure.* Only with the help of Hata's warden, the Proctor Chanel De Montrichard, did she escape? But it was at the cost of Chanel's and her two orderlies' lives. After all the Alpha had put her through, she found herself alone in the harsh mountains of the North Iron Belt, trying to survive. Only to be deceived into believing a god told her to return to her home of Oitilla, infested by the Children of Skaad. Finally, she came to the gateway deep in the earth that her father, Baal, had tried to cover up long ago. The very thing that had caused her family to be banished from Oitilla and her best friend-turned-lover to be murdered in cold blood by the village chieftain.

*Silja...my Silja...*Hata suppressed the agonising memory of her first love. After stepping through that Gate deep in the mountain, she found that man with four arms claiming to be the Primus himself. But he was just a man. *A powerful man, but still just a man.* It seemed the causes of most of her problems were contemptible men who wielded unfathomable magic power.

Her mind wandered to Joanna, her cellmate in the *Convent,* whom she had just begun to feel something for, and Saudett, the stunning soldier woman and the second person to ever love her. Hata wondered what they could be doing right now. Then, the massive gates on the mighty tower in the center of the courtyard, with its crystal veins spidering skyward, groaned and thudded open before them.

The room was filled with hundreds of people milling about, speaking in low voices to one another. All were finely dressed in colorful garments, sporting glossy waxed beards and intricately braided hair. Their skin tones were of all shades and complexions. At the end of the courtroom, sat upon a dais, was a stern, dark-skinned woman who leaned on one arm of her majestic crystal throne, chin on her fist, her sullen face expressing a hint of boredom. A breastplate of silver with a rainbow assortment of crystals embedded in the chest glimmered brilliantly on her torso. A white skirt parted on the sides revealed silver armored greaves and thick sabatons. She wore no crown, but her black curly hair was braided so tight to her skull that it formed many lines against it.

As the guard, Finn Sunstrider, led them stomping through the crowd, gently nudging people aside, Hata noticed the Queen tilt her head curiously at their approach and sit upright. As the guard finally stood at the base of the steps up to the throne, the Queen stood, her armored boots adding a good six inches to her height.

"Silence," the Queen's deep, melodic voice boomed over the crowd.

The conversations around them hushed instantly, and all turned to regard the Queen.

"Finn Sunstrider, Rorik Windbeard, and Bryn Sparkheart, are you coming to me yet again? And who is this lanky young lady who succeeds you?"

The guardsman, Finn Sunstrider, bowed and announced, "My Queen, Lady Raine Stormfall, I would have turned Bryn away this time for certain. But..." Finn turned and looked at Hata. "...this time, they found a traveler from a distant Lân."

"Queen Stormfall," Bryn said with a low bow. "Let me present the Sky-lass, Hata Vasara, the Sunstone of the Earste Lân. She brings fell tidings of Skaad."

There was a gasp among the listeners, and whispers rippled through the crowd.

"Skaad?"

"I thought those creatures had given up on our Lân."

"They are back in Ryk?"

"It's been nearly a hundred years."

"Enough," the Queen's voice silenced the room once again. "Speak, Sunstone, tell us these fell tidings."

Hata's mouth was dry as she tried to moisten her lips. "Queen Stormfall." Hata gulped nervously. Then, words from memory came to her from a time not so long ago.

"Etiquette..." The Proctor, Chanel de Montrichard, poked the willow switch into her back, causing Hata to straighten. Then the stick pushed her shoulders down and her chin up. "...is to announce one's strength. Should you young things ever find yourself in court, your decorum will mirror your own confidence. You must show those around you that you will not be intimidated or turned over by any man who would aim to use you. Show them, *my* pupils, show them that you are magi."

Hata's mind snapped back to the throne room. She straightened her back, and she took a deep breath. The Sunstone found her voice. "Queen Stormfall." Hata held the Queen's gaze steadily as she continued loudly for all to perceive. "Hear-fan Skaad and his Children of Skaad have come to your doorstep. He has invaded my home, the Earste Lân, and forced me to flee. His armies followed me here and will stop at nothing to get me back. Will you defend your lands?"

Murmurs expanded through the onlookers.

The Queen's mouth formed a hard line, her face brooding. After a moment, she said, "I will defend my lands. No thanks to you. The creatures of Skaad have left us in peace for nearly a century, and now you have brought back their destruction upon us."

She is right, Hata thought, but she pushed through. "Hear-fan Skaad would have turned his sight back onto you, eventually. I don't know what he's been doing for a hundred years, but he has been focused on conquering my home, the Earste Lân. Luckily, I was able to trap thousands of his Children there. They will not be able to come to his aid. Now is the chance to strike back at him. If all the Lâns were to resist, we could end him."

A handful of voices from the crowd called out in agreement., "The Sky-lass is right."

"It could be the end of Skaad."

Others were not so affable.

"Why should we fight for strangers?"

"Let's throw them out of our lands and sink the cursed feckin' island that archway is on."

Queen Raine Stormfall sat back down, her heavy armor audibly *thudding*. "We have no choice but to fight. I have not yet decided if it shall go further than defending our own Lân." She closed her eyes and leaned against her fist again for a long while as the silence held. Finally, the Queen stood once more. "To every rotor-wing we have. Find the Children of Skaad and report. Evacuate the citizens to Crystalia Keep immediately. Food and supplies are to be gathered here. Nobles, your bannermen and their forces are to prepare to defend the city below. My people. We *will* protect Aerion. Go forth."

The room burst into turmoil as people hurried about, shouting orders. Hata stood in awe and was unsure of what to do until the Queen pointed at her and beckoned her to follow. A set of spiraling stairs ascended the wall behind the throne to the next level of the tower. Hata followed the Queen of the strange new people, the Himin-dvergar, up the stairs.

Chapter Six

SEVER

Kiana Ahmadi stood over the body of the dead Xamidian slaver, Zalias Ershya.

"He was mine," Baal Vasara growled insatiably, his teeth bared as usual.

"By the Primus, why are you *murdering* people in Mister Nelon's home?" The beret-wearing steward wailed in bewilderment.

"I apologize, friend Baal." Kiana sighed in liberation. "The bastard had it coming." Zalias Ershya had been a black-market dealer of the highly addictive drug *grit. Oh, and not to mention slaves. Dear half-sister Saudett, wherever you are, I've avenged you. I killed the man who drugged you and nearly raped and sold you.* "The Earste Lân is now a better place without this disease within it."

"We must get friends and head north now to Oitilla," Baal grunted, dropping the housekeeper who had accosted them at their forced entrance to the home of the Magnus Huntsman, Jude Nelon. Baal had been effortlessly holding the man aloft all this time.

"What?" The steward brushed his fine clothing off with dignity and straightened his beret. "You're leaving me with this?" He waved at the body of the dead man.

"Apologies for the mess," Kiana said with a shrug, and nodded to Baal, and they both turned to leave.

"It's time Mister Nelon invested in a Skrull-damned volframi door," the man muttered as they stepped over the smashed and fallen entry.

"Aye." Baal barked a laugh. "Little man, you make the door of Vouri volframi ore. Not even silly magi break into this homestead."

Kiana looked back to see the steward dragging the body of Zalias toward the back exterior of the home, still muttering under his breath as he did so.

Anora Ahmadi's head thundered as people clamored into the little house. Her mouth was as dry as the Burning Sea. *I need more wine.* She stumbled to her feet as a wave of nausea nearly knocked her over. Taking a precarious step forward, Anora made for the doorway out.

There was a muted *snap* that sounded in the small room. "Vittu." Brena Vasara's voice hissed painfully in her native language of the Vouri.

"Good, now to sling it," Kaplan Mir's voice came to Anora through the haze.

Anora stumbled into the wall, knocking clay plates from a shelf near the hearth.

"Hettra's mercy, Third Otsoa, what are you doing?" Kaplan asked, appearing at her side and taking her by the arm.

"I...nee-need one more drink." Anora's words came out in a jumble.

"Please, Lady Third." Kaplan gently led her to a rickety wooden chair and sat her down. He then took a skin of water from his waist and aided her in drinking it.

Anora gulped it down eagerly. She breathed heavily when the last drops of water emptied into her mouth. "Thank you, my boy." She gave Kaplan's black-bearded cheek a gentle pat. "My daughter is in caring hands." Anora paused, looking about perplexedly. "Where are my daughters?"

"Daughters?" Brena snorted. "Friend, Saudett is far, far away from here. You should eat and rest. No more wine. Kiana found the slaver merchant, and she and my mate have left to seek out the Mangus Huntsman."

Things began to come back to Anora. *My daughter, Kiana? Ah, yes, she hates me. I made her become a whore when I could not do so myself.* She remembered why they'd come to Nidhaut, the capital city of Aurulan. *To rescue Hata Vasara from the Aerie magi.*

Kaplan placed a hard loaf of bread in her hands. "Eat now, Lady Third."

Jude Nelon, the Magnus Huntsman who had taken the Vasara's daughter. *That is why we came here.* "They know where Jude Nelon is?" Anora asked as she slowly bit into the bread.

"Yes, the merchant gave it up," Brena said. "They will scout it out and return here with news."

Anora finally looked at Brena. Her chain mail hung around her waist. Her upper arm was wrapped, splinted, and rested in a sling. Dark bruises riddled her bare, pale skin, blending with some of the black thunderbolt tattoos streaking across her body. "What happened to you?" Anora questioned.

"The slaver had some *protection*. Took a little fall in the Paon, nothing grave."

"Skrull, take me." Anora breathed. "If I had only been there, too. This could have been prevented."

"Bah." Brena grunted. "Look to your own words. Look forward, never back."

That is the creed I tried to live by, because every time I thought of Saudett, the guilt was overwhelming.

"You both should rest," Kaplan interjected. "I'll keep a lookout for their return."

Anora's eyes were heavy, but her stomach had settled, and the nausea had lessened. Kaplan helped her back to the straw bedding in the corner, where she soon fell asleep.

Kiana saw Kaplan Mir waiting outside the little shack they'd claimed as their home in the slum streets of Nidhaut. In the district of *Ville de Voleurs*. The tension between Kaplan and her had been palpable. She'd felt resentment that he had so quickly let her sell her body for the *greater* good. *To that point, so did Brena, who has been married for decades.* It was all for the sake of Hata. But things between Kaplan and Kiana hadn't been the same since. *He barely says a word to me anymore.*

As that thought came to her, Kaplan looked to Baal and asked, "Have any luck? Where is the merchant? Gods, did he escape you again, Baal? You lug headed dolt."

"Ha." Baal laughed, the sound booming from his broad chest. "Slithering grit man is dead at your mate's feet." The large man gestured with a massive fist to Kiana.

Kaplan glanced at her, then back to Baal. "I hope you found the Huntsman, then?"

"Joo. We know where my Hata is." Baal smiled toothily. "She goes home."

"Home?" Kaplan tilted his head. "To Dagad?"

"No, silly bookman. To Vouri home. To Oitilla."

"Ah, I see. Well, it seems we have a heading. The other two are resting. Shall we drop by a tavern for a cup?"

"You two pebbles, go play, perhaps walk the mountain," Baal said with a rumbling chuckle, and began trotting toward the homestead. "I will watch after my mate."

"Make sure my mother doesn't leave if you could, Baal," Kiana called after him.

"Joo." His deep voice echoed back, and then he disappeared into the shack.

The two stood awkwardly for a long moment. Finally, Kaplan took an audible breath and said, "I gave your mother water and bread, and we tried to convince her to stop this excessive drinking."

"Oh, so now you can address me?"

"My Otsoa—"

"No. I am not *your* Otsoa. You are not even of Hasiera. You have avoided me over the last few weeks. You sent me away to sell my body and said nothing. You didn't even care."

"Please—"

"By the Primus, I thought you loved me! You didn't think twice about me working as a whore."

"Kiana, it was a logical plan. You seemed on-board. I did not know you felt that way as you ceased speaking with me."

"*I* ceased speaking with *you*? Kaplan, you've said perhaps three words directly toward me since I began working at *La Maison du Paon*."

"This is childish. Come now."

"Do not fucking speak down to me. You're a disgusting old man!" Kiana shouted viciously. "Fucking hells, you're Skrull-damned twice my age." Kiana felt a revulsion ripple through her from letting herself willingly be with him. They had fought the Daanav together. Saved each other's lives. He was blunt and straightforward, but gentle and kind. He was knowledgeable. Then it dawned on her. *He reminds me of my father.* Rojas Ahmadi was stoic, gentle, loving, and did not take to inaction. Rojas was not only a caring father but an admirable man. *And Kaplan mirrors his qualities.*

Kaplan stood silently, his lips in a hard line.

"I can't do this anymore," Kiana continued in a fury, the word spilling out uncontrolled. "I can't stand another second with you." *Is it such a bad thing that he's like my father?*

Kaplan Mir did not answer.

"Say something, for fuck's sake."

"I am sorry, Kiana Ahmadi. I am sorry that I made you feel this way. Say the word, and I shall be gone from your life."

"Yes." Her lips quivered. *No, what am I saying?* "Yes. Go, get away from me." Tears blurred her vision. *No, I want to be with him.*

Kaplan Mir nodded, turned away, striding into the dark streets of the Ville de Voleurs, and disappeared into their shadows.

Come back. I need you. Kiana knelt, wiping away the streams from her cheeks, making herself as small as possible. She gripped her head and cursed herself.

Chapter Seven

LONGING

Fucking fucks...the damn demons have gone mad. The beasts shrieked and wailed in despair below where Jude Nelon sat on his horse on a jagged bluff, looking down at the chaos. *Skrull's fucking hells. What's gotten into them?* His eyes fell over the massive crater where the mountain had once stood. *That has got to have something to do with it.*

"They are dispersing in every direction," Joanna Ohlec said from where she sat just behind him.

She was right. Dark clouds still covered the skies as smoke rose from those massive six-legged blue-flaming beasts. The creatures were leaving the road they had followed fanatically until now. Running into the woods below or trudging up the mountain passes. He and this young woman had been keeping a reasonable distance from the path but traveling parallel to it. There was a commotion of branches snapping and rocks tumbling below them from where they watched on a higher level. They had climbed up here to find a good view of the surroundings.

One of the black-haired, deformed hulks burst through the scrawny mountain bushes. It screeched at the sight of Jude and Joanna, and a score more broke through the tree line. Hounds and hulks and a strange-looking grey one he'd never seen before. The creatures began aggressively climbing toward the two on horseback, screaming and wailing as they came.

"Fucking wonderful," Jude muttered. "Do you think you can handle them?"

"I don't know," Joanna said nervously. "Maybe we should just run?"

"In these mountains, the horses are slow and could break a leg. They will catch up eventually, especially those dogs." To his surprise, the bulky grey one was ahead of even the hounds, using its long arms to launch itself up the rocky incline. Jude dismounted. "Come, fighting on horseback up here will be too difficult."

Joanna hesitantly followed suit.

"Like I said, it's best to learn by doing. Try to stop that fucking ugly thing at the front." He pointed a dagger at the grey beast who was closing in.

Joanna nodded and sucked in a breath, raising her arms above her head. A sphere of flame exploded into life above her, and she shouted with effort as she flung it at the grey beast. It impacted with a burst that exuded heat so fiercely Jude felt it from where he stood. But the creature broke through the blast, its flesh sizzling and hanging away from glinting bones and its *metallic* skull.

"What in all the fucks?!" Jude flicked open his pouch of glimmering blue marbles. He pinched one and pulled his other palm across his dagger, swiftly splashing the fresh blood over the marble, then flicked it ahead of him. The beast was a dozen steps away when the tidal wave of seawater slammed into it. The wave crashed down the mountain, turning dark with debris and breaking trees and tumbling stones. All the Daanav before them, including the grey one, shrieked and reached out as they were sucked under the tsunami of water.

"You could use magic all this time? Why didn't you tell me?" Joanna asked in astonishment.

"Skrull's balls, girl. Do you think they would send an ordinary man to capture magi?" Jude grinned. "All right, now we run like fucking hells." He took up his horse's reins and led him in the opposite direction of the Daanav.

"Right." Joanna quickly followed after him.

Sometime later, in the darkness of night, they stopped to camp. They'd fled west, trying to descend the mountain range as they did so. Jude tied the horses to a thick, stubby tree nearby and began rolling out their blankets under the overhang of a shaggy pine tree. The needles would insulate them against the cold, somewhat, but he didn't want to start a fire, fearing the beasts would still be hunting them.

Countering his thoughts, Joanna ignited a small flame above her hand. It flickered brightly in the darkness.

Jude hurried over to her and covered the flame with both hands, extinguishing it simultaneously, grasping her open hand.

Joanna sucked in a small gasp as he did so. Their bodies nearly pressed together.

He looked at her in the darkness. A bright moon gave faint, lustrous light, and stars stretched across the horizon, showing Jude her face. *A warm, pleasing face. This girl has been through so much. She seeks true companionship. I can feel her need, like an aura around her.* Jude leaned closer, and inches from her lips, he whispered, "No flame tonight, Joanna. For we do not know if those things are nearby."

Her breath tickled his lips as she inched closer, her other hand joining their union. "All right, Huntsman. Then how are we to keep warm tonight?"

Fucks be to me. Jude had never been with a woman or a man. *Or anyone at all, for that matter.* He had been content to only work and otherwise relax in his garden. Not once had he the incline to pursue an attraction. "Uh—uh," he stuttered. *Skrull's balls, get your fucking act together, Jude.* "Um, I thought we could huddle close together under the pine needles there."

Joanna smiled genuinely, *beautifully*, her pale round cheeks reddening as she led Jude on, still holding his hands. She got low and crawled under the pine overgrowth. Her suddenly stimulating, shapely body moved suggestively as the woman crawled. Joanna turned, laying on her back, beckoning him to join her. She was remarkably round in all the right places, and Jude suddenly wanted to clutch her tightly against him and feel her unadorned skin.

He scurried in after her, twisting awkwardly to land on his back.

Joanna Ohlec immediately buried into his chest.

He wrapped his arms around her and held her. Cradling her head in a hand as she began to sob gently. "It's all right now," he whispered into her raven-black hair. "I'll keep you safe."

"You are too kind. You are nothing like *him*. Yet why do I feel guilty for being in your arms? Like I am betraying his love for me."

Ebras Corb, the Alpha. What did that Skrull-damned bastard do to you? "You really believe he loves you? Or that you can love a man such as that?"

"I don't know. I can feel that emotion pulling within me. My mind tells me that I *need* to be with the Alpha. For I am his."

"The man alters memories. He can anchor his will within your mind."

"No, it can't be." Joanna shook her head in disbelief.

"The arrogant prick has told me himself. Ebras wipes the memory of everyone I bring to him."

Joanna paused for a long moment as they lay together. Finally, she said, "I think you're right. There is nothing in my mind beyond the *Convent Enclosure*. Beyond waking up in that cage. I can barely remember my age, twenty-six summers, I think."

Only a few years younger than myself...But Jude's thoughts turned to all the people he had sent to the Alpha over the years. *Hettra's mercy. What have I been sending them to? I brought them to him for years, only for their memories to be stripped so they forget themselves.* Jude had been doing this task since his twenty-second summer. *Ten years of sending people to become the playthings of Ebras fucking Corb.* Thankfully, Jude hadn't been the one to capture Joanna. There were a few other Huntsmen in Ebras's employ. "I'm sorry, Joanna, truly. It could have been me who sent you to that place."

She lifted her head, her brilliant blue eyes looking deep into his own. "But it wasn't?"

"No, it wasn't," Jude reassured.

"I knew it couldn't have been." Her head inched forward, and her lips brushed his.

He lifted his head in response. Truly and tenderly returning the kiss.

She began to hurriedly unbutton his tunic.

He did likewise, his hands suddenly cupping her impossibly soft bare breasts. *Gods, I've never felt something so wonderful.*

She gasped and pushed her lips against his with impassioned fervor as he rolled atop her, and she began pulling at his belt.

Crack.

Jude bolted upright, pushing her down as he scrambled from the cover of the pine tree. A dagger darted into his hand.

The hulking brute's massive claws sliced into him. Jude tried to move, but it was too late. The razor-sharp points ripped into his arm.

"Fucking hells." He grasped the wound, blood spewing between his fingers. *Fucking fucks. The one time I let down my guard.* Jude stumbled backward, tripping over a branch and falling onto his back. His head slammed into stone, and all became black.

Chapter Eight

TRADE

"Bring Darkclaw Marah to me unharmed, and I will cooperate with you, Lord Skaad," Saudett demanded as she entered a hall. Her low-cut, sophisticated mauve and dusky dress cascaded about her feet. *Skrull's balls, I feel ridiculous in this.*

Sitting at the end of an extravagantly long dining table was the Lord Skaad. "Dear me, my Lady, such resolution burns within you." Hear-fan Skaad smiled as she approached. "It is admirable." He stood and clapped his two left hands together. "As she says, bring the creature, Darkclaw Marah, here immediately."

Damn, I had not expected him to agree. Now, what do I do?

Hear-fan gestured for her to sit, his eyes taking her in as he continued. "Dare I say, the gown suits you. You are truly an exquisite human."

Saudett flushed slightly. The dress pulled at places she was unused to and was constricting. Still, she had gazed at herself in the floor-to-ceiling mirror within her chamber for an absurdly extended time. Turning about, time after time, admiring her own features. It was odd. She loved how she looked in the gowns and other outfits she'd found in her chamber and, honestly, was feeling attractive. *Simon always said I was beautiful, even if all he had ever seen me in was my Shepherd's Eye regalia or his oversized men's clothing as I relaxed at home.*

"Don't just stand there, my Lady Saudett," Hear-fan said. "Have a seat."

Saudett snapped back to reality and circled the dining table. She chose a seat not directly beside Hear-fan but a few chairs down. More wing-tied servants began to dish up delicious-smelling food on a delicate silver platter in front of her. Filling a likewise silver chalice with a crisp golden wine. *Chilled wine.* She watched it sparkle in the light. She took a sip. A burst of flavor, sweet and bright with nuances of fruit and flower. Saudett savored each drop. *By the gods, that is perfect.*

"How do you find your chambers?" Hear-fan asked, lounging back in his seat at the head of the table. Swirling his chalice of wine thoughtfully. "Adequate, I would hope."

"It is exceptional," Saudett answered genuinely.

"I'm glad," Hear-fan answered with a smile. "I wish to make you feel comfortable. You may take a few days to settle in before I require your aid."

"My aid?"

"You have the air of a warrior about you. No, not a warrior...a soldier. From the way you walk and hold yourself, I can tell. I have some children who are intelligent enough to understand how to carry a weapon. Still, they need training and a leader."

"You would have me train and fight alongside your children? Against who?"

"Oh, you know, there are hundreds of primitive Lâns that would benefit significantly from subjugation."

"What about *my* Lân, the Earste Lân?"

"Of course, I would not send you against your own people. You humans are turning out to be quite the thorn in my side. Your people routed my forces in that blasted desert that the Wayfarer, Gaelin Yesnala, had bound my children to, and now"—Hear-fan Skaad's voice became increasingly exasperated and elevated as he continued—you have pushed me out of the Moreas Lân. Not that that festering swamp was of much use to me anyhow." He slammed a hand against the tabletop. "Confounded humans. If only I could bring you all into the fold as my devoted children."

"Perhaps you underestimate my people."

"Perhaps, and that is precisely why I need you, my Lady."

"There is undoubtedly a catch, no? I am to live in luxury here and train your soldiers, and that's that?"

"For now." He grinned roguishly, showing his pitch-black teeth. His teeth and inverted eyes were off-putting, but he was of fair grey skin, with a long jawline, and was oddly handsome. *He has been alive for thousands of years, yet he looks no older than Simon.*

"Is there any way I can persuade you to leave the Earste Lân alone?" Saudett asked doubtfully.

"Quite the bargainer you are," he said with a chuckle. "It is so pleasant to finally speak with an intelligent being. I will give you two conditions. First, prove yourself to me, train and lead my armies against my other foes. Second, if you or any of my children are to slay that Wayfarer, Gaelin Yesnala, who was charged with the Earste Lân, I will leave that Lân alone for eternity. But until then, I strive to bring him out of hiding by marching across its lands."

Saudett wasn't overly fond of Gaelin Yesnala. Still, how many people's deaths would be on her hands? *How many will be slaughtered at the hands of the armies I lead? But, if the Earste Lân is safe...then Simon is safe. My mother will be safe. It matters not how many others die as long as they are alive.* The faster she proved herself, the less the people of the Earste Lân would suffer.

"I will think about your offer, Lord Hear-fan Skaad," Saudett said. "Can I request one other thing?"

"Name it."

"My companion is to never leave my side."

"The wolfman?"

"*They* are Volkinn."

"Volkinn, so fascinating. How I would greatly like to study them. But alas, I shall bend to my esteemed guest's wishes. My home is yours."

There was an ear-splitting howl from one of the corridors, and a door slid open as Trije-fan Skaad pushed Darkclaw Marah into the dining room.

Marah was chained, and their canine golden eyes were wide and frantic, fangs bared as their head swung about, taking in the chamber around them. As they came to find Saudett, Marah's head tilted questionably, and they hissed questioningly, "What is the meaning of this?"

"Marah..." Saudett began.

"Release them, my son," Hear-fan ordered.

"This one cannot be contained," Trije-fan Skaad reproached. "It will attack if I release the bond."

"Do it." Hear-fan snapped.

Trije-fan's jaw locked under the shadow of his hood. He took a key from a pouch on his waist and clicked it into the lock on Marah's wrists.

As soon as the chains rattled to the floor, Marah leaped for Hear-fan Skaad, claws and fangs aiming to tear out his throat.

Saudett dashed in front of him, holding her arms out wide. "Stop, Marah. Please."

Darkclaw Marah skidded to a halt, inches from Saudett's face. "Why protect him? These things are shadow and hell incarnate. Can you not smell it?"

"I'm not protecting him. I am protecting *you*." Saudett pleaded. She reached out gently and put her hand on Marah's neck. The Volkinn's tension lessened immediately, and their neck and back hair flattened.

"Good, good," Hear-fan muttered unnervingly behind her.

Saudett leaned close to Marah, speaking quietly. "We will cooperate for now. But you have to trust me."

Marah let out a canine huff and nodded reluctantly.

"Darkclaw Marah, is it?" Hear-fan asked. "Please sit, eat." He waved his son away. "Leave us now."

Trije-fan twisted about lithely and swiftly glided out the way he had come.

Marah sniffed at the food, then hungrily devoured the contents while sitting across the table from Saudett.

"Dear me, what an appetite," Hear-fan said, resting his chin on his crossed hands. "Tell me, Darkclaw, what *are* you?"

Marah gulped down a bite and glared at Hear-fan. "We are Volkinn."

"And what is a *Volkinn*?"

Marah shrugged and placed a hand on their chest. "I am Volkinn."

Hear-fan sighed and turned back to Saudett. "One of few words, it seems. At any rate, Lady Saudett, please tell me of yourself. I wish to know about you. About your past, about the steps that have led you to me. What you dream of in the future. What makes you tick, as it were?"

Saudett couldn't help but speak. Her life story began to spew from her lips. She retold Hear-fan the tale of growing up in Xamid, in the Jewel of the East, the city of Al'Jalif, with absent parents. Training as a caravan guard. Searching the Burning Sea for the parents who abandoned her. Of being enthusiastically approached by Simon and eventually falling for him. Cautiously withholding their extracurricular bedroom activities. Finally, she told him of all the strange events leading her back into the desert to rescue Simon from the bandit nomads and how she eventually found him. She avoided telling him of Hata Vasara. *I abandoned her just as I have now abandoned Simon.* Continuing, she informed Hear-fan Skaad of her reunion with her mother and retold her mother's story of why she had left Saudett at such a young age.

Hear-fan Skaad listened intently.

As did Darkclaw Marah from across the table, all the while scarfing down food as they did so.

Lord Skaad smiled, gasped, and asked curious questions during her tale. *He is genuinely interested.* He had not once tried to harm her since their arrival, and Darkclaw Marah looked like their wounds had been tended to, and no more maltreatment had befallen them.

Saudett reached the point of the tale where she had taken the blow to her stomach. "My baby…" The words caught in her throat.

Hear-fan stood and gently placed a hand on her back. "Oh, my precious thing, I am profoundly sorry that something so grave could befall you. Enough talk for now. I think it is high time we retired for the day." He clapped his hands, and the servants appeared. "Shall I have a separate chamber prepared for Darkclaw Marah?"

Marah gave a low, guttural growl.

"Ah, I see. Then you shall share with the lady." He bent a flourishing bow. "I take my leave and look forward to seeing you both at breakfast tomorrow." With that, he strode from the dining hall.

The servant stood at attention next to Saudett and Marah and would not move until Saudett stood and looked about for the way she had entered. One of the servants croaked in a strange language and shuffled toward the wall. Saudett followed the winged being, and Darkclaw Marah, prowling in her wake, cautiously snarled at every uneven shadow.

Chapter Nine

HOME

Simon made a final inspection of the trench leading up to the Wayfarers Gate. They were ready to release the dam. He had repeatedly reviewed the plan regarding the gateway in his head. *If memory serves, the Wayfarers Gates can only be connected to one Lân at a time.* If someone tried to connect another Gate from somewhere else to the Moreas Lân Gate, nothing would happen as the Hasiera Gate was already linked. The only way to disrupt it would be for someone to physically go to either the Hasiera Gate or the Moreas Lân Gate and deactivate them or aim them at another Lân. *Skrull's hairy balls this is getting complicated.* Theoretically, once the water flowed through the Gate, they would never need to return to the Moreas Lân.

A group of Kadal lizard people made ready to break the dam. Simon and his people were to return to the valley of Hasiera and await the waters so they would not be trapped or need to swim through the underground tunnels.

"Do not break it until one hour after we leave," Simon reiterated, his voice rising a decibel higher as he addressed the gecko-like lizard blinking and nodding its head up at him. "Do...you...understand me?"

It kept nodding.

"By the gods," Simon muttered, rubbing his temples. "Where is Sir Kogs when I need him?"

The lizard twisted its head at Kogs's name. "Pah, puny Kogs is no match for mighty Yoz. Yoz will break the warlock-monkey's silly barrier."

"Oh, so you *can* speak."

"Yes," Yoz hissed. "Yoz is named the new king of Rawa. Of course, Yoz speaks puny warlock language."

Simon shook his head. *For the love of Hettra, let's just go home.* He held up his index finger. "One hour." He turned and hurried along the trench away from the barrier blocking the water from the large river.

Naurr and a linen masked, heavy-set Hasieran warrior awaited him at the Gate. The rest of his people had already returned to the Earste Lân.

"What's the rush, boss?" Naurr chuckled at Simon's frantic hustling. "Swamp creature on your heels?"

"No, far worse, I fear. I don't think the Kadal knows exactly what an hour is. Let's get out of here."

Naurr's eyes widened, and immediately, they heard the rumbling of rushing water.

"Oh, fucks." Simon placed his hands on the backs of the two men and whispered, "*Strangung.*" Simultaneously infusing himself with the spell as well. Then he pushed them through the Gateway, following behind quickly.

Naurr bolted through the small cavern and sprang up the rope ladder just as water crashed through the portal, sweeping Simon and the Hasieran warrior off their feet and slamming them against the wall.

The warrior's head glanced awkwardly off the stone, and he went limp.

The strength spell lessened the pain as Simon grasped the man's collar, and water filled the chamber. He looked up to see Naurr disappear over the ledge above. A dazzling light pierced down from above. *Thank Hettra, Naurr should have time to get further down the tunnel.* Simon internalized another spell. *Gebod.* "Keep going, my good man." Simon's voice, magically enhanced, echoed up the walls into the tunnel. "We are going straight up."

The river was pouring in, and Simon trod water desperately, trying to keep the unconscious man's head above it. They ascended with the tide. As they approached the corner leading down the tunnel toward Hasiera, Simon grasped that ledge with all his might and heaved the man above his head. "*Afléotan.*" The man drifted upward toward a hole in the cavern ceiling. *Now, how do I get up?* The water began flooding down the tunnel, nearly pulling Simon with it. He managed to get a foot on the ledge and kicked against it.

"*Afléotan!*" Simon cried again. He gasped for breath as he floated upward, bumping into the limp, drifting form of the man above. He gently guided the unconscious warrior up and through the bright light of the hole above. The scorching sun immediately caused Simon to wince and shield his eyes, nearly letting the man float away into the sky. Simon twisted clumsily mid-air, quickly grabbed the man again, dispelled his *Afléotan* incantation, and stepped onto the hard red stone. He paused to catch his breath from the exertion and took a moment to get used to the sweltering heat of the desert.

"We made it, my good fellow," Simon wheezed. The man didn't move, but he could see his chest rising as he breathed. "By the Primus, let's get back to the valley." Simon began to walk, holding the man by the belt as he floated beside him.

A few moments later, the man groaned and opened his eyes to see the earth moving below him. "What in Skrull's hell? What's happening to me.?"

"Calm down, my good fellow." Simon quickly dispelled the floatation spell.

The man flailed in the air momentarily and then thudded to the ground.

"Oh, gods, I'm sorry." Simon winced. "Should have thought that one through."

"Hettra's holy whores." The man rolled over, pulling the linen wrap away from his face.

The most handsome face Simon had ever seen. Brown skin, darkened by the sun, with a rugged look and confident smile. He was taller and more robust than Simon by a few inches and pounds, though he felt the taut muscles in the man's hefty arms as Simon pulled him to his feet. He wore a loose brown robe over his shoulders and a tight linen wrap covering his head and neck. A deadly curved sword hung at his waist, along with leather pouches across his chest. The Hasieran warrior found his footing with grace and agility.

"First?" the man asked as Simon stood gawking.

"Ahem," Simon cleared his throat inelegantly. "What is your name, my good fellow?"

"Zahir Al-Rashid," the man announced with a bow. "How did we get up here? I only remember the waters rushing in around us."

"A pleasure to meet you, Zahir Al-Rashid," Simon said. "Thank Qav's luck, I was there, or you and my good man Naurr would have drowned. Those Skrull-forsaken lizards couldn't wait."

"You saved my life, First Otsoa." Zahir knelt to one knee, took Simon's hand, and kissed it. "I owe you a life debt."

Simon felt his neck and cheeks flush. "Oh, no need for that." He coughed. "Though I would love to get to know *you* better, Zahir Al-Rashid."

"My Otsoa, I will be your steadfast sentinel and strive to protect you with my life." Zahir drew his sword with a flourish and held it out in his palms, still kneeling. His dark-brown eyes gleamed. "I shall never leave your side."

By the gods, what is the proper Hasieran etiquette here? This seems like a Xamidian custom. Simon recalled some texts he'd read about the Sultan of Xamid accepting warriors into his royal guard. He gently cupped Zahir's hands with his own. "I accept your pledge, Zahir Al-Rashid. You shall be my Rakshak, as the Xamidians say."

"I am your Rakshak." Zahir bowed his head once more, then got to his feet.

"Wonderful!" Simon exclaimed, putting an arm around Zahir's shoulder as they began to walk. Simon duly noted the man did not pull away or disengage from the embrace. "Now tell me more of yourself, Zahir. Were you born in Hasiera? Or *liberated*, as the former First Otsoa used to put it. Any family? *Lovers,* perhaps?"

"I would much rather make steadfast companions over lovers, Lord First," Zahir said with a stern smile. "And you are a lucky man. Your spouse is a formidable woman."

My spouse? Simon tilted his head at the thought of Saudett. *Oh gods, my wife.* "Skrull's fucking hells," Simon blurted. He had utterly forgotten about her during the turmoil of Gaelin's appearance and the work involved in setting the dam up on the river, the Wayfarers Gate, and everything else compiled on top. He released his embrace on Zahir. "By the Primus. Where is my wife?"

"Have you forgotten, First? The Lady Builder chased the winged man into the Skaad Lân."

How in the gods could I forget my own wife? Simon rubbed his temples. It wasn't enough. He began thrashing his head with his fists. "Stupid idiot. Fucking senseless son-of-a–Simon."

Zahir suddenly grasped Simon's wrists and stopped him from slamming them against his skull again. Simon turned forcefully to look deep into the man's dusky gaze. "My Lord First, worry not. You will think of something. This is the second time you have saved Hasiera. Your people will do anything to aid you. We *will* find your wife."

"I—" Simon started.

Zahir's dark hazel eyes shone, his expression so soft and full of empathy toward Simon.

Simon slowly raised his other hand and touched Zahir's rotund cheek.

Zahir smiled but took Simon's hand away from his cheek. Then he said, "Come, my Otsoa, let's go home."

Simon let the man lead him across the craggy red landscape toward the valley of Hasiera.

FORLORN

Hata stepped up the last set of stairs into the next level of the tower of Crystalia Keep and turned into a long hallway. The stairs continued upward, but Queen Stormfall awaited her at the end of the hall. The Queen beckoned again, pushed through a doorway, and disappeared as the heavy door swung back into place.

Hata hurried to catch up and fumbled into the door. The weighty, elegantly carved granite door groaned as she entered a large open chamber. Light flooded in from a large window of shining steel bars and colorful crystalline glass. Planters edged the base of the window, and many bright, vibrant flowers, bushes, and strange grasses grew there.

The Queen seated herself on a comfortable-looking divan in the center of the room. Other furniture surrounded a low stone ring where a ruby gemstone contraption glowed and hummed faintly in the center.

"Come, sit, Sunstone," the Queen said sternly.

Hata did so. Warmth emanated from the crimson, shining stone before her as she sat across from the Queen.

"I have a mind to destroy that Gateway and be done with Skaad and his Lân for good," the Queen announced as Hata settled in.

"It is your Lân and your right to do so, my Queen."

"You would name me *your* Queen so soon?"

Hata's gut churned, and her cheeks flushed. "Apologies, Queen Stormfall." *Gods, Chanel would've known how to act in the presence of royalty.*

"Save the formality when it is just you and me, my dear." The Queen smiled for the first time, her dark eyes sparkling with amusement. "Please, call me Raine."

"All right, *Raine*. But you are not upset that I have reignited Hear-fan Skaad's conquest of you and your people?"

"It was bound to happen, eventually. We were in denial as it has been nearly a hundred years since we encountered those creatures."

"The Children of Skaad."

"Abominations. Quite unnatural." Raine paused and thought for a moment. "I've only heard the tales. I was born fifty years after they had last been seen."

"Fifty years.? How old are you?"

"I am still very young in my people's eyes. Only forty-five rotations of Luminar."

"Forty-five..." Hata stared in disbelief. From what she could tell, the woman looked to be the same age as herself.

"By the look on your face, you think I am elderly." Rain said with a soft laugh. "I suppose the Himin-dvergar age slower than humans, perhaps."

"If by rotations you mean years, I am only over twenty-one." Hata had to stop and think. *How long was I in the Convent Enclosure? Months? Years?*

"Please, Sunstone, tell me more of these creatures of Skaad."

"Hata, you can call me Hata." Hata smiled at the Raine, taking in her sparkling eyes that seemed to burn with determination yet looked so tired. Her soft brown skin and slightly freckled nose and cheeks. Her lips...

"Hata?"

"Oh gods, yes." Hata shook herself out of it. "The Children. They are bound to him. He controls them with his devastating magical power."

"Such power must be held in check. But at any rate, I do agree that we should fight. Even join forces with other Lâns, as you suggested." Raine exhaled heavily, rubbing her eyes wearily. "Yet that Gate is the only way, and he controls it. How could we send word to others to go on the offensive?"

"I..." Hata started, but was at a loss. "I do not know. I am so sorry this has been forced onto you."

"Ha." Raine uttered a sound of exasperation. "I am Queen. This is merely another day with another problem to solve."

"Teras's stones, I do not envy your position."

Raine smiled tiredly again, slumping back in her seat and closing her eyes as she spoke. "It is stressful. I do not talk informally with my people, both commoners and retainers alike. It is a nice change to loosen up for a moment with you."

"By Teras, I can't imagine," Hata answered as she studied Queen Raine Stormfall. Raine looked stunning in her magnificent, polished armor. But oh, so weary. *She is such a strong leader and a strong woman. But I can tell she is stressed. She must be longing to relax and have an ordinary friendship.* Raine's dark freckled cheeks were dimpled slightly as she rested. *She is lovely.* Those dimples became more profound when the woman smiled. Hata found herself gazing at Raine's rosy, soft-looking lips once again. Hata rebuked herself internally. *No, she can be just a friend. She needs a friend.*

Raine opened one eye to look at Hata.

By the gods, that is charming. Hata blushed, turning her head away. "My Queen—I mean, Raine."

"Yes? Hata?"

Change the subject, you idiot. "The battle. Should we not be preparing?"

"That is the one good thing about being in charge. I told my people to prepare, and they will do it. I need only make the rounds in a few hours to boost morale, then we assess the situation and decide our next move."

"Well then, perhaps I should go find Bryn and Rorik."

Raine sat up hurriedly. "Oh, I was going to invite you to dine with me. We can't go to war on an empty stomach."

At the sound of that, Hata's own stomach growled immediately. *Teras's thunder, I haven't eaten in days.*

"By the sound of it, you need it. Come." Raine stood and strode to a small round table near the wall. An odd metal cone was fixed to the wall attached to a pipe that went up said wall and through the ceiling. Raine spoke into the cone, "Dinner, please, for two."

There was a clamoring sound and some unintelligible muffled cries on the other end, then a gruff female voice answered after a moment, "Coming right down, Your Majesty."

"They must be surprised I have company," Raine muttered, a half smile on her lips.

"You always eat alone?" Hata asked.

"I do."

"Well, as long as I am here, I would love to join you."

This time, Raine blushed. "It is not too much to ask? It seems you got on well with Bryn and Rorik."

"Ha. Those two are an adorable duo. Honestly, we should invite them to dinner, too. You would have a hoot." Hata couldn't help but giggle at the thought of the two men. "They are infatuated with each other, but both are in denial. It's so ridiculous."

"If only it were so simple. I could not effortlessly drop my persona before my people. I have meaning to them and can't have them thinking of me otherwise." Raine's eyes fell to the table's stone top, and she picked at it with a finger. "They do sound amusing, though."

She is so lonely. "Perhaps you—"

A door swung open on the opposite side of the room, interrupting Heta as a burly Himin-dvergar woman pushed a cart into the chamber.

The woman paused as she sighted Hata seated across from the Queen at the small table. "Luminar's bright beard," she exclaimed. "Your Highness, who is this lanky tree beast at your table? She's not one of them crystal elves now, is she?"

"Dvalinn," Raine said sternly, a frown creasing her brow.

"Of course, Your Majesty, my humblest apologies." Dvalinn began placing platters of food on the table. She leaned toward Hata and winked knowingly.

As the woman finished serving the food, Raine nodded to her in thanks. Dvalinn hustled back toward the door behind the Queen. She turned and smiled at Hata, put one fist up, and shook it while mouthing the word *yes.*

Hata's cheeks were aching from smiling. *Raine's people know she is isolated.* Hata nodded to herself in conclusion. *I will help fix that.*

The food was succulent roast meats and violet and crimson root vegetables seasoned with a hint that left Hata's palate with a burning sensation. Hata had scarcely taken three bites of the delicious meat when a barrage of banging at the door disturbed their meal.

"Come!" Raine called in answer.

The door swung open, and the guardsman, Finn Sunstrider, clamored into the room, sweating profusely. "Your Majesty." He panted heavily, gasping for breath to summon his words. "Our scouts have sighted the enemy."

CHAPTER ELEVEN

FIRST

"What? Kaplan Mir? He left?" Anora asked her daughter in astonishment.

"I obviously didn't mean that much to him," Kiana answered, her face sullen, but the skin around her eyes and nose was reddened from crying. "Let him go for all I care."

You do care. "I am so sorry, my daughter. I have been wallowing in my own self-pity and have not been here for you." She turned and addressed Baal and Brena as well. "For all of you."

"Is too bad," Baal grunted in response. "Baal liked puny bookman."

Kiana's brooding expression nearly broke down again as she snapped, "He let me become a whore so easily. How could you two do it? How could you let your mate fuck other people, Baal?" Kiana's questioning glare burnt toward Brena and Baal.

"I simply couldn't," Brena answered. "That is why you were the one to find Zalias, and you were the one to discover Hata's whereabouts. We thank you and owe you for that." Brena turned and looked at her husband for a long moment, then returned her gaze to Kiana. "You let me become a bouncer because I wasn't strong enough to do what I *must* to save our daughter."

"It is true." Baal nodded with his signature toothy smile. "We are now in friend Kiana's debt. We tried, and we would do anything to bring Hata back." Baal rested a massive hand on Brena's shoulder. "Anything for our daughter."

Brena gently touched her husband's hand and whispered, "Thank you, aviomieheni."

Anora cautiously approached her daughter, offering an arm. "Shall we go for a stroll? There is something I wish to speak to you about."

"You—" Kiana turned on Anora quickly, her face full of rage, but as her glimmering violet eyes, so like her father's, met Anora's, her daughter broke again. Her lips quivered as Kiana fell into Anora's arms. Burying her face into her mother's shoulder. "Why did he go? Why did he leave me?"

"Oh, my daughter, my Kiana," Anora whispered gently, holding her child. "I don't know. Love is a difficult thing to grasp. We choose who to love, and, in turn, they must *choose* to love us."

"You chose father? After all that happened to you in the desert with your first husband?"

"I did, but it did not happen overnight."

"Please tell me."

"Shall we walk and talk? I need the air. I've been cooped up in here for days."

"I'd like that," Kiana whispered as Anora led her out of the rickety homestead. Baal and Brena nodded and smiled knowingly in their wake.

"After the battle against Gaddaar Kafilah, I lay wounded in the desert." Anora began her tale...

Anora squinted blindly, the blazing sun's light piercing her vision. A slight silhouette of a figure walking along next to the cart she lay in. The shadows of massive sand dunes occasionally disrupted the sun's burning heat. Anora would wake in fits, pain coursing through her body. At long last, she finally awoke under a soft linen canvas, waving gently to a breeze.

"Does she live?" a gravelly low voice said from her side.

Anora groaned and turned her head to look. A man sat cross-legged on a cushion, *violet* eyes watching her. His head and face were wrapped tightly in tan linen, obscuring his facial features. Anora pushed herself up on her arm. Agony cut through her side, and she looked down to see her waist bandaged with a faint stain of blood seeping through. Her husband, Gaddaar Kafilah, had stabbed her in a last-ditch effort before he died with her own sword through his gut.

"Here, drink this," the violet-eyed man stood and moved to her swiftly, placing a sloshing water skin to her lips.

Anora gulped the water down desperately.

"You took quite a thrashing out there. That man we found at your side, I'm afraid, did not make it. You were so entwined we thought you had both succumbed to the Burning Sea and come together to hold one another in your last moments."

"You make it sound so romantic," Anora rasped. Her throat scratched like sand against a sword. "It was far from it."

"Well, until we pulled you apart to find your blade through his innards."

Anora grunted and lay back down. "Thank you for saving me, though perhaps you should have just let me die out there."

The man tilted his head curiously. "The past is forever in our wake. One must look forward to our future and strive to make it our own."

Anora closed her eyes wearily. "You sound like my philosophy professor at the Grand Library in Al'Jalif."

"Ah, so you are from Xamid?"

Anora squinted open one eye. "My skin color did not give that away?" She eyed the stranger. "You sound Xamidian yourself. Though I have never met anyone with such striking eyes."

"My mother is actually from Tal'tulu. That's where I acquired these unique eyes."

"Could you stop hiding behind your mask and reveal yourself to a new friend?"

"Friend?" he repeated gravely. "You may rethink such a statement after the tidings you will soon receive."

The memory of her caravan returned to her. Her guardsmen being attacked during the sandstorm. Gaddaar's faction against hers. Captain Blake of the Shepherd's Eye. He was overwhelmed by...wolves. *Yet, were they even wolves? Some had looked like people.* Anora sat up again, painfully. "What happened to my people? To my caravan?"

"Dead. All dead. The pack of man-beasts attacked your caravan before we could aid them. They travel with the storm to hide from us."

"Man-beasts?" Anora's head was thundering. "And who is *us*?"

"Indeed, so far as we can tell, they are part wolf, part human. We are in a bit of a struggle against them for dominance over the Burning Sea."

"You keep saying *we* and *us*. Who are you people?"

"I am Rojas Ahmadi, of Hasiera. We are the Hasieran."

"Hasiera? Hasieran? I've never heard of such a people."

"So it should be, for all who come to Hasiera, become the Hasieran. That or they die. By decree of the First Otsoa."

Anora rolled her eyes. "Skrull's unholy balls. You sure have a lot of titles for a *secret* nation in the desert."

"*Nation?*" Rojas Ahmadi snorted. "We are far from that. There are only a few hundred of us."

"By the Primus," Anora groaned again. Her eyes suddenly burnt with exhaustion. She slowly lay down once more.

"Yes, you need to recover your strength. Rest now...Lady?"

"Anora," she whispered her name as she soon fell back into darkness.

All who come to Hasiera become the Hasieran. The words echoed in Anora's dreams. *Or they die.* She woke again with a start. It was dark, only a faint grey light beginning to creep through the canvas sheets of the shelter she was in. She was alone. Painstakingly, she stood and explored the small tent. Some dried meat hung from a wooden pole in the center. Anora hurriedly gobbled it down, gnawing at the salty, gristly protein. She pushed the canvas aside and peeked out into the night. Dawn was fast approaching. Tents scattered about her, most dark, some with a faint glow of firelight within. Anora looked both ways on the small path that snaked through the pavilions. There was no movement. Cautiously, she skulked down the track, stepping lightly. She was surprised at the sight of palm trees, fern bushes, and long green grass growing lushly on her way. The glint of moonlight reflected off a small bubbling stream off to her side. Still, she crept away and soon found herself on the edge of the camp. A few dozen horses were tethered to poles here, and Anora caught a movement through their midst. She quickly ducked behind a low-growing fern and watched.

A young man became visible, walking with an odd stick over his shoulder and whistling quietly. The green wood of the shaft seemed to grow in foot-long sections.

That man, Rojas Ahmadi, said nobody could leave once they came here. I will knock this lad out, steal a horse, and go home to my sweet Saudett. She crept closer as the boy turned a corner, rounding a tied-up horse and strolling past her hiding place. His back was to Anora. *Now.* She surged forward with a burst of speed and leaped, wrapping an arm around the boy's neck and pulling tight with her other arm.

He grunted, dropping the stick he'd been holding, and, to her surprise, reached up and grasped her, suddenly rolling forward as he did so. She lost her grip as she flipped over his shoulders and was launched away from him. They both landed with a thud into the dirt. Anora swiftly came to her feet and spun about to face him.

The boy was already standing and picking up his fallen pole stick. He twirled it deftly and fell into a ready stance. Finally, looking at his face, she saw he was not really a *boy*, but a young man most likely of a similar age to herself. Xamidian heritage. His face dark and stern, the makings of a black beard beginning on his upper lip, yet his grin held a playful edge as he sized her up.

"Well…" Anora sighed. "You are not an ordinary stable boy."

"Is that any way to greet your rescuers?"

"I didn't ask to be rescued." Anora dashed in. The pole swiped out at her, and she ducked and let loose a side-kick to his legs.

He spun, dodging her kick, and twirled the shaft around to bring it down on her.

She crossed her arms before her and caught the blow. Pain rushed through her arms, but she pushed it aside and grasped the stick.

He yanked at it.

She did not let go.

"We can't let you leave, woman. If you should tell people of our home, we will no longer be safe." He changed his strategy and pushed forward.

She brought her knee up into his groin as he came within reach.

He grunted as he bent over, leaning against her.

"I need to go home to my daughter," Anora hissed into his ear. "Please let me go. I will not tell anyone of this place."

"No, you can't," he groaned. "You are free to live here as you see fit. We will provide for you and any needs you have. But that is the one rule I govern by. No one can leave Hasiera."

She disengaged, pushing him away. "*You* govern by? You are hardly a man."

"I am a murderer. I killed my father as he beat my mother to death, and I ran from Xamid into the Burning Sea. Running without supplies into this desert is a death sentence, so nobody gave chase. It is how the Sultan of Al'Jalif executes many criminals."

Anora stood, stunned. She looked about, the dawn light breaking over the dunes to the east. The warm glow lit her surroundings to see the richly growing oasis all around her. "And you found this place?" she said after a long moment.

"Indeed." The man nodded. "I also started to find many others like me over the years. Outcasts of the Earste Lân."

"What is your name?" Anora asked.

"I am Gidraltar Lein, the First Otsoa of Hasiera."

"And so, days turned into weeks and weeks into months. I was taken under the wing of your father, Rojas. I aided in cultivating the valley and tending the crops. I learned horse breeding and taming. I sparred with your father and the First many times in those early days. They took notice of my proficiency in combat. They soon had me training newcomers who came to Hasiera. I taught them how to fight and how to ride. I helped them build Hasiera into what it has become."

"And my father courted you during all this?" Kiana asked as they strolled through a garden in an agreeable section of Nidhaut.

"Gradually, we became close." Anora flinched as the thought of Gaddaar Kafilah came back to her. "The wounds to my heart Gaddaar gave to me were too fresh. It took a long time for me to even warm to the idea of being with a man again. I never loved Gaddaar, but I have come to love your father."

"I can't even imagine," Kiana exhaled. "Astonishing. I did not even know I had Tal'tulu heritage in my blood."

"You must speak with your father when we return to Hasiera and inquire with him. He said his mother would have become a sage of the isles due to her gift until your grandfather, a Xamidian corsair, seduced her into leaving."

"A corsair? Skrull's balls. Why does my family have so many secrets?"

"This is why I wished to speak with you, to get everything out. So, you, my precious daughter, can know about the things I have done."

Kiana snorted but grinned slightly. "You have become a different person since Saudett came back. Had she not, you would still be drilling the dance into my veins rather than speaking to me."

"I tried to speak to you during our training, but you were always so angry."

"Gods, I hated you, Mother."

"I know...and I am sorry. I can't take back what I've done to you."

"Look forward, not back, Mother." Kiana nudged her playfully.

Anora smiled sincerely. "People are fond of using those words against me."

"Though I wish to hear how my father eventually won your heart."

"Let's find a warm meal, and I will tell you."

CHAPTER TWELVE

KINDLE

Fucks...my head. Jude Nelon awoke to a blazing inferno about him. The entire mountain-side was on fire. He squinted to see the silhouette of Joanna Ohlec casting missile after missile of screeching, blistering flame at the fiends around them.

Pain glanced through Jude's skull, and his arm burnt. *By the fucking gods, what in Hettra's holy tits is going on? We need to get out of here.* The fire lit the night sky, and the shrieks and cries of the beasts echoed as they rushed up the mountain and died as they came like moths to the flame. Even so, there were too many of them. Jude painfully pushed himself to his feet and began fiddling in a pouch on his belt. *I need a teleportation stone to get us the fucks out of here.* As he reached into his pocket, a thick, grey ape-like beast roared and leaped at him from behind.

He rolled out of the way, pulling a dagger and sliding it along the belly of the beast as he rolled. Black blood oozed, and his magic-infused marbles scattered and bounced down the rocky terrain. The contents of his pouches were fleeing from the safety of their homes.

"Fucking fucks." Jude cursed as he dashed away, flinging a dagger at the creature behind him. The razor-sharp blade bounced with a *clang* off the Daanav's head. *Skrull's scrotum. What in all the fucks are these things made of?* He turned toward Joanna, fumbling in another pouch as he did so.

She spun abruptly at his approach, raising a hand instinctively. A flaming javelin gripped and ready to be hurled toward him. Her eyes widened, and her mouth opened in surprise as she saw him. Then she flung the spiraling scorching projectile.

The heat singed his skin as it boiled through the air and struck the grey ape-like Daanav behind him. The flaming missile drilled into its chest, melting its flesh and metallic skeleton alike.

Jude rushed to Joanna, pulling a translucent cloud-like bead from his pouch and embracing her. He exhaled with exertion and muttered into her ear, "Hell of a first courtship." With a grin, he covered the bead with blood that was leaking down his arm.

Hundreds of the dark abominations poured over the snow-covered stone toward them, their ominous yellow eyes weaving through the darkness.

Grasping her tightly by the waist, he leaped skyward.

"By the Primus!" Joanna exclaimed, squirming awkwardly in his arms as they floated gradually upward.

"I can't control where this goes. It only makes us weightless," Jude mumbled into her hair as he held her close against him.

Her soft cheek brushed his stubbly, unshaven face. "Let me handle that." She wrapped her legs around his waist and gripped the back of his shirt with one hand.

The next moment, Jude felt heat burst into life behind him, and their entangled bodies careered through the air.

Blasting flame exhausted from Joanna's outstretched hand. She clung to him as the freezing mountain air whipped at them. Even with the bitter cold biting his face and the blistering heat at his back, her body pressed against him felt Skrull-damned wonderful. *Primus, take me, this woman.* No one had ever made him feel this way before, and he hadn't had the care to bother with such attachments. When he really thought about it, he'd never been sexually attracted to *anyone* before. *On top of it, now she has saved my worthless life.*

They soared through the sky for several minutes, far away from the horde of Daanav. Finally, Joanna aimed their trajectory toward the ground. As they approached, he coated the same spell-infused bead in a bit of blood, and the effects of his magic wore off, and they fell the last few feet. But he managed to stay on his feet and steady Joanna as she tried to stand, leaning against him for support.

"Thank you," he whispered into her ear. "You save my life."

She half smiled, breathless with exhaustion. "I was merely trying to keep myself alive."

Jude took her chin in his hand and looked into her sparkling cerulean eyes. *Stunning.* "You are truly remarkable." He leaned in and kissed her. They had kissed before, but this time, it was like a dream became reality, a moment he'd not known he'd been waiting for. He felt her lips touch his, soft and sweet. His cold heart caught a spark of kindling. She wrapped her arms around him, holding him close, and he returned the embrace. Her breath was warm and fragrant, filling his senses. Jude felt a rush of emotion, a blend of happiness, nervousness, passion, and awe. *I want to make it last forever, holding her here...but I also want so much more.* It was the most beautiful and nerve-wracking thing he had ever done.

Distant howls and wails echoed through the greying dawn.

Jude broke their embrace. "Can you walk? We need to keep moving."

"I just need a minute—"

He placed his arm under hers, supporting most of her weight, and began to walk. After a moment, he said, "If I remember correctly...that woman in the Burning Sea, the Third Otsoa, she had said these creatures can't live in the light of day. We just need to keep moving until the sun is in the sky. *Then* we can rest."

Joanna whimpered but nodded and leaned even further against him. One laborious step at a time, they continued their descent.

Sometime later, as the light of day began to creep through the mountains of the North Iron Belt, they lay together, succumbing to enervation and hurt. Using each other for warmth, they slept.

COMMAND

Saudett enjoyed an extravagant lifestyle for weeks on end. She savored exquisite meals in the company of Lord Skaad, dressed in elegant new gowns and outfits. She soaked in the soothing hot bath in her chambers. She was even allowed to walk the halls at her own leisure.

Darkclaw Marah was not taking it as well. The Volkinn tended to stay in their room, pacing restlessly or simply sleeping the days away. Saudett had arranged for Marah's food to be brought to the Volkinn, but they barely touched it. Marah was beginning to look gaunt and undernourished. Their fur was becoming patchy and uneven.

"I don't know what is wrong with them," Saudett vented to Lord Skaad at one of many dinners. "They won't eat or even come out of the room."

"Not to treat the mighty Volkinn as a hound, but perhaps they must be taken for a walk. You know, stretch their legs and exert themselves a bit."

"No." Saudett reproached. *How can he say that?* "I will not treat them like a dog."

"Just a suggestion, my Lady." Hear-fan Skaad smiled genially.

She was getting quite used to that smile, even *pleased* by it.

"How about this," Hear-fan continued. "I think it's near time for you to begin your assignment of training the troops, as it were. Why not take Darkclaw Marah with you for this?"

"That's not a bad idea, my Lord." Saudett smiled back at the elegantly handsome humanoid. "Your halls are lovely and all, but I was beginning to get a touch bored."

"Oh, we cannot have that." Hear-fan raised his four arms in disapproval. "Then, on the morrow, you can begin. Stop by the armory on level forty-five to outfit the both of you, then meet me on the surface. You will be going to the Grot Lân to begin training my new soldiers in battle. They will have a very particular use in the Lân we are to surmount."

"I suppose it is time I returned your good favor."

"Your aid will be appreciated. Together, we will create peace throughout all the Lâns. I need an excellent commander to lead my armies into battle." He paused, his inverted eyes softening, nearly tearing up. "But more so, I find myself utterly enjoying your company, Lady Saudett, and dare I say, I desperately need a friend in my solitude here."

Saudett felt a pang of empathy for the lonely immortal man. *Driven out of his own home by his own people. Banished to this Lân of shallow waters and endless night. Yet he has built a magnificent hidden stronghold here.* "Well," she began, a half smile on her lips. "What else can we do as *friends* other than dine here day in and day out?"

"Entertainment?" He paused, pondering for a long moment. "I don't suppose you enjoy reading ancient texts in long-lost languages?"

"Not overly to my liking, no." Saudett stifled her laughter.

"We can travel to the few other Lâns I have made safe. The Wald Lân is a sprawling woodland with many lakes and rivers twisting about it. Do you hunt or fish?"

"I haven't done either of those things in years."

"Well, it's settled then." Hear-fan nodded in agreement. "Would Darkclaw Marah care to join us?"

"Perhaps they may be more comfortable in this Wald Lân you describe. I will inquire with them."

"Very well, my Lady. After you have settled into your assignment tomorrow morning, meet me for lunch at the gates above."

"I look forward to it." Saudett gave an awkward curtsy, still unused to wearing the elegant evening dresses that Hear-fan provided for her. They tended to promote her cleavage, and the cut up the side of the frock reached nearly to her waist, showing off an abundant amount of her thighs. Her tan legs flashed as she strode away. *But by Hettra's bouncing bosoms, I do feel alive.* Clothing had never been an interest to her. She wore her armor as a Shepherd's Eye soldier and comfortable loose shirts and trousers when not working. Before that, it was the maroon colors of Caravan House Kafilah. *I've always simply worn a uniform.*

Saudett found Darkclaw Marah pacing in their room. A cold platter of food was on the floor near the door, untouched.

"You need to eat, Marah," Saudett pleaded.

"We *need* to go home," Marah hissed in answer, spinning savagely toward Saudett.

"You know he will not let us. You could at least play along and bide our time until we find a way..." Saudett trailed off. *Do I even want to go home?*

"I smell your reluctance, your fear of going back. It sweats from your pores." Marah approached Saudett, breathing in her scent.

Saudett stepped back. "My husband, he...no, I can't. I can't bear to see him." *He will hate me.*

Marah huffed in frustration, then calmed, moved in, embraced Saudett, and said nothing for a long while. Finally, the Volkinn spoke. "It is all right to be afraid. Your husband loves you. I do not think that will change after you confess to him what happened."

Saudett imagined the interaction in her head. *I killed our baby.* The look of horror and disgust twisting across his face. She'd been trying to avoid thinking about this. Distracting herself with the new clothing and company of Lord Skaad. *I could try another distraction.* She focused on the person before her and inhaled Marah's scent as her head was in their chest. There was an off-putting smell of stale fur. "Skrull's hell, Marah, you need a bath."

Darkclaw Marah grunted disdainfully, moved to some sheets and blankets in the corner, and curled up inside them.

Saudett was tempted to invite them into the bath with her, to ask the Volkinn to have her. But since the loss of the baby, when she thought of sex, fear gripped her heart like a vice. *Never again.* She shivered dreadfully, a chill rippling through her. She grabbed a crystal carafe of wine and retreated to the warmth of the bath alone.

After the wine was long gone and her fingers pruning from the hot water, Saudett finally crept to her bed. First, she went to where Marah lay in the corner and whispered, "We are being assigned tomorrow to train new soldiers for Lord Skaad."

Marah sat up abruptly. "Why should we aid him? We should flee through one of those Gateways at the first chance."

"And become lost forever in some unknown Lân?"

"No." Marah sighed heavily. "We suppose that would be reckless."

"Please cooperate, start eating." Saudett insisted. "And I will think of something. I swear it."

"What do you swear upon?"

"On my life. I have nothing else."

Darkclaw Marah grumbled doubtfully and lay back down.

The clang of metal smithing rang through the blistering hot chamber. Saudett avoided looking at the hideous creatures working the metals on the forge. *The Daanav never carried weapons or armor when I fought them. They're all terrifying, deadly beasts. I suppose that will change as he has me training capable troops for him.* Saudett strapped on the black studded armor, glistening black steel bracers, and pauldrons. Then, she pulled on the tall black boots with plated shin guards. She donned a matching black steel helm that covered her nose and cheeks. A violet fringe sprang from the crest of the helm. *It all fits perfectly. How does Hear-fan Skaad know my size exactly?* All the gowns and outfits in her room fit flawlessly as well.

Darkclaw Marah growled low as they dressed in pitch-black leather and took up a thick, jagged two-handed axe. Saudett took a wicked-looking spear from the wall, testing its balance. She nodded and rested the weapon over her shoulder. "Skrull's balls, I can't wait to stretch the old muscles again." She glanced at Marah.

Darkclaw Marah's teeth were bared, and there was a savage, *hungry* look in their eyes.

"Let's return to the platform and meet our Lord Skaad at the surface," Saudett announced so all the strange creatures around them could hear.

Marah snorted derisively, but followed after Saudett.

The platform groaned and clanked as it slowly ascended. It stopped with a rusty *thud* as water pooled over it.

Hear-fan Skaad sat near one of the massive black and green marble Gateways on a simple wooden chair awaiting them. He was reading a book in one set of hands as the other set twiddled their thumbs below. He did not seem to take notice of them as they approached.

"Lord Skaad?" Saudett asked.

He startled. "Ah yes, Lady Saudett and Darkclaw Marah." He stood and paused to take them in. "You both look absolutely impressive."

Marah huffed and let a low, nearly imperceptible growl grow in their throat.

"I look forward to returning to the grind, my Lord." Saudett smiled, twirling her spear with expert aptitude.

"Indeed. Come now. Into the Grot Lân." He turned, his white robes flowing behind him as he vanished through a cloud of roiling grey mist.

Saudett couldn't help but hold her breath as she stepped through the portal into complete darkness.

Then, a faint violet light grew as an energy sphere appeared above Hear-fan's head. It revealed the environment before them. A cavernous tunnel with dripping stalactites like a wave of icicles covered the ceilings. A dark shape moved among the pillars.

"What's that?" Saudett alerted, readying her spear.

Darkclaw Marah crouched low, massive axe at the ready.

Hear-fan chuckled and called out in an odd beast-like clicking language.

The dark form crawled through the hanging spikes, then leaped down. Wings expanded from its back as the creature glided down and rested before them.

It was a male version of the beings who acted as servants to Hear-fan. Mighty wings like those of Trije-fan Skaad flapped and then folded behind the creature. Its skin was smooth and elegant. Its long legs were bent backward at the knee. Clawed hands and feet looked ready to slice her open. It clicked and growled menacingly, sharp teeth flashing and clattering as it spoke. It was dressed in primitive, hide-like clothing.

Hear-fan answered with calming gestures.

"Are these the creatures I am to train in combat?" Saudett asked uncertainly. "How am I to communicate with them?"

"Ah yes, of course," Hear-fan tutted. "I can help with that." He came and put his hands on both Saudett and Marah's shoulders. "*Scua Asecgan.*"

Something clicked in Saudett's mind.

"How are these flightless worms to teach the mighty Nyra to fight in a war when all they can do is stand on the dirt and watch as we dominate the skies?"

Saudett understood the words. "There will be times that flight is impossible during battle," she answered the being steadily.

"Pah." The creature sniffed contemptuously. "There's always space to take wing."

"What about inside a structure? When you must go in on foot to clear out defenders?"

It tilted its head questioningly.

"You do not have buildings or homes that you live in?"

"*We do,*" he hissed irately, and turned away. "Fine, let's see what the crawling thing offers the Nyra." He beckoned for them to follow.

Hear-fan Skaad leaned over and whispered in her ear as they trailed behind. "Excellent, simply excellent, my Lady. I was about to interject, as Nxyal can be a bit stubborn, but you handled that expertly, my dear."

Saudett shrugged. "You must show your soldiers that you mean business from the get-go. Otherwise, they will never respect you."

"Indeed? Where did you learn such a thing?"

"I've been a soldier all my life. The best officers were the ones who acted and took command with no hesitation, especially in combat."

"It seems I chose wisely when I recruited such a war veteran."

Recruited? Saudett contemplated. *Am I not a prisoner here? Though I honestly don't feel like one.* Aloud, she said, "Well, I've never been in a full-scale war, but it has been drilled into me since I was very young."

"There is no war in the Earste Lân?"

"There has not been a full-scale war for over a hundred years. Partly because no country wishes to defy the Council of the Aerie in Aurulan. I think the last real war was Aurulan trying to conquer the Vouri peoples of the mountains. It did not go well, but the Council was not around then. I believe that was over a century ago. Simon would know more about such histories." Saudett paused. *Unlike me, Simon is so intelligent and schooled in so much more than just how to fight. If I was more like him...I wouldn't have put our baby in danger. I wouldn't have been such a fool.*

"Hush now, my dear. I see the thought of him gives you no joy." Hear-fan Skaad held out an arm to her. "Come."

"My Lord," Saudett answered with a strained smile as she put her arm through his as they walked.

Marah gave a low growl behind them.

Skrull's hell, what is their problem? Saudett chose not to remove her arm from Hear-fan's as they strode through a long twisting tunnel.

Darkclaw Marah slowly fell further and further behind.

Finally, they emerged into a vast cavern, and Nxyal flapped his wings powerfully and took off into the air. Saudett let go of Lord Skaad's arm and took a few steps forward, captivated by the magnificent grotto.

The cave glowed with faint sapphire light emanating from some odd-looking plants on the rocky walls and cliffs of the cavern. Trickling water flowed and dripped down countless small waterfalls into a river on the far side of the crags. High among the hanging stalactites, round, hive-like structures stuck to the ceiling. Nxyal let out a screech, and suddenly, hundreds of Nyra leaped out of the hanging homesteads and swarmed the air. Like a black cloud, they fell in behind Nxyal and circled above where Saudett and company stood.

Then they dived.

The wind whipped and beat around Saudett, forcing her to cover her face. Razor-taloned claws susurrated past her.

Nxyal landed lightly on his clawed feet before her. "If you are to lead us," he snarled through fanged teeth, then tensed, baring his claws. "Prove yourself." He rushed her.

Saudett leveled her spear. She spun and ducked under the blade-like fingers as he came in with remarkable speed from a powerful wing thrust, launching him forward. *He is fast, but I have the reach.* She turned as he barreled by her and then flapped and drove skyward.

The shrieking horde was circling and *watching*.

He arched through the air and dived back down toward her; his taloned feet held before him aimed to gore her out on impact.

Saudett braced her spear. The spear tip reached out nearly four feet before her. She would impale Nyxal if he didn't stop. She watched his eyes as he swooped in.

He sneered as he halted his dive just before the weapon sunk into his chest.

The wind from his beating wings slowed his steep dive and buffeted against her, but she surged into action, charging forward with a leap. Twirling her spear in her grip to thrust with the butt end. It caught Nyxal in the hip, causing him to lurch forward. As her feet found the floor, she twisted and brought the shaft down on his back with a *crack*.

He screamed in pain and rage as he crashed into the rocky earth.

Saudett leaped onto his back, knees planting on his open wings, pinning him down. She pushed her spear shaft against his neck with both hands. She leaned close to his head and growled menacingly, "Now you understand, having flight is not a guaranteed victory in battle." She pushed harder against his neck, enforcing that he would be dead if she were genuinely earnest.

The shrieking horde was quiet as they descended. Landing and folding their wings on their backs. Ever watching and waiting expectantly.

Hear-fan Skaad came to stand next to Saudett and spoke, his voice unnaturally booming through the cavern. "My children. This is your Knight-Commander. You will listen to her every word and become the strongest of all my children."

Saudett stood, releasing her pin on Nyxal, turning to study the silent beings.

Nyxal huffed as he found his feet and moved before Hear-fan and her. To her surprise, he knelt.

"Knight-Commander, the Nyra will follow."

The entire swarm of Nyra knelt as the words left Nyxal's mouth.

I am to lead all these people into war. Teach them how to kill efficiently. I've been training for this my whole life. I'm needed here. Saudett beamed with self-satisfaction as she addressed the onlookers. "Warriors of the Nyra. My army. My Skaad Lancers."

The guttural hissing cry was taken up by all. "Skaad Lancers. Skaad Lancers."

Saudett raised her hand to silence them.

They did so.

Nyxal quietly asked, "What do they call you, Knight-Commander?"

Saudett Meridio laughed, authority flowing through her as the title seemed to emerge from nothing.

The Lord Skaad's hand was on her back.

"I am Gesche-fan Skaad."

Chapter Fourteen

OFFER

"I lost my wife." Simon slammed his fist against the sandstone wall he'd constructed in the valley of Hasiera. "How could I forget about my own Skrull-forsaken wife?" He struck the wall again, and pain burnt his knuckles. Blood smeared the sandstone slab before him. *Strangung.* He pulled back again and put everything he had into the next strike. With an ear-splitting *snap,* the wall caved and cracks spidered out of the center point around his fist.

"My Lord First Otsoa," a concerned voice came to him.

Simon turned to see that a small crowd of Hasieran had gathered. They watched him silently, *empathetically.* Upon his return to Hasiera with Zahir, he'd been greeted with cheers of celebration. The life-giving water had returned to Hasiera, and Simon, the people's First Otsoa, was responsible. He should be glad. He finally fixed the desert oasis that he'd broken. *I don't feel fucking happy. My pregnant wife is out there somewhere, in the hands of the enemy. Who knows what they're doing to her?*

"First Otsoa?"

Ah yes, Rojas, my wife's mother's second husband. By Hettra's saggy tits, that's a mouthful. Simon breathed, calming himself. "I need to find my wife, Rojas."

"How? Where did she go?"

"To Skaad. To the home of these abominations that we fight, the Skaad Lân."

"Hasiera stands with you, but we are weakened." Rojas's stunning violet eyes studied him readily. "We lost many in the battle for Hasiera and retaking the Moreas Lân for the

Kadal. Furthermore, Howler Thien and their kin have not returned from their expedition to the jungles of the south. We are in a dire state and need time to rebuild."

Simon closed his eyes in frustration. *Yet more problems to deal with. Will it never end? If only I could return to Dagad with my wife and child. Return to simple work.* He looked down at the white burn lines up his left arm from grasping and pulling that damned dagger from the Gate, which seemed like an eternity ago. He had brimmed with newfound knowledge and power because of it. But was it worth it? He was a ruler of a few thousand people. He was alive. *My father and mother are gone. My wife is lost, our child with her. Should I not do all I can here...for these people?*

Simon contemplated what it would take to find Saudett. He couldn't use the Wayfarers Gate in Hasiera without removing the valley's water source. He needed to find another Gate and point it at the Skaad Lân. *And then what? I'll need an army far more significant than what little Hasiera has left to offer.*

"First," Rojas advised. "Leadership is a heavy burden. Rely on those close to you for aid."

"And what aid do you have to offer?" Simon retorted. "Will you lead an expedition to find another Wayfarers Gate? Will you lead a delegation to bring our plight to the great nations of the Earste Lân?" Simon's voice raised higher with each question. "Will you rally an army against Skaad? Will you oversee Hasiera and nurse it back to health? Or run off to find Thien? Tell me, Rojas the Keen, what do you offer?"

"First Otsoa..." Rojas knelt before him, two fingers to his chin. "I will undertake any of those tasks should you command me."

Another man came forward and knelt beside Rojas. It was Ninth Otsoa, Shalasar Kaskin. Simon recalled he had led the cavalry against the Daanav in the battle for Hasiera. He was a stern-faced Xamidian. "As will I," Shalasar said with a nod.

Zahir came and knelt. Then another man. Then, a woman. A Volkinn. Soon, the entire crowd knelt before him, pledging their lives to him.

"Hasiera." Simon took a deep breath. "I do not deserve this. But I have come to care for you all and will strive to do what is right. We will rebuild the valley. *But.* We will no longer live separately from the outside world. We will send diplomats to Aurulan, Xamid, and beyond. We will seek allies against the Children of Skaad, as they are so named. We will seek another Wayfarers Gate to gather our forces and lead a strike against them." He lowered his voice nearly to a whisper. "And we will try to rescue my wife in the process."

Rojas stood and leaned close to Simon. "Here is what I offer." Rojas turned and addressed all gathered, "Let it be so. I will take a delegation to Xamid and perhaps Tal'tulu to seek information about the Wayfarers Gates and to convey our plight to the Sultan. I still know some people in Xamid. Second, I propose that the First Otsoa lead the delegation to Aurulan, as he is one of their people." Rojas paused as the crowd murmured in agreement. "Ninth Otsoa, find Howler Thien and bring them home."

Shalasar bobbed his chin in agreement.

"We will make Hasiera strong once more."

The small crowd answered with a cheer, "Hasiera."

Simon watched as they dispersed. Rojas and Zahir were soon all who remained. After a moment, he sighed heavily and sat on a large boulder. "My thanks, Rojas."

"Please watch for my wife and daughter when you are in Aurulan," Rojas implored. "I wish to know they are safe."

"Of course," Simon answered. "They should be in Nidhaut by now. Lucky for them, they traveled by Wayfarers Gate. We, unfortunately, do not have the same blessing."

"Is there not perhaps one of these portals closer to us?" Zahir asked hopefully. "In Xamid, perhaps?"

"My memory." Simon closed his eyes and tried to recall all that knowledge he had gained from the magical weapon. "Rather, *Gaelin's* memory has gone dark in my mind since he took back his arm. I only remember the things I learned while I carried it."

"The bastard." Zahir snorted. "I thought his purpose was to protect the Earste Lân."

"As did I, my friend, as did I."

"At any rate," Rojas said. "The other surviving Otsoa can stay here and care for Hasiera. We should set out as soon as possible."

Zahir stretched and nodded in agreement, causing his shirt to lift slightly.

Simon's gaze wandered across the warrior's body.

"Xamid is much closer," Rojas continued, "just over a fortnight's ride to the outskirts. I will gather my company and set out at dawn." He turned and began to stride away.

"My thanks again, Rojas." Simon called after him. "I will be on the lookout for Kiana and Anora."

Rojas raised a hand as he disappeared into the canvas tent town.

"I suppose we should do likewise, my new friend," Simon said, turning to Zahir.

Zahir held out a bamboo shaft toward him. "I think it is time for some training, my Lord. You should not only rely on your magic in times of conflict."

"But—"

"No *buts*, my Lord."

I was hoping to spend time with him doing something much more stimulating. Simon sighed regretfully and took the bamboo pole.

Zahir stepped behind him, adjusting Simon's shoulders and grip on the makeshift weapon. Then, using his hands, he widened Simon's stance.

The touch on Simon's thighs had his mind racing through the gutter, and he blurted, "Gods, Zahir, could we take this further in the privacy of a tent?"

"No, my Lord. I am here to be your loyal servant and protector. Your Rakshak." Zahir moved in front of Simon, readying his own bamboo pole. "That...and I have no desire for intercourse with anyone. It's not you, it's me."

Simon blinked. "You're not sexually attracted to anybody? At all?"

"No, my Lord. I find more satisfaction in making lifelong companions."

"Interesting. Thank you for informing me. I will now halt any further liaisons in your regard."

"Thank you, my Lord. Now...defend yourself." Zahir dashed in.

Simon stood stunned as Zahir's own bamboo pole whistled through the air at him. Instinctively, he put up the barrier. *Lind.* The weapon bounced harmlessly off it.

"You can't use magic for this, my Lord. Try again."

"Ah yes, sorry, it is so natural. I didn't even realize I was doing it."

Zahir nodded and readied for another strike.

This time, Simon tried to parry it.

Zahir's pole kicked up and thwacked against Simon's skull...

... Sometime later, Simon awoke to find himself in Zahir's arms. The man was dabbing with a cloth at a welt on his head. Simon winced in pain. "Gods, I do hate fighting in this manner."

"It's my fault, my Lord. I didn't expect you to parry upward. I should have held back."

"Nonsense, my good man. You are right. I do need to know how to protect myself. Please teach me, my friend. My Rakshak."

"I am yours, my Lord."

Simon leaned into the kind man and let himself be held. *I am exhausted and alone.* He closed his eyes and murmured into the man's stalwart frame, "I need you."

The sun's heat scorched down upon their company as it snaked its way through the dunes of the Burning Sea. "Skrull's sweaty balls. I forgot how much I hate this damned desert," Simon groaned as his camel bumped along. "But by Hettra's bouncing bosoms, it is lovely to be with you again, Marigold." Simon patted the neck of the gruff creature.

Marigold groaned listlessly.

"Well, don't get *too* excited, my good man. I missed you too." Simon reached up and scratched behind Marigold's ear. "Any luck in the romance department? A new man-camel in your life, perhaps? I have met a fascinating fellow in our time apart, but we are keeping things *civil*."

Marigold groaned again and shook his head to remove Simon's scratching fingers.

"I was ahead of myself in trying to seduce the fellow. He is strong and damned well gorgeous. He is loyal and honorable. He smells of the wind and the sand. He smells of spice and heat. He smells like home...like Saudett." Simon trailed off. He felt the anger resurfacing at his stupidity whenever his thoughts returned to his wife. Zahir was a nice distraction, even if the man had no carnal interest in Simon. He snapped out of his lull. "At any rate, what about you? Dear Marigold?"

"Are you talking to your camel, my Lord?" Zahir's rich, slightly elevated voice teased Simon's ears as the man rode up beside him.

"Ahem, of course not. What do you take me for, a sheep shagger?"

Zahir arched a brow playfully. "With your reputation, I wouldn't put it past you."

"My reputation.?" Simon gasped incredulously.

"Indeed, you're known as a bit of a tramp in Hasiera. It was rumored that you enjoyed the company of a particular camel, not to mention other *people* besides your wife. But I digress. At least introduce me to this former lover." Zahir leaned over and patted Marigold.

"This is my most loyal companion, Marigold Humphrey. We have been through hell together and have become fast friends. He is currently looking for a new man to love."

"You don't say?"

"Speaking of new men." Simon lowered his voice and led Marigold so they were nearly brushing up against Zahir and his desert steed. "Have you always had this lack of appetite for others? This condition?"

"It's not a condition. It's who I am. Take it or leave it."

"I'm sorry, Zahir, it's all new to me. I fear I am, as you put it, nothing but a tramp. My wife is missing, and I can only think about my next frisk. I'm a despicable man."

"I heard you and your wife had an arrangement in that regard?"

"We do...or we *did*, rather. Saudett had second thoughts about it, especially after finding out about the baby, and I was starting to agree with her. I think it just causes too much drama. It all stemmed from me not exploring my attraction to men thoroughly before I wed her. Even so, she supported me in that exploration. She also enjoyed other women, so it was a victory for both of us, as they say. When I think about those times before these ridiculous things started happening, I think things were going well."

"You need to examine your relationship and choose what is more important. Do you wish for some fun on the side above all else? Or a happy and healthy family?"

"Skrull's balls, you hit the nail on the head, Zahir. Simply settling down with the wife and child has been on my mind lately."

"Then that is what you want?"

"Yet more responsibilities are being heaped on my back after every passing day."

"I suppose the Primus took the reins and is guiding your fate."

"Pah." Simon snorted repulsively. "The gods are no more real than old stories of monsters in the night..." He trailed off.

"The Children of Skaad are very real," Zahir said. "And I believe the Gods are among us."

"To each their own." Simon sighed. "I simply do not agree with any religion. They cause far more harm than good, in my opinion. Aurulan, in particular, seems to have concocted the Primus to control the masses."

"I don't want to debate religion with you, my Lord."

"Of course, of course." *Though it is another distraction from thinking about Saudett.*

As the days passed and the journey stretched on and on through the desert, their company came close to a few dreadful situations. First, a mighty bird of prey, a kahytul, circled thousands of feet above them, following them for an entire day. Ever so slowly descending. Hour after hour. They began to prepare for battle, only to be saved by a massive wall of sand. The sandstorm ripped and tore at them. Everyone gathered to avoid losing anyone and waited for the storm to finish. It lasted through the night. Whipping and cutting at any bare skin. Sand crawled into all crevices. Their clothing, their eyes, mouths, ears, and nostrils. Simon did not get any sleep that night.

At long last, the storm cleared, and the sun climbed into the sky to burn down upon them once more. The massive vulture was gone, and Simon's company resumed their trek.

More blistering days and freezing cold nights drifted away. Zahir stayed with Simon in their makeshift tent as they traveled. Simon felt that Zahir did not trust him to be alone with himself. They would speak until Simon couldn't keep his eyes open any longer.

Sometimes, they would drink.

One such night, after too much wine, Simon's inhibitions were non-existent. He still found Zahir enticing and ached to strip both of their clothes off and entangle himself with Zahir's naked body.

Zahir was also a tad tipsy as he aided Simon with an arm under the shoulders as they stumbled into the small tent from a dim, cooling fire outside.

"S-Skrull's s-scrotum." Simon drunkenly made his plea. "I want you, Zahir."

"My Lord, are you trying to take advantage of me?" Zahir gently sat him down.

"Perhaps."

"You're drunk."

"Exactly. I am fully aware of my surroundings." Simon tried to focus on Zahir, but his head began to spin.

"Your wife...I thought you had made the resolution to choose only her."

The thought of Saudett instantly caused Simon's mood to plummet. Nearly sobering him up for a moment. One of the last things she had said to him was that she no longer wanted to share him. She wanted a more traditional marriage now that they were expecting a baby. *I am going against her desires with my pursuit of Zahir. Maybe if I hadn't left her behind. Fuck.* He lay down sullenly and said no more to Zahir. The room began to twirl around him, and he suddenly needed to vomit.

Zahir had swiftly passed out next to him.

Simon crawled out of the tent and spewed his wine-soaked guts out.

So, the journey through the Burning Sea continued. The only other thing to distract himself from the dark thoughts was his daily training with Zahir. Slowly and surely, Simon was becoming braver and more self-sufficient in swordplay.

Still, Simon's temperament was up and down, like the dunes they surmounted and descended each day. Over and over again.

After long last, they saw Dagad, Simon's hometown, in the distance from atop a patchy foothill on the edge of the Burning Sea. The square tan buildings with colorful canvases jutted into view.

Simon saw the dome structures he'd been working on just outside town. The place he'd been captured so many months ago by the very people he now returned with. *My father died right there.* He withdrew into himself. He barely noticed the commotion as they neared the town.

A thousand Shepherd's Eye soldiers rushed out from the Road's End and surrounded Simon and company. Weapons drawn and ready to kill.

Chapter Fifteen
Hunted

"We hunt the wolfmen down until none are still breathing," the young man, the First Otsoa, shouted as they road out of the valley of Hasiera. His golden regalia glimmering in the sun.

Anora rode by his side, Rojas on the First's other flank. Deep into the desert they went. Days vanished in the wake of their ride, and Gidraltar Lein finally halted them.

The First dismounted and approached a twisted dead tree and the corpse beneath it. A small cold fire scattered in the dust beside a person's torn, *devoured* body.

Anora joined Gidraltar, looking at the countless wolf prints in the sands around them. Some were nearly humanoid prints, but with claw marks in the powder. She knelt next to the body. She grasped a piece of fabric in her fingers from the pile of bones and dirt. Anora gasped. *Maroon fabric.*

"What is it?" Rojas asked as he joined them.

"This...this person was of my Caravan House. Company Kafilah. Why were they alone out here?" *Who could it be? Not Saudett, surely?* There was something awfully familiar about the ripped garments. *Skrull's hell, it could be anyone.*

"Odd for a caravan guard to travel alone," Gidraltar noted.

"We need to deal with these beasts before others befall the same fate," Anora said as she stood.

"Indeed," the First said with a nod. "These creatures are causing great difficulty in our efforts to bring more people into our fold."

Don't you mean enforced recruitment? Anora thought but kept it to herself. Gidraltar quickly became enraged when the topic of his golden rule came into question.

"Shall we follow the track?" Rojas broke the silence.

Anora leaned over and nudged Rojas in the ribs. "Stating the obvious again, oh, *keen* one?"

Rojas rarely smiled, but he did as his eyes met hers. Those violet pools twinkled with delight at her jest. "Someone must do it, or we shall stand around all day."

"Rojas, ever the one to keep us on task." Gidraltar chuckled as he swung back into the saddle of his white-speckled stallion. "Yet, he is correct as always. Let's ride."

Anora noted one set of horse prints leading away from the dead tree, heading east as the wolf prints gathered and moved north. They followed the tracks of the hundreds of paw prints and footprints leading through the dunes. Often, packs of wolves would break away from the main trail. They continued north, where the desert became more of dry red rock than that of waving sand dunes. The tracks were becoming dispersed and challenging to follow on the craggy landscape. They entered a canyon where they managed to see a few prints. It became oddly quiet as they crept along. The sound of their horse's hooves seemed to echo down the canyon. Bones riddled the gorge base as they picked their way through the narrow path.

A distant howl reverberated and swept over them before fading away.

"I think we're near their den, First Otsoa," Rojas cautioned.

Anora caught a glimpse of shadowed movement in the rocks above. "They are watching us."

"Indeed," Gidraltar agreed. "I thought I caught sight of wolves in the dunes as we traveled, keeping pace with us. They always kept their distance yet were near enough to keep an eye on us. It seems the beasts are expecting us. Dismount and tread lightly. We can't fight on horseback in this narrow canyon."

They tied their horses together, left them behind, and continued on foot. The canyon ever narrowing as they went, causing them to traverse the gorge nearly single file. The First, Rojas, and Anora finally emerged into a large gap. Numerous dark holes in the cliff side surrounded them.

The howls suddenly burst into a cacophony around them. The wolves appeared, leaping out of the entrances to their caves, yowling and snarling at the humans. Completely surrounding them. They blocked the path back. Only a handful of Hasieran warriors had made it through the tiny crack in the gorge to this prominent area.

Anora's hand rested on the hilt of her blade nervously. They were cut off from their company.

The First strolled forward confidently. Almost *arrogantly*. "Do the beasts have a voice? Can one speak for you? Or are you nothing more than animals?"

One massive wolf crouched low and prowled out before them. Then it stood on its hind legs.

The yipping and howling of the others quieted as the creature stood and spoke.

"Leave us be, humans, lest you wish to feed the pack." The creature bared its fangs from its nearly humanoid face. They were gaunt, lean muscled, with a woman's breasts and mangey hair or *fur* covering most of their skin. Ribs protruded on their sides. It wore a ragged covering around its waist. *Hettra's mercy. It looks half-starved.*

"So, you are more than simple beasts," the First answered. "Yet you hunt and kill humans who travel the desert without remorse."

"We must eat," the being hissed.

"Why not move out of the Burning Sea and hunt in the rich forests to the north and west, or even south to the jungle lands?"

"We were cast out of those lands by your kind. You know nothing, human." The wolf-like person stepped forward, clawed hands at the ready.

"Wait." Rojas stepped up beside Gidraltar. "We need not shed more blood. It would be a bloodbath for *both* sides if we fought here and now. If you consider yourselves more than just savage beasts, then we can come to an agreement."

Gidraltar tilted his head curiously at Rojas's words, then grinned. "Indeed, if you lack food, we can offer it."

The creature paced repeatedly, seemingly debating whether to pounce on the two men. Finally, they asked, "You would feed us? Feed us meat? What does the human wish in return for this? Is it bait? A trap to kill the Volkinn?"

"Volkinn?" Gidraltar questioned. "Is that what you call yourselves?"

"We are Volkinn," the Volkinn gave a deep growl. "And you did not answer our questions."

"We tend sheep, goats, and pigs," Rojas reassured. "We do not lack meat. We raid caravans and take their goods and sometimes their people. Usually freeing their prisoners should they be slavers."

"We offer sanctuary for all outsiders of the Earste Lân," Gidraltar continued. "We would welcome your people with open arms. What is your name, if I may ask?"

"I am Howler Thien, and before we may trust you, we must test your strength." Suddenly, Howler Thien leaped forward.

The surrounding Volkinn yowled in bloodlust.

Rojas rolled out of the way, his sword flashing from its scabbard as he did so.

Gidraltar Lein did not even flinch. He stood as Howler Thien breathed into his face, neck fur bristling, fangs dripping hungrily. Teeth at his neck and claws inches away from spilling Gidraltar's innards to the dirt, he stared the powerful Volkinn down. Calmly and slowly, the First Otsoa raised his hand and rested it on Howler Thien's shoulder. "You and your people will be safe with us. You will be home in Hasiera. You will be one of my Otsoa."

Howler Thien panted heavily, their eyes never leaving Gidraltar's. Finally, their tension faded, and they crouched down low once more. With an exasperating sigh, Howler Thien answered, "That is all we wish. To eat well and not fear being hunted by humans any longer."

"Then come with me," the First put his other hand on Howler Thien's opposite shoulder. "To Hasiera."

Howler Thien nodded.

The watching Volkinn howled, but the cries were elated. *Joyful.* They rushed down, standing on two feet, seeming more humanoid than ever. They approached and stood a respectable distance away from the group of Hasieran. Seeming unsure to advance further and greet the humans.

Anora stepped forward and strode toward them, extending a hand to the first one she met. A sturdy, grey-furred person. "I am Anora. It is a pleasure to meet you."

The Volkinn gave a snarl-like smile but took her hand awkwardly and shook it. "I am Silverfang Zilarra."

The two groups intermingled and became one.

Anora sat by the fire that night, stirring a pot of goat curry, when Rojas sat beside her with a satisfied groan. She smiled as her eyes caught his. "You did well to de-escalate the strain with the Volkinn," she commended. "I think Gid was ready to fight them to the death before you stepped in."

"Now and then, our First Otsoa thinks with his sword before he uses his head. Sometimes, he just needs to hear another option, then quickly takes it up."

"I have noticed that Gidraltar is quick-tempered and rash at times."

"Quite so. But on the other hand, you were fearless to be the first to approach the Volkinn back there."

"I don't fear for my life. Someone has to take it by the horns and be the first to break the bull, as they say."

"Who says such an expression?"

"Honestly, I just made that up."

Rojas gave a surprisingly hearty laugh.

It tickled and delighted Anora's ears, causing her to blush. *That is the first time I have heard the man genuinely laugh.*

"Anora, it is strange. I don't usually talk to anyone as much as I have spoken to you. For some reason, I am oddly comfortable in your company."

"You are comforting to me as well. A breath of fresh air compared to my late husband..." Just the thought of Gaddaar caused her mood to darken. Which led her to think of Saudett, alone out there, with no parents and no one to love her.

"I'm sorry. I know your past is a sensitive subject," Rojas said tenderly. "Let's look forward to the future. Forget the past for now."

Look forward, not back. Anora repeated the words within herself. She turned to regard Rojas, his handsome dark face, those violet eyes reflecting the warm glow of the fire. *But I do wonder about your past, oh violet-eyed man.* "Wait a minute." She leaned over and nudged him with a shoulder. "What about you? Come now, surely you have known some lovers in your time?"

"A long time ago, when I was very young. One brilliant summer, I traveled with my mother to Tal'tulu, her homeland. That's where I met Keeya on those soft white island beaches. God's, those isles were something to behold. I've always dreamed of going back there." He took a handful of red sand and let it fall through his fingers. "Nothing like this place of endless strife, survival, and death."

Anora tried to keep him from going further into dark thoughts and instead moved for more information about him. "Your mother was Tal'tulu?"

"Indeed, she lived with my older brother and me in a small town north of Al'Jalif. And my father...should he rarely return to port."

"Wait, what about this girl? In Tal'tulu?"

"Ah yes, she was my first and only love. Keeya Saros. We were young, perhaps fourteen summers old, and it did not last long. Somehow, I convinced her to come back to Xamid with us. Little did I know, she would never return to Tal'tulu."

"What happened?"

"I got her killed." He shook his head, his face distorting in disgust at himself.

Anora touched his arm gently and then cleared her throat. "Let's change the subject. What of your father? Was he a sailor? A captain?"

"Pirate. Father's *business* eventually got back to us. It's why Keeya is dead. It's why my mother is dead. It is why I fled into the Burning Sea."

"Please, if you are comfortable, tell me more. I wish to know why you are in Hasiera and loyal to the First. I still think daily about running away and finding my daughter."

"Yes, you should know the real me." He leaned forward, looking into the flames of the fire for a long while. "It is quite simple for me to stay in Hasiera, as I have nothing to return to elsewhere. My mother is dead, and I know not of my father and brother. Xamidian royal bounty hunters came to our home one day with their shining, pointed silver helms. This was right after returning from Tal'tulu with Keeya. My older brother was long gone, joining my father in the business. They were waiting for us. The guards had broken down our door. When we arrived, they confronted us, demanding the whereabouts of my father. There were three men, and I had a knife. They were laughing as they began beating and raping my mother. One of them held Keeya, readying to do the same. The third man, who was watching with such a satisfied expression at my mother's wailing, I stabbed him in the gut and pulled the blade across his belly. Everything poured out of him. With trousers around his ankles, the second man fumbling atop my mother died as I stabbed into his back repeatedly. His damned pointed silver helm rolled into a puddle of his blood as I pulled his dead corpse off my mother. She had somehow held him atop her, giving me time to get to him after murdering the first man. My mother did not survive. Keeya had distracted the one holding her. I turned around to see her laid out, bleeding on the floor. The last guard chased me. I ran into the streets covered in blood, where more guards awaited. I ran. I ran into the desert and never looked back."

"Hettra's mercy." Anora exhaled in astonishment as Rojas concluded his tale.

"This is why I don't enjoy thinking of the past."

They sat in silence for a long moment. Finally, Anora gathered the courage to ask, "Do you think you could ever find love again?"

Rojas's violet gaze flitted toward her in the firelight. "I've never told anyone of my past, not even Gid. Yet now I have told *you*."

"Thank you for telling me." Anora nestled in closer to him.

Suddenly, his hand took her chin and turned her face to his. "I think, perhaps, I *could* find love again."

Their lips pressed together in a tender touch. Anora had never felt anything like it before.

Chapter Sixteen

PROPEL

Hata followed Queen Raine Stormfall across the bridge from the tower and onto the battlements. The massive turret that looked out on the city and surrounding floating islands was wide enough for a dozen strange flying contraptions to land on its surface. Crews of Himin-dvergar engineers bustled about the flying machines with extensive metal tools while they shouted at one another. White-clad armored soldiers manned the wall. A massive ballista swiveled on gears as red and blue crystal gases exhausted from vents on its sides. There was a seat for the soldier pilot, who cranked levers to turn the weapon. Hata saw him looking through a long tube on top of the contraption.

Raine marched directly to the ballista. "Report," she called over the turmoil.

"Aye, my queen," the burly Himin-dvergar answered, keeping his eye fixed on the tube. "There is something out there. I've seen shadows moving around the islands and through the clouds. I suppose the bastard Skaadlings can fly now."

"Any more details?" Raine asked.

"Nothing—" The man stopped suddenly and cranked a lever to turn the massive weapon. "Oi. A rotor-wing is fleeing, and some creatures are attacking it."

Hata covered her eyes and squinted in the direction. A hand full of dark specks was all she could make out from here.

"Luminar's light," Raine cursed. "To the rotor-wings, to their aid." Raine beckoned for Hata to follow and rushed to the nearest flying contraption.

There was a thrumming sound, then a massive *clunk* behind her. Hata turned to see an enormous steel arrow explode from the ballista, red steam trailing it with unnatural speed and accuracy. It soared into the distance, and she watched as one of those tiny specks puffed out of existence.

"Ha. Take that, you Skaadling shite!" the Himin-dvergar man behind the weapon shouted.

"Hata, come now." Raine's voice was urgent.

Hata rushed to her. The queen was settled in the front divot of one of the rotor-wings. The other dozen or so machines were already ascending around her. The air *thumping* with the sound of their propellers whirling.

"Get in."

Hata climbed over a solid wing, noticing the razor-sharpened steel on the front of the wing blades for the first time. She clamored into the back seat, knees squishing into her face, barely fitting in. A lever in the front of the chair began to move between her legs as they lifted from the ground with a jolt. "What is this stick?." she called out to Raine, who sat before her. But Hata's voice was drowned out by the screaming propellers.

Raine turned her head and touched her ear as if to say, *I can't hear you.*

Hata noticed Raine had donned some goggles over her eyes. Hata squirmed in her uncomfortable position, but she found a pair of goggles on a hook beside her, and a small crossbow was tucked below her feet on the other side. She pulled the goggles on. Surprisingly, they fit. Then she fumbled with the crossbow, unsure how to use it. Finally, she looked ahead to where they were flying.

Shrieking bat-like people with spears, swords, bows, and armor as black as night swarmed and swooped down on a fleeing rotor-wing. Smoke billowed from the machine, and its elevation was slowly declining. They were still some distance away, but Hata saw it was Rorik and Bryn in the craft. One of the creatures was latched on as Bryn desperately tried to fight it off with a hammer.

"Hang on." Raine's voice scarcely touched Hata's ears, and their aircraft suddenly dived toward the battle.

Hata's body was pushed back against the seat. Her stomach twisted and turned. *By Teras's mountain, this is senseless.* Suddenly, a black hissing swoosh exploded through Hata's vision. A massive ballista bolt hit one of the creatures, and the beast burst into a mist of navy-colored blood.

The queen maneuvered their craft to begin spinning like a barrel as they dived into the midst of the flying Children of Skaad. The sharpened blades on the aircraft's wings tore through the enemies. They cut through the creatures like a scythe to hay.

That bluish blood splattered across the machine and all over Hata. She coughed and spit the foul-tasting gore from her mouth. Then she wiped it from her goggles so she could see again. There was another sudden jolt. Her stomach lurched, and her body was pushed back into her seat even further. She saw stars and black clouds on the edges of her vision. As suddenly as it started, the sensation stopped. Hata blinked and got her bearings. They were slowly ascending again. Rorik and Bryn's rotor-wing descended at an angle toward a small island above Hata and Raine's craft. Bryn dislodged a creature as they passed over Hata and Raine. The beast screamed and plummeted down, nearly colliding with their propellers.

Raine ascended to the lip of the island, holding the craft level with it. She pointed at the smoking heap of Bryn and Rorik's craft.

Hata nodded and leaped out, careful not to slide along the sharp blade on the front of the wing. Her clothing was covered in blood as she rolled across said wing. Finally, her feet found the ground, and she ducked and ran toward the wreckage of Rorik and Bryn's rotor-wing.

The Queen took off behind her to rejoin the battle.

Hata ran up to find Bryn struggling to pull a heavy chunk of metal off Rorik's body.

"Blasted bright beard." Bryn cursed, groaning as he strained against the metal. "I've got you, Rorik. Don't worry. I've got you."

Hata focused on the mixture of minerals made of a sheet of metal. It lifted, hovering above the two Himin-dvergar, and Hata tossed the chunk away with her mind.

Rorik lay still, eyes closed. His face was deathly pale.

"No, Rorik!" Bryn cried. "My Rorik."

Hata knelt beside him and put a finger on Rorik's neck. His pulse was strong.

"What is it, Sky-lass?" Bryn pleaded, his voice breaking. "Is he gone?"

Hata watched as Rorik stifled a grin, then laughed. "Nearly I was."

"Luminar's light." Bryn pulled Rorik to a seated position and embraced him. "Don't be worrying me like that."

Rorik blushed as Bryn squeezed, not letting go. "I—Bryn. I didn't know you cared so much."

"Of course I care," Bryn cried, tears in his eyes. "You damned cheeky fool."

"Eh, you're making me blush, calling me cheeky."

Bryn's voice calmed, and a whisper that Hata could hardly hear came out. "I'll call you more than that. You know I love you, even if you're an idiot."

"What?!" Rorik exclaimed, pushing away from Bryn. "You love me?"

"Aye, that's what I said. You don't return it?"

The widest smile Hata had ever seen stretched across Rorik's face. "Of course, I love ya. I've loved you for ages."

"Nay, I can't believe it. You're always spitting insults at me."

"Aye, 'cause I love you."

"And you're always criticising my work."

"Aye, 'cause I love you."

"But—"

"By the bright beard, shut up already and kiss me."

It was Hata's turn to blush as she looked away and examined some crystalline trees. Then a shrieking creature swooped in from behind her. A glinting spear tip pointed and hungry for her flesh. Hata managed to dodge the weapon's point, but the creature's taloned foot caught her shoulder as it passed overhead, ripping into her. She cried in pain, clutching her shoulder as blood welled through her fingers and the hurt throbbed. Hata sucked in a breath and turned to ready herself as the beast landed a few paces away, spinning its spear in an oddly familiar fashion. It reminded her of Saudett. *Besides the wings, claws, and bluish-violet skin, these creatures look nearly human. They even wear clothing. They are nothing like the hulks and hounds and massive smoking abominations we have faced before.*

There was another shriek, and Hata heard the wings flapping behind her.

Turning her head an inch was all it took for the creature before her to leap into action.

Hata raised her hands, and the solid walls of earthen rock erupted around her. Hata *pushed* the walls outward. More shrieks came to her from beyond her walls, this time of agony, as the barrier of earth rumbled and crushed into the first winged beast. She turned to see the other beat its wings and thrust itself skyward right before the wall overtook it. Then it realigned and dived toward her once again.

A crossbow bolt sunk into its head, causing the bat-like humanoid to go limp and crumple into the ground as it crashed at Hata's feet.

"You damned freakish flying rat. That's for wrecking my baby." Bryn scorned as he ran over and kicked the dead beast for reassurance.

Rorik limped up behind him. "Me or the rotor-wing?"

"My rotor-wing, of course."

Hata found herself on her knees as faintness washed over her. The blood still gushing from her shoulder.

"Sky-lass. You are…"

Hata collapsed onto the bloodstained dirt and closed her eyes.

"Tyttäreni," a voice whispered.

Hata groaned. *Is that my father's voice?*

Baal's deep voice echoed in her mind. "We will always be together."

"We must protect each other." It was her mother's soft tone.

"What would you know?" Saudett's voice was full of frustration. "You're just a child."

Hata blinked awake. Raine Stormfall stared back at her, gazing into her eyes as she was seated beside her bed.

"Thank the light, you're awake." Raine exhaled. "I thought we might lose you."

Pain pulsated through Hata's shoulder. She touched the bandage. A crystal was wrapped beneath it as a slight bloodstain soaked through. The memory of the encounter came back to her. "What happened? Did we win?"

"For now, the enemy retreated. It was a probing force, nothing more. The next time, they will come in vast numbers and bring us into this war, like it or not."

"Teras grant us fortitude. Will we be ready?"

"I do not know." Raine leaned back in her chair, thoughtfully crossing her arms across her chest and closing her eyes.

Hata noticed she wasn't wearing her armor anymore, and her formfitting blue and white tunic caused Hata's eyes to wander curiously.

Finally, Raine sighed. "I fear we will lose many in this war."

Hata tried to sit up, but the ache stopped her. "Damn, I can't believe I was hurt. I should be better than this."

Raine smiled. "Well, next time, we'll get you better protection for your body, my Sky-lass. Something that can take a hit or two. Though I heard you saved Rorik and squashed one of the creatures with your powers."

"How are they? Rorik and Bryn."

"Ha. They've been arm in arm since their little escapade, or so I'm told."

"Thank Teras." Hata breathed, then smiled as she recalled their confessions to one another. "They are so cute together."

"Are they? I am unused to noticing such things."

"Oh gods, the tension between those two before the skirmish was thicker than honey. I bet they are having fun right about now."

"Fun?"

"You know, as *lovers* do."

Raine blushed and stood. Turning away from Hata and speaking under her breath, she said, "I wish I did."

"Wait." Hata grabbed Raine's arm before she could go. The pain in Hata's shoulder blossomed at the sudden movement. "Ah, uhm...Raine, stay a bit longer. I very much enjoy speaking with you."

"I appreciate your company as well, Hata Vasara. But you must rest. I will return shortly."

Raine left her there as Hata's thoughts considered showing Raine what lovers do firsthand. But soon, her eyes became heavy, and the exhaustion and pain caused sleep to overtake Hata once more.

CHAPTER SEVENTEEN

DISGUST

The Nyra warrior, Nyxal, lunged forward, his dual wooden training swords lashing out from each of his hands quickly. His mighty wings propelled him, adding ten times the force of a typical strike.

Saudett had to dodge, or her spear shaft would snap in two, that, or her fingers would be broken if she miscalculated her parry and took the strike on an exposed hand. She rolled to the side and thrust out to counterattack at his unprotected side with the blunted end of her training pole.

Nxyal twisted unnaturally and deflected the jab as he spun through the air and landed on his feet.

Saudett set her jaw and came in with a flurry of blows. Twirling the hewn pole skilfully, she struck in quick succession. A diagonal left crosscut followed by a twist of her body as she jabbed forcefully toward his head. A turn and swipe at his legs. Then a leaping kick.

Nyxal deftly caught each of her attacks or dodged them outright. The Nyra seemed to have heightened senses compared to a human. Add vigorous training to their repertoire, and they become exceptionally formidable. *Nyxal especially. His talents surpass that of the other Nyra.*

Still, under Saudett's onslaught, he was forced to back step, and his footing suddenly slid on some loose stone in the massive cavern of the Nyra people.

She summoned a surge of energy to take advantage of the misstep. Feinting a high arching swing toward Nyxal's head, she spun into a round-house kick, and her booted foot *thwacked* his chin.

He tumbled and sprawled onto his back, dazed.

Saudett took a deep, renewing breath.

"Gesche-fan Skaad," Nyxal groaned and sat up, hissing in frustration. "You're kin to a persistent cave rat, crawling into the slightest of cracks. A worm. May Zalak, the winged one, cast you into the abyss."

"I'll take that as a compliment," Saudett said, nonchalantly resting her training spear on her shoulder. She gave him her most self-assured smirk.

He gave a sharp-toothed smile in return. "I *will* best you next time." He cast his gaze about the gathered Nyra soldiers who were watching intently. "If you have time to stand gawking, you have time to be sparring."

The Nyra startled and scattered back into their sparring pairs to return to training.

Nxyal is a natural officer. He will be valuable in the coming war. Saudett pondered. Aloud, she ordered, "Continue the drills, Warrior Nyxal. I will return tomorrow, and we will try a large-scale battle formation."

He nodded and strode into the throng of his kind, shouting curses and correcting forms.

Battle formations. Saudett had very little combat experience in this aspect. She knew a little from a few old strategy manuals her father had left in their estate library back in Al'Jalif. A memory came of her father ordering the cracked, weathered tomes of war and combat to be thrown out with the waste in the alley behind their estate grounds. Years later, Saudett had a crash course on formations and large-scale combat after joining the Shepherd's Eye. But the Shepherds were there to enforce the law rather than wage all-out war.

As she pondered all this, she walked through the dark tunnel to the Wayfarers Gate. Her stomach growled. *It is terribly difficult to tell time in the shadowed caves of the Grot Lân.* She stepped through the Gate into the Skaad Lân, the starry sky twinkling above.

Hear-fan Skaad sat in a small chair, a woven basket on his lap and a fishing rod propped against the back of the chair. "At last..." he exclaimed on sighting her. "You must be famished. Come, I have freshly baked bread and some cherry preserves. Let's hope you can catch a fish to add to our luncheon."

"I would like to freshen up and change into something more *comfortable*, my Lord."

Hear-fan Skaad arched a brow inquisitively. "Of course, I await you with vast antici-pation."

Saudett's stomach growled again. "On second thought, let's just go."

Saudett's appetite subsided after the delicious fresh bread, jelly, and fish. She leisurely reeled the fishing line in, readying to cast it again. Having already caught a large, colorful fish, she was not interested in acquiring another, but the repetitive nature of fishing relaxed her after the morning of exertion. As they sat in the heart of the Wald Lân, the beauty of their surroundings left Saudett in awe. The lake shimmered in the sunlight, its crystal-clear waters reflecting the serene blue sky. The sweet melodies of woodland creatures echoed through the air, creating a peaceful ambiance. With its dense foliage and towering trees, the forest seemed to stretch out endlessly before them, beckoning them to explore its hidden wonders.

Hear-fan Skaad sat quietly on the woolen blanket beside her, reading from a tome.

Saudett sighed heavily. *Contently.*

He looked up from his studies. "Something on your mind, my dear?"

"Oh, nothing. I am simply enjoying life at the moment."

"Indeed, relaxing after a long day of effort is enjoyable. It certainly is, Gesche-fan Skaad." He smiled warmly at her. "Are the Nyra cooperating with your tutelage?"

Weeks had gone by since she began training the Nyra. They were shaping quickly into a formidable fighting force. "They learn quickly. I couldn't ask for better students."

"Quite right, that's precisely why they also make excellent servants. If I do say so."

"My only setback is that I wish I could fly with them."

"Oh really." Hear-fan tilted his head curiously. "Do you truly want that?"

"By the gods, it would be incredible to soar through the skies along with them." Saudett paused as Hear-fan's eyes flashed with a sudden violet sheen. His face changed, his black teeth appearing behind ravenous lips. Then it was gone.

Saudett recoiled internally, keeping her own expression in check and outwardly friend-ly. *Skrull's hell, what are you? You can't hide your deranged practices from me. You modify your Children however you see fit.* Another thought came to her, and she said aloud, "That begs the question, why chain the servant's wings? Assuredly, they are loyal?"

"A simple precaution, my dear. Why leash a hound or cage a captured bear?" His gaze returned to the thick book he was reading.

Saudett pondered the answer. *He sees the Nyra as no more than animals. How does he see me, I wonder?* She finished reeling in the line and placed the fishing rod down. She then shuffled over to Hear-fan and pulled the book down from his nose with one finger. "Is that how you see me, my Lord?" she asked, biting her lip temptingly. "Like an animal to be caged and used?"

His eyes narrowed, but he smiled knowingly. "Is that how you wish to be treated?"

Saudett contemplated leaping onto him, pushing him onto his back *like an animal*. Mounting the Lord of Shadow, Hear-fan Skaad. Simon's face suddenly flashed before her eyes, and tension churned in her gut. She held back. *I can't. I'm not ready. I don't think I ever want to risk bringing a child into this world again.*

"My Lady, fear not," Hear-fan said, caressing her cheek tenderly. "I find you to be a fascinating woman. I will not hide that I would enjoy exploring you further. Your body and your mind. But only if it is at your own pace."

*How can such an ambitious man be this kindhearted? Maybe just this once...*Saudett leaned in closer, her lips brushing his. Simon's face came to her again. A look of utter disgust and revulsion twisting upon its features. She jolted away from Hear-fan. "I'm sorry. The feeling is mutual. It just...after the baby and my husband—"

"Of course, of course. At your own pace, my dear. At your own pace. Perhaps some wine will loosen your senses." He produced a fine bottle and two crystal goblets.

"Perhaps," Saudett said, taking the goblet eagerly. *Anything to stop thinking about Simon.* She quickly downed the first glass and held it out for a second helping.

Hear-fan obeyed, pouring her another. Only sipping from his own goblet.

They chatted as Saudett nearly finished the bottle on her own. When they talked, Hear-fan's gaze would often become distant, his mind far off. Sometimes, she would have to repeat herself as if he didn't hear her. Other times, Hear-fan Skaad would mumble under his breath as if he were speaking to someone else. Saudett swore she heard him mutter the word *Primus* multiple times. Still, she stared at the magnificently stunning being, Hear-fan Skaad. Months in his company had made her increasingly curious about him, even sympathetic to his causes. Sorry for the hardships he has been through. What his people, the Iban'mael, did to him. Gaelin Yesnala was one of those people. *He is so sad and lonely...ah fucks, why not? I will have you, Lord of the Skaad Lân.* Her reservations dissolved like salt in water. She began to work at the buttons on his robe.

His hands stopped her. "You're inebriated, my Lady Gesche-fan. I think it's time we head home. Perhaps a bath will sober you up."

"But I want—" Saudett's gut began to churn, and her surroundings did not like staying in one place.

"Next time, my pretty little human, next time."

The marble walls around Saudett shook violently. Her head still throbbing, she vaulted from the steaming hot bath and into her sleeping chamber. *What in Skrull's hell is that?!* She was nearly under her bed when the shaking finally stopped. She donned her armor, grabbed her spear, and looked out into the hall. Nyra servants were rushing about frantically.

Suddenly, Trije-fan Skaad was thundering down the aisle, pushing servants out of his way.

"What is it?" Saudett called as he dashed passed her.

He turned his gaze, sneered at her, and continued until he vanished down the hall.

Trije-fan had barely said a word to her since her arrival. *I'm confident that man wholly despises me.* He gave her dark looks and disgusted expressions if he happened to meet her in the halls. He played nice if his father, Hear-fan Skaad, was present. Even so much as smiling at her, though it was more of a mocking leer than a genuine smile. There was a sense of spite when Trije-fan looked at her. *Skrull's hell, why is he not the Knight-Commander of the Nyra? He can even fly.*

Shaking the thoughts of Hear-fan's son from her mind. Saudett hustled down the hall, snaking through intersections and passing many chambers until she found herself before the lift to the surface. It was absent. She touched a runic panel on the wall and waited. After an agonizingly long time, the platform groaned to a halt at her level. It was full of stone debris and puddles of crushed black blood, the remains of *many* dead Children of Skaad. The dais itself was at a slight angle. *By the gods, what is going on?* She stepped onto it cautiously. It began to rumble and shake as it climbed once again. It stopped, and a dozen hulking creatures with massive bloated arms boarded with her. A few of the Skaad hounds sulked their way on as well.

"I hope this thing holds until we reach the surface," Saudett mumbled.

"The Sunstone did this," one of the creatures gurgled.

Saudett was startled when it spoke. She hadn't heard one of these things talk since back in the Burning Sea. *Did it say Sunstone?*

"Our father has burnt her image into our minds. We *loathe* her. We must extinguish the Sunstone." The beasts began to shriek and howl, working into a frenzy as the lift finally stopped on the surface.

The Sunstone? Hata? Saudett reeled as she took in her surroundings. Massive boulders of stone and rubble were everywhere. Dust filled the air. She had to cover her face as the dry-stone powder filled her tastebuds and nostrils. A violet radiance exploded nearby, shining brilliantly, and Hear-fan Skaad burst from underneath a massive pile of rubble. Blood dripped from his head.

Trije-fan swooped down and landed before the wounded man. "Father, you're hurt."

"Get away from me, you damned fool!" Hear-fan bellowed furiously. His voice was harsh and devastatingly loud. "Go. Capture her. Find out which Gate she went through. Now!"

Trije-fan Skaad turned and pointed at one of the gates. The hounds and hulks rushed toward it. The trio of hounds, well ahead, leaped through a cloudy portal, shrieking as they went. Trije-fan himself beat his wings powerfully and disappeared through another gateway.

Saudett saw the source of the debris. It seemed to have ejected from one of the Wayfarers Gates. Crushed stone spewed from its mouth until one could no longer see the portal as the rubble piled up in front of it and across the waters of the Skaad Lân. Two other gates across from it were also nearly covered in debris.

Hata was here? Was she standing right here? Saudett stumbled about in shock.

"Knight-Commander." Hear-fan Skaad's voice boomed through the settling dust. "Gesche-fan Skaad."

Saudett turned and found Hear-fan strolling toward her, a yellow-violet light glowing from his hand, which rested upon his head. A black gemstone pendant was clutched tightly in one of his other hands. The gash on his head closed up as he approached.

She stiffened in a soldier's attention.

At that moment, one of the hulks stumbled through the portal it had entered a moment before. "Father. She is here. The Sunstone slaughtered more of our kin and escaped."

Hear-fan turned toward the portal, his face contorting in rage. "The Ryk Lân. Of course, she would be so lucky to choose that despicable world."

"My Lord?" Saudett queried.

Hear-fan composed himself, facing her once more. "Gather your forces, Commander. It seems the time to enact our theater of war has come sooner than expected."

"Yes, my Lord." Saudett nodded and moved to enter the gateway to the Grot Lân, which had luckily avoided the destruction.

"Insufferable disgusting human Sunstone." Hear-fan Skaad cursed venomously behind her as she stepped through the portal.

Disgusting human? Saudett walked into the Grot Lân and soon found herself again in the massive cave home of the Nyra. Nyxal landed lightly next to her as she entered. He was clad in black armor like herself and carried two wicked-looking swords instead of his training ones.

"What news?" Nyxal greeted her. "Drills were complete for today."

"It has been months since our training began. It's time to put that training to the test. The Nyra people are ready."

Nyxal bared his sharp fangs and let out an ear-piercing shriek. The cave filled with the beating wings of the Nyra as they swarmed like a cloud into the tunnel toward the Wayfarers Gate. Saudett strode after them, Nyxal at her side. *Darkclaw Marah should be on my other side.* Saudett thought as he flanked her. *I wonder where they are?* The Volkinn had taken to disappearing for days at a time since Saudett had begun training the Nyra in the caves. She knew that Marah had taken a liking to the Wald Lân, a world nearly completely covered in a vast forest and a scattering of lakes. *Come to think of it, when was the last time I saw the Volkinn?*

Darkclaw Marah tracked the strange-looking deer through the woods. Marah crouched on all fours, then became deathly still as the deer's head suddenly looked up from grazing. Marah licked their lips. *We can taste it.* As the deer lowered its head once again, Darkclaw Marah surged forward and sunk its teeth into the deer's sweet, delicious neck flesh. Blood filled their gullet. Marah's mighty clawed hands snapped its neck effortlessly, and they drank deeply before dragging the kill toward their den.

CHAPTER EIGHTEEN

RANGER

Fucks...we're being hunted. Jude's muscles strained as he supported Joanna as they descended a treacherous cliffside. *In another day or so, we will be out of these Skrull-forsaken mountains.* The creatures were insatiable. They would not give up the chase. Jude and Joanna would move in spurts, day and night. Take some rest for a few hours, then continue on. The Daanav could move through the earth during daylight but could not surface as they would melt in the sunlight.

After some time, and Jude's arms and legs screaming with agony, they reached the bottom of the cliff. Exhausted. He couldn't take another step. A quick look around, he deemed it safe enough to camp and get some sleep.

Joanna lit a small fire and roasted a scrawny squirrel Jude had lodged into a tree trunk with one of his daggers. They had lost their provisions in their flight from the Daanav. They shared the stringy meat and settled down, readying for rest, the light dimming by the minute as dusk fell.

The beasts attacked. Three enraged abominations burst from the ground around them, screaming and bloodthirsty.

Jude cursed as the hound darted toward him, and he leaped to his feet, scattering their small campfire. He had lost most of his magic-infused stones back at the collapsed mountain. He grasped a dagger, and with a flick of his wrist, it darted through the air and pierced directly into the hound's exposed eye. It squealed and retreated, the pommel of his dagger protruding as it shrieked, lost its footing, and dropped to the rocky earth.

Fucking bastard. Jude dived on its back, gripping the dagger, pulling it free with a spray of black blood into his face. He stabbed repeatedly until it finally lay still. *Just fucking die and leave us alone.*

There was a flash of heat behind him. Jude turned to see Joanna casually finding a seat where they'd started to make camp. Two sizzling corpses of the massive, bloated hulks were crumpled and smoking behind her. She tossed some branches on the spot where Jude had strewn their firepit about and flicked her fingers, and the wood ignited before her.

"Thank fucking Hettra you're on our side, Joanna," Jude panted, gasping for breath.

Joanna shrugged. "The Alpha will not share your optimism at our failure to retrieve the fledgling—I mean, Hata."

"Well then, the bastard should have chased her down himself."

"Do you think he will punish us?" Joanna asked nervously.

"Has he punished you before?"

"More times than I can count."

"Then I fear the answer is yes."

Her face fell, and she began to tremble.

Damn fucking Ebras. Jude sat beside her, awkwardly putting his arm around her.

She leaned into him, her head on his shoulder. After a moment, she whispered, "Have you ever thought of leaving?"

"Me?" Jude questioned.

"Why keep capturing people to have them abused or murdered under the guise of training magi? Why keep helping such a vile man?"

"Ha, because, Joanna, I'm no better than him. I've always done the job and refused to think about what he did with my captures. Not to mention, he pays extremely well."

"He promised me power and authority to be a sorceress in the king's court. But if I fail this one task, I fear he will extinguish my flame...forever." Joanna's face contorted suddenly with a rage. "If only I knew where that treacherous ginger bitch went." Then, her face softened once again. "We had a good thing going, Rose and me. Why couldn't she have just stayed in the *Convent Enclosure*? Is she dead under that mountain?"

A twig snapped.

Jude leaped to his feet and turned, two daggers appearing in his hands.

Joanna did likewise, flames gathering on her palms.

A hooded man stepped out from behind a scrawny pine, a sizeable, curved scimitar resting on his shoulder.

"Did you say ginger?" the man asked. "I don't know her as Rose, but did I hear you say 'Hata' earlier?"

"You know her?" Joanna exclaimed.

"I do," the hooded man answered. "But how do *you* know Hata?"

Jude eyed the hooded stranger. His black, slightly greying bearded face was shadowed, yet he seemed oddly familiar. He bore a faded arm braid of the Shepherd's Eye soldiers from Dagad. Xamidian skin tone. It came to him. This man had been leaning against the wall with the Third Otsoa's daughter after the battle against the Daanav. Jude eyed him coldly as he said, "You were in Hasiera."

"As were you, Jude Nelon." The man reached up and pulled back the hood, revealing a dark, middle-aged face. "We've been looking for you."

Jude immediately scanned the environment for more intruders. It was nearly completely dark now. "Ha, you can't fucking bluff me. You're alone. Who are you?"

"True, I come alone, and my name is Kaplan Mir. I am a ranger of the Shepherd's Eye. But my party left Hasiera looking for *you*, Jude Nelon. Looking in turn for Hata Vasara, the Sunstone."

"Well," Jude scoffed. "Your search ends here, my friend. The girl is undoubtedly dead. We tracked her to the mountain village of Oitilla. A Vouri village. But there was no village left. No mountain where it was to be."

"No mountain?" Kaplan Mir's head tilted questioningly.

"It was gone. Collapsed in on itself," Joanna said, her voice still rattling with her own disbelief. "It was impossible."

"The Sunstone is stronger than you can imagine. It must be her doing. These mountains are crawling with the abominations of Skaad. Perhaps she used the mountain against them?"

"No," Joanna sucked in a breath. "There's no way she is that powerful. She could barely hold up against me—"

Jude touched her arm to silence her.

Kaplan Mir studied each of them in turn and then nodded. "I would like to see this mountain. Search for clues."

"Fucks man, it's suicide," Jude rebuked. "There are thousands of those creatures between us and that mountain."

A howl drifted through the air of the mountain peaks. Followed by the guttural cries of the Daanav on the wind.

The ranger's head twitched at the sound. "They're close. We must flee." He beckoned to them. "We're nearly out of the mountains. Come, I have a few horses not far from here."

Joanna stepped after him.

Jude grabbed her shoulder and whispered, "We can't trust him. He is an ally of this Hata? Didn't you say she betrayed you?"

The cries of the Daanav were becoming louder and louder.

"I don't think we have a choice right now, Jude. I just want to get out of here."

Jude sighed heavily but nodded. "All right, just be careful, Joanna."

She smiled delightfully up at him, and he couldn't help but grin at her attractiveness.

They followed the man for over an hour. The cries faded behind them. Finally, they came to a makeshift camp with two horses and a pack mule tied to a tree. Silently, they made ready to mount and depart. It was a lower elevation here. The woods began thickening as the landscape changed from mountains to foothills and lush evergreen forests.

Jude scanned around, alert for more creatures lurking up on them. Suddenly, he caught a glimpse of blue light through the trees. "Fucks!" he shouted as the massive arachnoid crashed through the woods, knocking trees aside as it charged directly toward them. The humanoid torso with its four arms, two of which sported giant scythe-like blades, screamed as it caught sight of them. *Skrull's balls, not again.* Jude fumbled in his pocket for a magic-infused marble. He came up with only a water bubble and an invisibility spell. *Skrull's fucking balls...*

"Together," the ranger called, his scimitar flashing with the reflection of the blue flames. To Jude's surprise, the man rushed in to meet the creature. He deftly dodged and rolled away from a swinging scythe arm. Kaplan's scimitar cut deep into one of the abomination's six tree trunk-sized legs.

It shrieked and barreled toward the ranger as he dashed away.

A piercing flaming javelin struck it in another leg.

The creature screeched and spasmed, stumbling in every direction.

Joanna was readying for another attack when the beast suddenly surged toward her.

Jude crashed into her, nearly too late, grasping and pushing her out of the way. He felt a sudden tug upon his leg. Then, a cold sensation. He looked down. His foot and part of his leg had been sheared off. A bloody red stump was all that was left.

"NO!" Joanna screamed, such an excruciating cry.

I've never heard such a painful cry before. Jude Nelon, the Magnus Huntsman, saw a light in the sky. Like the sun had suddenly returned in the middle of the night. *Gods,* he thought, *relaxing in my garden and having tea under such a warm sun would be perfect right now. Fucking perfect.* Then, heat washed over him. Then, finally, a chill engulfed him, along with the darkness.

Chapter Nineteen

REFLECT

Simon was finally *home*, though, with a heated welcome. The soldiers of the Shepherd's Eye surrounded his company of Hasieran at the edge of Dagad.

Captain Cad Dermont stepped out of the line of soldiers and shouted, "Drop your weapons and kneel. In the name of the King, you are all under arrest."

Simon stepped forward, his hands outstretched. "Cad. It's me, Simon."

Cad's mouth fell a gap in shock, and then he rushed forward. "Simon." He had a slight limp as Simon came out to meet him. The handsome, middle-aged captain of the Shepherd's Eye soldiers was no stranger to Simon. He was a regular *companion* to Saudett and him in their home. They embraced as they met.

"By the Primus, Simon." Cad breathed into his shoulder. "I feared you were long dead. You and everyone else who went after you."

"I survived," Simon reassured. "As did the company sent after me."

"Thank Hettra." Cad untangled himself and put his hands on Simon's shoulders. "How is Saudett? Where is she?"

"Well, she also survived. But...we were separated. She is somewhere far away from here."

"Please tell me everything." Cad looked past him at the rag-tag group of nomads. "Are these not the bandits who attack Dagad? Wait, is that Naurr Andiges I see?"

Simon's burly foreman smiled as he approached, followed by many others of Simon's workforce. Though some had stayed behind in Hasiera to help rebuild, those who were willing and had nothing tying them down to Dagad, like a family.

"Cenna," Naurr bellowed out. A crowd of villagers had gathered behind the Shepherd's Eye soldiers. "Noa."

A child pushed through the legs of the onlooking soldiers and dashed directly toward Naurr. "Papa."

Naurr knelt, and the boy ran into his open arms. "My boy." Naurr's eyes glistened. "My boy, by the will of the Primus, I'm with you now."

A woman came and joined them. Her greying-black hair was tied in a curly bun and wrapped in a colorful scarf.

"Cenna." Naurr hoisted Noa with one arm and took his spouse in the other. Holding them both as if to never let them go again.

"We feared the worst," Cenna murmured, tears dripping from her eyes, but she smiled and touched her husband's face. "We were all alone. I...I didn't know what we were going to do."

"Don't worry now, my dear Cenna. I'm home, and I swear I will never leave you again."

Other workmen rushed to find and greet their families in the crowd.

The nomads of Hasiera shifted uncertainly, watching the homecoming.

"You are certain it is safe to bring these people into our home?" Cad asked, gazing back at the Hasieran suspiciously.

"They're as much my people as the townsfolk of Dagad," Simon answered. "I am now the leader of these poor lost people."

"Leader? Who are these people, Simon? Did they not kill your father?"

"No," Simon said coldly, his eyes darkening. "*They* did not. One man did that. And that man has paid for his transgression by my own hand."

Cad eyed him steadily. "It seems much has happened to you since your unfortunate kidnapping."

"Gods, my man, you have no idea." Simon chuckled, trying to lighten the mood. "Come, this is a joyous event. We are home. Let's celebrate."

Cad turned back to his soldiers. "Let them through."

The soldiers parted but watched cautiously from the sidelines as Simon led the group into town.

"You can have these people camp in the barracks grounds until we can find lodging for everyone," Cad added as he walked with a clipping stride beside Simon.

"No need to find long-term housing. I am afraid we will not be staying for long."

"What? Why?"

"There is a threat to the entire Earste Lân, and I go to Nidhaut to seek an audience with the King and his council of magi."

"By the Primus," Cad muttered, shaking his head. "I haven't the faintest idea of what is happening. Come to my office, start at the beginning."

Simon paced through the small room as he retold his story, stopping to sip some wine at intervals. He retold the tale of his capture by the nomads, of how he was forced, or *persuaded*, into building them a wall against these creatures, the Daanav, now known as the Children of Skaad. The battle for Hasiera. The Wayfarers Gates. The Wayfarer himself, Gaelin Yesnala, and his eventual betrayal. Simon told the captain how Saudett had chased after one of these humanoid Children of Skaad through one such Wayfarers Gate. Finally, he spoke of the party sent to Nidhaut to find the young woman, Hata Vasara, The Sunstone.

"I aim to gather an army, find another Wayfarers Gate, and attack the Skaad Lân." Simon finished and downed the last of his wine, quenching his parched mouth.

"Skrull's unholy hell," Cad said in astonishment. "You've been through the gauntlet, my friend."

"I didn't ask for any of this," Simon rebuked. "Now. To top it all off, Saudett is pregnant. I want nothing more than to bring her home and settle down. Continue with life, happily ever after, as they say."

"Well, some congratulations are in order then. Finally, a little Meridio will be joining the family."

Simon brought the image of cradling a tiny bundle of a babe in his arms, her soft round cheeks rosy red as she smiled up at him, with a thick mop of black hair and dark brown eyes just like her mother's. He imagined handing the babe back to Saudett for nursing. His wife would be humming a Xamidian lullaby as she rocked their daughter in a comfortable wicker chair. *Gods, I want nothing more than this. Why did you run away, Saudett?*

Cad poured Simon more wine from a jug, then filled his own. He took a swig and sighed contently. "At any rate, Kaplan Mir has gone to Nidhaut, as you said. But I did not hear during your story of my other ranger, Taryn Drel. What became of her?"

"Taryn Drel?" Simon tried to recall a face to the name, but nothing came to mind.

"She set out with your wife to find you."

"Oh dear, she was not with Saudett and company when they came to me. Though that was after the battle..."

"Skrull's fucking hells," Cad cursed. "Say no more. Drel was a damned good soldier."

"We've lost so much in the last few months. One way or another, I mean to end this."

"I'll go with you."

Simon tilted his head questioningly. "Surely you cannot abandon your post?"

"Don't worry, Simon, I'll put a lieutenant in charge of Dagad. From the sounds of it, we will need every able-bodied soldier for the battle to come."

"Thank you." Simon placed a hand on the man's muscular bare arm. "You're a good man, Cad Dermont."

"Ha, far from it." Cad's face twisted slightly.

Simon felt something connect through his touch, and his mind found Cad's thoughts momentarily.

I tried to take your wife the moment you were gone. I was hoping to comfort her in her loss and make her mine. Gods, she was a good fuck.

Simon felt his jaw clench, but he quickly pivoted and smiled. "Oh, for the good old days. I remember that awkward first time you joined us one night."

Cad grinned mischievously. "That was your first time with a man. If I remember correctly. By Hettra's saggy tits, I remember it like it was yesterday. Saudett watching me have my way with you. Working her into a frenzy. I had you both that night."

The image of that night came through Cad into Simon's mind. Cad's gaze never looked away from Saudett, even as he used Simon's body.

Simon pulled his hand away, and it instinctively went for the magical dagger that was no longer there. *The man is in love with her. He cares nothing for me and would sooner see me dead. He was hoping I was.* Simon looked back to another memory, his own memory...

"Dear wife," Simon said as he watched his spouse wash herself under the slow-release water drops he'd designed and built in their home. It wasn't much more than a bucket with holes drilled in the bottom, which simulated rain. The hard part was getting warm water into the bucket.

"Husband?" Saudett answered curiously, the lemon grass ash soap bubbling in her hair as she scrubbed away. The frothy liquid slowly made its way down her flawless curves, glistening as it traced every contour of her body.

Simon shook himself out of his ogling and cleared his throat. "I was just thinking, what would you say about adding a bit of spice to our bedroom? I've always regretted not experimenting with men before getting hitched, as it were."

"You've been hinting at this for months," Saudett said with a smirk. "I can't say I'm not curious myself. Who says it is wrong to limit oneself to a single partner?"

"I'm sure marriage is a religious construct. Not many animals mate with one partner for life, you know. That being said, I still wish to be married only to you. It's just we could add an element of fun, of *heat*. We simply can try some things out with other people. If it's not for us, we can wash our hands of it."

Simon moved to hand his wife a towel as the hot water stopped dripping out over her.

"Let's try it. There's a handsome man at the barracks whom I have in mind. He has not hidden his desire for me and has also told me he enjoys both men and women."

Simon hesitated. *She already has someone in mind? How well do they know each other?* "Is it wise to bring someone in who desires only one of us?"

"I mean, this won't work otherwise." Saudett shrugged as she dried herself, finally wrapping her head in the towel. "How about we set some rules."

"What did you have in mind?"

"We are allowed to be intimate with others. In or out of our home. With or without both of us present. But we always come home to each other."

"So, we can foster genuine relationships with these others? I thought it would just be for the sex."

"The deed is more enjoyable with someone you can connect with."

"I suppose that's true." Simon held back other words. *As long as I am attracted to them, I could just live with having sex and nothing more.* "I think the first time we should partake together, though. In our own home."

"I'll invite Cad over tonight."

"Tonight.? Skrull's balls, I'm not ready."

...Simon returned to the present. *Cad has always been in love with her and only her.* Simon boiled internally. *But that's what we agreed upon. We were free to love and be loved by others.*

"Something wrong, Simon?" Cad queried, taking another sip of wine.

Simon shook his head and rubbed his eyes. "Oh, I'm simply tired after a long journey. I apologize. My mind wandered."

"Go home, get some rest."

Simon nodded. "That sounds like an excellent idea." He drained the last of his wine and went to open the door out of the office.

"Simon," Cad called after him. "I'm glad you're back. I *really* did miss you."

Simon turned his head and smiled fakely, then closed the door on his way out. *Did you really miss me, you fucking bastard?*

Zahir was waiting outside for Simon. "My Lord First."

"I've made my decision. Saudett is my one and only. I will not be fraternising with anyone else from this point forward."

"Well said, my Lord."

"Ah, my faithful Rakshak." Simon gave him a hearty pat on the back. "Come see my home."

"Of course, my Lord."

Another thought came to Simon. *By the gods, will I even be there when Saudett gives birth? What if I don't find her in time?* Simon's mood began to darken once more, his teeth grinding. He brooded as he led Zahir to his house. By the time they arrived, all he wanted was to be alone. He found the extra key to the door in the front garden bed, the plants and flowers long dried up and dead. He patted the dirt from the key and placed it into the lock. It was stiff, but finally, with effort, it clicked and turned. The door squeaked open. *I'm home.* He looked about the dusty, dim interior. It looked exactly the same as when he had left it. Everything reminded him of one thing. *Saudett, my star.* Simon clutched at his heart. "I can't do it. Let's go to an inn. This place only reminds me that I lost my wife."

"Oh gods, I'm sorry. Do you want to stay here alone? I think taking time and thinking about her would help you."

"I think I'd rather distract myself lest I become overcome with doom," Simon exhaled. "But perhaps you are right. Perhaps I should take some time and think about *everything*."

"I'll see you tomorrow then." Zahir nodded reassuringly and strode into the shadowed streets of Dagad.

The door closed behind Zahir, and Simon stood *alone* in the darkness of his home.

CHAPTER TWENTY

DOUBT

I'm a horrible mother. The baby would not stop crying. Anora was exhausted. It'd been two months since she gave birth to little baby Kiana. Two months with very little sleep. *I don't remember Saudett being this difficult.* Rojas tried to help Anora during the long nights when Kiana would awaken nearly every hour on the hour, crying for milk, or rather the comfort of Anora's breast. Rojas walked with the child, which sometimes calmed her down, but if he stopped, sat, or tried to place her on some bedding, she would immediately wake and begin screaming.

At times, Rojas would offer to relieve Anora to let her try to get some rest, but it would only worsen things. This caused both of them to get no sleep, and they became increasingly irate with each other. Anora was left alone during the day as Rojas would attend to the First Otsoa's assigned tasks and oversee his Otsoak, his section of the Oasis camp, and its people. Gidraltar had begun naming his most loyal followers and giving them the responsibility of governing an area of the tent town of Hasiera.

Anora was utterly isolated. The memory came back to her. A few sleepless nights when Saudett was very young. But Anora was forced to put Saudett with paid caretakers a few weeks after her birth as Gaddaar had wanted Anora to return to work on the caravans immediately. Anora had not seen her first daughter grow up. *I will not make the same mistake with Kiana. I will raise her myself. I will teach her how to defend herself. She will be tenacious.* Still, nothing had prepared her for the difficulty of mothering a baby. *It is so lonely, just me and you all day and all night.* She only managed to get any sleep when Kiana was attached to her nipple, and she would dose off in her makeshift chair of cushions and pillows. Then, she would awake with a start, fearing the child had fallen off her or suffocated while Anora slept.

"I can't do this anymore, Rojas." Anora pleaded at her wit's end. "I need help."

"I know, I know. I am *trying* to help you." Rojas's voice was strained as he tried not to raise it in return. "But nothing I do is enough for you."

Tears welled in Anora's eyes. "No, my love, you do plenty. But this is so hard. It's more mentally and physically demanding than I ever imagined. What do all the other women with children do in Hasiera?"

"Of course." Rojas exclaimed and clicked his fingers. "Why hadn't I thought of that before? Considering what you told me about your first daughter, I assumed you wanted to do this independently."

"Thought of what?" Anora asked hopefully. She would be grateful for any help at this point.

"The pregnant women, those with newborns, and those with young children all gather to help each other. Numerous older, more experienced women help them out. I've even heard that there are women whose children have long since stopped drinking their mother's milk, but these women still take turns nursing the others' babes."

"Skrull's hell, Rojas, why didn't you mention this a month ago? We've been on the edge around one another for weeks. I've been so frustrated sometimes I wanted to grab you by the neck and throttle you."

"I know, Anora. I'm sorry. With the exhaustion and tension, it slipped my mind."

"It's fine." Anora sighed heavily. "Just bring me to them."

With that, Rojas introduced Anora to the group of lively women. They gathered under a wide linen sheet near the river that gave life to Hasiera. The group was chatting, washing clothes, sewing garments, and nursing babies. Toddlers ran about, some splashing in the water while others kicked a leather-bound ball about in the dust.

"These women are of my Otsoak," Rojas announced as he bowed before the group. "Ladies, this is Anora, my partner. We are in desperate need of your experience and company."

"Ah ha, so this is the famed Anora we've heard so much about," a middle-aged Tulu woman said. "Don't just stand there gawking. Come, hand me that child."

Anora hesitated, unwilling to hand over her child to a stranger.

Rojas touched her arm reassuringly.

"Come now, I don't bite," the woman said as she stood and came to Anora, offering her hands to take Kiana.

Reluctantly, Anora handed Kiana over, and it felt like a weight lifted from her shoulders, and a twist in her gut unraveled. Kiana immediately began to cry, and the feeling of anxious tension flooded back into Anora. She reached out to Kiana. *God's, I am the worst. I'll take her back.*

The woman immediately popped her breast out and began nursing Kiana. "Though I can't say the same of this little one, my Skrull-damned tits are nought but mutilated mounds after a decade of child-rearing."

Anora breathed a sigh of relief as Kiana settled in. "Thank you. What is your name?"

"Nina Bahari, I am."

"Thank—"

"Now, go get some sleep, come back when you're well and rested."

Anora stopped, looking at her baby quietly nursing. *I can't just leave her. What kind of a mother would do such a thing?* She voiced her reservations aloud, "Surely I can't leave Kiana alone."

"Not alone. She is with me. With us." Nina beckoned to the other women gathered about. They smiled and nodded in agreement. "With your people. This little young 'un will survive a few hours away from you, my dear."

Anora took a deep breath and closed her eyes. She was so tired she could barely open them again. *I just need an hour, then I will come back.* "All right, Nina, just a little sleep."

"Come, Anora, back to bed with you." Rojas began to usher her off.

Anora let herself be taken back to their tent. She crashed into the hide skin bedding and was soon fast asleep.

She awoke to the darkness of night and sat up with a start, remembering she had abandoned her baby. "Kiana."

Rojas snorted awake next to her. "What is it?" he asked groggily.

"Where is my baby?" Anora didn't wait for Rojas to answer. She rushed from their shelter.

Nina sat outside their home before a small fire, the baby bundled in a makeshift cradle beside her. Sleeping soundly.

Shocked, Anora opened her mouth to speak.

Nina held a finger to her lips in a shushing motion as she stood up. She came to Anora and leaned close to her ear. "Join us again tomorrow. If the little one wakes tonight, feed her, but do not let her fall asleep while suckling. Place her in the cradle and soothe her until she sleeps alone."

"But what if she keeps crying, no matter how much I soothe her?"

"Then resort to what is working for you. You are doing good, lass. You are a remarkable mother."

The words struck Anora like an arrow. *I'm a good mother?* She couldn't hold back her tears as she nodded more to herself than to Nina. *I'm a good mother.*

Nina hugged her and then ushered her to the chair she'd been seated in. Anora sat, her cheeks aching with a smile and streaked with tears of gratitude. "Thank you so much, Nina," she whispered.

Nina smiled back at her, then turned and disappeared into the night.

From then on, Anora spent her days in the company of the other women of the Otsoak. She soon returned to training newcomers and left little Kiana with the women for the day. Anora was named Third Otsoa, and life in Hasiera became busier with new responsibilities governing the ever-growing population. She made sure to always make time for Kiana every day. When the child was old enough, Anora began training Kiana to use a sword.

You need to be strong. Don't let anyone take advantage of you. Or force themselves upon you. Ever.

Some twenty years later, Anora looked at her daughter, whom she had hurt so badly, trying to impose that resilience within her.

"I think I understand now, mother," Kiana said, poking at a plate of food before her. "I appreciate you telling me all this."

"It is the first step in repairing what I have broken with you."

"All right, enough talk, let's gather the others and go find Hata."

They paid for their meal and exited the tavern into the market street of Nidhaut. A commotion immediately caught their attention. A large group of *Hasieran* were moving through the street. With the First Otsoa, Simon Meridio, at their lead.

CHAPTER TWENTY-ONE
DISTRACTED

Hata strolled across the battlement for the hundredth time in a few days. She spent much time up on the walls of Keep Crystalia, watching for the enemy. Her newly fashioned tungsteel-tinted armor glistened in the sunlight. A massive amber gem was embedded in the burnished-colored metal's breastplate. When she called upon her magic, the gemstone burnt bright, and power rushed through her. Amplifying her spells. How that was possible, she did not know. The different colored gems of the Ryk Lân had many uses. Some powered the flying machines, lifts, and other contraptions that the Himin-dvergar had invented. Others gave boons to weapons and armor, some even increasing the user's physical strength. When Raine presented the armor to Hata, she said that amber was connected to the sun and earth and channeled their life force and wisdom. Hata touched the large gem. It was warm and relieved unease, like being wrapped in a warm blanket next to the hearth on a cold mountain night.

A hand rested on Hata's lower back, and Raine's voice snapped Hata out of her musings. "Have the scouts returned?"

It had been a handful of days since their skirmish in the air with the Children of Skaad. The enemy had yet to attack since then. Hata blinked and turned to Raine. "Not yet, my Queen. I've been watching for them, but I fear I should have accompanied the scouts."

"They are capable of the task, Sunstone," Raine addressed her formally while she was in front of her soldiers.

Hata was more excited to spend time alone with the Queen later that evening. Slowly, Raine had been softening to Hata's attention. Raine was craving affection, and Hata was more than willing to give it. *We need to break down the barrier of her being above or separate from her people. Maybe we should find an alehouse tonight and go out together.* Bryn Sparkheart and Rorik Windbeard had invited Hata out on multiple occasions. She had yet to take them up on the offer, as Hata always had dinner with Raine. *What was the name of that ale house they'd said to meet at?*

"Scouts returning," one of the Himin-dvergar soldiers shouted as he manned one of the many massive arbalests, looking down the long sighting tube.

Three rotor-wings soared into view. Hata held her breath, waiting for a score of the flying creatures to appear in pursuit of the scouts. None came. She released her breath.

"Luminar's light, they made it." Raine also exhaled in unison with Hata.

They watched as the three crafts descended toward them and landed on the massive battlements. Rorik and Bryn jumped out and raced toward them. Nudging and bumping each other, trying to be the first to get there. Rorik mischievously tripped Bryn and became the victor.

"Lady Stormfall," Rorik puffed as he stood at attention. "The Skaad Lân forces have camped on one of the larger islands near the Gateway. We couldn't get too close as those flying ones are all over the skies near there. They're building massive chain bridges to connect the islands. They are gathering their army."

"So it has come to this," Raine grumbled. "We must strengthen our defenses. We have a better chance at winning if we defend from Crystalia Keep."

Bryn plodded up behind Rorik. "If only there were a way to break those chain bridges while the bastards were on them. That would make them think twice about coming for us."

"If I can get close enough, I may be able to do something about that," Hata said.

"No," Raine rebuked. "It is too dangerous. We need you here to help with the defense."

"What can I do from atop this wall? There is no earth to manipulate. I would have to use the wall itself as a weapon. Destroying it in the process."

"The Sky-lass is right, your Highness," Bryn agreed with a nod as he scratched at his curly beard. "She won't be of much use standing around here. They could use her on the front in the city below. When they send their great chains across, maybe our Sunstone can deal with it there."

"Or drop me on their side from above," Hata suggested enthusiastically. "I could truly let loose if no allies are around me."

"Hata, you would be surrounded and alone," Raine cautioned. "We do not know what weapons the enemy has. What if this Hear-fan Skaad were to show himself the minute you are secluded?"

Hata remembered the violet-tinted fire boring through her shoulder. There was a star-shaped scar there that still itched along with her wound from the flying humanoid. The Ryk Lân magic-infused crystals had healed her quickly. *Raine's right, what if he is here and I go out alone? Still, am I not the only one with a chance against him?*

"I say we assault the slimy bastards where they gather. Strike them when they least expect it," Rorik urged. "Bryn has been experimenting with red spinel and amethyst. The poor bloke has singed his curly whiskers more times than I can count."

"My whiskers? By the bright beard. If you would stop looking over my shoulder when I'm trying to work, the feckin' things would have been done ages ago."

"But you're so *serious* when you tinker," Rorik said, grinning at Bryn good-humoured-ly. "I can't help but stare. It's endearing."

Bryn blushed and mumbled quietly, "I suppose it wouldn't be the same if you weren't at my side."

This time, Rorik blushed. The two couldn't take their eyes off each other. "Cracked crystals, Bryn, I want to jump your bones."

"Enough." Raine's voice was strained with impatience.

The two Himin-dvergar lovers jolted out of their trance and bowed their heads toward the queen.

"Apologies, my Queen." Bryn bowed repetitively.

"Back to the matters at hand." Raine sighed wearily. "I think it too dangerous to go on the offensive. We will defend the city of Aerion. We will continue to prepare and to wait."

Bryn and Rorik nodded and bowed once more in unison. They stood awkwardly in silence.

"Dismissed."

The two turned and hurried back to their flying machine.

"You shouldn't be so hard on them, Raine." Hata leaned in close and nudged her playfully.

Raine closed her eyes and rubbed her temples with both hands. "I know, but they do press my patience with their antics. Luminar's light. I need a drink."

"About that…" Hata strived to remember the name of the alehouse, and then it clicked. "*Iskaldur.* The alehouse, we should go there for a drink."

"Ha." Raine snorted distastefully. "I can't mingle in such a place. My people would think less of me."

"Or perhaps the opposite," Hata proposed. "Do you ever stop to think they would like to *see* their ruler join them in their merriment?"

"I…" Raine hesitated. "I don't think it's a good idea. I can see it now, I walk in, and everyone stares at us silently. Stares at me. The entire mood of the place will be sullen. They will not be their true selves before me."

"Bah!" Hata barked a laugh. "That's the glory of an ale house. They will be far too into their cups to care you are even there. I guarantee it. Come on, it will be fun. You'll have fun." Hata pulled on Raine's arm enthusiastically, causing Raine's head to come within inches of Hata's chin. She smelled of a cozy morning by the hearth with a tinge of the forge fires drifting through the window. Raine's scent both comforted and excited Hata.

"All right, Hata," Raine said, looking into Hata's eyes. "I'll do it for you."

"Joo." Hata cheered. "Let's get changed and head there now."

Hata donned the fur-lined cloak over a delicate olive blouse and graceful skirt. *This reminds me of my people's feasts in the Chieftain's hall back in Oitilla, like the feast honoring my first successful hunt.* She had worn the skin of the mountain bear she had slain to that feast. It was the last feast she would ever see in her hometown. That image of Silja Vastaan's body swinging from the eaves of the longhouse returned to Hata's mind. Silja's mate, Ota Vastaan, had murdered her in cold blood.

A knock at the door interrupted Hata's dark thoughts, and Raine's muffled voice crept through. "Are you ready?"

Hata shook herself from the memories and called, "I am, come in."

Raine shyly stepped through the doorway to Hata's chamber.

Hata's jaw dropped.

Raine wore an elegant black dress, cut low on her chest, with a silver beaded choker-like collar connected to the center of the 'v' between her breasts with a strip of black lace. Feathered, poofy shoulder pads with inlaid silver embroidery and long laced sleeves.

Accompanied by a wide silver belt around her wide waist with matching earrings and nose studs. Finally, her flowing, nearly translucent shadowed skirt showed a silhouette of Raine's robust thighs and calves.

By Teras's stones, she is Skrull-damned gorgeous.

Raine stood awkwardly, waiting for Hata to say something.

"Uhm..." Hata cleared her throat, her cheeks flushed. "You look amazing, Raine."

Raine smiled shyly in answer. "Thank you. You look pleasant as well."

Excitement flitted through Hata, and she moved and took Raine by the arm. "This is going to be fun. To the alehouse."

The alehouse went silent as they entered, all eyes turning to stare at them.

Raine was frozen in place and began stuttering, "I—I can't do this, let's get out of here—"

"Sky-lass." Bryn Sparkheart's voice boomed over the silence. "Raine Stormfall. Your tankards are full to the brim, chilled and waiting to be had."

Rorik appeared next to Hata and Raine and ushered them to a round table where Bryn awaited them along with the guardsman Finn Sunstrider. As they moved through the crowd, the din began to return to normal, yet many of the Himin-dvergar still eyed the queen.

"My queen—" Finn started, but Bryn's open hand smacked him across the back of the head.

"There's no rank in the alehouse, you nitwit, only friends and good beer."

Raine sat silently, staring at the mug of ale before her.

Hata sat on the stool, her long legs causing her knees to touch the underside of the table. She turned and sat sideways for better comfort before grasping the handle of the massive tankard of ale. She took an enormous swig of the cold brew and gasped at the taste. It was thick, fluid, and bubbly and had a crisp scent. "By the gods, that is delicious."

"I knew you'd like that one, Sky-lass." Rorik chuckled. "That's Gildrik's Crystal Lager, a peated malt brown ale, a Himin-dvergar delicacy."

"I love it. Reminds me of the Vouri stout back home." Hata gave Raine a slight nudge as she leaned over and whispered, "Try it."

Cautiously, Raine took a sip from the large tankard. Her eyes widened. Then, she took a few more long drafts of the beverage.

"Looks to be a first for both Raine and the Sky-lass," Finn Sunstrider said, a broad smile on his bearded face.

"Honestly," Raine muttered. "I've begun to get sick of the wine in my tower."

"Ha ha." Rorik laughed heartily. "I bet that is the truth, ain't it, Raine?"

"Luminar's light," Raine chuckled. "It feels odd not to be addressed as Queen."

"There are no queens in *Iskaldur.*" Bryn lifted his tankard and toasted, "Only friends and ale."

"Friends and ale." The five clanged their cups together in unison.

"Now." Rorik suddenly was on the tabletop. "You two newcomers, you can't come to *Iskaldur* and not learn an alehouse song." Rorik gestured to all those around them and began to stop his foot to a beat.

We're the Himin-dvergar, we live up in the sky
We dwell among the crystals, that sparkle and that shine
We drink our ale with gusto, it makes us feel alive
We dance and sing with joy, we're happy and we're fine

Bryn and Finn stood up and joined in the chorus.

So come and join the party, it's a celebration time
We'll drink until we're tipsy, and leave our woes behind
We'll cheer for our friends, and for our country too
We're the Himin-dvergar, we're splendid, and we're true

Suddenly, the entire alehouse joined in the song, instruments began to accompany the music, and people cleared tables and began dancing in the center of the room.

Hata stared in amazement and clapped her hands along with the beat. She watched Raine out of the corner of her eye.

The queen was beaming, following along with the song's words as they came, trying to take them all in.

We're the Himin-dvergar, we shine with brilliant light
We honor our forefathers, who gave us this delight
We're the Himin-dvergar, we're loyal, and we're brave
We'll defend our home, we'll never be a slave
So come and join the party, it's a celebration time
We'll drink until we're tipsy, and leave our woes behind

We'll cheer for our friends, and for our country too

We're the Himin-dvergar, we're splendid, and we're true

The alehouse erupted in a cheer, and people started coming over and greeting Raine with joyful expressions. Then, the music broke into another song.

"Dance with her lassie." Rorik called to Hata as he pulled Bryn forcefully onto the dance floor.

Hata's cheeks were aching from the merriment and warm from the ale. She grabbed Raine by the arm and swept her into the cleared area where a throng of Himin-dvergar bounced and twirled along with the music.

Raine was laughing as she looked up into Hata's eyes. Their hands were clasped together, hopping and spinning along with the upbeat tune.

She is beautiful, Hata thought as the music ended. Panting and exhilarated, Hata led Raine to their table and drank deeply from a fresh tankard. Their hands were still held together.

Once they'd quenched their thirst, Raine eagerly pulled Hata back to the dance floor.

The next song was slow and elegant.

Raine leaned against Hata's chest, uncaring of her onlooking people, as they swayed like ripples in the stream around the room. "Thank you for this," Raine murmured into Hata's chest as they danced, then she looked up.

Raine's hazel brown eyes, looking so profoundly into Hata's, ignited a need within. *Those eyes. Those lips.* Slowly, Hata leaned forward, brushing their noses together. She could feel Raine's breath. Her warmth.

Raine closed the distance by standing on her toes, and their lips came together.

Suddenly, a massive *crash* resounded through the air above them.

The dancing ceased, and everyone looked around in confusion.

Hata inspected the ceiling and saw smoke beginning to seep through the rafters.

The doors at the front of the alehouse burst open. A Himin-dvergar man rushed in, shouting, "We are under attack. They're dropping blue fucking fire on us!"

The crowd poured out of the alehouse, pulling Hata and Raine along.

Explosive *crashes* and *thuds* echoed through the air around them, like clay jars shattering. They saw the sapphire flames smash against rooftops and burst into life.

Queen Raine Stormfall began shouting orders, "To the rotor-wings, we must take the fight to them. Drive them from our home. Make teams to combat the flames."

Bryn and Rorik appeared before them, panting with exertion. "My Queen," Bryn said as he gasped for breath. "We'll escort you to the keep, then make for our rotor-wing. You coming, Sky-lass?"

"I will stay and help with the fires. Go quickly."

With that, the three Himin-dvergar disappeared into the chaos of the night.

Hata ran to the nearest burning building. The wooden roof crashed in as the blue flames consumed it. People ran screaming from the entrance.

"My husband is trapped inside!" a young woman shrieked, her face soot-covered, clutching the bundle of a baby in her arms. "Somebody help."

Hata clenched her teeth as she rushed into the burning homestead, blue flames lashing out at her. The Himin-dvergar man lay under a pile of collapsed roofing, a heavy beam pinning him to the ground. The flames were creeping toward him.

Hata leaped and slid toward him, simultaneously erupting the earth in a dome-like shield around the man and herself. Protecting them momentarily from the flames and the collapsing structure. The man lay still under the debris as Hata used her mind to dig beneath him enough to dislodge him. Using all her strength, she grasped him under the arms and pulled him free. She tried to breathe, but only smoke filled her lungs. The dome had trapped it inside. She released the dome, and the heat immediately seared at her exposed body.

Teras, grant me strength.

She continued to drag the unconscious man from the wreckage. As she approached the entrance of the homestead, it became nearly impossible to move forward. Air sucked in through the archway so powerfully she couldn't contest its pull.

A beam crashed down beside her and exploded in an azure blast. Embers scattered against her right arm and hand, down the body of the man. Pain tore through her, and she screamed in agony. She collapsed under the man.

I'm going to die.

An image of Hear-fan Skaad's mocking smile played in her depleted vision.

No. I will not. One last push. Hata concentrated on the earth around them. *If I can't go out the front door, I'll just have to go up.* The earth shook, and then the floor cracked in a jagged circular pattern around them. The earth erupted skyward, crashing through what little remained of the structure's charred second floor and roof. There was more pain as Hata shielded the man with her own body as they crashed through the flimsy remains.

Cool air rushed into her lungs as they broke the surface. Yet even up here, the heat was blistering hot. She detached the top of her makeshift pillar and guided it away from the flames toward the keep. The city burnt blue beneath her. People flocked to the lifts and into the open gates by the thousand, but it was slow goings.

Hata imagined Raine, Bryn, and Rorik had got stuck waiting for the lift up to the keep. But she heard the thudding of hundreds of rotor-wings in the air as she approached Crystalia Keep. There was a battle raging in the night sky. Only a few patches of blue burnt in the keep grounds and along the battlements. Not nearly as much as the city below.

She released her hold on the earth as she touched down on top of the walls. Exhausted, still trying to catch her breath, pain rippling through her skin, she pleaded for help. "I need healing." She tried to scream the words, but her throat was hoarse, and it came out as merely a squeak. "Somebody. Anybody."

Two Himin-dvergar soldiers noticed her, and the man sprawled out before her. They rushed over.

"What happen—"

"Quickly, he needs help," Hata rasped, cutting the soldier off.

"Go get a healer," the other soldier woman ordered.

The first nodded and ran off to find help.

Hata took a deep breath and pushed herself to her feet. *I need to go back down and help. To save anyone I can.* Her legs shook with the effort, and she winced as she steadied herself on the wall parapet. Her right hand and all along her arm were blackened in places, the skin peeling away painfully. She suddenly felt dizzy as each pulse of her blood caused the burns to throb. *Let me rest for a moment.* Hata slumped against the bastion wall and leaned her head against it, focusing on everything but the pain.

Chapter Twenty-Two

REASON

Saudett watched as the blue flames spread through the darkness miles away from the island where she overlooked the destruction. *Hata is down there somewhere. But what can I do except fulfill Lord Skaad's orders? I can't reach Hata on my own. If only I could fly like the Nyra.*

She focused back on the task at hand. Once satisfied with the attack, Saudett signaled to a Nyra woman, wielding a long spear and a twisted-looking horn of some beast on her belt, to sound the retreat.

The winged woman put the horn to her lip and let loose three eerie blasts into the night.

Soon, they *heard* more than saw the wings of their comrades, the Skaad Lancers, returning overhead. The repetitive thumping of the enemies' flying contraptions echoed in the distance, unable to chase their foes through the darkness. The Nyra, as Hear-fan had graciously informed her, could see in the dark, had superhuman hearing, and could communicate with one another over great distances in their language. Unlike the other Children of Skaad, the Nyra did not have an aversion to sunlight, but it distorted their vision and confused them somewhat. They preferred staying in their shadowed under-ground homes or taking to the skies at night.

Excellent, I'll continue these night raids to demoralise the enemy. Saudett turned and began striding across a chain bridge, one of the dozens set for their ground troops to traverse from island to island. She returned to the massive island where they made their war camp. The Nyra had built many nests in the canopies of the crystal-like trees of this land. Thousands of the Children gathered. The hulks, hounds, greys and more. The behemoths that spewed navy smoke stalked around the island, providing eternal darkness for the Children. That same blue fire was now being used to barrage the short humanoid peoples of this Ryk Lân.

When she'd queried Hear-fan for more information on these people and their Lân, he admitted he didn't know much...

"They excavate and utilise crystals and minerals for use in magic. I've only sent a few scouting parties here in the past as I was too preoccupied with other *things*. It was a long time ago in human life spans. Only one such scout returned, clutching this obsidian gem in its jaws as it died at my feet." He pulled a shining silver necklace from under his robe. The center was a gem that was as black as night itself.

Yet as Saudett studied the obsidian stone, she swore something moved within.

"But the obstinate people of the Ryk Lân gave chase through the Wayfarers Gate," Hear-fan Skaad continued. "They had the aid of another Wayfarer. The one assigned to their Lân. She came at me with full force, and I lost this shadow-stone, but not before wounding her mortally, sealing her ability to heal. Still, she managed to escape with the stone. To your Lân, the Earste Lân. She left a cluster of Ryklings to be slaughtered by my Children. That glimpse of power I felt from this stone back then caused me to turn all my attention to retrieving it from the Earste Lân. The trouble with Wayfarers Gates is that you must know the location of another in order to connect with it. I only knew of the one in that confounded desert, and it had been tampered with. Only recently did I discover the Gate in the mountains of the Earste Lân, which enabled me to return this shadow-stone to me. Finally, after a century of looking for it...I have it back." His look of utter gratification was disturbingly sickening.

"It would seem this Ryk Lân would have abundant resources to use in our further conquests."

"Indeed. But these Ryklings are not to be underestimated. Their species is surprisingly ingenious."

So Saudett had witnessed. Their flying contraptions were incredible, and the massive fortress she had spied from afar was a formidable obstacle. Capable of launching projectiles with insane precision thousands of feet through the air. It would be suicide to attack during the day when their flying crafts and defenses had the advantage of vision. *We will continue the bombardment.* Saudett stepped into her command tent and sleeping quarters past two Nyra warriors who stood guard outside.

A makeshift map of the islands had been drawn up and pinned to a table in the center of the room. A hammock stretched between two poles was her bedding. *Gods, I miss my luxurious chambers in the Skaad Lân.* She began removing her armor and prepared to sleep for a few hours when one of the guards announced the arrival of Trije-fan Skaad and Warrior Nyxal.

"Enter," Saudett permitted as she stood over the map, putting on an air of inspecting it thoroughly.

"Knight-Commander." Nyxal saluted as he came before her. "The raid was successful. They could do nothing against us. They are blind in the darkness."

"Excellent, Nyxal," Saudett said with a nod of acknowledgment. "You and your people did well."

"All that you did was throw flames upon them in the night," Trije-fan Skaad rebuked, his shadowed lips curling in contempt toward her. "This accomplishes nothing."

"Nothing?" Saudett asked incredulously. "What, Primus tell, would you have done differently?"

"Simply begin the assault in full. Decimate the Ryklings in one night and leave them begging for my father's forgiveness."

"You believe we could take that monstrous keep in one night? What if we are unable to move the smokers in before dawn arrives? Should the sun come out and destroy our ground forces. What then?"

Trije-fan bared his teeth, his voice raising incrementally, "You needn't worry if I were to lead the attack. I would unleash such a hell upon them that they would cower under the brutality of it."

"As you did in the Moreas Lân?"

Violet energy flared from Trije-fan Skaad's hands as he stepped forward.

Nyxal stepped in front of him, blades raised. "I will have the Nyra swarm you like flies to shit should you touch the Knight-Commander."

Saudett held Trije-fan's sweltering gaze, desperately wishing she was closer to her spear.

Finally, the son of Skaad unclenched his fists, and the violet glow dimmed. Without another word, he turned and exited the command tent.

Saudett finally exhaled. "He would have killed us both, Nyxal. He is more than capable of it."

"Then the entire might of the Nyra would have befallen him."

"Why do you follow Hear-fan Skaad?" Saudet asked genuinely, slumping into her chair. "Why do your people abide by him?"

"The Lord of Shadow annihilated one of our colonies single-handedly when he first discovered the Grot Lân. Thousands died, and he *laughed* as he slaughtered us. We bent the knee to him in the end, vowing our loyalty. It is better to save more lives by being enslaved for eternity than to be wiped out entirely. It would've been a genocide."

"How did he find your Gate? I thought one could only point them at a Gate by knowing the location of another."

"There was one of his kind in our Lân. A friendly person who enjoyed studying the plants, animals, and rock formations of the Grot Lân. A peaceful being. He was loved by the Nyra. This Iban'mael would go through the Gate, back to his home, the Lân of Hiel, with many others to share knowledge with other Wayfarers. One such time, he went and never returned. A few weeks later, the Lord of Shadow appeared and subjugated the Nyra by force."

"I'm sorry this happened to your people, Nyxal."

"We're alive, and we will fight on under Hear-fan Skaad, or free of him should the chance arise. Are you not a loyal soldier of Skaad, Knight-Commander Gesche-fan?"

How honest can I be with Nyxal. I trust him, and he has put his life on the line for me now. "I'm conflicted," Saudett deliberated. "Of course, of his aims, I also feel sympathy for him. He was banished by his people to a wasteland. For what? I do not know. Yet he has shown me only kindness since my arrival. He is ambitious and intelligent. Until he shows me otherwise, I will follow him."

"And the Nyra will follow *you*, Knight Commander."

Saudett smiled and clasped Nyxal's forearm in her own. "My thanks, Nyxal." *Perhaps I can use this,* she pondered as the Nyra left her tent.

Saudett awoke to the sound of that repetitive *thumping* in the air and the screaming of the metallic wings diving down from high above the island.

Dressing in her armor as quickly as possible, she ran outside to a scene of complete chaos.

The Nyra swarmed the air as hundreds of the propeller-driven crafts swept in.

The Rykling flying machines spun as a handful of Nyra Lancers met them, the sharpened blades on the contraption wings shearing through her Skaad Lancer's flesh by the dozens.

Some of the Nyra's spears met their marks as they collided with the aircraft. Three machines lost control and struck the earth, while others missed the island entirely and fell into oblivion below.

Projectiles whistled down into the screaming horde as the machines dived. Piercing through hounds and hulks in scores, leaving them wailing and bleeding in the dirt. The Children shrieked, yowled, and thrashed about, unable to do anything against the flying contraptions.

The crafts reached the vertex of their dive and began climbing once more. *Slowly.*

A dozen muscular grey, ape-like children leaped into the air, latching on to a few of the lowest flying crafts. Their weight careened the contraptions out of control, crashing them into the ground. Some burst into flames as blue and red mist exploded from them. A stout humanoid hopped out of one of the down crafts and began striking about with two hammers, cracking skulls before he was overwhelmed by the horde and ripped to shreds.

The flying machines were inclining slower, and the Skaad Lancers swarmed them and killed many of the beings piloting them. Each craft seemed to have two short, stout people huddled in them. The second would defend the craft with a crossbow, axe, hammer, or sword.

Many of the Nyra fell from the skies, dead on the winds of this Ryk Lân.

I need to do something. Saudett paced in frustration as she watched the battle. There was nothing she could do.

A second wave of aircraft appeared from above, their wings screaming. More of the Nyra and Children fell to their onslaught.

A craft came soaring in, smoke billowing from its rear, directly toward her. A crossbow bolt whistled past Saudett's ear and thudded into the earth beside her.

The machine did not stop.

She dived aside as it crashed into the ground. Saudett rolled to her feet to see two stocky humanoids jump from the burning craft and charge toward her, shouting in a different language. Yet she understood it. She recalled Hear-fan Skaad's speech enchantment.

"We are Himin-dvergar. We'll never be a slave, you Skaad bastards."

Gesche-fan Skaad leveled her spear and counter-attacked.

The first Rykling came in with a massive tool with a 'u' shape on each end.

Saudett deflected the blow. It rattled through the shaft of her spear and into her hands. *Little bastards are strong.* She flicked her spear and caught him in the jaw with the butt end, causing him to stumble backward.

The other appeared and loosed a crossbow bolt at nearly point-blank range.

Twisting, it glanced her side, *panging* off her armor and ricocheting into the dirt.

Her spear impaled the man's chest.

He stared down at it in disbelief. Blood dripped from his lips down his curly, dark beard. His eyes flamed, and he grasped the spear shaft with both hands. "Fucking Skaad bastard." He spat blood at her. Those were his last words.

"Borin!" the other Rkyling screamed as the metal tool smashed into Saudett's leg.

She buckled in agony, releasing her grip on the spear.

Tears streamed down the stout man's eye into red whiskers as he raised the heavy metal again to bring it down on her skull.

Nyxal collided with the man, his talons digging deep into the Rykling's chest. At the same time, Nxyal's dual swords beheaded the man as he pinned him to the ground with his feet.

The impaled Rykling man stood stiffly, grasping the spear shaft as his eyes stared ahead in death.

Chapter Twenty-Three

SHAME

Simon knelt before the grave of his father and mother, Yakeb and Teresa Meridio. Simon wasn't a religious man and doubted the existence of gods altogether. But his parents, especially his mother, were devout followers of the Primus. Simon had never told his mother he didn't believe anymore because he knew it would break her heart. *She would have been on her deathbed worrying that I was going to Skrull's hell.* It was better for her to die happy, thinking her child would join her in salvation. *If the Primus is so loving and powerful, why did He let Mother get sick? Why does He let murderers and rapists do what they do? Why does the Primus cause storms that destroy people's homes? Why does he let His clergy of men abuse their power? Why is there suffering in the world?*

The list goes on and on. After Simon's mother passed, he often debated religion with his father. Her death truly made Simon's mind flee further and further from his upbringing in Primus Dogma. The memory came back to him...

"Many people follow the guidelines of the Primus and his lesser gods to find their morals." Yakeb sat before the hearth in their family home, nursing a cup of wine as he continued, "His teachings tell us not to kill, steal, and many other guidelines that make humanity virtuous."

"If people need a god to tell them how to be good, and that's the only thing holding them back from *murder,* then their own humanity is very flawed. I murder as much as I wish, and that is not at all."

"That is a very logical outlook on it, my son. It's lovely that you can look at life from such a rational point of view. But what is there to live for without seeking what comes after death?"

"That's just it. Nothing comes after death. Do you remember anything before you were born? No. You won't even know you're dead. I wish to make the most of the life I have."

"Perhaps, but faith comforts people, and I can empathize with them in that regard," Yakeb said. "No matter the god or religion."

...Simon sat before the gravestone. Death had come to his family again that day on the outskirts of Dagad when the First Otsoa had beheaded Yakeb. Simon remembered his father looking directly at him and smiling fondly. *Father was always so happy and so proud of me. And now I'm a murderer.* His parents would be devastated. *So much for not needing the moral guidelines of the gods. But I avenged you, Father. I killed the First Otsoa.* Simon had murdered the leader of Hasiera slowly, in cold blood. At the time, he had felt nothing, but as he looked down on the stone tablet with his father's name etched into it, he felt wholly gratified. *I'll see you in Skrull's hell, you bastard First.*

That satisfaction soon faded as he further reminisced about his father. He sat alone in the graveyard in the woods of Aurulan. A rickety shack was the only building in the small clearing. The escort of Hasieran and Captain Cad Dermont with a few hundred Shepherd's Eye soldiers had gone further up the road to make camp.

Simon finally let his grief emerge from its shackles. He had been holding it in since the day he saw his father die. At the time, Simon had been so full of rage that the only thing he could think about was vengeance. After accomplishing that, he had been so busy that he didn't have time to reflect upon the loss. Finally, he let it sink in. His father was gone.

"Fath—" the word stuck in Simon's throat. "I'm so sorry. I didn't treat you kindly in the end. I told you to leave me alone, and I never had the chance to apologize. Gods, I wish I could make it right. If you are up there, somewhere, with Mother, I miss you. I miss you both...I love you."

The light of day began to dim as he knelt before their tombstones and recalled all the beautiful things about the two people who had brought him into this world. Finally, when no more tears were left, he stood, stretched, and turned toward the road.

The door on the rundown shack squeaked open, and a greying old man appeared. "Terribly sorry for your loss. Simon, is it?"

Simon stopped. "How do you know who I am?"

"Your father spoke much of you," the old man said. "He was a regular visitor to his dear Teresa."

"Ah," Simon answered. "I suppose that makes sense."

"Can I show you something quickly, dear sir?"

Simon yawned and stretched. "I'm quite tired. I need to catch up with my company and get some sleep."

"It will only take a moment." The grey old man beckoned him toward the shack. "Please, please, come inside my home."

A handful of crows perched on the roof of the building, watching with an eerie silent intent.

Simon sighed as he stepped into the dim light of the wooden boarded shed.

The man was arranging some clay jars on a table that looked like it had been broken and put back together on numerous occasions. He then let out a nearly crow-like cackle. "Petre has been practicing. He is a great sorcerer now. Look here, Simon Meridio." He waved his hand over the jar, and a string of water rose from it slowly before falling back into it as the old man pulled his hand away, a bead of sweat dripping down his forehead.

He looks about to pass out. "Remarkable," Simon said sardonically.

"Have you ever seen anything so powerful?" the man croaked excitedly. "I have not witnessed such a thing since that girl moved the earth. But I am the bearer of this mighty power now. That ignorant Alpha will kneel before me." The man's voice elevated with each sentence, maniacal laughter following in its wake.

Simon froze. *Hata?* Cautiously, he asked, "A girl that moved the earth?"

"Buh ha ha. Yes, that red-headed witch has nothing on me. Reported her to the Alpha, I did. Got her where she needs to be, I did."

"You, yourself, reported her to the Alpha?"

"Yes. Haven't you been listening, you damned peasant."

Windan.

The old man split in two at the waist, shrieking as his two halves fell to the floor.

Simon strolled from the shack, casually closing the door behind him, the screams dulling as he walked down the road to rejoin his company. *Like I said, First, I'll see you in Skrull's hell.*

They came to a quiet little town a few days after the graveyard named *La Vierge*. It was surrounded by orchards of fruit trees, fields of golden wheat, and pastures with speckled cattle grazing peacefully in the sun. A man introduced himself as the mayor of the little village. He had a long scar running just under his eye and down his cheek, causing him to look grizzled and menacing. Though he was quite young to be mayor, in Simon's opinion.

"Welcome to *La Vierge*." The young man met them with a friendly greeting. "I am Aaron Marion, newly appointed mayor of this little town. How can we be of service?"

"We can pay for food and lodging, my good man," Simon answered as his people filed into the town. "But please, point us to an unused field to make camp. There are far too many to find beds for all."

"We can move benches aside in our temple. We've done it before." Aaron said with a smile. "There should be enough room in there."

Simon looked at the large building with the symbol of Hettra depicted in stained-glass above the large entrance doors. He had read the meaning of this symbol long ago in one of his father's texts. The symbol consisted of a heart shape with a dove inside it. The heart represents love, compassion, and kindness. The dove represents peace, harmony, and freedom. The symbol also has a circular border with four petals at the corners. The circle represents unity, wholeness, and eternity. The petals represent beauty, grace, and joy. The symbol was colored in pink and white, which were the colors of Hettra.

"It's seen far worse than a few sleeping people," Aaron said reassuringly. "It's Our Lady Hettra's temple. She welcomes everyone and anyone into her home, even with all our differences."

Oh gods, more religious mumbo jumbo, Simon thought as he followed the young man into the temple. Zahir and a handful of others joined him. People were sitting in the pews listening to a middle-aged Tulu woman preach. She stood before a statue portraying the Goddess Hettra. The statue was a woman with long flowing stone hair, nursing a babe in one arm, with the other outstretched in a welcoming gesture.

The Priestess acknowledged them with a nod as they entered and continued her speech, "Welcome, travelers, my beloved brothers and sisters, to the Temple of Hettra, our Goddess of love and peace. We are gathered here today to celebrate the divine gift of love that Hettra has bestowed upon us and to share it with one another. Love is the most incredible power in the Earste Lân and the source of all life and happiness.

"Let us take a lesson from Hettra that teaches us that love knows no bounds and is meant to be shared. We should not hold it back or try to control it but give and receive it generously. Love is not meant to be divided or restricted. It is a unifying force that brings us together. We should welcome it with open arms. There is no room for fear or hate when it comes to love. Instead, we should trust and cherish it, for it can heal and transform our lives beautifully.

"Hettra is a loving and accepting mother who warmly welcomes all who seek her love, regardless of their background, gender, sexual orientation, faith, or anything else that is perceived as different or unusual. Hettra loves her children equally and desires them to love one another. She does not judge or condemn but instead offers forgiveness and healing. She does not demand or command but inspires and guides us towards our best selves. Regardless of our faith or lack thereof, Hettra supports and blesses us unconditionally.

"Let us hear the call of Hettra and follow her example of spreading love and peace throughout the Lân. Hettra encourages us to be kind and compassionate to one another, to be generous and grateful, and to show respect and tolerance towards everyone. She urges us to be honest and faithful and to remain humble and hopeful in all situations. Our Lady Hettra invites us to live a joyful, playful, adventurous, curious, and passionate life filled with love and empathy for those around us.

"She challenges us to rise above our fears, doubts, anger, resentment, greed, selfishness, pride, and arrogance. Hettra encourages us to confront challenges and difficulties and face our mistakes and failures with courage. We must also acknowledge our losses and grief while keeping our dreams and aspirations alive.

"She promises to always be with us, in our hearts and minds, in our words and actions, in our relationships with friends, family, lovers, partners, enemies, and strangers, in our connection to nature and the environment, in our past, present, and future, and even in our life and death.

"May we offer our prayers to Hettra, the embodiment of love and peace, and express our gratitude for her boundless affection. Let us raise our voices in song and honor Hettra for the tranquility she brings. As we listen to her wisdom, may we be guided by her example and follow in her footsteps. Let us cherish Hettra, the Goddess of love and peace, and emulate her love for one another."

To his surprise, Simon was nodding along in agreement with the words of the teaching as the sermon ended.

"Go with love." The priestess blessed the gathering, dismissing them as she did so. The villagers filed past Simon, Aaron, and company.

The priestess approached with a welcoming smile. Her black, greying hair was tied into a neat bun, and she wore the plain beige robes of Hettra. "Welcome to the Temple of Hettra." She leaned to the side to look past him in the town square where his people gathered. "Quite the parade you have. It looks like you'll require lodgings for the night."

"Our humblest apologies, Priestess," Simon said with a bow. "We humbly thank you for the abode."

"Don't be thanking me. Thank our Lady Hettra. She would have us offer all peoples generosity and kindness."

"So I heard," Simon said, then paused. "You would even offer such kindness to a known murderer?"

"It is not our place to judge others. Perhaps they had a rightful reason to kill. But if we know they do it simply for pleasure. For downright evil. Then. Then, we kindly show them to Skrull's door."

I enjoyed killing the man in the graveyard. But he caused all this. He sent the Magnus Huntsman after Hata. He deserved to die.

"What's your name, boy?" the priestess repeated.

"Hettra's bouncing bosoms, I apologize." He renewed his bow. "Simon Meridio, Meridio Enterprises, First Otsoa of Hasiera. At your service."

"Well, that's a mouthful indeed." The priestess chuckled, a broad smile creasing her face. "I'm sure the Goddess is laughing at your colorful use of her name."

Simon reddened. "My gods, I'm sorry it just slipped out."

"It's fine, my child." The priestess reassured. "I am Priestess Amahle. Come, let's get these benches moved aside. You all must be exhausted from your travels."

Some of his people and the townsfolk helped them move the heavy pews to make room for their bedrolls. They made short work of it, and there was plenty of room for Simon's entire company in the large temple building.

Simon was restless that night and noticed a light peeking under a door near the back of the temple. He crept over and knocked gently.

"Come," the priestess's voice muffled through the doorway.

He entered. The Priestess Amahle was sitting at a small table. A loaf of bread and a jar of honey sat half-eaten beside her as she wrote on a parchment.

"Couldn't sleep?" Amahle asked as she pulled a wooded stool from beneath the table and pushed it toward him with a foot. "What troubles you, Simon?"

He sat and pondered that question for a long moment. Finally, he let it out. "I'm the murderer."

She did not even flinch as she continued writing. "Did you do this in cold blood? For no reason other than taking pleasure in it?"

"Oh, there were plenty of reasons. I have done it twice now. I can't say I didn't find some satisfaction in it. Yet I can't help but feel this immense sense of shame. I am a hypocrite punishing them for what they have done to others."

"My dear child. You are suffering and struggling with what you have done. I know that you feel guilty and ashamed for taking the lives of others. We live in a Lân where, unfortunately, evil exists. Greed exists. War exists. Power-hungry magi exist for Skrull's sake. I know that you wish you could have done things differently. I know you fear what others will think and say about you. Yet still, you told me of these deeds. I do not judge you but offer you love and forgiveness. I know that you are haunted by the images and sounds of killing. I know that you are hurting and broken. Can you tell me why you killed these people?"

"The first man killed my father and enslaved me. The second man caused a young woman to be kidnapped by the Council of the Aerie. Skrull knows where Hata is now—"

"Hata?!" the woman exclaimed, her stool tumbling back as she found her feet.

"You know her?" Simon asked in disbelief.

"Indeed, I do...She and her family helped us a few years back with a small bandit problem."

"That's remarkable. It really is a small Lân, as they say."

"Ha. She was such a passionate girl. You say she's been captured by the Council?"

"Unfortunately, yes."

"This is where you are headed? To Nidhaut?"

"Honestly, Hata is a secondary objective. We sent a group to try to find her months ago. Hopefully, they succeeded. Our real reason is of far greater concern." Simon told the woman everything, starting from his father's death to the magical Wayfarers Gates and the impending threat from the Skaad Lân.

Amahle sat in silence, pondering his story. Finally, she spoke. "I will help you. One of the council members is a devoted follower of Hettra. I'm overdue a pilgrimage to their tower."

"You don't need to do such a thing," Simon said, shaking his head. "We'll figure it out when we get there."

"Better at least one connection before bringing your plight to the Aerie, is it not?"

"Skrull's balls, woman, I can't argue with such sound logic."

"Ha. That is another teaching of our Goddess, Hettra. She teaches us that humans are not fixed or determined but dynamic and evolving. She teaches us to grow and develop our physical, mental, emotional, and spiritual capacities and to pursue our passions and interests. She teaches us to embrace change, challenge, and learn from our mistakes..."

Simon leaned his head against the wall and began to doze as the priestess rambled on and on into the night. *By the Primus, this is why I hated going to the temple.*

Chapter Twenty-Four

IRE

Hata was sick of being wounded and in pain. She was fed up with recovering in bed while the Himin-dvergar raided the Children of Skaad's location on one of the isles. *I should be out there with them.* She was fed up with being useless. The burns on her arm and hand were wrapped in bandages with flecks of emerald gemstones underneath. She had saved one man from the fires before she had passed out. *I did nothing…* At this moment, a fleet of rotor-wings was assaulting the enemy, and she was lying in bed. It was too much. The anger broke from her lips in a furious outburst, "Fucking hells."

"I think that's the first I've heard such colorful language out of your mouth," Raine said as she entered the room.

"They are fighting and dying out there," Hata exclaimed desperately. "How can you be so calm? We should be out there with them."

"Our strike is not meant to destroy them. It is to tell them we will not cower in fear of their flames. We retaliate to show them what the Himin-dvergar are made of."

"Then why not send everything we have against them? Why not send me?"

"I will fight on my own terms, not theirs. We have the advantage of Keep Crystalia here. They will be hard pressed to conquer this fortress."

"But they will continue to come at night and cast the fire down from the skies. What about the common people?"

"They will spend the nights in Crystalia. They can go back to their homes during the day."

"If they have homes to go back to," Hata muttered.

"What would you have me do?!" Raine shouted, startling Hata with her sudden cry. "I am Queen, Hata Vasara, not you. We could've responded faster to the attack if I hadn't been a fool dancing about in an alehouse. I will not take orders from the likes of you."

Hata's lip quivered as Raine's words cut at her. "Raine—"

"I will not play your games of acting like a commoner anymore. I am not a commoner. My people need a Queen."

"Raine, please—"

"No," the queen silenced her with a glare. Raine's eyes glistened with moisture as she continued. "I will move your lodging to the barracks. If you still wish to help us, report to Finn Sunstrider for active duty. He will make use of your skills. Farewell, Sunstone." With that, Raine turned and marched briskly from the chamber.

Hata wiped the tears from her eyes on her sleeve. *What have I done? Why does she hate me?*

Sometime later, Hata rolled over in the wooden cot that was far too small for her. Her long legs uncomfortably sticking out over the end of it. The music of snoring soldiers all around her scratched at her ears. Irritated and restless, she sat up, and her head *thumped* against the bunk above her.

"Fucking hells," Hata cursed, the compounded anger still bubbling within as she rubbed at her head. "Teras, toss me off the mountain."

Himin-dvergar soldiers sleeping nearby grumbled and snorted at her sudden outburst. But soon rolled over and began snoring once more.

"They sleep like Skrull-damned logs," Hata mumbled as she picked her way out of the barracks and found a spiraling staircase leading up to the bulwark of Keep Crystalia. *I just need some air.* Stars glimmered in the night sky, and two crescent moons, one slightly bluer than the pale white glow of the other, shone brightly as she strolled along the battlements. The city below was dark and lifeless as all the citizens had been evacuated into the keep for the night. The walls were still busy with activity. The massive ballistas swiveled on their platforms and scanned the sky's darkness. Luckily, the moons and stars seemed extra bright this night. Hundreds of soldiers camped in the courtyard below as there was no room within Keep Crytalia's structures.

Himin-dvergar engineers toiled and rattled away at the damaged rotor-wings that had returned from battle. They'd counter-attacked the Children of Skaad, and lost many lives. But from the stories she heard, the Children had taken far more losses.

Hata saw a familiar figure as she neared one of the flying contraptions.

Rorik Windbeard turned and hooted in surprise as he sighted Hata. "Sunstone."

Bryn Sparkheart's goggle-covered face popped out from behind the rotor-wing, and he gave a toothy grin in greeting.

"Hello," Hata answered meekly.

Rorik clapped her on the back. "Why so solemn, little Sky-lass?"

"I don't know how you can sleep in the barracks with all that snoring."

"I don't." Bryn barked a laugh. "I prefer to sleep with my dearest darling." He gave a sensual caress to the fuselage of the rotor-wing before him.

"Excuse me, Bryn Sparkheart?" Rorik stomped over to him, and he recoiled. "Your dearest darling?"

"I–I meant my *second-most* dearest darling, of course." Bryn stuttered. "Rorik Windbeard, you are far and beyond at the pinnacle of my compassionate consideration."

Rorik narrowed his eyes at the oil-stained Himin-dvergar man. "That's a lot of fancy words you're twisting about to try to confuse a simple laddie here, isn't it? Bryn Sparkleheart."

"Sparkleheart." Bryn snorted. "Well, I oughta give you a whoppin'."

By this time, Rorik had rounded the aircraft, and Bryn was retreating away from him, ever keeping the rotor-wing between him and his partner.

Hata stifled her laughter.

"You." Rorik turned on her abruptly. "Quit your moping and help me catch this gear-grinding griffin."

Hata jolted in start at Rorik's demand and looked at Bryn, who was looking right back at her, shaking his head to dissuade her.

"Don't do this, Sky-lass," Bryn cautioned. "Don't let Windbeard's rotundly good looks persuade you into doing anything rash."

"Get over here, Bryn Sparkheart!" Rorik hollered as he sprinted around the aircraft.

Bryn's only option was to run away or come in Hata's direction. He decided it wasn't worth the risk and retreated down the bulwark away from them.

Rorik stopped his pursuit and returned to Hata. "Give her time, Sky-lass. She'll come round. Next thing you know, you'll be chasing our queen around her bed chambers, smacking one another with duck-down pillows."

"Wh–what?" Hata stuttered in surprise. "The Queen? Raine? Pillows?"

"A little pillow tussle always leads to far more *entertaining* activities," Rorik said with a mischievous grin.

Hata felt her cheeks flush, imagining that scenario. Frolicking around Raine's rooms in their nightgowns, feathers flying and poofing through the chamber as they miraculously tumbled into bed together, faces inches apart. Their lips...their hands...

"Oi. You in there, Sky-lass?"

Rorik's voice brought Hata back from her daydream. "Oh, uhm, yes. What were you saying?"

"Once this war ends, you'll have plenty of time to spend together."

"She hates me, Rorik." Hata sighed. "I don't think she ever wants to see me again."

"Nay, she doesn't hate you, lass. She has responsibilities that come above all else. Even before the wonderful thing called love. Rather, her love for her *people* comes above all others."

"I know," Hata said, almost inaudibly. "Still, she blames me for bringing her to *Iskaldur* when she should have been in the keep."

"None of us could have known the bastards would do that," Rorik reassured. "Even so, the Queen's presence at the keep would not have changed the outcome."

"Well, I wish someone would tell *her* that. She avoids speaking with me now." It had been a couple of days since Raine had dismissed her. "She ignores me if she sees me."

"Oh, my dear lass, young love is a trying time. Come, let's find that Sparkleheart and have a sip of brandy." Rorik ushered her away in the direction Bryn had fled, where they soon found him drinking with a handful of other engineers and rotor pilots.

"Couldn't keep up with Bryn 'The Swift' Sparkheart, could you now, Rorik Wind-beard?" Bryn greeted them as they approached.

"Pah." Rorik retorted. "I could've planted my foot up your arse had I the inkling to do so."

"Have a seat. Join us, Rorik Windbeard and Sunstone Hata," one of the other Himin-dvergar women said. "Have a cup."

"Don't mind if I do." Rorik took a seat and poured two mugs of brandy. She handed one to Hata, who took a seat nearby.

The woman who had spoken raised her own mug and said, "To our fallen brothers and sisters who gave the bastards hell."

"Aye, aye." the small group cheered in unison.

"To Borin Stoneshield and his mate Hakon Fireheart," another woman said.

"And Elin Silverhair and Thora Thunderwing."

"Magnus Cloudmane and Ingrid Hardhand."

Always in pairs, the Himin-dvergar toasted their fallen rotor-wing comrades. Hata sat in silence, listening to their sullen memories of those lost. *So many have died since I discovered I had these powers. Before I had them. It all started in my village with Silja. Then, Taryn Drel, the Shepherd's Eye soldier. The countless people of Hasiera who died at the claws and fangs of the Children of Skaad. That old man who had protected me on the valley's walls during the attack on Hasiera. Then Luftan and Tomas. Chanel de Montrichard. Now, these innocent people in this Lân fighting for their lives.* Something twisted within her, scraping to get out. *Rage.* Rage and loathing at the man behind all this. *Hear-fan Skaad.*

Hata stood up without a word and walked away from the group of Himin-dvergar.

"Hata?" She heard Rorik call after her but ignored it.

I need my armor. Hata returned to the barracks, silently donning the heavy ivory breastplate with the glowing amber gem embedded in it. The gem pressed against the skin of her thorax. Immediately, her sense of the earth heightened. The stone of the keep, with its flecks of crystal and gems, was like a living being, encompassing and comforting her. Once dressed, she made her way to the lifts at the exterior of the keep and descended into the abandoned city of Aerion below.

Chapter Twenty-Five

TIDINGS

"We should be getting close to the Wayfarers Gate," Simon announced to the gathering. "We will form a long line and comb these woods until we find it."

Rakshak Zahir led the Hasieran on one side of the search party, while Captain Cad Dermont led the Shepherd's Eye on the other half. Simon searched his memory for the location of the Wayfarer's Gate, used by Kiana Ahmadi's group, which consisted of her mother, Anora, the ranger, Kaplan Mir, and Baal and Brena Vasara. *Oh, and don't let me forget the merchant, Zailas Erhsya.*

Simon wondered what they had been through since their departure from Hasiera. *I hope things have gone better for them than they have for us.* He returned his thoughts to the Gate, which was deep within the woodlands of Aurulan, far from the main roads that led across the country. They had veered southwest after leaving the town of *La Veirge* behind. Simon recalled the approximate location when he had tuned the Hasiera portal to this one using Gaelin Yesnala's memory. It was in a secluded thick forest, between some jagged rock formations. Passing by, one would not notice the gateway without studying it closely. Unless it was open and attuned to another portal.

Still, he knew he was headed in the right direction. It was like an itch in the back of his mind, ever guiding Simon forward. The feeling grew as they journeyed on. Finally, a commotion erupted in the line ahead. Simon jogged to catch up and broke through a tree line to find Zahir being confronted by a large group of Aurulan soldiers dressed in the white and yellow surcoats of the King. They had weapons ready as more Hasieran flooded behind Zahir, readying their own arms defensively. Simon could see the tension readying to turn into bloodshed.

"Halt!" one of the soldiers shouted. "Put down your weapons and state your business in Aurulan."

Zahir did not drop his curved sword and round spiked shield, glaring at the man intensely.

Unexpectedly, the Priestess Amahle was there, smiling sincerely at the Aurulan soldiers as she addressed them. "Peace, friends, we come in peace. We are simply passing through on our way to Nidhaut."

"Well, this is a roundabout way to the capital. Why not take the main road?" the soldier retorted and gestured to the Hasieran. "And these people are dressed in outlandish clothing. This could be an attack against our kingdom."

"We have come from Dagad and beyond," Simon said, finally joining the disruption. "From the Burning Sea. We seek an audience with the Aerie as we have grave news of an impending attack on the Earste Lân by creatures of shadow himself."

The soldier paused, and others in his guard looked at him knowingly. Then he returned his attention to Simon. "What news of these beasts do you bear? How do you know of them?"

Captain Cad Dermont appeared with a handful of Shepherd's Eye soldiers, and to Simon's surprise, the Aurulan soldiers immediately saluted Cad and stood at attention. "At ease, sergeant," Cad said with a nod. "What's this I hear of beasts?"

"Captain, it's not my place to say."

"Spit it out, soldier," Cad ordered.

"Yes, Captain, the beasts attacked northern Aurulan. They came out of the North Iron Belt in the wake of the fleeing Vouri peoples."

"How goes the war?"

"The beasts have scattered, but they roam the countryside when darkness falls. And thousands are left crawling about the mountains. It is no longer a safe place for anyone." The sergeant shook his head disbelievingly. "We have reports of small towns and farmlands being overtaken and slaughtered on the farthest outskirts of north and west Aurulan and beyond. But how do you know of these creatures? Dagad is so far from the mainland."

"Ah," Simon pondered aloud. "So Aurulan already knows of the Children of Skaad."

"Take us to your commanding officer," Cad barked.

The soldier saluted again and turned, nodding at his squad to lead the way.

Simon and his company of nearly five hundred followed the two dozen soldiers further into the woods. As they entered the tree line, the sergeant stopped at a broad tree, looked up, and spoke to the abovementioned branches.

"Hold your fire. They're on our side...for now," the sergeant muttered.

"Those are the Shepherd's Eyes out of Dagad," the tree answered. "What're they doing all the way out here?"

Simon squinted into the branches and could vaguely glimpse a man dressed in olive and tan clothing, blending nearly seamlessly with the canopy. He held a long bow, notched and ready.

"Skrull's balls, if I know," the sergeant answered, "but I'm taking them to the magi."

"Have at it, I'll pass on the word to my men." The figure in the tree let out a shrill whistle that sounded somewhat like a bird call. After a moment, an answering call returned.

As they continued following the sergeant, Cad caught up to him and asked, "How many rangers do you have stationed out here? We're in the middle of nowhere."

"Perhaps a thousand are scattered about the artifact."

Simon's ears perked up at that word.

"Artifact?" Cad asked.

"You'll see, Captain."

With that, they moved into a large man-made clearing. Trees had been felled in a massive circle around a jagged rock formation, their freshly cut stumps dotting the landscape. Three watchtowers were in mid-construction, and a crude wooden sharpened palisade pointing inward aimed at the rock formation. Hundreds of tents surrounded the barrier, and soldiers milled about. Some aided with the construction, while others drilled formations or played kickball if they weren't on duty. There were thousands of soldiers here.

Simon knew where they were. *The Wayfarers Gate.*

The sergeant halted and turned to address Simon and company. "Essential personnel from here on out. There are a few tavern tents around the camp, so your people can mingle."

Captain Cad Dermont nodded and dismissed his soldiers, who immediately greeted and began circulating with the onlooking Aurulan soldiers.

The Hasieran hesitated before one of the Shepherd's Eye ushered a nomad into the throng, introducing him as they went, which broke the awkwardness.

Simon, Zahir, Cad, and Priestess Amahle followed the sergeant toward the Gate. They passed through the barricade to find a handful of robed individuals bustling about.

One of the figures noticed them and approached. Clothed in black robes trimmed in silver, the man was perhaps Simon's age, early thirties. The mage was quite handsome and had unruly dark hair and pale skin. Simon noticed some crisscrossing scars on his neck before they disappeared into his robes.

"What have we here?" the mage asked suspiciously. "An odd foursome indeed. Clearly a Priestess of Hettra, a Captain of the famed Shepherd's Eye out of Dagad, and a desert Xamidian?" The mage paused, studying Simon. "And last but not least, a very *ordinary-looking* man. You have brought quite a riffraff of others here?" He gave the slightest inclination to indicate the rest of Simon's group that was in the camp.

"Excuse me?" Simon retorted, stepping to the forefront of his little group. "Simon Meridio, Meridio Enterprises. I am the leader of this riffraff and find myself far from *ordinary* these days."

"Apologies," the man gave the slightest of bows. "Simon Meridio, of Meridio Enterprises, successor of Yakeb Meridio."

"Apology accepted—" Simon stopped. "How do you know my father? How do you know that?"

The man laughed contemptuously. "Education, my dear Simon. I've studied the history of the Earste Lân at the *Seminary Enclosure* for quite some time. Your family business has made a name for itself outside of Nidhaut."

Simon felt an inkling of pride at that, swelling his ego. "Well, well, who'd have thought? You seem like a respectable young man. Tell me, nameless magi, have you figured out how to use the Wayfarers Gate yet?"

The man's handsome features warped at Simon's comment. "How do you know this?"

"It is a long story. Tell me, how did you find it?"

"We were told where it was."

"By who?" Simon asked curiously.

"The Alpha would not say," the mage answered. "He simply ordered us to study it, protect it, and kill and destroy anything that came through it."

"A wise man, this Alpha."

"An incredible man," the mage said with a look of approbation.

"If you say so," Simon muttered, keeping other thoughts to himself. *The incredible Alpha who steals young people away from their families?*

"Why are you here, Simon Meridio?"

"The same reason as you, it would seem. I'm here to protect the Earste Lân."

"The First Otsoa speaks the truth," Zahir reassured. "The Children of Skaad seek our oblivion."

"Skaad?" the man queried incredulously.

"Ah ha." Simon sighed obnoxiously. "Perhaps we should take this up with your superior. Is the Alpha to be expected? Can I speak with him?"

The man's face flushed in frustration. "No. He is not. You cannot speak with him. I am his acting acolyte, Lohan Perrault. Anything you have to say can be relayed through me."

"Well, *acolyte*, this is sensitive information," Simon said mockingly. "I do not think a mere *acolyte* will keep such important information safe from unwanting ears. You've already revealed much to me without even knowing me. We must defer to his majesty the King and this Alpha of your council."

Simon could nearly hear Lohan's teeth grinding in his skull as his face became increasingly red. A vein appeared on his forehead. Just as Simon thought it couldn't get any worse, the man began to breathe raggedly, and his eyes began to change color from a pale blue to a vibrant jade. Suddenly, his lower jaw extended with a *crack*, and his incisors grew into long, pointed tusks. His robe ripped and stretched as his body grew to double the size. Powerful, reddish-brown fur-covered muscles pulled through the fabric effortlessly. Spittle dripped from Lohan's gaping mouth, and his voice transformed into a deep guttural roar. "I am Lohan the Mammoth. You listen to me, little man." The magi extended a massive furry hand toward Simon.

Simon's loyal servant, Rakshak Zahir, and to his surprise, Cad Dermont sprang before Simon, blades drawn.

Lohan hesitated.

"So your magic makes you big and strong?" Simon taunted. Gesturing to them to stay calm, he stepped between his two protectors. He stood directly before Lohan, looking up into his furious jade-tinted gaze. "Is that all you got?"

Lohan bellowed in fury and slammed his clenched fists into Simon.

Stragnum. Simon caught the massive hands by the wrists as Lohan attacked.

Lohan's eyes widened in surprise as he strained against Simon. Try as he might, he could neither pull away from Simon's grip nor overcome him.

"You're outmatched here, acolyte," Simon susurrated menacingly. "Tell us everything you know, and then summon your Alpha."

"I can't summon him. He comes and goes as he pleases. I do not know when he will be back."

Simon tightened his grip, and Lohan winced in pain.

"I'm telling the truth," Lohan pleaded. "I'll tell you everything. Just let me go."

Simon released his grasp.

Lohan stepped back, and his tusks receded, his body returning to hide within the ripped, torn, oversized robes.

"Who informed your people of this Wayfarers Gate?"

"Someone met with the Alpha, and the next thing I knew, I was assigned here to study and protect it until further notice."

"And, have you learned anything from studying it?"

Lohan looked at his feet shamefully. "Nothing. I can't get the blasted thing to activate."

"Let me see it," Simon ordered.

"Right this way." Lohan led Simon to the portal.

It was carved into the stone, barely visible if you did not look closely. Simon put his hand against the curvature of the archway. *How had Gaelin constructed this one to look like stone?* As he touched it, he realized the thinnest layer of a spell was upon it. Something that caused the illusion of stone. He knew beneath the illusion that was runically carved atop the Gate was the same green and black marble crafted from the bones of something or someone. He raked his memory. Simon had been linked to the man's consciousness when he had the dagger that Gaelin had made from his arm. He could recall Gaelin Yesnala's vast knowledge when holding the dagger. Now, there were only strands of that knowledge left to Simon. *But it is still in there, far away. I had it, but I just need to remember it.*

He focused on the Wayfarers Gateway. *What can I do with this? I know of the portal to Moreas, this one in Aurulan, and the Hasiera Gate.* Had Gaelin mentioned any others? He stretched his mind. He remembered Gaelin speaking of the Skaad Lân. His mind formed an image of a vast world of water and night. Six massive Gateways in a circle. All but one activated and connected to other Lâns. Each glowing with a different hue of colored mist. *I can use this. We can counterattack from here.* Simon removed his hand from the Gate and turned back to his followers.

"We can invade the Skaad Lân from here. To stand a chance against the Children of Skaad, we must first gather allies and form a stalwart coalition.

"A coalition?" Lohan asked incredulously. "With whom? Aurulan is more than a match for anything these creatures can muster against us. We defeated them once already."

"Did you?" Cad Dermont spoke up this time. "Your sergeant was saying they still roam the countryside, murdering the common folk."

Lohan's face darkened. "These soldiers need to keep their tongues in check."

"These soldiers *are* your people," Cad hissed. "And they only want to protect Aurulan and their loved ones, wherever they might be. Have some empathy for fuck's sake."

"I've heard all magi, especially the council members, have a stick up their arse," Simon added.

Rakshak Zahir blurted a laugh.

Cad's words brought the memory of Naurr Andgies and his family seeing Simon and company off as they had departed Dagad. His son, Noa, perched on Naurr's sturdy shoulders. Naurr's wife was ever at his side. It warmed Simon's heart. *This is what we fight for.* He had left Naurr with a bank draft, paying him and all the other workmen who had returned to Dagad for their time away, multiplying it for the endangerment of life and extended leave from loved ones. His account was looking quite dry by the end of it all. *These insane adventures through the Earste Lân are not very profitable.* Should they need it, he had a draft written up to withdraw what little he had left once he came to Nidhaut. The Hasieran had pillaged a large stockpile of gold over the years of raiding caravans even though they did not use currency in the valley.

"We must work together, Lohan the Mammoth," the Priestess comforted. "Hettra's mercy looks to us to do what we must to aid our Lân."

Simon snapped back to reality. *Skrull's unholy balls...she always has a way of sneaking in Hettra and her teachings into a conversation.*

Night had fallen, and Simon sat alone in a tent in the military encampment. Tossing and turning, he could not sleep as he pondered what to do next. *We need the entire might of Aurulan behind us.* It sounded like they had had a brutal battle against the Children of Skaad. Even with the council members taking part directly, they had lost thousands of soldiers, with a seemingly endless supply of the enemy constantly emerging from the mountains. Then, they suddenly stopped coming. Something had caused the Children to flee in all directions. Regiments of Aurulan soldiers were still patrolling, trying to clean up the stragglers, but the reports said the Children were akin to ants overrunning the North Iron Belt.

They would soon be a problem for other countries of the Earste Lân. Xamid to the east. More Vouri villages in the mountains and foothills further north. He doubted the Children would ever cause havoc across the sea, in the Isles of Tal'tulu, or past the North Iron Belt, where the mountain range nearly touched the North Sea at its furthest reaches. Crags and rolling hills slowly turned to rocky cliffs overlooking the often frozen North Sea. Some people lived on the ice flats even further across that sea. A researcher from Xamid once traveled there to study them and wrote a volume about the people there. Simon had heard of it but never actually read it. All he knew was the frozen country they claimed as Nunara called themselves the Nunarat. It was said the Vouri traded with the Nunarat in their most northern town-states.

Something itched in Simon's memory. No, not Simon's. Gaelin's memory.

He saw the image of people trudging through deep water, wearing the furs of hunted game animals, and living off mainly fish. People perched on sleds behind packs of barking dogs. Smoke steaming from round wooden homes. The image of a Wayfarer Gate, its green and black marble silhouetted through a terrible blizzard.

"There is a Gate in Nunara. Should I seek the aid of the Nunarat as well? If Aurulan is stretched so thin, we may need all the help we can get." Simon stood and paced about his tent, pondering aloud. "I am optimistic that Rojas will fare well in Xamid. Skrull's hell, I hope he succeeds in convincing them."

Speaking of convincing. Simon needed to consider what he would say to this Alpha of the Aerie. The man was responsible for abducting magic sensitives throughout the entire Earste Lân. He coveted all things magic.

"I suppose I am also magic-sensitive," Simon said aloud. "Will this Alpha try to take me, too?"

"Simon?" It was the Priestess's voice from outside.

"Yes," Simon cleared his throat in surprise. "What is it?"

"I couldn't sleep. I have a bottle of Xamidian spiced I'm willing to share."

"Oh, thank Our Lady Hettra. Come in, come in."

Priestess Amahle pushed through the curtain, a bottle under one arm and two wooden mugs in her hands.

Simon gestured for her to sit as he found a candle in a chest at the end of the bedding. He lit it on a standing torch just outside the tent and returned. They sat cross-legged on the dirt-packed floor.

Amahle poured the crimson wine and handed Simon a cup. She took a sip and sighed contently.

Simon did likewise. The wine was the perfect combination of sweetness and tartness. It had hints of cardamom and saffron. Simon breathed and focused on the flavors. There were notes of dark fruits, such as plum, cherry, and blackberry, as well as floral and herbal nuances. It had a long and satisfying finish, leaving a pleasant aftertaste of spice and sweetness.

"How are you holding up, Simon?" Amahle asked after a moment. "You have a lot on your shoulders."

"I honestly don't know why I have ended up responsible for saving the Earste Lân. If it were up to me, I would be at home with my wife, working and raising our children."

"You have children?"

"One on the way," Simon said, smiling weakly. *Will I ever see my star Saudett and our child?*

"Congratulations," Amahle toasted, taking a long draft of the wine. "Where's this wife of yours now, back in Dagad?"

"No, no. Saudett went through one of the Wayfarers Gates. I assume she's in the Skaad Lân. A prisoner of the enemy."

"Perhaps my commendation was too soon. I apologize."

"No harm, no foul, as they say."

"So, you are an unwanting leader. At times, the person who least wants the responsibility would have the most success in that position."

"Skrull's hell, I wish it were someone else. But the fact is I feel responsible for the Hasieran. Many of them died because of me. They fled into a tunnel I was supposed to excavate, and I didn't do it because I was too focused on my problems. And because of that, nearly all of them would have died when the river stopped running because of me."

"But from what I've heard, you saved many more. You built a wall that kept the bulk of the creatures at bay. The Hasieran have nothing but praise for you. I've asked many, and all were positively inspired by you."

"Surely there must be someone out there who doesn't like my face?"

"Ha ha." Amahle chuckled. "There was some talk of your lack of faith in your wife, while others defend your *actions* outside your marriage bed."

"Oh gods, that's still causing a fuss, is it? If you look at the animal kingdom, very few other species mate with one partner for life. Are we not also animals? I simply don't believe it is human nature to not want to fuck more than one person in our lives."

"I would argue that no, we are not animals. We have developed the capabilities to differentiate such things. But I see your point of view. Of course, our Goddess Hettra encourages all different types of love. Nothing in her teaching forbids multiple partners, along with *many* other things. On the other hand, the Primus is a bit contradictory to that."

"Don't get me started on the Primus..."

The conversation continued as the bottle of wine was drained. Simon enjoyed speaking with the Priestess. Her intelligence was beautiful, and as the wine flowed, her smiling face with its creased laugh lines and the little jokes she told became increasingly attractive. She was a couple decades older than Simon, but it mattered not to him.

"I've heard that a Priestess of Hettra is not prohibited pleasures of the flesh? Is that true?" Simon asked naughtily.

"I spoke to Zahir," Amahle said with a laugh. "He said you had pledged yourself to your wife and only your wife once again."

"I did say that, didn't I?" Simon sighed woefully.

"Simon. You know it is possible to have relationships without getting naked."

"It is?." Simon threw his hands in the air in exaggerated surprise. "Lies. Blasphemy."

Amahle stifled her laughter. "You are a fascinating man, Simon Meridio. A humorous and charismatic man. I would love to continue our friendship."

Simon exhaled in resignation. It had become a routine since she had joined them on the journey. She would come and talk to him for hours each night. The Priestess was never shy to consul Simon in his grief and relationships. It was even enjoyable to debate such things as religion with her. It reminded him of his father. *She is right. I will focus on Saudett. If we ever find her.*

"Friends, it is then." He downed the last of his wine.

"So, what is your plan for this Gate, and are we still going to Nidhaut?"

"Skrull's hairy balls, that's why I couldn't sleep in the first place."

CHAPTER TWENTY-SIX

WINGS

Saudett limped toward the extravagant dining table.

Hear-fan Skaad sat at the head, leaning over a scroll, sipping some wine from a crystal goblet.

She cleared her throat. Saudett hadn't even dressed in one of the delicate gowns he supplied her with as she was in too much pain to care.

He looked up from the scroll, and she noticed his eyes dart down her body and his lip twitched before he stood and extended *three* hands in greeting. "Ah ha, Gesche-fan Skaad, my favorite human, how goes the battle in the Ryk Lân?"

"Not well. The Ryklings retaliated after we dropped the fire upon them during the night. We lost many Children."

"So I heard from my son. No matter...my Children can be replaced. What is your next move? Trije-fan has been adamant that he could handle matters far better than my appointed Knight-Commander."

"And where the *fuck* was Trije-fan when the Ryklings attacked?" Saudett asked spitefully. "We could have used him. Their flying contraptions are remarkable and deadly. Not to mention that their people are ferocious and strong-willed. The Children could do nothing from the ground against them. I could do nothing."

"Should the general of my armies really be participating directly in the battle anyway?"

"They were on our doorstep. What would you have me do? I can't command the Nyra from the ground." Saudett paused for a long moment, dreading her following words, but she needed an advantage in the battles to come. "Give me wings like your son."

"Is that truly what you wish? The process is," he trailed off, studying her for an uncomfortably long time, "painful."

"Yes, I've made my choice."

His face twisted with an anticipatory smirk. "Let it be so."

The shrieks and screams echoed through the darkness as Saudett followed Hear-fan Skaad through the damp, cavernous halls. She had never been on this level of Lord Skaad's underground citadel. No marble tiles, warm lighting, or artistic pieces were decorating the halls as there were in Hear-fan's quarters. No luxurious dining rooms, libraries, or steam baths. A few of the blue-flamed torches lit the darkness at intervals. The only company was the cries of agony and despair as they continued through hell.

They bypassed many massive chambers, crawling with the Children of Skaad. Creatures she had never seen before. These ones were small, hulk-like, but lesser and deformed. They seemed to be tending to many of the tasks. They were the ones who had been working the forges crafting weapons and armor. Saudett glimpsed inside a room to see large pools of yellow-green muck bubbling and steaming. She paused to see one of the hulking Children slowly pull itself out of the muck. Though it was not fully grown, its limbs were muscled like cords, its black fur thin and growing in patches. Then, a hound arose from another pool. *Is this how the Children come to life?*

As if hearing her thoughts, Hear-fan Skaad answered her question. "The Children were aimless creatures when I found them wandering the Skaad Lân. But I studied them. Watched them for years. *Dissected* them. Did you know there are males and females? It is relatively challenging to tell the difference. The different sexes move in separate pods across the surface. They spawn when the females drop their pebble-sized eggs in the waters of the Skaad Lân. The males trudge along not long after, crushing many eggs while fertilising hundreds of others. When they finally hatch, the children are too weak and small to follow and need sustenance. They devour one another, leaving only the strongest to follow after the adults.

"Then what are these pools doing here?"

"I have infused these pools with the needed nutrients, circumventing the Children's need to consume one another. It also accelerates the development process. They emerge more vital than they do on the surface, and I lose far less this way. Only the ones who donate their eggs and sperm for reproduction are unfortunately lost in the procedure."

"That is...interesting," Saudett said aloud but internally shivered with horror.

"Indeed, I do find it all very fascinating. I've since added modifications and bred them with species from the different Lâns."

Saudett noticed a hound sulking about the pools. It was deformed and small, walking with a limp.

"What do we have here?" Hear-fan asked to nobody in particular. He whistled and crouched low, clicking his fingers for the hound to come to him. "Here, boy, come."

The hound whined and limped over to the Lord of Shadow.

The second he grasped it, Saudett saw his forearms surge with strength, veins suddenly bulging from them. He snapped the hound's neck. "I do not have time for failed experiments." He stood, ushering her to follow, leaving the dead beast behind.

Saudett followed fervently after him, uncertainty simmering within her gut at the thought of being under this contemptuous man's knife as he surgically connected Nyra wings to her. *What if he fails? Will he kill me as well? What of the Nyra that is donating their wings?*

Her reservations increased as they entered a stale, dimly lit chamber covered in dank bloodstains. Two wooden tables were stained with tacky black and crimson fluids. Metal chain manacles were attached to both slabs. A variety of tools hung on the walls. Bone saws, scalpels, hooks, and drilling apparatus, among many other tools. The room reeked of rotting death and pungent fecal matter.

"Here we are," Hear-fan said matter of factly. "Remove your clothing and lay on your stomach."

Reluctantly, Saudett complied, and the metal shackles connected to chains were locked in place around her wrists, ankles, and head. She could not move as she heard the muffled shrieks of a Nyra woman being forcefully pulled into the chamber. With her head strapped down and facing the other table, Saudett watched as the Nyra woman was pushed down upon it by two of the hulking beasts. She could still understand the words through a gag around the woman's mouth.

"No. No." the Nyra screamed, her grey eyes pleading to Saudett. "My children need me. Knight-Commander. Please."

"Oh gods, no." Saudett tried to wriggle free but was locked in place. "Lord Skaad, I've changed my mind. Isn't there another way? Could you not use one of the fallen Nyra for this?" Saudett begged of Hear-fan Skaad. "There are many casualties in the Ryk Lân."

"Ha, of course not, my dear." Hear-fan Skaad laughed cruelly. "This only works with the freshest of specimens. The blood must be pumping throughout the wings for a successful transplant surgery. This is what you wanted." He circled about so his back was to Saudett, blocking her view of the Nyra woman. "There's no going back now."

She heard the sound of flesh and bone being rendered. Blood spurted before Hear-fan as he worked.

The Nyra woman's legs and head spasmed as she shrieked in agony.

Then suddenly, there was a sickening sucking sound, then a *pop*, and Hear-fan quickly turned with a wing in his hands, its dripping rounded joint bone exposed. He handed it to one of the awaiting children, then leaned over Saudett's back with a scalpel in one hand, steel tongs in another.

He began to cut and murmured enchantingly, "Scua besmidian baan, befégan bréostloca."

She screamed at the intensity of the pain that engulfed her, growing and growing as he continued to cut and pull.

"Scua besmidian baan, befégan bréostloca." He continued to speak in a trance-like state as he cut away her flesh.

Saudett cried in anguish, her arms and legs shuddering from the shock and pain. Her vision began to blur.

"Scua besmidian baan, befégan bréostloca..." Hear-fan intoned as he worked. A violet light filled the chamber.

Saudett felt two of his hands enter her flesh, and part it forcefully open, then the cold steel tong slid into her and held. Her vision flashed bright white, then violet, and finally, nothingness.

When Saudett awoke, there was a burning sensation in her back. She lay face down on soft, silken sheets. She groaned as she pushed herself to her knees. She felt her wings against the bedding behind her, and she subconsciously raised and opened them. With an odd tingling sensation, she realized she was controlling them. Cautiously, with a dull pain still throbbing through every inch of her, she stumbled to the massive mirror in her bed chamber. She gasped in awe as she saw the dark wings attached to her unclothed body. She turned so her back faced the mirror and looked over her shoulder. Blood dripped slowly from where the wings were connected just under her shoulder blades. A sweltering impression seared at the base of the wings as she opened them, like flexing a muscle.

She stared in awe. *Primus, take me, I have wings, and they are beautiful.* She gave them a mighty flap to test them and left the ground momentarily, but pain coursed through her again. She immediately lurched back to bed and lay down. As exhaustion overpowered her, she had a fleeting thought of the woman screaming on the table across from her as her wings were torn from her body. Unable to hold her focus, the thought faded away as she fell back into sleep.

REUNION

Kiana Ahmadi pushed through the gathering crowd toward her people, the Hasieran and Simon Meridio. Her mother followed closely on her heels. She reached the front of the crowd as Simon was accosted by a handful of town guards.

"How did you get through the Gate?" a guardswoman demanded. "Who are you people?"

A soldier stepped up beside Simon. He had the look of the Shepherd's Eye warriors from Dagad. The man in question appeared to be in his middle ages, with a striking appearance. He had well-groomed salt and pepper hair and a beard, adding to his authoritative stance and sophistication.

"Bring us to the Alpha's tower immediately, Lieutenant," the man ordered. "We have urgent matters to discuss."

The guardswoman stammered, realising the man's rank, she saluted. "Right away, Captain." She turned abruptly to lead them away.

"Simon." Kiana called as she pushed forward.

Simon did a double take, looking around frantically before his gaze fell upon her. His sullen face brightened, and a genuine smile flourished. "Kiana Ahmadi. And my dear mother-in-law, Anora, too." He rushed to meet them, as did a few others from Hasiera who saw Anora and Kiana.

"By the Primus," Kiana embraced Simon as they met. "I'm glad to see you."

"As am I, little sister, as am I." He squeezed her tight, then opened an arm, gesturing for Anora to join them. "Come here, mother."

Kiana's mother came into the embrace, tears in her eyes as the three held each other. "My dear son-in-law, what in Skrull's hell are you doing here? What happened in Hasiera? Did you fail to find water and flee?"

"Oh, gods," Simon said as he broke the embrace. "It is truly a long and grueling story. But the essence is that we restored the water to the valley and now seek the aid of *all* peoples in the Earste Lân for our fight against the Children of Skaad."

"You'll have to tell us everything," Anora necessitated.

"Of course, of course, but later, over wine," Simon reassured. "And what of you? Did you manage to find Hata Vasara's whereabouts?"

"We only recently discovered that she traveled north back to her homeland of the Vouri," Kiana said. "She was heading for her village, Oitilla. We were just readying to depart. By the Primus, Baal and Brena must be getting anxious. It's nearly a week's ride to Oitilla."

"Ah yes, the mighty Vouri warriors. Where are they?" Simon cast his gaze around the crowd, expecting to see them.

"They're back at our makeshift home," Anora replied. "I'll go fetch them and meet up with you all. Kiana, stay with Simon."

"Well, we are heading directly to this Alpha's tower," Simon said. "Let's pray to Qav he is home."

"Be careful, my son," Anora cautioned. "From what we've heard, he is a dangerous man."

"Worry not, dear mother," Simon reassured, a cocky grin playing on his lips. "I have a trick or two up my sleeve."

"If you say so." Anora sighed. "I'll meet you at the base of his tower. Please don't go in without me."

"Of course, my dear. At any rate, I have an inkling for a warm meal first." He held his arm out in a gentlemanly manner. "Come, dear half-sister-in-law, let's find an eatery near this tower if possible."

"Oh, I just ate." Kiana laughed as she nudged him in the ribs. "But I'll have a drink."

Anora came to their little shack to find the door broken in and the contents of the house ransacked and destroyed. Baal and Brena were nowhere to be found. There was a relatively fresh smear of blood on one wall, like someone's bloody hand had grasped at it as they were pulled out of the doorway. *Skrull's hell, where could they be?* There were other bloodstains on the floor. *Are they dead?* She closed her eyes and breathed deeply, imagining the dance of the blade in her mind, and composed herself. Anora opened her eyes. *If there is blood here, then perhaps...*

She exited the small shack and crouched outside, looking for signs of a blood trail. Nearly on hands and knees, she scoured the dusty, dirt-packed street of the *Ville de Voleurs* district around their home. Finally, she saw it. *There.* She found a trail of droplets in the dirt heading into a shadowed muddy alley. Finding traces of blood in the alley with the muck and very little light would be difficult. She fixated on the task and crept into the dark back street.

"Captain Cad Dermont, it's a pleasure to meet you." The handsome captain of the Sheperd's Eye took Kiana's hand and kissed it.

"Kiana Ahmadi," she said. He was quite the man. A well-built, handsome, and charismatic man. *Why do I find these older men attractive?* The thought of Kaplan Mir flooded through her, and she grimaced and pulled her hand away. *I'm done with old men.*

"You look very familiar," Cad pondered aloud, not noticing her disgust when she pulled her hand away. "Have we met?"

"She is my wife's half-sister," Simon answered for her. "And from what I last knew, she was in a committed relationship."

The captain stared at Kiana, his eyes wandering up and down her, not hiding his ravenous ogling. Then he blinked as he processed Simon's words. "Simon. Why would you say such a thing? I'm merely introducing myself."

Kiana shivered under his gaze.

"Well, you've done so," Simon said flatly. "Now, do you mind giving us some privacy? I have some personal matters to speak with my sister about."

Cad Dermont put his hands up defensively. "Hettra's sagging tits, *Simon*. I'm sorry, don't let me be a nuisance then." He turned and retreated to a group of Shepherd's Eye at the company's rear.

"He is delightfully disgusting." Kiana breathed in relief once he was gone. "He seems overly friendly with you."

"Ha." Simon snorted. "That's what happens when they've been inside you. Suddenly, they think they own you."

"Him?" Kiana asked in surprise.

"Indeed," Simon said with a grin. "He was a regular in our bed chambers. My wife and I enjoyed his...*companionship*. Alas, I fear he has had ulterior motives this entire time."

"What could he possibly want? He had you both."

"He would have preferred it if I was out of the equation. Has a thing for Saudett. *More than a thing.*"

"Ah, I see." *Skrull's hell, is that why he was staring at me so oddly? I look like my sister.*

"Anyhow, what is that smell?" Simon interrupted her thoughts. "Gods, I'm famished."

They followed the smell to an open seated tavern on one side of the busy street. With Simon's mix of Shepherd's Eye soldiers and Hasieran warriors, they soon filled the tables, and nearly half the group had to continue to find food elsewhere.

Kiana sipped on an ale as Simon drooled over a roasted stuffed pheasant with potatoes and beans placed before him.

"Praise be to Hettra. It's been far too long since I've had a meal like this." Simon, ever the gentlemen, cut into the pheasant's breast and sliced a clean piece with his fork and knife. He moaned in pleasure as the poultry entered his mouth, and he chewed the tender meat.

"Eat quickly," Kiana urged. "It shouldn't take Mother long to gather Baal and Brena and meet us at the tower."

"Right you are," Simon mumbled through a mouthful, placing his utensils neatly to the sides of his platter. He then took a leg of the pheasant and ripped it off, unceremoniously gnawing on it to his heart's content.

The trail twisted and turned through the streets of Nidhaut. Someone was bleeding profusely. Anora continued on, the tower of the Delta Passeriform stretching high above her, becoming ever nearer. Finally, the blood stopped in one of the alleys, seemingly vanishing. She continued to see if it would pick up again at the other end of the alley but found nothing. She backtracked and could find no other way except from the direction she had come. She crouched and leaned against the wall, staring at the end of the blood trail. *What now? Should I go back to Simon?*

Anora sat for a long time, pondering.

A drunken beggar came stumbling through the alley. His dragging feet cut through the bloodstains in the dirt. He did not see her crouched in the shadows and was talking aloud to himself as he disappeared around the corner.

Dusk began to fall. Just as Anora was about to stand and return to Simon and Kiana, she heard a *click*. Then suddenly, the wooden slat wall across from her was slowly swinging inward. Swiftly, she scrambled away and hid in some refuge further down the alley. A robed duo, a woman and a man, emerged with torches from the opening. They looked both ways, then hurried down the alley, luckily in the opposite direction of Anora.

She leaped up, sprinted to the doorway, and slipped through just before it closed in her face. Darkness surrounded her, and she felt her way along and found that she was descending steps into the earth. Hundreds of steps. Finally, she reached the bottom, and the way forward turned into a tunnel. The walls were thick black wood, and posts were set at intervals along the tunnel, supporting the ceiling planks. Then, she came to an intersection with three directions to choose from. *Gods, which way should I go?*

Kiana paced back and forth. Dark clouds had rolled in overhead, and it was nearly nightfall as they awaited her mother, Baal, and Brena at the base of the obsidian black tower that reached skyward and expanded at its peak.

"We can fill our dear mother in on the details once she arrives. We can't wait any longer, Kiana." Simon reiterated once again, staring at the doorway to the citadel.

"But why is she late? It is not like them, Baal and Brena especially." *Did Mother stop by a tavern and get drunk again?* She palmed the hilt of her sword petulantly. "What could have happened?"

There were a handful of others with them. A priestess of Hettra had left Simon's company to seek a different council member to join the discourse. She, too, had yet to return. That left Cad Dermont and Zahir Al-Rashid, who had taken the title of Rakshak, Simon's personal protector, along with a regiment of soldiers and nomads.

Suddenly, the doors to the tower groaned and opened a crack, and a head popped out. "You have been standing out here for hours. What in Skrull's unholy hell do you want?" The voice came from an elderly woman dressed in black robes, her white hair braided tightly against her head.

"Ahem, madam," Simon said, clearing his throat in surprise. "We wish to speak with the Alpha and the entire Council of the Aerie. Not to mention the king."

"The Alpha is away. Come back tomorrow." The door began to creak closed.

"Wait." Simon called after her. "Do you know—"

The door slammed shut.

In frustration, Simon slammed his fist against it, then pulled on the golden rings that made up the handles. The door didn't budge. Kiana heard him mumble the word *Strangung* as he wrenched at the round pieces of metal. Then a ring popped off in his hand, and he stumbled onto his back. "Pah. Plated copper...what a cheap bastard this Alpha is," Simon muttered as he picked himself up and dusted off his trousers.

"Shall we return on the morrow as instructed?" Zahir Al-Rashid inquired. "It's getting late. We could all use the rest."

"I suppose you are correct." Simon sighed. He took a sizeable coin pouch from beneath his nomadic robes and handed it to Zahir. "Find lodging for our people, my faithful Rakshak. My sister and I have one errand to attend to." He turned to Kiana. "Let's find our mother."

The first raindrops began to drip as Kiana led the way down the street toward the *Ville de Voleurs* district.

CHAPTER TWENTY-EIGHT

DELTA

Baal Vasara awoke in chains. Hanging by the wrists, the metal dug into him painfully. He was on his knees, arms extended above his head. He found his footing and stood, the chains allowing him to move somewhat when standing. The pain instantly lessened as the tension lifted from his wrists. His stomach rumbled with hunger. A stone wall was behind him, and an iron-barred Gate was to his left. A dim light lit the hallway further down, leaving his prison cell in shadow.

He recalled his last moments before a high-pitched shrieking sound had echoed in his head so strongly that he had blacked out. He still felt a faint, constant underlying ringing in his ear. He touched his affected earlobes and felt dried blood there. *What happened? We were attacked by many people, armored soldiers, and...magi. Brena. Where is my Brena?*

He rattled in his chains, straining against them frantically. "By Teras's justice," Baal cursed. "I will break the neck of whoever is responsible for this."

"Bah...ha...ha..." A deep yet hoarse voice startled Baal from within his chamber. Chains rattled across from him in the dark. "Baal of House Vasara, how Teras has cursed our people to put me in the presence of such a dishonored man once again."

Baal peered into the darkness toward where the oddly familiar voice came.

A man leaned into the light. A blonde-white beard appeared, stained, ratty, and long. His once stout, scarred face was gaunt from malnourishment. His pale blue eyes looked hollow in the dim light.

The *rage* took Baal's reins as he roared the man's name, "Ota Vastaan." The cry echoed down the halls. Baal leaped forward, hands outstretched to wrap them around the chieftain's neck. "You killed Silja. Your own mate. My daughter's friend." Baal was halted by the chain, only halfway across the room from where Ota sat back against the far wall.

"The conniving little bitch deserved far worse," Ota wheezed. "She should thank Teras that I swiftly put her out of her misery. Well...that is after I had beaten the life from her and filled her with my glory."

Baal bellowed in fury, his voice booming down the halls of their prison. He strained with all his might against the chain manacles. They cut at his wrists, and he felt the blood begin to ooze.

"Try as you might." Ota laughed at Baal's struggles. "You'll never be free. Never be free to kill me, Baal, dishonored of the Vouri."

"The only one who lacks honor here is you, Ota of House Vastaan," Baal growled, relinquishing his strain against the chains. "I swore to my daughter that I would take your life should I ever meet you again."

"A strong vow for a weak man. I triumphed over you once. I can do so again."

Baal heard footsteps approaching from down the hall.

"Now you went and caused a fuss," Ota cackled maniacally. "Enjoy the thrashing."

Two guards dressed in navy-white surcoats appeared.

"Who's making all that racket?" The guard asked as he tapped a solid straight club against the bars. The noise clanged and echoed down the halls. "Oi, geezer, did you not tell the newcomer the rules? The Delta absolutely despises overly loud commotions." He rattled the bars once again, louder this time. "Oi, stop that." he directed his order at Baal.

The other guard fiddled with a key in the locked Gate and opened it.

"This one is out of line." the first guard shouted as he closed in on Baal. The club lifted to strike.

Baal backed up just enough to have some slack on the chains. He faked fear as he raised his arms to cover his face from the blow. As the first attack fell upon his shoulder, Baal took the hit, then lashed out, grasping the man's arm that had swung into reach. He pulled the man in.

The guardsman's eyes widened in terror, and he stammered a cry, "Wait, no—"

Baal took his head and slammed it into the wall with such force the guard's skull caved in. The dead man slumped to the floor at his feet.

"Delta. Lady Delta. The other guard shouted, retreating from the chamber. He closed the Gate hastily, the keys jangling on his belt as he ran away down the hall.

"You were right, Ota Vastaan. I did indeed enjoy the thrashing." Baal gave the sickly, sad-looking man, once mighty clan chieftain of the Vouri village of Oitilla, his most toothy snarl.

"You've only made your punishment worse for yourself, fool," Ota rebuked. "Now, the Auru bastards will hang you by the feet and have their way with you."

"Let them try." Baal spat onto the stone floor. He focused on the dark shape of the man who had banished his family from their home. "Tell me, Ota Vastaan, how have you come to be here in chains?"

"This is your fault. It was your greed that caused the fall of Oitilla, Baal Vasara. If you had brought forth your findings in the mountain, the Vouri of Oitilla would still be alive." Ota's voice caught in his throat. "We would still be free."

"You speak of the Gate?"

"Yes, you fool." Ota shrieked hoarsely. "They came from there. Those creatures, the foul beasts of night. We could have secured and protected the tunnels with a band of the warrior caste if we had only known it existed. Had you simply told your chieftain? Why Baal Vasara? Why did you keep it a secret?"

Baal thought back to that day, the red light deep within the mountain. He had been digging in one of the many mine shafts and came across the strange gateway with glowing crimson mists. His first thought had been to cover it back up and leave it be. It was unnatural and not of Teras and his stone. He had been hungry and tired, and he had made his decision. He had gone home to prepare for his daughter's feast of the hunt and had not had a moment to think of the Gate. *Ota is correct. I should have told him immediately, but Alvar Kovaa had his way before I could act.* He imagined his second, the miner Alvar Kovaa, going on about precious gemstones. He imagined him uncovering the Gate after Baal and his family had left the village. Ota would have been there with him. Fury boiled up within, and Baal clenched his fists against the chains. "You're the fool, Ota Vastaan. If you had left the Gate buried in the ground, none of this would have happened."

"Bah. I may have done just that if I had only fucking known of it." This time, to Baal's surprise, Ota was on his feet, rattling the chains as he surged forward. Ota's chains pulled taut just a foot from where Baal stood. A fire burnt in Ota's eyes, but his body was fragile. His once broad chest and massive arms were emaciated. His breathing was ragged. Yet his fury burnt bright in Baal's direction.

"So you aren't dead yet, chieftain." Baal gave him a toothy smile. "This is good. Let's get out of here, and we can settle our differences once you are nursed back to health."

Ota stared furiously into Baal's eyes, then his gaze fell, and he slunk back into the shadows. "There's no way out. All of the Vouri who fled Oitilla were captured and held. I do not even know if any of them still live." Ota curled into a ball against the wall. "It's impossible. *She* hears all."

"Who hears all? What are you talking about? And why? Why hold the Vouri here?" Baal tried to pry *something* out of the defeated man.

At that moment, footsteps echoed down the corridor outside their cell. A single pair of footfalls fell to the cobbles with resounding *clicks*.

Baal saw the source: tall, high-heeled black boots attached to a woman dressed in a delicate navy skirt. Her bronze midriff was exposed as she wore a fine crop-top jacket of the same deep navy blue trimmed with white. The woman wore an odd-looking helmet or mask of azure metal, her lips and mouth visible below the mask. Her dark eyes drank in the scene before her. The mask covered her head and ears protectively. She stood staring at Baal for a long moment, her head tilting as her lips curled into a smile. She strode into the prison cell as the guard from before worked the lock for her. Her eyes never left Baal's. She came within striking distance of him, looking him up and down.

Finally, she spoke in a low, sultry voice, "Such a stout Vouri man we have here. You're oh so similar to your mate."

"Where is my Brena?." Baal bellowed, lunging for the fragile little woman.

Something exploded in his vision as a high-pitched shriek filled his skull. He clutched his head, thrashing back and forth frantically. He fell back, the chains pulling tight on his wrists, leaving him dangling. The high-pitched sound faded slowly but never seemed to go entirely silent.

"Now," the woman hissed, her calm demeanor gone. "No more commotions or killings or shouting or so much as *shitting* loudly. Be a good boy, be quiet, and try to survive. Eventually, I'm sure the Alpha will indefinitely allow all the Vouri to be released from their confines...if they still live."

Baal couldn't focus. His vision blurred, and the room spun. He couldn't understand her words. He tried to stand but lost his balance. He tried to speak, but his words were jumbled. He tried to crawl toward the vile woman, to grab her by the ankle, but could not reach her. He watched her black boots recede into the hall. He couldn't hear the *clicking* footfalls.

CHAPTER TWENTY-NINE

BESTOWED

As Hata soared through the stunning night sky of the Ryk Lân, she clung tightly to a small piece of earth, feeling the rush of the cool breeze blowing past her face. She was determined in what she needed to do. The stars twinkled above her, casting a glittering spell on the darkness, and the moons shined brightly in the distance, illuminating her path. The breathtaking scene left her in awe of this magical Lân. She went from island to island as quickly and silently as possible. Her mind focused on the task at hand. *I will find the main island where Hear-fan Skaad's forces gather, and I will destroy the entire island. The problem is if I can make it there before being noticed.*

It was a cloudless starry night sky, even peaceful, as she glided through the cool air on the chunk of earth she controlled. Keeping an eye for any hint of movement, she scanned the horizon. Hata noticed a more significant island among the many that spread out before her, and she leaned toward it, deciding to investigate it. Hata flew down toward the massive cone-shaped island ahead. She thought she saw a flicker of blue fire through the crystalline trees before it disappeared. She touched down on the edge of the isle, hopping off her little floating platform and creeping forward into the tree line as quietly as her heavy armor allowed.

As Hata turned her gaze to the tree line, she suddenly caught sight of the mesmerising azure flames flickering once again. Her heart skipped a beat as she was drawn toward the enchanting dance of the fire, captivated by its mysterious glow. Closer and closer, she stole through the woods.

Something rustled in the canopy above.

Hata came to a sudden halt, her feet rooted to the ground. She tilted her head back, gazing at the magnificent sight of the branches adorned with myriad colorful leaves. She stood there in complete stillness, straining to hear even the slightest rustle of the leaves, but there was only silence. *It must have been just a squirrel or some wildlife of the Ryk Lân.*

She breathed and nodded to herself and began pushing forward once more. The blue light grew closer. Finally, she spied a clearing ahead, with a black iron brazier in its center burning with the azure flames. Two dozen of the hulking Children of Skaad stood like statues around it. Unmoving. All facing in one direction, regardless of their orientation around the brazier. Then she heard a low undertone of sound. Deep within the creatures' throats, an undulating wail rose and fell with a strange melodic rhythm.

Hata placed her bare hands on the grassy soil at her feet, extending her senses toward the singing hulks. Closing her eyes, she felt where they stood. When she felt the connection reach the creatures through the earth, they all simultaneously turned toward her and gave a blood-curdling scream.

With their ear-piercing cries and wailing, they surged directly toward her. At the same time, the trees above came to life with shrieks and cries. The winged humanoids emerged from the branches in the hundreds.

By Teras, there are so many of them.

More hulks and hounds appeared out of the woods, rushing toward her.

But Hata breathed and focused on the amber gemstone power source in her chest, and time seemed to slow around her. Her hands were still to the earth as she took hold of the entire island and *shook* it. The ground rumbled and cracked, and things burst into motion around her. Children fell into crevices that opened and swallowed them. Others were forcefully knocked from their feet, one toppling into the flames of the tipped brazier, screaming as it burnt alive. Massive, sharpened pillars of rock erupted about her, spearing the swooping winged beings as they dived at her. Chunks of earth broke free and floated skyward as the island broke apart around her. The amber gemstone in her chest flared so brightly with a warm yellow light that she could barely see around her.

Suddenly, a winged man weaved through the projectiles of earth and slashed out with two swords.

Hata deflected one blade with the masterly crafted bracer of one arm, then extended her other hand and gripped the metal minerals of the second blade with her mind. Inches from her face, the razor-sharp sword halted.

The creature's jagged teeth hissed with exertion, trying to push the blade against her and into Hata's flesh.

She tilted her head inquisitively and grinned. The metal weapon began to turn on its owner.

He lashed out again with the first blade.

Hata halted it likewise and slowly turned it against the man again.

Realising the weapons were lost, he released them and let out a double-footed kick to her middle, using his wings to add extra strength to the strike.

Even with the armor, Hata flew back with the breath knocked from her lungs. The rumbling and tearing of the ground halted, and the massive chunks began to fall as she lost her concentration.

The entire island began to fall.

Hounds and hulks shrieked in terror as the ground vanished below them.

The flying Children of Skaad dodged falling stones and earth as they fled the chaos.

The man Hata had been in combat with was nowhere to be seen, and she realized she was falling along with the debris. Instinctively, she reached for the closest earth, stone, and crystals and willed them toward her. As she stood there, she drew the earth towards her. It raised up in chunks of terrain that enveloped her like a cocoon. The ground formed a sturdy shield around her, creating a protective sphere that kept her safe and secure.

The Sunstone watched as the enemy fell to their deaths into the abyss below or flew into the distance as the last of the debris was only a trail of dust, descending into nothing. "I did it," Hata exhaled aloud. "I took them out. I destroyed the island."

Suddenly, a discordance of shrieks and howling filled the air around her. Sapphire flames came to life on the hundreds of islands surrounding her. She saw dark silhouettes of thousands and thousands of abominations crying out at her. The stars and the moons began to blot out as the wings of uncountable flying Children of Skaad streaked into the air from the surrounding islands in massive trails of black clouds. Hata saw colossal chain bridges connecting many of the islands together.

The winged creatures swarmed toward her like rats to a carcass.

No! There are so many on every island. I've accomplished nothing. She began to retreat with the earth surrounding her, but the enemy was swift. Calling more earth to her, she closed the sphere-like shield tighter around her, leaving only a crack at her eye level open to let her see where she was going.

Suddenly, Hata was surrounded. The protective earth rattled with countless impacts, the crack before her darkened with numerous beating wings, and the creatures' shrieks and hiss-like whistles rang through her.

She pushed forward, concentrating on keeping her hold on the defense while simultaneously plummeting through the air. She picked up her pace and felt the sphere crashing through the enemy's bodies. Their bones and wings snapped like twigs against her shield of rock and gemstone. But with each concussion, she felt her stamina waiver. *Teras, grant me the strength of your mountain,* she prayed as her grip on the earth slowly weakened.

Hata caught a glimpse of the lit bulwarks of Keep Crystalia through the crack in her shield. *Still so far away.*

At that moment, a hand penetrated the earthen barrier beside her with a forceful burst of dust and stone. Violet glowing vapors pulsated from the hand as the fingers managed to grip her arm.

The armor at that spotted began to corrode away rapidly, and an overwhelming pain tore at her arm. She gasped in shock and lost concentration on the protective barrier and the earth keeping her afloat.

The hand, connected to a hooded, winged figure, released its grip as the weight of her armor suddenly pulled her down.

Hata plummeted into darkness, the shining safety of Keep Crystalia vanishing from sight. Her right arm flapped limply in the air as she twisted her body to look toward her fall. Only the two crescent moons reflected back at her as they became closer to the ocean world below. Try as she might control her descent, she looked desperately for land to try to aim for, to fall into the clutches and comfort of the dirt and stone that would once again come to her aid. There was nothing but the wind whipping at her face and darkness.

Is this truly the end? After all my struggles and hardships, is this how I die?

She was falling, fast and furious, toward the endless depths of the seas of Ryk. She had no earth or minerals to save her, no solid ground to catch her. She felt helpless and hopeless, a speck of dust in the vast starlit skies. Hata heard nothing but the wind in her ears and even the roar of the waves below as they loomed upward. She saw nothing but the blur of shadows. She felt nothing but the fear in her heart and the cold in her bones.

With her heart pounding and her gut twisting, she took a deep breath and shut her eyes tightly, bracing herself for the inevitable collision that was about to come.

But then, Hata felt something else. A warmth in her chest, a pulse in her veins. A familiar sensation, a gentle reminder. The smell of a cold mountain night filled her senses, the stones under her feet. That first time, she had felt others around her by touching the vibrations of their footfalls in her very soles.

Use it. The words came from deep within. *Use the Sunstone.*

She opened her eyes and beheld her armor. The amber gem was like a radiant fire. *The armor was forged from the mountain itself.* The armor was made of earth and minerals, which she could control. *It is of Teras.*

Hata Vasara, the Sunstone, took hold of the armor and the amber power source and slowed her descent. As she coasted downward, the waves washed peacefully over one another. She let herself float down, reached out her finger, and touched the water. It was surprisingly warm and rippled at her touch.

"Thank you, Teras," Hata whispered aloud, then turned her gaze skyward. "I'm not dead yet." She gathered the energy into her armor, letting it converge into a vast supply. Then she let loose the power and detonated into the sky. The shock wave burst into the waves below her in a massive circular expansion, and a streak of pressurised air followed in her wake.

Her thoughts were on the hooded man who had felled her and made her arm useless. Its limp form still dangling at her side. *I'm coming for you, Child of Skaad.*

Saudett could hardly make out what was happening in the darkness. *If only Hear-fan had given me the Nyra's vision along with their wings.* Then she shuddered at that thought. *Would he have taken the eyes right out of the woman as well?* It looked like one of the floating islands had broken apart and fallen away. A dark shape soared through the sky, back toward the enemy stronghold. The Nyra made chase, swarming around the thing. Saudett saw a streak of violet energy shoot after it as both projectiles vanished into the distance as they left her sight range. *Skrull's hell, what was that?* Cautiously, she stepped to the island's edge and surveyed the chaos. Nyra circled in massive clouds, eager to assault the city.

Saudett shook her head, then pulled on the black-armored helm she had held under her arm. She let Knight-Commander Gesche-fan Skaad take over as she commanded, "Do it!"

The Nyra woman let the horns resounding blast loose, and the swarm of Nyra circled back to her. Thousands of them flying overhead.

Gesche-fan Skaad flexed her wings, then stepped off the edge. She dived, then opened her wings and swooped upward. Behind her, the swarm of Nyra lifted two massive chains upward, then across the sky to the nearest island. Sharpened spikes the size of a horse were dropped from the sky, falling and exploding into the earth below. Hundreds of Children pulled the chains tight on the opposite end, causing the spikes to dig deeper into their holds. The Children, the deformed creatures she'd seen in Hear-fan's breeding chambers and forages, crawled across the chains, fastening metal planks to them as they went.

Excellent, Gesche-fan Skaad mused as she beat her wings, keeping her steadily above the procession. *We will soon be one island away from that massive fortress and begin our siege.*

They had connected almost all the islands from here to the Wayfarers Gate. Even so, the ground forces moved across slowly. The massive insectoid creatures that spewed dark smoke teetered perilously on the chain bridge. Waylaying the congregation of hulks, hounds, greys, and molten rock-like creatures.

Warrior Nyxal appeared at her side, the horn blower hovering on her other.

"Knight-commander," Nyxal said with a salute. "A powerful magi attacked one of the islands we'd occupied. She destroyed it. She used the very rocks and earth against us."

Saudett flooded back in, and she nearly gasped aloud but calmed herself as she asked, "What did this woman look like?"

"Pale skin, bright red mane. Heavy armor. If not for Trije-fan Skaad, she would have escaped us. He took her down before she could reach the enemy fortress."

Impossible... Trije-fan took her down? He killed her? Saudett blinked in shock beneath her helm. *Hata is dead? No.* Saudett quickly recomposed herself even as the *hatred* for Hear-fan Skaad's son overflowed. "The magi is dead then?"

"She plummeted to the sea below," Nyxal answered. "We did not follow. We assume she has drowned with the weight of her armor."

No. As simple as that, Hata is gone? After all this? Aloud, she said, "Send a patrol to confirm. The magi may have clung to a piece of earth that had fallen before her. If she lives, bring her to me alive."

"It will be done," Nyxal said with a nod, then pumped his mighty wings to see out her orders.

Hettra's mercy, please be alive, Hata, Saudett prayed. *If that bastard Trije succeeded, I will end him.* The morning light began to warm the horizon, while behind her, the shadows grew as thick spewing navy smoke filled the skies.

CHAPTER THIRTY

FLICKER

Fucking hells. Jude awoke with a chill in his bones. He was shivering uncontrollably as he tried to get his bearings. *What in Skrull's hell happened? Where am I?* He turned his head to see he was in some sort of cave. A shadow moved before him. *One of the demons?* He strained to sit up and grab for a dagger, but pain shot through his leg down to his—*My foot.* He felt suddenly dizzy with shock. His foot and half his shin were gone. The sudden urge to scream permeated within him.

The shadow moved closer, and a small flame flick appeared on a fingertip. "Shush, Jude, you're all right. It's me, Joanna. I'm here."

Jude tried to answer, but his mouth was dry as dust, and his throat burnt. He managed to strain out one word, "*Leg.*"

"I'm sorry, Jude," Joanna said, her eyes glistening on the brink of tears. "You saved my life, and it cost you dearly. I'm so sorry."

It all came back to him. He'd pushed Joanna to safety, and the scythe-like blade had cut clean through him. How they had managed to escape after that was all a blur. Then he was waking up here.

"Where?" He rasped the word.

Joanna put a water skin to his lips and let him drink. He gulped it down eagerly, and it soothed his parched throat.

"The ranger man distracted the creatures and led them off to allow us to hide here. He said he would be back, but I fear he is dead. We lost the pack animals, too. There were just so many of them."

"We need...we need to get out of here, get back to Nidhaut." Jude urged weakly.

"We had to backtrack. The beasts had cut us off from going further toward the Auru mainland. We carried you further into the mountains again."

Fucking hells. Gods, I wish I had a teleportation stone.

"And we can't leave without the ranger," Joanna continued. "I can't carry you by myself, Jude."

Jude looked down at the stump where his lower leg and foot had once been. He would have thought it was still there if he hadn't known about it. He tried to wiggle his phantom toes, and the stump tingled with an odd, somewhat painful sensation.

"I burnt the wound shut. The creature did make a clean cut, but I had to stop the bleeding. I'm sorry, Jude."

Jude managed to push himself to a seated position and lean against the cave wall. He gave her his most insufferable smile. "Hells, stop apologising. I'm just glad you're all right." *Huh,* he shrugged inwardly. *Who'd have thought I would care more about someone other than myself?* "You'd have been dead had I not stepped in when I did."

The tears rolled down Joanna's cheeks, gleaming in the small light of her finger candle. "Thank you, Jude. So much, I don't know how I could ever repay you."

"You can start by getting us out of here alive so we can tell the Alpha to go fuck himself."

"Ha," she blurted out, covering her mouth and whispered urgently, "Skrull's hell, shush. Those things could hear us."

"I'm done with this fucking shit, Joanna. You and me, let's ditch the Alpha and find a cottage somewhere...somewhere that we can grow a garden."

Joanna stared at him in the darkness for a long time, saying nothing. She opened her mouth a few times as if to say something, then closed it as she thought better.

"Come, woman, spit it out," Jude insisted.

"I—I honestly wouldn't mind that. A part of me longs to run away with you. But it is like something is tangling my mind, telling me I still need to serve Ebras Corb. Another part of me does not want to give up the position and the power I have risen to."

"You're nothing more than a disposable puppet to him. As am I. As is his entire council of magi. He will use you up and toss you aside when he's finished with you."

Joanna paused again before saying, "I know you speak the truth, but my heart will not let me leave."

"Have it your way. As for me, I won't be hunting magi in this condition anymore. Let's return to Nidhaut, report to our Lord Alpha, and be finished with it. Then I can retire."

The sound of pebbles and stones moving nearby startled them.

Jude gripped a dagger from his belt but could not move from where he sat.

Joanna's flame brightened on her hand.

The ranger, Kaplan Mir, stumbled into view. He bore many bloody gashes, and his cloak and clothing were ripped to shreds. He took an unsteady step and then collapsed before them.

Joanna Ohlec did what she could to bandage the man's wounds and get him to eat and drink a little, but she felt it wasn't nearly enough. She let the ranger sleep. Jude also slept fitfully, moaning and groaning in his sleep. *What will I do with two men who can't walk because they are hurt?* Jude was sweating and shivering at the same time. She leaned over and patted the sweat from his brow with a torn piece of her cloak. Then she curled up next to him to try to keep him warm, still too afraid to make a fire should the light draw the attention of the creatures outside.

I've failed in my mission to find that betrayer, Hata. How dare she deceive me. How dare she betray the Alpha. But what will Ebras do when I return empty-handed? Punish me terribly, just like back at the Convent Enclosure. All those beatings...the abuse. Yet after every encounter with the Alpha, Joanna's will came away invigorated to please him. To be his faithful, loyal companion. *His slave.*

As she sat there, lost in thought, her mind seemed to unravel before her eyes. Suddenly, a faint glimmer of something caught her attention – a memory, a feeling, something that had long been buried deep within. Slowly, it began to take shape, like a mist rising from the depths of her consciousness, until it finally coalesced into a clear and palpable form. The longer she was away from Ebras Corb's company, the less hidden her mind became. The memory returned to her...

The waves were crashing on the sea, and fishing boats were coming into the harbor of their little town. *What was the name of it? Marteau Marin* on the coast of the *Mer d'ombre*. Western Aurulan. *Yes, it was true. This is where I grew up.* Her father, Phillipe Ohlec, was a fisherman, out all day filling his nets along with many of the other men of the village. Her mother worked…no, she *ran* the docks. Madame Marteau was the woman's nickname, though her proper name was Marie. Joanna had simply called her Ma. Joanna remembered sitting on the docks mending nets as her mother bustled about giving orders. She was a sturdy woman with sunburnt skin and calloused hands. Ma wore a simple dress of blue linen stained with salt and greasy fish scales. Her black hair was always kept from her eyes with a headband, and her blue eyes danced as she worked. She had a leather apron around her waist, where she kept her knives and hooks. She worked tirelessly, gutting and cleaning the fish the men brought from the sea. Ma was not afraid of the blood or the smell, for she had been doing this since childhood. Ma knew every fish by name and how to prepare it for the market. She taught Joanna their names and showed her how to clean them.

Joanna recalled a cold winter's day in *Marteau Marin*. Frost made the pier slick, and the wind was biting. Joanna was no longer a little girl and always dreamed of life away from the village. She was sick of fish, sick of guts, and sick of the smell.

By the Sea Hammer, Marec, I wish I was near a fire, Joanna pleaded internally as she shivered. She was helping her mother with the fish as usual and wished she had a warmer coat and a fire to warm her hands. Joanna recalled looking at the pile of wood stacked near the dock, waiting to be sold or burnt. She had wondered what it would feel like to have a flame in her palm, to feel its heat and light. Then, closing her eyes, Joanna imagined the flames and felt a strange tingling in her fingers. She opened her eyes and gasped. There was a small fire in her hand, flickering and dancing. Joanna dropped the fish she held and stared at the flame, amazed and terrified. She tried to shake off flames, but they stayed on her open palm, and she felt a surge of panic and screamed.

Her mother heard her scream and ran to her side. She saw the fire in her daughter's hand, and her eyes widened. She grabbed a bucket of nearly frozen water and threw it at Joanna, hoping to extinguish the fire. But the water had no effect. Only drenching and chilling Joanna to the bone. The fire remained, and Joanna felt a sudden pain in her hand. She cried out in agony and fell to the ground.

The flame went out.

"It's all right, *ma petite flamme*, everything will be all right," Ma whispered as she hugged Joanna, trying to comfort her.

But it wasn't all right. The villagers were staring at them, some with curiosity, some with fear, some with anger. Her mother took her home and hid her away. When her father returned from fishing, the villagers glared at him and cursed him on his way home. The villagers did not let Ma and Pa access the docks from that day forward. They belittled and harassed them incessantly.

A week went by, and then another. The family was short on food and becoming desperate. Once they had finally decided to leave *Marteau Marin* and find somewhere new to start over, where no one knew of Joanna's powers, a knock came on their door.

A hooded man dressed entirely in black with two wicked-looking handaxes on his belt grinned and leaned on the door frame. "Give me the girl."

Ma grabbed a long boat hook from the wall and, with a shout, lashed out at him ferociously.

Joanna's father stood dumbfounded.

The black-clad man moved so quickly that Joanna pulled away at his sudden outburst. He dodged the hook with a low sweeping manoeuvre, his cloak billowing as he surged past Joanna's mother and stepped toward Joanna.

Her mother turned, and one of the axes was embedded in her chest. She looked Joanna in the eyes, and blood gushed from her mouth as she tried to speak.

Joanna's mother. The Madame Marteau. Marie Ohlec collapsed on the floor of their home in a pool of her own blood.

Joanna screamed.

The man reached out for her with one hand, a yellow-golden round stone in his other hand.

Her father fell to his knees and began to babble.

The man stopped and *tsked* to himself, then turned and retrieved his axe, blood spurting from her mother's chest as he did so.

Her father did not even look in her direction as the man in black gripped Joanna by the neck.

The next thing Joanna knew, she was awakened in that iron cage in the enclosure with the black-and-gold-cloaked magi, his slick, shiny black hair, and that leering face with his sharpened goatee.

Joanna Ohlec awoke and forgot who she was, where she came from, or even her parent's names.

Someone nudged her awake. Joanna thought of Ebras Corb, groping at her as she opened her eyes to see the ranger, Kaplan Mir, crouched over her. She flinched and sat up defensively.

He raised his hands and backed off. "I'm sorry, magi. I was just awakening you. Light has come, and we should move."

"I'm sorry, ranger." Joanna breathed. "You startled me."

"It's always good to be wary," Kaplan said matter of factly. "But at any rate, thank you for tending to my wounds."

"I hope you are feeling well enough."

"The old bones are creaking, but I'll be all right. Shall we try to wake this one?" The ranger nodded at Jude, who lay next to her. "He has been asleep all night, muttering about tea."

Jude groaned and rolled over. "Fucking hells, some fresh camomile and ginger would get me right fixed up this early in the morning."

Joanna stifled a laugh. Jude was rough around the edges, but his obsession with tea and his garden was endearing. Joanna nodded to the ranger, Kaplan, to help her sit him up. They did so.

"So, Kaplan Mir, what's your plan?" Jude sighed incredulously. "The redhead is long gone, and we're cut off from Aurulan. Unless we climb the mountains east or west to try to descend into Aurulan further along. Sounds right fucking impossible in my condition."

"You're correct, Huntsman," Kaplan said in agreement. "It would be difficult. Our other option is to go further north into the mountains. I have found a well-trodden road leading in that direction."

"Won't it be crawling with those creatures?" Joanna asked.

"We will stop well before nightfall and look for secluded caves or something similar where we can hide through the night. It will be a long, slow journey."

"And what will we find to the north?" Joanna tried remembering the maps that the Proctor, Chanel de Montrichard, had taught her about.

"Ice, sea, and fucking rocks," Jude groaned. "Perhaps a few more Vouri villages along the way."

"Yes." Kaplan nodded. "All the Vouri villages near Oitilla were evacuated or slaughtered, but there may be some further out who were unaffected by the Daanav."

"Well, I have a task for you two before we start." Jude cracked his knuckles impatiently. "Get me a log or something we can tie to this stump so I can damn well walk on my own."

CHAPTER THIRTY-ONE

OUTSET

Simon drank from his goblet as he paced petulantly through the tavern. This *Alpha* was nowhere to be found. Anora, Baal, and Brena were also gone with the breeze...*as they say*.

"Skrull's balls, why is nothing ever just fucking simple?!" Simon cursed aloud.

Some early morning patrons looked up from their cups at him curiously.

Simon paid them no heed as he announced, "That's it. I'm going directly to the king."

"Hear hear." One of the patrons raised a cup. "To the king."

Oh gods. Simon knit his brow and rubbed his temples with both hands.

At that moment, the door to the tavern opened, and the Priestess Amahle hurried in with an entourage in her wake. The Priestess held the door open as an elegantly dressed person strode confidently into the tavern.

They wore a high-collared peach blouse with a sharp neckline that cut down nearly to their navel. There were swirling, colorful patterns adorning the ivory-smooth skin of their chest and arms, twisting up their neck, merging perfectly with their stunningly made-up face. Pristine bleach white trousers and high-heeled leather shoes. They were decorated with fine silvers and golden jewelry, many with a rainbow of different colored gems worked into their craftsmanship.

"This is the Epsilon council member, Rofous Hornero," Priestess Amahle introduced.

"A pleasure to make your acquaintance, Rofous," Simon said with a flourishing bow as the person approached.

"The pleasure is all mine." Rofous took Simon's hand and kissed it tenderly.

Simon felt his face flush.

"A friend of Amahle is a friend of mine," Rofous continued. "Though the tidings you bring are dire indeed."

Simon blinked, shaking his attention out of the sewers. "Ahem…" He cleared his throat and asked, "Has the kind Priestess informed you of our plight?"

"Indeed, can you believe our mighty leader, the Alpha, has not called upon the entire council to address this issue? He called upon us to fight a battle against the beasts in the north but has not addressed the issue further. I have sent messages to all council members. We are to meet in the council chambers of the King in the *Château de Nidhaut* in the afternoon of the morrow. That should be sufficient time for all members to gather. We'll ensure the King, Guignol Gaucher, is at that meeting. If we can get the king on our side, we may be able to help you."

"Many thanks, Epsilon, this is terrific news." Simon clapped Rofous on the shoulder. "I've been pulling hairs out of my arse, trying to figure out what to do next."

The Epsilon tilted their head curiously, looking Simon over. "That paints a thought-provoking image in my mind."

Simon blushed again. *Skrull's hell, no.* I need to find Saudett and focus on our family.

"Meet me at the gates to *Château de Nidhaut* around noon tomorrow. I will see that you and your advisers are seen in without issue. But I'm afraid I must be off. Prepare yourself, Simon Meridio. You will need to be extremely convincing. The Alpha does not enjoy others telling him what to do. It's his way or the throughway, as they say."

"Ha. I've never heard that one. It's a good one." Simon chuckled. "I will be ready."

With that, the elegant Epsilon turned and glided back into the streets of Nidhaut.

Simon returned to his seat at one of the tavern tables and sighed, picking up his discarded cup and drinking again.

Amahle came and sat down next to him. "Rofous informed me of a few more things, Simon. The Alpha is a ruthless, cold-blooded narcissist of a man. He would sooner kill you than have you speak against him. By Qav's lucky coins, Rofous has not seen him since the battle against the *Children of Skaad* to the north. He should not be aware of you, but we must be careful. I think we should move until the meeting tomorrow. We don't know what he is capable of."

"This is sound advice. This man sends sellswords to capture young people with a magic affinity for his own opulence."

"Rofous told me he was looking for someone. The Alpha had confronted him about an old necklace that the Epsilon had enchanted long ago and given to one of the Alpha's subordinates. The pendant was of charmed gemstone marbles, except the fine-cut obsidian at its center, which apparently took no hold of the spells Rofous tried to infuse. He had liked how it looked, though. The Alpha had demanded Rofous on where one of the teleportation stones was configured. The location was the North Iron Belt."

"*Hata.*" Simon breathed. "He is still out looking for her? Kiana said they were ready to go after the Magnus Huntsman, who also departed for the North Iron Belt nearly two weeks ago."

"Perhaps that is where the Alpha's focus is at?"

"Well, if we are moving, I must send someone to find Kiana and Zahir. They are still looking for her mother and the two Vouri warriors." Simon had seen the little hut where the party had been staying. It was a dreary little shack. *How long had they been living like that? Did they spend all the gold we sent with them?* Aloud, he said, "I think we can stay the night here and await Kiana here. The first thing we will do tomorrow is set out and bide our time until the meeting. I need to concentrate on what I will say to the council right now."

"Very well, Simon." Amahle smiled reassuringly. "You'll figure it out. I have great confidence in you. I'll be here if you need someone to bounce notions off. I do write the odd sermon here and there."

"Thank you, Amahle. You are a dear friend." Simon took a long drag from his wine, emptying the cup. He strolled to the tavernkeeper and asked for a refill, a warm meal, parchment, ink, and quill. He took another sip as he settled himself in, the din of the early morning tavern a relaxing background ambiance as he began to write down his thoughts.

"What happened to her? Where in Skrull's hell could she be?" Kiana backtracked the muddy streets around their little shack for what felt like the hundredth time. It had started to rain during the night when they returned to find the hut ransacked and abandoned.

"Someone took them by force, and the trail has gone cold," the man, Zahir, said as he crouched low, inspecting the muck.

"What Otsoa do you serve?" Kiana asked the Hasieran.

"Formerly, the Fourth Otsoa, Gaspar Haytham. I am now Rakshak to the First."

"Sorry for your loss. Gaspar was a good man."

"He was like a father to me."

Kiana paused to observe the man. He was heavy-set but looked stout, definitely not lacking in physical ability, even if he had a bit of a belly. His shoulders, arms, and legs were thick, almost cut from stone. Yet the man had soft facial features, almost elegant through a thin dark beard and mustache. The way he crouched and moved was different. It dawned on her after a moment. *He is...or was a she.*

Zahir stood and looked back at her. "What should we do, Sixteenth? We have no clue where they were taken to."

Kiana decided not to confront him about his gender. "Honestly, let's get back to Simon. Maybe he will have an idea. I'm starving. Perhaps my mother and those other two will show up eventually. It's not a simple undertaking to hold Baal and Brena Vasara captive."

Baal could see the guard's mouth moving, but the words were muted and distant. A handful of them had come and cleared out the corpse of the man Baal had smashed against the wall. They had kicked and beaten Baal as he struggled in his shackles. They would shout at him, but Baal couldn't understand, and they would beat him further. He couldn't even defend himself anymore after what that woman had done to him. There was a constant pain in his head and ears.

The guards left Baal hanging in his chains, leaving a half loaf of stale, mouldy bread behind to be shared by both prisoners. Baal lifted his chin slightly, his stomach twisting with hunger as Ota snatched the bread and gobbled it down in a few bites. Baal tried to protest. Whatever he tried to say did not come out, and there was only an odd vibration in his throat and chest as he spoke.

He saw more than heard Ota Vastaan's mocking reply, his scraggy, stained, white beard shaking as he laughed.

Baal let his head sink back to his chest, too weak to object any further.

Anora crept through the passageway, which suddenly, she realized, had changed into a sewage way as the nauseating stench washed over her. It opened up into a labyrinth of complex tunnels. She immediately turned around and backtracked in the direction she had come from for nearly half an hour, back to that intersection she had first encountered. *I'll try another path. They wouldn't have been taken into the sewer system of Nidhaut. Would they have?*

As she approached the intersection, she heard voices and saw a light ahead. Cautiously, she moved closer. The light was coming down the passage from the direction of the surface. Anora held back, praying they wouldn't turn onto her route. Pressing herself against the wall, she held her breath and waited.

The two cloaked figures she'd seen before appeared with torches in their hands and turned down the opposite tunnel away from her. The two moved wordlessly down the hall, only their footsteps echoing through the dark.

Anora waited until they were just out of sight around a bend before removing her sandals to move quieter and follow after the duo. *I can keep my distance and always have their light in view.* She came to another intersection, barely seeing their light disappear through the lefthand passage. Anora picked up her pace. A few minutes passed as she hurried after them. She turned a corner and saw the two navy-robed figures standing before a dead end. She halted and stepped back, peaking around the corner.

Some strange metal bars were protruding from the wall. One of the figures took out a small knife and tapped it in a delightful rhythmical tune, the different bars giving off diverse tones as they were struck. As the last note was played, there was a *clunk*, and the wall began moving. Splitting down the middle following the uneven lines of the stones stacked upon one another. The wall parted like a toothed mouth opening sideways.

The people continued, and the secret doorway began to close as soon as they stepped through.

Skrull's hell, Anora nearly hesitated. The song had been too complex for her to follow and remember. She dashed after them, her bare feet slapping against the floor. *They will hear me.* She unsheathed her curved sword. She squeezed through the opening just in time to fit through. It clamped shut with a *thud* behind her.

The two had turned around and watched as she rushed through barreling toward them.

Anora did not wait for them to react. Without stopping her momentum, her blade danced in. She charged forward, her sword moving with lightning speed. Before her opponents could even react, her blade sliced through the air with deadly precision. The man was about to shout as his throat was severed and blood poured out of him.

As the robed woman stood there, she appeared more composed than her counterpart. She slowly lifted her hands up in the air, and suddenly, a complex network of roots emerged from the ceiling, rapidly extending towards Anora as if they were alive and had a mind of their own. The roots were thick, twisted, and gnarled, with tiny tendrils and branches that seemed to be reaching out for anything they could grasp.

Anora continued the dance, spinning and slicing through the roots like a scythe to hay. But the tough plant fiber slowed her advance enough for the woman to turn and flee as more roots grew from the walls and pushed through cracks in the floor. Anora had to cut her way through as she gave chase.

"Delta. Delta!" the woman cried out repeatedly as she turned a corner. "Help me. Somebody."

The hallway they traversed was finer than before the secret door. These halls were lit with candles and lanterns, with doors along it. Further ahead of the fleeing mage, one of these doors opened, and two guardsmen dressed in blue hurried out with weapons drawn.

The woman pointed back at Anora. "Help me. She's going to kill me."

"Halt. Stop where—"

Anora's chest heaved as she drew a deep breath, steeling herself for the impending fight. With a sudden burst of energy, she propelled herself forward, her blade glinting in the torchlight as she weaved toward the enemies.

The first man raised a spiked mace to strike her, but she cut through the tendon in his forearm. Blood sprayed across the walls.

He screamed and released his grip.

Her second strike glided, razor-sharp, across his thigh, and he buckled to the floor.

The second man guarded himself with a stout shield and sword. He stood, watching her, waiting for her to make a move.

Anora faced the guardsman, her elegant sword gleaming in the candlelight. She could gauge that he was a formidable opponent. He carried the scars of many battles on his face. *A trained soldier.*

Cautiously observant, he stood his ground, waiting for her to make a move.

Anora smiled, her eyes sparkling with anticipation. Her blood pumped, and the adrenaline rushed. She took a step forward and breathed deeply, catching her breath from the pursuit. *Good, he is giving me time to recover.* Within another second, she dashed in, swinging her sword in a wide arc.

The guardsman raised his shield, blocking her attack. He countered with a thrust of his sword, aiming for her chest.

She sidestepped, avoiding his blade. She spun around, slashing at his back.

He turned quickly, parrying her strike. He pushed her back, creating some distance. He studied her movements, watching for an opening.

She falsified a limp on her left side as if an old injury was affecting her.

His wary eyes flickered to her leg.

Will you take the bait?

He feinted to the right, then switched to the left. He swung his sword at Anora's leg, aiming to cripple her.

Praise be to Skrull. Seeing his play, Anora surged, leaped over his sword, and barreled into him.

He took her body with his shield, and she rolled over him, landing behind him, and slashed at his neck.

The guardsman ducked away by a hair's breadth and elbowed her in the face, making her stagger. He followed up with a kick to her stomach, knocking her down. He raised his sword, ready to deliver the final blow. He grinned triumphantly down at her.

Not yet. Anora rolled to the side, dodging his sword. She kicked his knee, making him fall. She sprang up and let loose a dragging slash that sparked along the floor before it met his exposed face.

The guardsman tried to block, but it was too late. Her sword cut through his flesh, his lips, his nose, and his eye. The blood spurted out. He screamed and clutched at his face.

She silenced him by puncturing both lungs with some well-placed stabs. Anora breathed heavily, feeling a surge of adrenaline fade as the man bled out on the floor. Noticing some keys hanging from his belt, she removed them and tucked them away in her linen wraps. She looked for the woman who had retreated through the door from which the guardsmen had come. Cautiously, she approached the door.

A crossbow bolt thudded into it right next to her face.

Brena Vasara heard the sound of fighting down the hall from her cell. Straining against her chains, she tried to manoeuvre to see but was unable. *By Teras's mountain, what is happening?* Her arm ached with pain from the fall she had taken at *La Maison du Paon.* Her sword arm had broken in the fall.

Suddenly, a woman ran by, a curved sword dripping with blood.

"Anora!" Brena cried out as she realized who it was.

Anora skidded to a halt. "Primus, take me, Brena." Without a second thought, Anora began fiddling with a jangle of keys. "There are two dozen soldiers on their way, not to mention a Skrull-damned sorceress. We need to hurry." The lock clicked after a few tries, and Anora hurried into the cell, precious seconds slipping away as she tried at the manacles around Brena's wrists.

"My mate is in here somewhere," Brena said urgently. "I heard his shouts. I have never heard him cry out like that. He must have been in intense pain."

"Will find him and get you both out."

"My people are here, everyone who survived from my village, Oitilla. Or at least what's left of them." Brena nodded to a lifeless bundle of rags across from her.

Click. The manacles fell to the cold stone floor.

"Come, let's be off," Anora whispered, slipping back into the hall.

As Brena emerged, rubbing at her wrists, a group of navy-blue-clad soldiers appeared, charging toward them.

"Run." Anora shouted as she retreated down the hall.

Brena could feel the anger build as she gritted her teeth, trying to contain the fury threatening to spill over. She struggled to resist the urge to lash out at her opponents and unleash chaos upon them. Instead, she turned on her heel and followed Anora, her emotions roiling beneath the surface.

Hands reached out of the barred prison cells, pleas for help echoing in their wake. They were all Vouri. People from Brena's village. All of them were half-starved and on the brink of death. It caused the fury to boil over, and she halted and bellowed in a vengeful cry after Anora. "We must fight."

Brena did not see if Anora had stopped or even heard her. She turned back and met the pursuers head-on. With a roar, she was among them.

The guards hesitated, not expecting the fleeing women to turn and fight.

Brena crashed into one as a spear reached out for her. She gripped the shaft at the same time, crushing her shoulder into the man's chest, wrenching the spear free of his grip upon impact. Pain shot through her broken arm, but she bellowed in rage and ignored it.

The man fell on his back.

Brena slammed her foot down on his skull.

A crossbow bolt zipped past Brena's ear, slicing the flesh. She hissed in fury and returned the spear with a mighty heave, and it took the crossbowman in the chest. He slumped back, pinned against the wall.

Three more soldiers rushed toward Brena with a mixture of deadly weapons.

Amid the chaos, Anora emerged like a blur, her sword flashing in the dim light. She displayed an otherworldly grace with each move, her body moving with a fluidity that seemed almost impossible. The enemy soldiers lunged at her with their weapons, but she evaded their strikes with ease, her movements so precise that she was able to paint them with their own blood. It was a sight to behold as she continued to dance through the battlefield, leaving a trail of destruction in her wake.

Brena picked a handaxe off the belt of the felled soldier at her feet, his neck crooked at an unnatural angle. She waded in with the rage for her people bolstering her, splitting flesh in a whirlwind of steel and fury. Brena chopped into a woman's skull like lumber, sending blood and brains flying. She hacked away at a shield until she met the flesh of an arm, and it dangled from a string of bloody gore. Brena Vasara, warrior caste of the Vouri, hewed, carved, punched, and kicked her foes, ignoring the minor wounds that began to slice her own flesh. She laughed wildly as adrenaline and fury fuelled her assault and red clouded her vision.

Chapter Thirty-Two

SIEGE

Hata soared through the air. Dawn had come to the Ryk Lân, but the skies to the west were darkened by clouds of thick smoke and thousands of the flying creatures of Skaad. War had begun. Hata aimed her flight toward Keep Crystalia, praying to Teras that she would make it in time.

Queen Raine Stormfall stood on an elevated platform on the walls of Keep Crystalia. Thousands of her people stretched out around the entire circumference of the massive bulwark. More still were readying to defend the city of Aerion below. The creatures were carrying across immense chains to create a bridge to the edge of their island's capital city.

The ballistas were launched with a loud thundering sound, and their projectiles hit the flying creatures with great force, creating clouds of gore. However, the creatures seemed innumerable as they kept coming, swarming the skies like an army of locusts. Despite the intense onslaught from the massive arbalists, they held the massive chains with an iron grip, determined to achieve their objective at any cost. There was a moment of silence as the spikes fell from the air and crashed into the earth.

There was a stiffness in her people, looking out at the immeasurable mass of beasts seeking to slaughter them. They stood like statues awaiting their fate. The feeling pulled at Raine's chest, constricting her breathing ability. *I must be strong. I must shine so my people can rally against this doom.* She lifted her brilliantly crafted sword, embedded with a substantial fire-infused ruby. It glinted in the morning light.

Raine inhaled deeply, then called out to the Himin-dvergar, "My brave and loyal people. Today, we face the greatest threat to our existence we have ever known. The *Children of Skaad* have come to our doorstep to destroy us, to smother Luminar's light, and take away *our* freedom. They have brought a vast and terrible force that will not halt until the last of us lay dead.

"But we are not afraid. We are not *weak*. We are not *alone*. We are the Himin-dvergar, the children of the sun and the stars. We have built our fortress, where we can enjoy the beauty and the prosperity of the Ryk Lân. We have forged our weapons and machines where we have harnessed the power of the elemental gems gifted by the isles. We have trained our warriors, engineers, and pilots to show our enemies the skill and courage of the Himin-dvergar.

"I will stand at your side. I will fight at your side." Raine lifted her sword higher, pressing the gem, igniting the sword in flame, and screaming the determination in her heart, "I will die at your side. For we are the Himin-dvergar, and we will not surrender. We will not fall. We will not fail!"

"We are the Himin-dvergar!" Her people resounded in answer, continuing the words passed down by their ancestors. "We will rise! We will shine! We will prevail! For the Queen! For the light of Luminar! For the Himin-dvergar!"

"Sound the call!" Raine ordered, and a dozen soldiers put gem-infused horns to their lips and blew.

The call was taken up across the entire wall, and down in the city below, a force of Himin-dvergar rallied out to meet the oncoming horde. Hundreds of rotor-wings took to the skies, and the ballista renewed their reverberating thrumming shots.

The horde of creatures poured across the bridge of chains and met a battle line of heavy Himin-dvergar pikes. Like waves crashing into a cliffside wall, the creatures broke their bodies against her front line's pikes, heavy shields, and armor.

But even as they died, more *Children* filled the gaps and were relentless, clawing, biting, and tearing at the Himin-dvergar line with their fangs, horns, and talons. The winged beings swooped in with spears, skewering soldiers too busy looking ahead to worry about the skies.

The second wave of monsters crashed into the phalanx, impaling themselves on the sharp points of the pikes but slaughtering many of Raine's people with the suicidal method.

The Himin-dvergar pushed back, trying to keep their formation intact, but slowly, they were cut down. Abruptly, the three quadrilateral shapes of the phalanxes on the front tightened. And through the opening in the line, charged battle-crazed men and women, Himin-dvergar berserkers, with flaming dual axes or ice-crusted hammers. They wore lighter armor and moved swiftly and with brutal ferocity, hacking and slashing at the beasts with their magic-infused weapons. Blood and gore splattered the battlefield as limbs and heads flew in the air, some burning with hot fire and others breaking apart in chunks of flesh and ice.

Raine looked to the sky. Another battle raged on. The snaking clouds of the flying *Children of Skaad* trailed after her outnumbered rotor-wings. It almost looked like smoke trails chasing the flying contraptions, but she knew it was not.

Still, the rotor-wings sailed through the clouds of enemies, their sharpened wing fronts slicing through bone and flesh. Blood burst across their wings and cockpits, covering pilots and engineers alike in the visceral fluids.

I should be up there with them, Raine thought as she surveyed the scene. *In my own rotor-wing, they need my help.* She had no further time to ponder it as hundreds of the flying humanoids soared into the air directly before her. They had flown low under the wall and ascended upward, appearing at the lip and slicing and stabbing at Himin-dvergar manning the walls. Still more, flew higher, turned back, and dived toward the defenders.

"Defend the keep!" Raine bellowed and lifted her shield as one of the creatures lunged at her from the air. The *bloodstone* infused with her armor activated, its green and red mineral blazing to life as it strengthened her body. She slammed the shield into the creature as it reached her.

Bones snapped and limps crumpled against the metal as if the thing had flown head-first into the walls of Keep Crystalia itself.

Raine followed the blow through and flung the crumpled corpse aside. She got her bearings. The wall was in chaos. Many creatures had landed and were fighting in unison, with military precision, cutting her people down. Their blackened weapons and armor were smeared crimson with the blood of her people.

Raine felt a surge of anger and grief, and she cried out in wrath and rushed at one group of organised enemies, throwing herself into them. Her flaming sword seared through flesh and bone, a wing went tumbling away, and the creature shrieked, lashing out with a wicked black axe. Raine deflected it by lifting her knee, trusting in the craftsmanship of her armor. The axe bounced off painfully, the force behind the blow still formidable.

Raine struck out with her shield arm, smashing the edge of it into the creature's neck. Its throat crumpled behind the blow, and its mouth opened wordlessly as it clawed at its own neck and collapsed.

Something collided with her square in the back, and she stumbled forward, tripping on the enemy she had just felled. Raine rolled as another blow struck where she had been atop the creature a second beforehand. The head of a massive two-handed hammer thudded into its own ally's chest, concaving the ribcage inward.

Raine looked to see the foe, a large male of the flying species.

It effortlessly lifted the hammer, raising it above its head to deliver another strike. Even her armor would not hold up long under the punishment of that weapon.

There was a cry from nearby, and a handful of Himin-dvergar soldiers led by Finn Sunstrider appeared. "Protect Her Majesty the Queen."

The hammer-wielding creature turned to meet them, lashing out with a mighty blow at Finn, who led the charge.

Finn Sunstrider seemed to speed up as the blow came in, and suddenly, he was sliding below the hammer's arc. Finn struck out with his two-handed axe, slashing through both knee joints of the creature.

It screamed and toppled, dropping the heavy hammer.

The other Himin-dvergar soldiers swarmed it and finished it quickly. Then Finn Sunstrider and his guards were around her, helping her to her feet while striking at any enemy who came too close.

"Are you all right, my Queen?" Finn asked, panting with exertion.

"I am. Thank you for coming to my aid."

"You would have done the same." Finn scanned the battlefield for a split second, then continued, "They are trying to destroy the ballista. Come with us, your majesty. Let's put a stop to them."

"Lead the way." Raine fell into the company as they hacked their way through.

Gesche-fan Skaad aimed her body to cut off the flying machine. Curling her wings around her to hasten her fall, she dived through the sky toward it. As she came in at a high angle, she reached out with the tip of her spear as she shot past. It caught the Rykling in the front seat of the machine, slicing through its face, neck, and shoulders. Then, she was far below the contraption, opening her wings to halt mid-air. She twisted around to watch as the machine began to rotate on its axis and fall from the sky. It exploded into a crowd of enemies below, causing death and destruction.

Gesche-fan Skaad studied the battle below. Her ground forces had still not broken through the line of Rykling soldiers defending the city, nearly right where her bridge connected with the island. They were bristling with weapons and armor far more advanced than her own forces. *Fucks, we need to take the lower island before we will ever conquer that fortress.* She signaled to her hornblower, who was never far from her side, even amid battle. "Send in the smokers. They should be able to break that line."

The Nyra woman let out a rapid succession of blasts, and not long after, Gesche-fan Skaad saw two dozen of the blue-flamed abominations stomping toward the front. They began to pick up the pace, uncaring of their own kin. Hounds and hulks were crushed under their log-like limbs as they thundered across the bridge.

She saw the battle line of Ryklings wavier in the chaos below. She saw them hesitate and even backstep away from this new threat. *This is it. We have them.*

Hata ripped through the metal planks of the bridge, exploding skyward. Children were flung from the safety of their bridge as they waited to cross. One of the massive burning creatures lost its balance and tumbled into the hole she had left in her wake. She arched back through the air, seeing more of the enormous creatures charging toward a line of Himin-dvergar. Summoning the power of the Sunstone in her armor, Hata burst down, and her feet fractured the stone street as she crashed to the ground in front of the Himin-dvergar defense.

A moment's pause of awe rippled through friend and enemy alike.

Then, the burning abominations were upon them.

Using the armor to control her wounded arm, Hata slammed her fist into her open palm, then lifted her hands to the sky, and a thick wall, hundreds of feet long, of rock, earth, and gemstone veins exploded before her. She closed her fists and *pushed*. The wall rumbled forward. Crushing both burning beasts and lesser *Children* alike.

A cheer erupted behind Hata as Himin-dvergar berserkers burst forward, cutting down any stranded enemies on this side of the wall.

She could hear the shrieks and cries as the Children retreated, sure that many were falling off the side of the floating island with each forward push of the wall.

Suddenly, there was a high-pitched sound, as if something was moving unnaturally fast through the air. There was an enormous impact and a pause as Hata looked with horror at the violet cracks snaking from an epicenter in her wall. A second later, the center of Hata's wall exploded in violet fire.

The wall began to crumble as the hooded man, both fuming hands outstretched, soared directly for her.

Bryn Sparkheart wiped at his blood-covered goggles. He stared in awe over the side of the rotor-wing as the auburn glowing Sky-lass pushed hundreds of the Skaad bastards into the abyss. "She's doing it, Rorik. Our feckin' Sky-lass has finally shown up."

Rorik tilted the craft and looked where Bryn was pointing. He nodded, and Bryn could tell he was grinning behind his bandana-covered face.

Then, a horde of flying beasts was upon them. Bryn's heart pounded as he fired bolt after bolt from his crossbow, desperately trying to fend off the unrelenting onslaught of enemies. But no matter how many he took down, more just kept coming, and he wondered if they would ever make it out alive.

Bryn held on for dear life as Rorik's instincts kicked in, and he piloted with precision and grace. With a skill honed over years of practice, he expertly evaded the creature's attacks, darting and weaving through the air. His machine's wings sliced through the air with a whooshing sound as they twisted and turned, leaving trails of dead enemies in their wake. Bryn couldn't help but be awed as Rorik remained focused, his skills fluid and deliberate, as he continued to outmanoeuvre the creatures and stay one step ahead of them.

Out of the corner of his eye, Bryn saw a burst of violet light below that streaked toward the Sky-lass's countering amber glow. He reached out and tapped Rorik twice on his helmet and pointed.

Rorik nodded again and climbed momentarily before turning the craft back toward the battle below and into a screaming dive.

Bryn readied his new toys.

Saudett hovered mid-air in shock as Hata Vasara decimated the *Children* below. *She is alive. What should I do? I must show myself to her. But what will she think? I am her enemy.* Before she could contemplate further, Trije-fan Skaad counter-attacked. The wall exploded and then crumbled, and he tore through the air toward Hata. His violet light clashed with the warm orange light that Hata emanated. *She truly is the Sunstone.* As the two met, a violent shockwave of magical energy detonated outward from the epicenter of the two forces colliding.

Should I help that fucking bastard Trije-fan? Or let him die? Her eyes watched as the two lights shot apart and ascended into the sky. More explosions rained down on her *Children* on the bridge. Gesche-fan Skaad hissed in frustration and considered her next move.

Raine cut down the last creature crawling on the side of the massive ballista. She ground her teeth in fury and heartache for the unfortunate engineer in the gunner seat who had perished before their company could come to his aid. His body had been stabbed countless times as he lay limp in the chair. Then, the creatures began hacking at the controls, gears, and anything they could handle to disable the weapon. She did not know if they had succeeded or not.

A *bang* echoed through the air, and Raine twisted her head to see violet and amber light shining blindingly from the front line in the city below. "By Luminar's light." she shouted. "What is that?"

"It's the Sunstone," someone called out from further down the wall. "She fights with us."

There was a cheer, and her forces began to rally.

Thank you, Hata. Raine stepped down from the elevated step pad the ballista sat upon and turned her attention to the wall. *Thank you for being here with me.* "To me, Finn Sunstrider, they're still attacking the other ballista. To me." Raine Stormfall, Queen of the Himin-dvergar, charged down the wall, killing her enemies as she did so.

Hata caught both his wrists as he collided with her. She wrapped the earth around her legs to steady herself and halt him in his tracks. She called upon every reserve of strength left in the *Sunstone* to her aid.

His black teeth snarled at the unexpected stop. The violet energy snapped and crackled like lightning around him concurrently, fuming out of him like steaming clouds. His eyes glistened white under his hood. "Vile human," he hissed. "You're all repulsive. That human man in the Moreas Lân. He acted like he was one of the conceited Iban'mael Wayfarers. Now, that disgusting insect of a woman who licks at my father's feet. And you. The Sunstone, they call you? All you humans are nothing compared to my father."

"Then you'll enjoy this little *human* trick." Hata gave her most father-like grimace and smashed her forehead into his face.

His head snapped back, and blood burst from his nose.

With lightning speed, Hata pulled his arms towards herself and launched a powerful kick, magically propelling her armor-booted foot right into her opponent's midsection. The impact was so intense that it almost felt like the ground shook momentarily. She released her grip on him.

The hooded man flew back, crashing into the ground and skidding across it. But he suddenly righted himself and shot up into the air with powerful thrusts of his wings, flying higher and higher.

A rotor-wing swooped in above the renewed horde of *Children* who poured over the bridge. Hata saw a multitude of red-orange gemstones glint and fall from the craft. A second later, a score of explosions burst in amongst the horde of creatures, and their shrieks and screams echoed over the battlefield.

Thank Teras, that will give the Himin-dvergar time to regroup. Hata took a deep breath and leaped from the ground, flying after the hooded man.

When she approached, the hooded man turned mid-air and pointed his finger at her. Black-violet fire shot out from his finger in a sizzling line.

Hata veered, narrowly missing the string of unblockable energy.

He fired another, then another.

Hata had to change her course to fly at an angle, scarcely avoiding the malevolent spell each time. She looked to see him stop in mid-air and raise both hands above his head. Hata steered up in an arch toward him.

"Scua Ad Cliewen," he screamed out as she neared. A sphere of violet flame grew to triple his size above his head. Then he hurled it at her.

Hata dodged it quickly and scoffed internally. *Is that all you got?* It was slow but picked up speed as it went. Hata turned her head as it soared by to follow its path and realized it was aimed directly at one of the ballista contraptions on the wall. "No." She turned and flew after it, unsure what she could possibly do to stop it.

The heat from the blast buffeted her as it melted the ballista and many of the Himin-dvergar around it. Their skin and bones were blackened charr as they were cooked alive in their armor.

Finn Sunstrider, running ahead of Raine, halted at the sight of the flaming sphere. Lightning quick, he turned and screamed, "Protect the Queen." He pushed Raine as hard as he could.

Raine fell onto her back, and her soldiers leaped on top of her. Then she felt the heat as the air was sucked out of her lungs. She screamed and struggled for freedom even as she felt the heat on her face. "Finn. No. Let me go."

The Himin-dvergar guards on top of her did not move. Even after the heat had subsided.

To Raine's horror, she realized they lay dead atop her. Struggling out from under them, she saw the armor on their backs melted into their flesh, the pained last expressions on their faces twisted and frozen. She looked up to see Finn Sunstrider, his hand stretched out with his back to the flames. The blackened metal of his armor reached around him.

Raine walked to his side and saw his entire back, arms, legs, and head were *gone*. The flesh melted off and seeped down in a burning pile of waste.

"Luminar's light, this can't be happening." Raine fell to her knees, and tears dripped down her cheeks. "Why die for me?! My people are dying all around me, and I can't help them."

At that moment, Hata touched down and stepped up to her, putting a hand on her shoulder. "You are their queen. They love you more than anything." Hata's words caught in her throat. "I...I love you more than anything."

Raine looked up through her blurry tears into Hata's blue eyes. Raine's lip trembled as she stood and wrapped her arms around Hata. "And I, you, Hata. I love you too—"

"Then you can die together." Another voice screamed with unholy fury.

Raine looked past Hata to see a man with wings and a hood pointing two fingers at them.

"Scua Bael Cnytells." the man shrieked venomously.

As Hata held Raine close to her chest, she saw Hata's eyes light up with a fierce amber glow.

Hata took off into the sky without hesitation, holding Raine tightly, soaring away from the assault. Black-violet fire lines hissed through the air where they had been standing a second before.

Hata moved calmly, holding Raine aloft, ever watching the hooded man.

He didn't move or try to attack them again.

Slowly, Hata lowered Raine back down to the wall. "I need to finish this," Hata whispered in her ear.

Raine nodded and gave Hata a slight kiss. "I'm sorry I doubted you."

"It's all right, *my* queen."

"Now go fucking kill that Skaad bastard."

Hata grinned a toothy snarl and shot into the air directly toward the waiting figure.

"So she loves you, does she?" A woman's voice came to Raine's ears. "Oh, how nice it must be to have the ever-fleeting desires of a child."

Raine turned to see a humanoid woman dressed head to toe in dreadful black-steel armor, her face hidden by a wicked spiked helm. Black wings folded down behind her as she strode eagerly toward Raine. A bloodstained spear spun and readied in an underarm grip. The woman's pace quickened, and suddenly, she was rushing toward Raine, intent on killing her.

CHAPTER THIRTY-THREE

COUNCIL

Simon entered the extravagant floor of the Council of the Aerie chambers. Eight tall back seats were elevated, four on each side of the room. One smaller seat was at floor level directly before Simon.

A man sat there, a golden crown lopsided on his greying hair. The man looked exhausted and slumped back on his *throne*. He did not look weak or frail, but the dark bags under his eyes said otherwise. A black-robed woman stood somewhat behind him. Simon could instantly tell she had the air of a magi about her.

Cad Dermont, Rakshak Zahir, Kiana Ahmadi, and the Priestess Amahle funneled in behind Simon. Simon looked them over momentarily, glad of their presence as he pleaded to the council. *But should things go tits up, they will not be of much use against a roomful of powerful magi. Their weapons will be useless here. Not even the Priestess's clever tongue for negotiation will be of aid.*

As he stood there, he could hear the faint sound of doors creaking open, and his ears picked up the shuffling of people taking their seats on the elevated platform above him. *Just like birds,* Simon thought as he stifled a chuckle. Then he looked up to see the gorgeous Epsilon sitting on the chamber's left side.

Not long after, an elderly, greying man in flowing white robes sat beside the Epsilon.

A stunning woman entered on the right-hand side in a vibrant jade and bright yellow dress cut low on her powdery white chest. Her golden blonde locks curled around rosy cheeks. Simon felt his eyes widen as she leaned over the rail, flaunting her ample cleavage in the low-cut dress. Her lips curved into a seductive smile as she met his stunned gaze.

He quickly looked away, feeling a surge of heat in his cheeks.

A young man trailed behind her, his face hidden by a dark hood and cloak. He moved with a stealthy grace, blending in with the shadows that seemed to cling to him. He sat silently, his body rigid and motionless as a statue.

On the opposite side entered a handsome man, Simon, determined to be nearly his own age. His oval brown eyes and unnaturally golden hair blended with his skin tone. His hair was spiked upward in an odd fashion. His fine golden tunic shone brilliantly with an emblem of the Primus, the sun, the crescent moon, and an eye-opening between them on his chest. He studied Simon for an awkwardly long time before taking his seat.

At last, a woman of regal bearing entered the hall, clad in a flowing gown of pure white. A dazzling diamond brooch shaped like a swan sparkled on her chest. She glided gracefully to her chair and sat beside the mysterious hooded man.

Two seats were left empty.

"Why are we here?" the handsome golden man asked, a hint of irritation in his tone.

The old man in white cleared his throat, leaning toward the railing. "Should we not wait for the Alpha and the Delta?"

"Ha, ha." The colorful woman laughed light-heartedly. "As if the Alpha has the time or the desire to attend this council."

There was a murmur from the king, and the woman in black behind him came, leaned in close, and listened. Then she stood and announced, "He will come. The Alpha promised our King Guignol Gaucher that he would deal with this...*problem*." The woman waved a hand dismissively at Simon.

"And what precisely is this?" the woman with the jeweled swan brooch questioned.

Simon looked at the powerful magi elevated above him, his eyes resting on each in turn. When they met the Epsilon's eyes, Rofous Hornero smiled warmly and nodded, encouraging Simon to take the floor.

I can do this, but by Skrull's hell, I wish Saudett were here by my side. Simon breathed slowly. Gathering himself, he began, "Honorable magi of the council, thank you for allowing me to speak to you today. As I am sure you know by now, creatures of darkness have invaded the Earste Lân. My name is Simon Meridio. I come before you, not as a leader of a desert tribe or an architect of a decently profitable construction company. No, I come as a fellow inhabitant of this Lân. A Lân that is in grave danger.

"You've all by now heard of the *Children of Skaad*, the monstrous creatures ravaging the countryside of northern Aurulan. They revealed themselves first in the vast desert of the Burning Sea. We have fought them." Simon gestured to Kiana and Zahir in their desert garbs. "You've seen the reports of their atrocities, their brutality, their hunger for destruction. You may have even taken part in the battle against them. You've witnessed the refugees, both Vouri and Auru alike, fleeing from their homes, seeking shelter and safety. You've felt the tremors of the *Children's* march, shaking the very foundations of our world.

"We scattered the creatures to the wind," the magi of golden attire rebuked. "They were no match against the might of this council. They are no longer a threat."

"Yet they still roam free, killing our people," Simon continued. "They will not stop there. Do you know who is behind this menace? Do you know who commands these beasts? The being who unleashes them upon us? The man who seeks to conquer and enslave us all? His name is Hear-fan Skaad, and he is no ordinary foe. He is a dark sorcerer, a master of forbidden arts, and a wielder of ancient and terrible power. He is the enemy of all life, the destroyer of all worlds. He is the Lord of Shadow."

The hooded man stirred uneasily in his seat as if the final words had struck a nerve. The shadows that enveloped him grew darker and thicker as if they were trying to hide him from sight.

Simon did not falter. "This Hear-fan Skaad has already annihilated and conquered many Lâns, subjugating their people, draining their resources, and corrupting their worlds. He has amassed an army of thousands, a horde of horrors, a legion of doom. And he has set his sights on the Earste Lân. I fear we are the only ones left to stand against him. The Lord of Shadow will not stop until he has crushed us under his heel, until he has extinguished our flame, and until he has devoured our souls.

"We cannot let this happen. We cannot stand idly by while Hear-fan Skaad approaches our gates, while he prepares his assault, while he plots our doom. We must act, and we must do so now. We must unite, and we must fight. We must defend our world, and we must save our future.

"That's why I'm here today to ask for your help, plead for your aid, and beg for your support. I'm not asking for only myself but for all of us. For our people, for our land, for the Earste Lân. I am asking you to join, stand, and fight with me. I ask you to lend me your power, wisdom, and courage. I'm asking you to lend me your magic.

"You're the most powerful magi in the Lân, the guardians of our realm and humanity's protectors. You can shape reality, bend the elements, and command the forces of nature. You can make a difference, turn the tides, and change the course of history. You can stop Hear-fan Skaad, defeat his legions, and save our world.

"But I can't do it alone, and neither can you. We need each other, we need to work together, we need to combine our strengths. We need to form an alliance, a coalition, a pact. We must join forces with Aurulan, Xamid, and the Vouri. We must gather the bravest and strongest warriors in the Eartse Lân to defend our borders and be champions of our cause. We need to form a united front, a solid wall, a formidable military. We must face our enemy, strike him as one, and defeat him. This is not a time for hesitation, doubt, or fear. This is a time for action, for resolve, and for courage. This is a time to show Hear-fan Skaad what humanity is capable of.

"So, I implore you, honorable magi of the council, to join me in this noble mission, stand by my side in this war, and fight with me for this cause. By the Primus, I ask you to say yes for the sake of our Lân. For all people's sake and for our futures. What say you?"

There was a long silence, and then, from behind Simon, a slow clap came...

...once...twice...thrice...

Simon turned to see a man striding into the room as he continued his slow clap that was somewhat muted by his black leather gloves. His robes were pitch-black with golden trim, and his black hair was combed back and shining. He smiled wickedly at Simon through a well-trimmed goatee.

"Did you rehearse that?" the man said as he glided forward. "Tell us, *Simon Meridio*, who are you exactly, and what could you possibly provide that we of this council do not already possess?"

Simon faltered. *This must be the Alpha. The leader of this council, and I'm just a nobody. I'm a simple architect. A man who wishes to find his wife and go home.*

"He is nothing," someone shouted out Simon's exact thought. The voice sounded like it was right beside him. And it sounded far too familiar.

"Who's there?" the woman in white yelped in surprise.

"Show yourself, Wayfarer," the Alpha ordered.

Gaelin Yesnala blinked into existence, standing next to the Alpha.

Simon's jaw immediately clenched in anger, and he fought the urge to throw a *Windan* spell directly at Gaelin and cut him in two.

"What is going on here, Ebras?" the golden-robed man demanded, his striking face an expression of outrage. "Who is this, and why have you been absent during these dire times?"

"Zeta, Sol Oriole," the Alpha belittled, his sudden glare causing the Zeta to flinch back in his seat. "All will be told to gratify your insignificant chirping." The Alpha began to levitate and floated up into the chamber's center so he could look down on everyone. "I will let the Wayfarer explain himself."

Gaelin floated up next to the Alpha, hovering just below his level. He gave a flourishing mid-air bow with all four arms moving in unison. "Indeed, I will explain myself. My name is Gaelin Yesnala of the Iban-mael. We were a race of people who worshiped knowledge above all else. We were travelers of the Lâns. Wayfarers of the worlds. For the most part, we simply studied these Lâns. Unfortunately, our curiosity got the better of us when we discovered a new world of perpetual darkness. He was there, waiting for a way out, and we gave it to him. He invaded my world, the Hiel Lân, and reduced it to rubble."

Something itched in the back of Simon's mind. *He isn't telling the truth. This is not quite the correct memory.* There was a lingering image of a figure striding through knee-deep water, but Simon couldn't quite see who it was.

"So, Wayfarer, do your goals not align with what the man Simon has just said?" It was the old man seated next to the Epsilon. "You both wish to go to war against this Hear-fan Skaad, correct?"

"Ha." Gaelin sneered contemptuously. "This man is of no concern to us. He has no power and no influence. He leads a handful of untrustworthy bandits who will be of little use against the overwhelming forces of Hear-fan Skaad. Dismiss him, and I will aid you in devising a plan with the best chance of defeating the enemy."

There were murmurs amongst the magi as they leaned in toward one another.

"I would have to agree with the Wayfarer," the Alpha announced. "We have no use for this *Simon* and his band of criminals. As a matter of fact, we have heard that many Aurulan caravans have been lost to these nomads of the Burning Sea."

Kiana stepped forward, a hand on the hilt of her sword. "Hasiera only takes what's needed, and we never kill anyone needlessly." She glanced at Simon when she said this.

Well, not now that the former First is in his grave. Simon withheld a sarcastic grimace, still fuming over being in the same room as Gaelin Yesnala. *I should strike him down here and now. I'll show him who's nothing.*

"We shelter those of your society that you deem different or strange," Kiana continued. "People who do not abide by the Primus's dogma of one man and one woman. Or people who have been abused and ridiculed by their peers. Even an entire race of peoples who were hunted like animals."

The Epsilon stood, a knowing smile on their lips. "This sounds like a beautiful sanctuary far from the prejudiced eyes of our country. They have not done any true harm. Indeed, I would like to visit this Hasiera, oh lady of the desert."

"And we shall open our borders under Simon's guidance." To Simon's surprise, it was Zahir who spoke. "He has led the Hasieran against the Children of Skaad, while this man"—Zahir pointed at Gaelin—"killed friend and foe alike during the battle of the Moreas Lân. He does not care if humanity lives or dies. He only seeks vengeance for his people."

"Well, that is quite dispiriting," the blonde, colorful woman said with a distasteful look in her eyes. "The safety of the Earste Lân comes before your petty thoughts of retribution."

"I agree with the Gamma." It was the old grey man again. "Well said, Lila."

The ample-bosomed woman, Lila, smiled and winked at the old man.

"Enough!" the Alpha shouted abruptly. "Revenge or not, The Wayfarer has his uses. He knows the enemy better than any of us. And he has knowledge that would put all of your weak attempts at magic to shame. He is far more prominent than a man playing as king of a tribe."

I need to do something. I need to say something. Simon had been fumbling about and gawking since the Alpha and Gaelin had shown up. Simon glared intensely at Gaelin, who was completely ignoring him, rotating in the air slowly, looking at each council member.

"This council is not without its faults," Kiana spoke again. "You abducted the young woman, Hata Vasara, because her ability to use magic awakened. What gives you the right to capture and control anyone who shows signs of magical ability?"

The other council members looked at one another uncertainly but stayed silent.

The Alpha reddened, and his face distorted in rage. "That insolent girl is *gone*, dead for all I know or care. My fledglings flee like rats with wings. Both the cardinal and now my fat little magpie are gone."

"Where?" Kiana urged. "Please tell us where she might have gone, to the north? To Oitilla?"

"How do you know this?" The Alpha's composure was slipping away, his voice rising by increments as each word left his mouth. "Who told you this?"

"Indeed," Gaelin answered Kiana, ignoring the Alpha's mounting temperament. "I believe she used the Wayfarers Gate under the mountain. Reports show that the mountain has collapsed atop the village of Oitilla and the Wayfarers Gate. A shame, really, we can no longer use that portal."

So Hata has traveled to another Lân, Simon pondered. *Where could she have gone? Skrull's balls, it's like chasing a thorne in a wheatfield, as they say.*

"At any rate," Gaelin continued, smirking at Simon. "Dear Alpha, Simon Meridio is a *nobody* if not thanks to me. I led him to the desert tribe and rid the Moreas Lân of the filth who had taken up there. I will be far more useful in the battle to come." Gaelin lifted a hand and said, "*Leoma.*" A globe of light grew from his outstretched hand and floated upward.

The golden man snorted. "You're not the only one who can play with light." He held out his hand, and the light from Gaelin's orb was sucked into it. Then, after a moment, a brilliant flash of light blinded the room.

A second later, a cloud of darkness, like tentacles, groped and clutched at the light. Suppressing it. The hooded man on the opposite side of the chamber held out his hand as the dark tendrils of shadow snaked out of it.

"We know you all have massive cocks. Now stop this." It was the woman in white with the swan pendant.

The Alpha flicked his hand, and both men of light and dark were flung back into their chairs. The chairs shattered under the sudden impact, and both men skidded across the floor behind their designated seats.

"Honestly, Kuro," the Epsilon sighed, rubbing their forehead. "I can see Sol acting like this, but I thought you had more class."

Both men, groaning, slowly picked themselves up and dusted themselves off before returning to stand by the railing.

"My apologies, Alpha," the Zeta said. Or Sol, as Simon had come to understand. "Still, a bit of light is merely a trickster's game."

"Show him," the Alpha said flatly. "Show us all what you are capable of, Wayfarer."

Gaelin's black teeth appeared as he smiled so wickedly that Simon was taken aback. Gaelin aimed his finger at the Priestess Amahle. "Bael cnytells."

The white fire was too fast for Simon to react. It hit Amahle directly in the chest. Burning through her flesh and bone. Directly through her heart.

Amahle stood, her mouth a gap, her lips moving up and down in a suspended shudder. Her eyes were wide with terror, then they clouded, and she crumpled to the floor.

"No!" Simon screamed. *Maegen. Strangung. Windan.* He summoned the three incantations simultaneously. *Maegen* caused Gaelin to become instantly heavy, pulling him to the floor with a sudden impact. *Strangung* strengthened Simon's body, and he sprinted like a wolf to prey on the fallen Wayfarer. *Windan* blades cut a path before Simon, slicing out at Gaelin Yesnala.

The Alpha appeared in front of Simon. The razor-sharp winds of magic impacted against him. Yet he stood unphased. Then he lifted a hand, and Simon was hurled directly into the air.

Kiana and Zahir's blades flashed out at the Alpha, then glanced off of nothing mere inches from the man's exposed face.

Simon felt himself begin to fall as Kiana and Zahir danced about the Alpha raining blows down upon him. Before he could think of the *Afléotan* spell, he was caught in a dark web of black tendrils. To his surprise, Simon was lowered and placed gently beside the man controlling the shadows.

The hooded man grunted and nodded at Simon. "I, Kuro Raven, Beta Council."

A beam of light struck Kuro, and he flew back and burst through a stone pillar.

"He attacked the Alpha, you fool. Kill him!" the Zeta shrieked and pointed an open-palmed hand directly at Simon.

The grey old man touched the Zeta nonchalantly on the cheek.

The Zeta began to spasm, his face turning pink and his veins extruding from his neck and head. His arm shot upward, and the light beam shot from his hand and tore through the ceiling like a massive sword cutting through stone.

Rubble and stone began to fall from the roof.

The Epsilon was suddenly beside the old man. Rofous fiddled with a bracelet, and a brown gem was quickly covered in blood. Thick trees surrounded all three people in a dome-like shield, protecting them from the falling debris.

Next to Simon, a glacier of ice exploded above him as the brick and stone crashed and slid off it harmlessly away from anyone standing below. The woman in white, her eyes aflame with blue light, held her hands up high as the frost overgrew the entirety of the damaged ceiling, creating a completely new one of solid ice.

Simon stared in disbelief. *These magi are truly unmatched.*

A burst of air whistled up from below and exploded into the rail before Simon.

That was a Windan spell. Simon looked over to see Gaelin floating up toward him. He glanced and saw Kiana and Zahir hurled across the room and through the massive entrance doors to the council hall.

Cad Dermont was nowhere to be seen.

"Hello, lovely." Something soft touched Simon's cheek. He knew a woman's lips when he felt them. He turned to see the blonde woman, Lila, smiling back at him. "This should give you some time." She stepped back, and to his surprise, she turned into him. He watched as he, himself, Simon Meridio, ran away around the railing toward the opposite side of the chamber.

Gaelin shot up into the air past the railing and took no notice of Simon. He soared toward the fake one, readying to cast white strings of fire into the poor woman's back.

Simon realized the woman had also made him invisible. *I won't let anyone else die.* Simon renewed his *Strangun,* then cast *Afléotan.* He lunged into the air after Gaelin. *Maegen.* Simon used the gravitational pull to propel himself even faster toward the Wayfarer. He collided with Gaelin's back, and the man's head whipped back with the impact.

Simon wrapped his arm around Gaelin's neck, securing it with the other, and squeezed.

Gaelin sputtered and clawed, with four hands, at Simon's arms vainly, managing a few words between strained breaths. "You—des—despicable human."

Simon tightened his grip further, but out of the corner of his eye, he saw the Alpha coming.

The Alpha, Ebras Corb, had a look of utter wrath as he glided up slowly, menacingly toward Simon.

Simon knew he could not compare to this man. "Wait. I will let him go. Let me and my companions go. You can keep this bastard for all I care."

The Alpha slowed to a stop, his gloved hands clenching and unclenching repeatedly.

"I stand by Simon!" someone called out. It was Rofous Hornerno, the Epsilon. They stood upon a jeweled plate of silver as they glided up to stand mid-air next to Simon.

"As do I, Theta of the Aerie Council," the grey old man said from his place below. Seeming unable to fly.

"I, Sol Oriole, will die by the Alpha's side, or I am unworthy of the title of Zeta." His entire body glowed brightly, and the golden man hovered beside Ebras Corb.

"So will the Eta, Nix Swan." A sheet of ice grew into a staircase as the woman in white elegantly stepped up beside the Alpha. "Shall I freeze the whole lot of them?"

"Gamma and Beta, which side will you choose?" Ebras said so sternly that the last two magi balked where they stood.

Simon watched as the Alpha's fury seemed to boil over, and he screamed, spittle dripping from his lips. "Who will you choose?!"

"Surely we can figure this out," Lila pleaded. "We all want the same thing. To protect the Earste Lân."

The hooded man Kuro nodded in agreement.

At that moment, a soldier came crashing through the door. "Lord Alpha. Lord Alpha. The Delta is dead. Murdered in her own tower."

CHAPTER THIRTY-FOUR

MOUNTAIN

Baal saw the desert woman Anora, and then, to his incredible surprise, his mate, Brena, sprinted past his cell. Seconds later, a dozen soldiers followed them, their mouths open with shouts Baal could not hear and weapons raised to strike. *My Brena.* Baal tried to call out but heard nothing from his gullet. He saw movement across from him.

Ota Vastaan appeared, stretching his neck to see what was happening. Ota said something, but Baal heard no words.

Frustration at his inability to understand turned to fury at the sight of his Brena in danger. Baal stood from where he had hung lifelessly in his shackles. *By Teras's mountain.* He summoned every bit of strength and pulled against the chains. *By Teras's strength.* His arms and legs tensed and screamed against the metal restraints, as did his silent voice. *By Teras's honor.* He knew his voice was bellowing in rage at his chest and neck vibrations. Still, he heard nothing.

My Brena. My Hata. My everything.

Something gave behind him, and he was suddenly face-first on the floor.

Gaunt fingers clutched at his arm. Baal looked up to see Ota Vastaan's sickly face staring back at him as his bony fingers gripped at Baal's sweating skin.

Ota's mouth was moving, and there were tears in his eyes.

He pleads for my help. What a despicable man. Baal formed his answer in his mind. He knew he could speak even without hearing the words he said. "Did Silja beg for her life like this?"

Ota's eyes widened with realization and terror as Baal tore his arm free from the man's sickly fingers.

Baal couldn't hear the man sobbing, pleading, and cursing him out as he turned away and craned his head against the bars to see down the hall. What he saw astonished him. A dozen men lay dead, and two women stood, covered in blood and gore. Gasping for breath.

"My Brena."

Brena felt a sudden jolt as the wooden roots snaked out and coiled tightly around her arm, refusing to let go as she tried to bring it down to finish one of the soldiers.

With great effort, the soldier attempted to crawl away on his hands and knees, desperate to escape Brena's wrath. However, his movements were too slow, and he was soon caught by the glint of Anora's dancing blade. The sword slashed through the air with a sharp whistle, cutting through the soldier's armor and leaving a deep gash on his body. He let out a cry of pain as he fell to the ground. Anora stood over him, her sword at the ready, waiting for more signs of resistance.

The magi screamed, and more roots reached up from cracks in the stone floor toward Anora. Some managed to wrap around the desert warrior's feet, tripping her up. She struggled to move, to break free. The tendrils only seemed to tighten their grip, threatening to drag Anora down into the earth below.

Brena's face contorted with anger as she flexed her arm firmly against the roots. With a sudden burst of fury, she yanked her arm free, letting out a bellow that echoed through the hallway. The sorceress was the last one standing. Brena leaped forward, clear over dead soldiers, and slammed her fist into the woman's face with an audible *crunch*.

The magi's eyes rolled back, and she fell to the floor, unconscious. As she fell, the plant roots ensnaring Anora slowly began to loosen their grip and recede back to the earth from where they had come. It was as though the sorceress's control over them had been entirely severed by her sudden loss of consciousness.

Anora stood there, momentarily stunned by what had just happened, before cautiously approaching the fallen figure to see if she was still breathing.

Brena gasped for breath and hissed in pain, her broken arm hanging limp at her side.

Suddenly, there was a deep, labored shout from down the hall.

Brena knew that voice. She heard her husband's call, the tears welling in her eyes as she ran to him.

His arm was outstretched through the bars, chains still attached at the wrist.

She clutched at it, reached her arm through, and wrapped it around his head, pushing her forehead against his through the bars. "*Aviomieheni...*" she whispered, letting all the fear drain from her as they held one another.

Baal mumbled something incoherent.

"What's that, my mountain?" Brena asked.

Anora appeared and jiggled a key in the lock. Not long after, the door squeaked open.

Brena pulled Baal out of the cell, wrapping her good arm around him, afraid to let go.

A man was holding his head in his hands, sobbing uncontrollably behind Baal in the darkness of the prison cell.

Brena leaned to get a closer look. *Is that Ota Vastaan?*

"We need to keep moving before more show up," Anora urged.

Brena was about to confront the crying man when, at that moment, a slow click of hard-heeled boots rang down the corridor toward them. Approaching unhurriedly. A woman in a navy-blue outfit and a familiar mask stepped into the torchlight.

"Dame Personne," Anora gasped in astonishment.

"My *name* is Dawn Héron, Delta of the high Council of the Aerie, and you have far gone past violating the Alpha's bidding."

"You helped us," Brena mumbled, still taken aback. "You were kind to us. Why do this now?"

"You let us work in the brothel," Anora added. "Which let us find the man we were looking for. Why take us now?"

"Brothel?" the woman sneered, tilting her masked head. "*La Maison du Paon* is no mere brothel. It is a place of fine art and exquisite pleasure. I will not answer your questions. Simply know that the Alpha rules above all. Now, I'm afraid, my lovely Personne's, you must die."

Brena was facing the Delta, Dame Personne. Suddenly, a deafening shockwave of sound erupted from the Delta's mouth, causing Brena to cover her ears and step back. The high-pitched shriek was so mighty that it seemed to rattle her entire skull, leaving her disoriented and vulnerable. She fell to a knee.

Anora sprawled on the floor, covering her own ears in agony with her back-arching as she screamed wordlessly.

As white light fogged Brena's vision, she saw her husband's broad silhouette. The man she had dedicated her life to, the one who completed her in every way, stepped forward through the pulsating shockwaves of sound that reverberated around them. *My partner. My mate. My mountain.*

He pushed forward through the vibrating repercussions of ear-splitting noise.

Baal stalked toward the woman who stood there dumbly, staring back at him from behind her strange mask. Her mouth was opened wide like she was screaming. He heard nothing.

The woman took a step back as he moved forward.

Baal felt increased vibrations in his chest and limbs but ignored them as he continued, step by step.

She backed up again, and the vibrations increased. Her eyes were wide with terror behind the mask. The sorceress backed up into a wall and jerked her head around in surprise.

Baal reached out his massive hands and seized her by the throat, the chains on his wrists dangling and *clanging* against the floor as her black high-heeled boots left the ground.

The vibrations stopped, and she feebly scratched and pulled at his forearms. Her legs kicked sporadically, thudding into him with little effect.

Baal Vasara held the helpless woman from the floor by the neck and effortlessly squeezed the life out of her bulging eyes.

Her hands fell to her sides, and her legs ceased kicking.

CHAPTER THIRTY-FIVE

DOWNFALL

Hata took control of fallen axes, spears, hammers, and swords in a cloud of deadly weapons. She struck out at the winged man cloaked in violet plumes of smoke as they both soared skyward.

He retreated, firing rays of black fire at the oncoming weapons, melting many of them away as he flew higher and higher.

At this rate, I will run out of weapons and have nothing to use against him. The islands were becoming distant shapes below them. The air was becoming chilled and challenging to breathe. Hata began to worry as dread crept into her. *There is no earth within my reach.*

He abruptly twisted around without warning, and a burst of violet light emanated from him, propelling him directly at her with even more force. Out of nowhere, the man came hurling towards her with great speed. She could see his hand fuming with violet fire in that split second.

Hata could feel her heart racing with fear and uncertainty, but she unleashed a barrage of spinning weapons aimed straight at him. But just as they were about to strike, a sudden explosion of violet magical energy surged forth, creating a shockwave that deflected the weapons away. The once-deadly weapons were reduced to mere dust. She was left defenseless and alone.

Raine deflected the lethally fast strikes of the spear as best she could. The woman spun and stabbed in such quick succession that Raine was doing her all just to keep the weapon at bay. Thankfully, her armor was nearly impenetrable, but her face was unprotected as she had lost her helm earlier in the battle, and the deadly spear tip seemed to be intent on her exposed flesh at every opportunity.

As Raine raised her shield to deflect the incoming spear, she felt a surge of frustration building up inside her. Despite her magically enhanced physical abilities, she struggled to keep up with the speed of her opponent's attacks. As she tried to launch a counterattack, her movements felt sluggish and uncoordinated, and she couldn't help but wonder at the level of skill this woman possessed. Despite her doubts, however, Raine found resolve within her duel. *I'll never give up. For my people. For Hata.*

The winged woman gracefully danced back, flapping her wings to create distance between them. She kept a watchful eye on Raine's movements, waiting for the right opportunity to strike. Suddenly, she leaped into the air and soared over Raine's head, her spear tightly grasped. With a swift motion, she brought the spear down in a long arch, aiming to strike Raine from above.

Raine sidestepped, and the weapon glanced off her shoulder pauldron, sending sparks flying. Again, Raine charged forward as the woman landed and spun to meet her. With a shout, Raine slashed out with her flaming blade, putting all her might behind the blow.

The black-armored woman reeled back, taken off guard for the moment, raising her spear shaft to deflect Raine's sword.

The magic-infused blade seared through the shaft of the spear at an angle, and Raine cried triumphantly as the bladed end of the spear twirled into the air.

The woman's helmeted head tilted conceitedly, and in seconds, she spun the broken shaft in her hand, gripping it to stab, and brought it down ferociously directly on Raine's inside elbow joint where the armor was weakest.

Pain tore through Raine as the jagged, heated tip pierced through the soft armor and into flesh. She gave a seething hiss and pushed through the pain. At the same time, she struck out with her shield arm, the gemstone armor still empowering her strength. The heavy metal plate *crunched* into the woman and sent her spinning through the air to land with a painful cry, sprawling onto her back.

Raine touched the metal bar, jutting into her arm, and agony rushed through her. She realized, to her horror, that the shaft had penetrated clean through to the other side. Blood gushed and dripped from the tip of the spike.

Hata strained against the overwhelming power of the corrosive fumes, evading the hooded man's strikes by magically jerking her armor and body, along with it, away from him. Sometimes, with such force, her neck strained painfully in distress from the sudden movements.

He was relentless. Never giving Hata even a moment to breathe.

She retreated.

His hands touched the tungs-teel plates of her armor, and they blackened and steamed away, dissolving when contacted by the violet energy. He was grinning wickedly, halting for a moment before outstretching his hands and unleashing a torrent of corrosive fumes.

Hata tried to evade, but she was too late. The fumes pummeled against her armor, eating away at the metal. She felt a surge of pain as the fumes reached her skin, burning and blistering it. She screamed in agony, losing control of her flight, and began to freefall.

The hooded man swooped down after her.

At the last second, Hata used what was left of a piece of her armor and formed it into a knife in her hand.

He crashed into her and gripped her in his corrosive hands.

They shot toward the islands below.

The vile man's face was inches from her own. Hata saw his eyes for the first time. They were inverted to human eyes, black surrounding white pupils. They glowed with violet light and looked bursting with malice and pure hatred.

"You are the Sunstone," he yelled into her ear as they fell. "And I am the Son of Shadow. You are the light, and I am the dark. You are the earth, and I am the night sky. You are nothing, and I am everything."

Hata clenched her jaw and stabbed, pulling the metal-shaped blade through his gut.

He screamed.

Both of them plummeted from the sky, twisting and turning as they struggled against one another.

The black-armored woman picked herself up. One of her wings dangled unnaturally on her back, seemingly broken. Slowly, the woman reached up, removed her helm, and threw it to the ground. Raine saw a beautiful woman with flushed bronze skin and short, tousled, midnight-black hair. But the abysmal expression in her eyes and her grimacing curved lips that had been cut and were bleeding were heartbreaking. She looked nearly on the brink of tears.

"You're *human*, like our Sunstone. Like Hata?" Raine asked as she tried to catch her breath. "Why do you fight for the abomination, Hear-fan Skaad?"

"*Your* Sunstone?" The woman leaned down and picked up a discarded axe. "Would you treat her as a possession, like a pet or an object to be owned? Did you make her promises of love and loyalty and bare your soul to her, only for her to leave you behind?" Tears began to cascade down the woman's cheeks, cutting lines through the sweat and grime of the battle.

"You knew Hata?" Raine asked again as she circled, dropping her shield and taking her sword on her unwounded side. "You loved her?"

The woman closed her eyes. "I did. I still do. I want her to be safe. I vowed to protect her and failed her miserably. I promised to be the sole partner at my husband's side, but in return I killed our—"

With a deafening roar, the wall shook as an explosion detonated a few hundred paces away. The ground beneath Raine's feet quaked, and she and her opponent were both thrown off their feet and fell to the ground.

Raine shielded her eyes as dust and stone pelted at her body. A second later, through the haze, she saw a violet glow in a depressed crater of the wall. She stood and ran to the edge. Below her, Hata lay limp, pinned below the hooded, winged man. He knelt on her chest with a heavy knee.

Hata look dead, her eyes closed. Her armor was riddled with corrosive holes, and the amber gemstone in her chest was shattered.

No. She can't be dead. Raine stepped forward.

Visibly, in great pain, the man grimaced, holding his stomach as blood seeped through his fingers. He ignited his other hand with violet-black plumes of corrupt energy and reached down to grip Hata's head.

Raine was sprinting toward Hata with all the strength she could muster just as the man's fingertips brushed Hata's ear.

The black-armored woman reached him first. Her axe burrowed into the back of his neck and hacked through flesh and spine.

His head rolled, blood sprayed, and his body fell limp atop the Sunstone.

Chapter Thirty-Six

TREATY

Simon released his grip and pushed Gaelin away as the Wayfarer lashed out with a *Windan abrecan.* The slashing sphere of wind nearly tore into Simon's flesh.

"Enough!" the Alpha bellowed. His face was pink with fury. "That's enough, Wayfarer. Do not make me repeat myself."

Gaelin halted his next spell at the Alpha's words.

The Alpha had removed a glove and put two bare fingers to his temple. To Simon's surprise, the Alpha visibly calmed himself. "One of our council members is dead, and we may lose more if things continue on this course. We cannot be fighting amongst ourselves when the fate of the Earste Lân is at stake. We would lose too much power."

Slowly, the magi lowered their hands, and everyone descended to the floor.

There was a murmur behind them as Simon found his footing.

Then the woman in black, still standing beside the king, said, "So you have all finally come to your senses."

The Alpha strode over to the king and rested a bare hand on the man's head, cupping his ear in a gesture of fondness. "My king, I have everything under control." The Alpha smiled and gave him a very improper pat on the cheek.

The king mumbled something that Simon couldn't hear.

"I leave it in your capable hands," the woman answered. "I will take my leave." With that, the woman in black helped the king to his feet and escorted him from the chamber.

The Alpha turned back to the congregation of magi. "We will divide our forces. Zeta Sol Oriole and Epsilon Rofous Hornero will join me with the Wayfarer and prepare our assault at the Aurulan Gate. Call upon your acolytes and personal guards to meet us there." The Alpha paused, and his dark eyes met Simon's. "You will be sent to the closest Gate to Xamid that our Wayfarer has constructed. That *was* in your desert oasis, but now I fear you will be sent to the Isle of Tal'tulu. From there, you will secure the Gate and travel by ship to Al'Jalif to plead for the Sultan's aid."

"You would send me alone in this?" Simon asked skeptically. "With only my own people?"

"Theta Cynge Caladrius and Gamma Lila Parakeet will accompany you with their retainers. You will set up a pylon at the Tulu Gate, allowing us to be in contact. Epsilon, see that they are provided with the pylon."

"Of course, Alpha," Rofous said with a bow.

"Eta Nix Swan and Beta Kuro Raven will hunt down and exterminate the remaining beasts roaming the north. As soon as the Xamidian forces are ready, we will launch a two-pronged assault on the Skaad Lân."

Simon breathed a sigh of relief. *Skrull's hairy balls, it was nice for someone else to take charge for once.*

There was a moment of silent anticipation before the Alpha turned his head to Gaelin and spoke again. "You *lied* to me, Wayfarer." The Alpha's cold glare sought a terrible punishment upon the four-armed man.

Gaelin flinched away under that stare.

Even he fears the Alpha, Simon thought.

"Simon Meridio, you are nearly as powerful as he," Ebras Corb continued, his tone hinting at deference. "The Wayfarer said he let you borrow his power, then stripped you of it. But here you are, wielding it with uncanny efficiency. You have proven yourself a worthy mage, Simon Meridio, the *nobody*."

"Ha." Simon barked a laugh. "Gaelin is a deceitful, lecherous bastard. You shouldn't trust him. I'm sure he has some greater aim behind all these cries for vengeance."

"Silence, fool human!" Gaelin cried out rashly. "I made you. I gave your life meaning as you wasted your intelligence away, always gawking after your next sexual encounter. Humans are truly disgusting."

"I've heard enough of this." The Alpha waved a hand, and Gaelin was knocked from his feet, skidding along the fine marble floor with a squeak. "Be gone, Simon Meridio. I will send a messenger to your inn with instructions."

Simon looked down at the still body of Priestess Amahle. Anger bubbled up within once more. *I will kill Gaelin Yesnala if it's the last thing I do.* "What about the priestess?" Simon asked vindictively. "She was murdered in cold blood."

The Alpha snorted in contempt. "An ill-fated casualty. Now get out of my sight before I change my mind." The Alpha didn't wait for Simon's reply and turned to his council members with a glare that could freeze over Skrull's hell. "Those of you who aided this foolish man against your Alpha, come to me. *Now.*"

Simon hurried out of the chamber, thankful to not spend another second in that man's presence. Kiana and Zahir met him on the way out and retreated with him. He looked back to see the Alpha reaching up to touch the head of the magi, Kuro Raven, as the doors closed behind him.

Baal could see his mate's lips moving, tears streaming down her cheeks as he pointed at his ears. He made a gesture as if to listen, then shook his head. He saw her soft lips quiver, and she embraced him, pushing her face into his chest. Her shoulders raised and fell as she wept against him.

Baal stroked her long, tangled blonde hair and comforted her. "*Vaimoni,*" he said, taking time to form the words. "We are together."

Her head nodded repeatedly against his chest.

Anora unlocked cage after cage of imprisoned Vouri people. Once all had been unshackled, they were ushered into the hall and made ready to depart. Anora stopped before the cell where Baal had been held.

The white-haired man, with his patchy stained beard, looked up at her in desperation. "Please, I beg you, let me go. I'm the chieftain of this clan." He held up his shackled hands. "I'm of a mighty Vouri House."

"Leave him." Brena's voice came to Anora. "He has dishonored the Vouri and does not deserve a quick death. House Vastaan is no more. Let him rot."

Baal looked from Brena to Anora and then into the cell. He gave a menacing growl.

"Have it your way." Anora sighed. "We can't stay here any longer. Follow me."

Just over a hundred Vouri refugees crept through the darkness in Anora's wake, Baal and Brena at their head. The refugee's quiet murmurs longed for freedom and sunlight.

As they crept past the room where the guards had filed out, Anora spied a massive, blue-edged hammer with intricate runes etched upon it.

Baal grinned toothily when he saw Anora pointing at it. He strode into the chamber, plucked it effortlessly from where it leaned against the wall, and propped it on his shoulder before rejoining them. His smirk did not recede as they found their way to the midday streets of Nidhaut.

Kiana pushed through the market to see what the commotion was about. As she broke through the crowd, she cried out in surprise to see her mother leading a large group of very hungry-looking people. Then she sighted Baal and Brena, tall forms in the crowd. "Oi!" Kiana shouted at them. "Where in Hettra's bouncing bosoms have you been?"

Anora and Brena turned their heads to look at her.

Baal did not take notice.

"My daughter!" Anora cried and ran to her.

Kiana embraced her shortly before accosting her. "What happened? The shack was in shambles, and you were nowhere to be found."

"The magi captured and imprisoned Baal, Brena, and all the Vouri from Oitilla. But we managed to free them. Unfortunately for us, we killed one of the council members in the process."

"Kiana Ahmadi." Brena came and hugged her as well.

Baal placed a large hand on her head and tousled her hair like a child.

Kiana was beyond relieved to see him grinning with his big dumb smile.

"It was Dame Personne," her mother whispered. "She was the Delta all along. The entire council will be out to get us now."

Kiana's eyes widened in shock. The head whore of *La Maison du Paon* was a council member of the Aerie. "Fucking hells, mother...that is absurd. How could she be? She was a kind woman."

"It's true," Brena said in agreement. "She was keeping all my people in the base of her tower even as she let me work in the brothel house." Brena cracked her knuckles in anger, and then she looked at Baal. "Now, she has taken my mates hearing from him."

Kiana blinked in surprise. *He lost his hearing? Yet he seems so pleased.*

"Make haste, my daughter," Anora urged, nudging Kiana down the road. "Let's get off the streets."

"The council shouldn't be an issue," Kiana said. "Simon has made a deal with them."

It was her mother's turn to blink in surprise. "You've already treatied with them? How did it go? What happened?"

"Let's just say it was an *impassioned* conversation." Kiana smiled and then looked at the hungry faces of the Vouri refugees. "Let's get these people a warm meal and somewhere to rest. Come on, this way."

The tired trio fell in behind Kiana, the throng of starving Vouri close behind as she led them to the inn district of Nidhaut.

CHAPTER THIRTY-SEVEN
TRICK

Fucks to these fucking mountains. Jude Nelon groaned in pain as he pulled himself up the near-vertical stone path. *Fucks to this fucking cold.* His stump, where his lower leg used to be, was burning in agony. It had been too painful to attach a makeshift leg to the end of it until it had healed fully. Instead, the ranger had fashioned him a crutch for under his arm. Still, it was nearly impossible to progress through the mountainous pass's rising and falling without the constant aid from one of his two companions.

Joanna gripped his wrist and pulled as Kaplan pushed him up from below. Finally, with a mighty heave, they got him over the ridge and onto the next part of the so-called *path*. He sprawled out on Joanna, who had fallen back as she pulled him up. He lay catching his breath as she sat with his head in her lap, panting with exertion.

Kaplan quickly hopped over the ridge, which hadn't been more than a five-foot incline. Dusk began falling, and the sun soon disappeared behind the mountain range, which always surprised Jude. One minute, it was as bright as day. The next, they were under deep shadows. And where there were shadows, there were those creatures on the hunt.

"Let's find a place to camp for the night," Kaplan Mir suggested, scanning the surroundings. Then he pointed. A jutting cliff and a divot were in the rock face on one side of the gulley path, nearly thirty feet up.

"Skrull's hell, I will never make it up there," Jude said sardonically.

"I will climb up and secure a rope. You two can follow. If you need to use your magic to help you, Joanna, do so quickly before night is truly upon us." The ranger did not wait for an answer and began free climbing up the cliffside.

"The Primus's blessing has sent this man to our aid," Joanna reflected.

"Ha." Jude snorted. "Why did the Primus get us into such a mess in the first place, dear magi? Is he not also responsible for the horde of flesh-eating beasts that now roam the lands, slaughtering helpless peasants?"

"Well, if you put it that way," Joanna muttered, her shoulders slumping. "I just wanted a little hope during all this bleakness..."

"We're responsible for our own lives." Jude's leg pulsated terribly, and his irritation at Joanna's useless prayer grated on him. "There ain't no fucking gods going to do fuck all about it."

Joanna went silent at his harsh words.

"All right. Come on up." A rope came dangling down from above.

Joanna said nothing as she put an arm under Jude's shoulder and propped him up.

"How are we going to do this?" Jude asked doubtfully.

"Let's not talk about the gods anymore, all right, Jude? If I say a prayer, it is out of a need for comfort and habit. Don't *yell* and look down at me for my beliefs."

Jude turned his gaze and saw the tears in her eyes. *Skrull's sodden balls, what have I done?* "I'm sorry, Joanna, it's this damned leg. It's killing me, and it's causing me to be more of an ass than usual. You can pray all you like to whatever god you wish."

She half smiled. "It hurts watching you in such pain."

"I'd be dead tenfold if not for you, my love." He leaned over and kissed her gently on the cheek. Joanna's skin was delicate against his lips, and her scent was warm and soothing. He inhaled her, the sudden wish to lay in her arms and never leave again overcoming him.

Her cheeks dimpled as she smiled back at him, her blue eyes twinkling affectionately. *Hettra's mercy...*

"You two better hurry," Kaplan called down once more.

"Right, hold on to me, Jude," Joanna ordered.

Jude leaned on her back, arms wrapped around her, and she strained under his weight. Then he felt the heat.

Fire blossomed to life from her feet and hands, then exploded in a blast that sent them both skyward. The sound of the detonation echoed down the gorge. They soared directly at the jutting cliff, and Kaplan came suddenly into view.

The ranger's eyes widened in shock as he opened his arms. Jude and Joanna crashed into him, and all three tumbled back into the recessed rock. Kaplan groaned as they slowly untangled themselves from one another and found some space to sit with their backs against the walls.

Kaplan Mir opened his eyes at the sound of snarls and growls from below. Slowly, soundlessly, on his stomach, he inched toward the edge of the small cliff and peaked over. Kaplan heard more than saw the movements of many creatures in the darkness, the sounds of the hound-like one sniffing and scratching at the ground. Time crept by as he watched and listened. After what seemed like an eternity, the sounds of the beasts moved off further down the gulley.

He was just beginning to doze off once again when the same sounds returned, coming back from the direction they had moved on to. Once again, the sound gathered directly below them. It dawned on him. *They have our scent. They moved further to see if the trail would pick up again and found nothing. They know we're here somewhere.*

Rocks skittered, and something scraped against the rock. The sound became closer and closer.

They are coming. Kaplan shook Joanna awake and said urgently, "They are coming. They are here." He unsheathed his sword. There was barely room to move on the small plateau where they had camped.

Joanna bolted upright at Kaplan's urgency.

The Magnus Huntsman won't do us much good here, Kaplan thought as he shook the man awake.

Jude sucked in a gasp as he groaned irately with the abrupt awakening.

A scattering of stone came from the cliff edge.

Joanna ignited her flames and lit up the night. Shrieks erupted from down in the gulley at the sight of the light.

One of the grey-skinned beasts bared its fangs and leaped over the edge with a roar.

Kaplan readied his scimitar, but Joanna struck first.

The sphere of boiling flames hit the beast head-on and took it far over the edge. It screamed as its flesh melted, and both sphere and monstrosity plummeted into the gorge below. Joanna ran to the edge, her hands outstretched, a look of concentrated fury on her face. There was a blast of light from below. Flames licked up thirty feet into the air. The shrieks of the burning creatures undulated into a crescendo, then abruptly halted.

All was quiet except for the crackling and sizzling of flesh and bone.

Then, a howl and answering discord of cries reverberated from further down the path.

"More are coming," Kaplan said.

"Thank you for stating the fucking obvious as usual," Jude answered cynically.

"We can't flee with him in this condition," Joanna said, looking at Jude.

"Leave me. Fucks, I'm going to get us all killed at this rate." Jude said, struggling to stand. "You both can survive. I will distract them for as long as I can."

"You idiot." Joanna slapped Jude across the face, and the man blinked in shock. "I'm not leaving you. I just found you."

"Honestly, our best course of action is to defend our current position," Kaplan stated. "The hounds and the hulking creatures will not be able to reach us here. Only those damned durable grey ape-like ones."

"I can deal with them," Joanna said resolutely. "Even bones made of metal melt when heated enough."

"You are both insane," Jude said, then chuckled maniacally. "I may have something that can help us." He fiddled in one of his sleeves and revealed a hidden pouch. He pulled out three glass-like marbles. Crystal clear. "These are my last three magic beads. These will make us invisible to the naked eye."

"Always a trick up your sleeve, Huntsman," Kaplan said approvingly. He felt a hint of admiration for the man, even if his profession was less than moral. *The fellow is good at his job.* "This is how you captured the Sunstone back in the valley of Hasiera."

"Fucking rights I did," Jude grunted. "Followed you muddling fools straight to the ginger lass, I did."

The cries from below began to grow louder.

"All right, they will still come here to look for us, so we can't make a noise," Jude said as he pricked his finger on the point of a dagger. "Use your own blood and coat the bead with it." He held out his hand, and Kaplan took one from him. Joanna did likewise.

Jude rolled his last marble on his bloody finger and vanished. "Come, press against the wall. We must take up as little space as possible up here." They heard him laboriously getting into position, panting with the exertion.

Kaplan held out his scimitar to Joanna.

She placed her finger on the sharp edge and yelped in pain when she slid the flesh along it. Then she was gone.

Kaplan followed suit and stumbled into an invisible body as he moved as far back from the edge as possible.

They held their breaths as the creatures came shrieking and yowling down the gulley. The cries grew and grew directly below as the beasts found the melted pools of black muck where their kin had burnt to death.

Not long after, there was a scream and scratching and scraping as they heard something climbing the cliffside. In the dark, they saw the glowing, milky eyes of the two grey beasts. As they crested the ridge with guttural shrieks, they halted abruptly when they found no one in the slightly recessed rock cave.

One of the creatures stepped forward, sniffing as its glinting metal fangs dripped with saliva. It huffed and growled, stepping yet closer.

Inches from where Kaplan pushed against the wall, it bent down and touched a spot of blood that had dripped from one of their fingers. It sniffed the blood, its head tilting curiously as it did so.

The one behind it grunted impatiently and leaped back over the side.

Kaplan felt the creature's hot breath as it screamed an intense rebuttal and turned and bound away, gripping the cliff's edge and throwing itself over as both beasts descended into the night.

The cries waned and soon dispersed down the valley.

The trio dared not move or come out of their magical cloaks until the light of day began to warm the skies once more.

Chapter Thirty-Eight

CHIEFTAIN

Simon let the note fall to the ale-stained tavern table beside the large pouch of gold coins. An apparent apology of the council for the death of the Priestess Amahle. He doubted the Alpha was behind this generous condolence.

He picked up the note and began to read it once more.

The burial of Priestess Amahle Okorie will be held in the Cathedral of the Primus tomorrow afternoon regarding her years of service to the people of Aurulan and Our Lady Hettra, the Goddess of love and peace...

...Sincerely, Rofous Hornero.

Simon closed his eyes to suppress his hatred and outrage for the appalling creature, Gaelin Yesnala. *She did not deserve to die. Amahle was a woman of peace. She was kind and empathetic and loved everyone. Above all, she was my friend.*

The door to the tavern clattered open, and Kiana pushed into the room, followed by her mother, Baal, and Brena. Then, more and more people filtered into the room after them.

Simon stood to greet them as the room began to fill to capacity.

"Tavern keep, get the stoves hot, and prepare a feast. We have many hungry mouths to feed," Kiana called to the man behind the bar.

"You're alive." Simon gently embraced his mother-in-law and then held out a hand to Baal.

The massive Vouri man sported a hammer on his shoulder that was equally proportionate to his body.

Skrull-damned big.

Baal gave a toothy grin and gripped Simon's hand painfully.

"By the gods, man." Simon winced and tried to free himself. After a moment, Baal released him. "It's good to see you, mighty warrior Baal."

Baal tilted his head in confusion and then looked at Brena.

"Baal has lost his hearing in the confrontation against the Delta," Brena said, likewise painfully squeezing Simon's hand.

"What confrontation?" Simon asked dully.

"All these people were being held under the Delta's tower in the district of *Ville de Voleurs,*" Anora said. "Thank the Primus that Baal and Brena caused such a struggle in our little shack. There was plenty of blood for me to follow their trail to a secret entrance to the prison."

"I heard the Delta was killed not long ago," Simon said in amazement. "You did battle against a magi of the council? How are you all still alive?"

"She was the one who subdued us in the shack, but I did not see her then," Brena answered. "She attacked with magic from outside. Her soldiers must pad their helms against the sound because it was agonizingly loud. Even so, Baal fought through it and wounded many of their men even as I fell unconscious from the echoing shriek in my head. Yet now, after facing her again and *killing* her, he has lost all hearing."

"Skrull's forsaken hell, you never cease to amaze me, you Vouri." Simon breathed. "So these are your people?" He waved to the crowd of thin, starving individuals.

The tavern keeper began to bring out large platters of cooked meats and pieces of bread with the help of a serving woman, placing them on the bar before them. As one of the Vouri reached out to take a glistening slab of fatty pork, the tavern keeper bellowed over the din, "No one eats a morsel until I see some coin."

"Ah, right," Simon mumbled as he pushed through the crowd and dumped a handful of gold on the bartop. The coins clattered and rolled around.

The tavern keeper's eyes widened in surprise, and a look of excitement crossed his face. He reached out quickly to snatch up the coins, his fingers closing around them tightly. The sound of the coins clinking against one another filled the room, and the tavern keeper couldn't help but grin at the sight of such wealth.

"Will that be enough to feed all my fellows for this night?" Simon asked.

The tavern keeper repeatedly nodded and said, "Indeed, gracious sir. Breakfast as well. I'll have a mighty feast prepared for all."

"My thanks to you, my good fellow." Simon smiled appreciatively, then paused as he thought of something else. "Add a few rounds of ale to that order too, if you will. Vouri dark if you have any."

"Of course, master, right away, master." The tavern keeper turned and glared furiously at the serving maid. "You heard him, Vouri dark for all. I'll handle the vitals. Hettra, bless your divine little arse. Now move it."

The woman squeaked and scurried into the back.

It didn't take long for the little tavern to be in an uproar of levity. Mugs of ale clashed together as the Vouri filled their empty stomachs and cheered to Baal and company for their rescue.

"Praise Baal of House Vasara!" one man cried out. "By Teras's might, he liberated us from that vile woman."

"Praise Brena of House Vasara!" another woman cheered. "By Teras's justice, we were freed from that hell."

"Had we heeded House Vasara's warning in the first place, none of this would have happened," said another rebukingly.

"Ota Vastaan is the traitor, naked of his honor. He fled from the mines without so much as warning us. Many of us watch as he galloped away down the mountain pass alone after coming out of the mines."

"Then those beasts were upon us. We were caught off guard, and many were slaughtered."

The Vouri retold their tales of being overwhelmed by the creatures in the night. All that was left of their village were those who managed to escape and now stood before them.

Simon shook his head in disbelief at the tales. Brena retold her story of the night that Baal had discovered the Wayfarer's Gate deep in the mountain of Oitilla. Though they did not know what it was at that time. Baal had decided to close the mine shaft and keep the Gate a secret but was confronted by Ota Vastann and the mine's second-in-command, Alvar Kovaa, at Hata's feast of her first hunt. House Vasara's honor had been questioned, forcing Baal and Brena to challenge their accusers to a fight to the death. Baal had challenged Ota, while Brena had issued hers to Alvar. Alvar, a small, dishonorable man, poisoned Brena before they could fight. Baal had fought against Ota and lost. Brena forfeited her duel as she was unable to do battle. Their family was banished from Oitilla.

"Then Ota decided to reopen the mineshaft, and the *Children of Skaad* swarmed into Oitilla," Simon finished the tale. "It's a wonder any of your people survived. Why was the Delta holding the Vouri?"

One of the survivors piped up. "I overheard the guards talking one night, long ago. It was on the order of the Alpha. He didn't want anyone in Aurulan to know what was happening in the north. The Delta appeared that same night and silenced those guards for gossiping. Never saw them again. Never heard another word of rumor from another guard after that."

"The Delta heard everything that went on in her tower," another Vouri woman said eagerly. "If you made too much noise, you would be escorted out and never seen again. A few of my kinswoman crying for their babes disappeared like that."

A murmur of shock and vengeful curses toward the Delta rippled through the listeners. The entire room seemed intent on the conversation.

"The honor of House Vasara is renewed," a stout man with a greying beard and a scarred face announced. "By Teras's will, Baal and Brena have given us salvation." The man fell to a knee and put a fist to his chest. "On my house's honor, I will follow House Vasara."

A woman beside him went to her knee. "On my house's honor, I will follow House Vasara."

Then another and another. All the Vouri were on their knees one by one, pledging to Baal and Brena. "House Vasara." they all finally shouted in unison.

Baal stared out at the crowd, a pained expression on his face.

Brena placed her hand on his back comfortingly, then answered her people, "We will take you, Vouri of Oitilla. We will lead you home. Voitoon."

"Voitoon." the Vouri roared, and the tavern walls shook with the chorus of battle cries and shouts. Fists banged against tables, and feet stomped as the cheer elevated.

Baal held up a hand, and the Vouri fell silent. He gestured at his ear as if to listen, then shook his head. Then he grasped his mate's hand and held it high. His words were slow, but they rang out over the concourse. "Chieftain Brena. Voitoon."

"Voitoon. Chieftain Brena. Voitoon." The Vouri again took up the cry, swearing Brena as their chieftain.

Soon, the drinking started again, and the Vouri celebrated and ate to their heart's content.

After the uproar had calmed again, Simon murmured to the table where Kiana, Zahir, Anora, Baal, and Brena sat. "I'm afraid no village of Oitilla is left to return to Chieftain Brena. The mountain collapsed. Apparently, it was your daughter's doing."

Brena sat up abruptly in her seat. "Hata was there? How do you know this?"

"The council, well, that bastard Gaelin Yesnala said they had had reports that the mountain collapsed. That was the last place they said Hata had been. He assumes she used the Wayfarers Gate under the mountain to escape."

Brena shook her head in disbelief. "How could she do this? Is she capable of pulling down a mountain? Destroying her own home? Where could she have gone?" The questions raddled out of the mother in Brena.

"I have a few thoughts on the matter," Simon answered. "First, Hata must have destroyed many of these *Children of Skaad* when she destroyed that mountain. Second, the under-mountain Gate is now unusable. It would take years to dig it out."

Brena took a very long, anxious swig of her ale.

"That doesn't tell us where she went," Kiana added incredulously.

"I'm getting there, dear *sister*." Simon grinned and nudged Kiana in the arm playfully. "Third, Hata would not know how to configure the Gate to another Lân. That leaves one prominent location in my mind. The Skaad Lân. The very place these fell creatures are spawned."

Brena's face darkened, and Baal looked at her and then from one face to another at the table. He began to huff with irritation.

"We will not assume the worst," Simon reassured. "The lass brought down a fucking mountain for Skrull's sake. I think she can handle far more than we give her credit for. She may have escaped or, pray to Hettra, she might have killed the mastermind behind all this. However, that is doubtful. Alternatively, she is being held captive by *him*."

Brena slammed her fist against the table, and Simon jolted in his seat.

Baal jumped to his feet at the action, gripping his massive runic war hammer, unsure what to do next.

"That is also our destination, isn't it, Simon?" Kiana asked. "Aurulan plans to invade the Skaad Lân from the Forest Gate while we look for another."

"True," Simon said, then sighed regretfully. "Though I have yet to hear from the Alpha on his so-called *directions*."

"We will go with you, Chieftain," the Vouri man who had first fallen to his knees before Baal and Brena said from their side. He had been mingling in the crowd but had stayed within earshot.

Brena turned and looked at the man. "Edvard Aalto, I remember Baal knocking your lights out once when we were younglings."

"Aye, then you promptly put the big lout in his place, if I recall," Edvard said with a mischievous smile.

"Our people have been through enough," Brena answered. "I don't want to put them through further hardship."

"And what would the Vouri do if we do not follow you? Like this scrawny laddie said?" Edvard slapped Simon on the back.

Simon spluttered and coughed wine at the sudden impact. The vibrant red wine staining as it dripped down his linen shirt.

"We have no home left to return to." Edvard took no notice of Simon's sputtering. "If we idle here, the magi may seek vengeance upon us while you're all off galivanting in the Lân."

"He has a point," Anora said, "and we will need all the help we can get."

"Hasiera and Vouri together as one," Zahir said, nodding in agreement.

"A few Shepherd's Eye soldiers as well," Simon added. "By the way, has anyone seen Cad Dermont since that unfortunate council meeting?"

"The fool ran at the first sign of trouble during the meeting." Zahir snorted in disgust. "Better off without such a coward."

"He has his uses," Simon muttered under his breath. *The man probably wants me dead.* "He got us into Nidhaut using his authority. But I agree, I'd be wary to bring him to any more tense meetings we are so destined to have."

"Not to mention a real battle if he is so craven." Zahir snorted again.

"So it's settled?" Anora asked. "All roads lead to the Skaad Lân." She looked empathetically at Baal and Brena. "To Hata. To the Sunstone."

"If that bastard, Ebras Corb, gets off his ass and sends his orders," Simon hissed frustratedly. "On another note, I will attend the good Priestess's funeral tomorrow afternoon if anyone is interested in joining me."

At that moment, the doors banged open, and a hooded woman clad in black leather, followed by two heavily armored soldiers, pushed into the chamber. The crowd turned and quieted, and the hooded woman asked, "Where is Simon Meridio?"

"Here I am," Simon said, standing as the din went silent.

The woman strode toward him. The Vouri seemed hesitant to let her through, but the guards carried large glaives and created a wide berth for the woman.

Simon's party of companions, Anora, Kiana, Baal, Brena, and Zahir, all stood to meet them, their hands resting on the hilts of their weapons.

The woman stopped and sized him up. She had a belt full of pouches, a long knife, and a hand crossbow fastened to her leg in a holster. "I am Magnus Hunstman, Céline LeCouteau, speaking on behalf of the Alpha. You are to meet at the Alpha's tower at dawn tomorrow. The council members and their retinue will be there, and you will all depart for the Wayfarer's Gate in Aurulan immediately and be transported to Tal'tulu from there. Be ready."

"First thing in the morning? Can he not wait a day for us to prepare and gather supplies?"

"No," the woman said sternly, her eyes shadowed under her dark hood.

"What about the funeral? That bastard Gaelin killed Amahle in cold blood."

The woman tilted her head questioningly. "I know not what you speak of. You must be at the tower first thing in the morning or be left behind."

Simon's anger began to overtake him. His fist clenched, and he imagined casting the white-hot strings of fire straight into the woman's chest from point-blank range.

A hand rested on his shoulder.

Simon turned his head, and Anora's reassuring gaze met his own. *It is so much like Saudett's.* He thought of his wife. *She's probably being tortured in prison by Hear-fan Skaad himself. Or worse. Has the baby come? It's been months. It's nearly time.* These thoughts worried him but focused him on the greater goal. "Fine." He breathed. "We will be ready."

The woman nodded, turned on her heels, and hurriedly exited the tavern, followed by her guardsmen.

Simon sat back down with a huff. *I'm sorry, Amahle, but I won't be there to see you off to Hettra's loving embrace. I loved you as a dear companion. I pray you're at peace.*

CHAPTER THIRTY-NINE

INFIDELITY

Raine stood staring at the woman in black armor, cradling Hata in her arms, weeping. "It's all right, Hata, I'm here. I did it. I protected you."

Three winged creatures appeared out of nowhere, their wings glistening in the sunlight. They landed gracefully before the human woman holding Hata. The creatures ignored Raine's presence as they spoke to the woman in a language Raine couldn't comprehend. Suddenly, they began pulling the woman away from Hata.

"No. Leave me be. I need to stay with her." Then, the woman continued shouting in the same language as the winged ones.

The creatures restrained her and took flight. All the while, the woman screamed and reached toward Hata.

There were multiple blasts of sound from the enemy's horns, and Raine looked out over the battlefield. The Children of Skaad were retreating...*for now.* Relief washed over her as she turned back and fell to her knees at Hata's side. She took Hata's head and brushed her damp, bloodied crimson hair out of her face.

"Luminar's light." Raine pressed her lips to Hata's forehead. "I pray for your safety, Hata, my love. I'll never tell you to leave me again. So please, don't die on me. *Please.*"

Hata's eyes fluttered, and one squinted open. "Raine? I—I dreamed of Saudett." Her eyes closed again, and her face contorted in pain.

"Help!" Raine shouted. "Help, I need healing!" She called for an eternity until a regiment of Himin-dvergar soldiers came rushing along the wall to find them and carry them to safety.

Saudett blinked her eyes open. Her head was pounding, and she reached up and felt a large welt on the back of her head. *Fucking hells, Nyxal hit me hard.* Then she remembered Hata, lying beaten and burning, on the brink of death. Saudett leaped up and began to hurry out of the command tent. A chain rattled, and cold metal tugged at her ankle, and she fell to the ground.

"Knight-Commander, please calm yourself." Nyxal's voice came from the other end of the chain. He stood and walked toward her from where he had been sitting nearby. The chain was fastened to his own ankle.

"What's the meaning of this, Nyxal?" Saudett demanded. "You've defied my orders and now fasten me to you like a chained hound."

"We watched you kill Trije-fan Skaad," Nyxal said, his voice low. "We saw you protect that human woman."

Saudett stopped, weighing the words of the Nyra warrior. *Will he report me to Hear-fan? Will I be executed or worse?*

"Your loyalty does not lie with our benevolent Lord of Shadow?" Nyxal took another step toward her.

Saudett could not tell if his last words were a question or a statement. "You're wrong," She blurted. "Lord Skaad saved me. I will serve him to the end—"

"Our loyalty does not lie with him either." Nyxal placed both hands on her shoulders to calm her.

Saudett looked up into his glowing yellow eyes. They stared at her with such sympathy that tears began to well within hers. She slumped in his grip, relief flooding through her.

"We hate him," Nyxal continued. "He enslaves our people. He slaughters countless innocent beings. The Nyra simply wish to return to our caves and be free."

"But what can we do?" Saudett pleaded in desperation.

"First, we tell him our foes bested his son and killed him. He will want to regroup and renew the assault. He may even come himself to the Ryk Lân to seek his vengeance. If *you* can get close, strike him down when he least expects it. That is our greatest chance."

Saudett thought back to Hear-fan Skaad rapidly healing his wounds after being crushed under rubble. "Do you think it's possible? Can he even be harmed?"

"It must be a decisive blow. Try to remove the vile bastard's head."

"Difficult to do with a spear," Saudett muttered incredulously.

"I will be watchful should you try to take him in the open. I will ensure he does not survive." Nyxal bared his sharp teeth eagerly.

"Betrayal does not befit you, my dear Gesche-fan Skaad," Hear-fan Skaad's voice came from outside the tent. Then he pushed the curtain aside and strolled in casually.

With a blood-curdling shriek, Nyxal launched himself at the Lord of Shadow. Clearly, their plans had been thwarted, and Nyxal was not holding back. His swords glinted in the dim light as they appeared in his hands, and he swung them fiercely at his opponent.

However, the Lord of Shadow was not unprepared. With a swift hand motion, a barrier of violet light appeared before him, effectively blocking Nyxal's blows. The impact of the swords against the barrier caused a reverberating sound to resonate through the chamber, and Nyxal was thrown back by the force of the barrier.

"*Scau Windan,*" Hear-fan said flatly, flicking his wrist as he did so.

The blast of sharpened violet wind struck Nyxal as he found his footing. He sucked in a breath as his torso fell from his legs, and two pieces of his wings flopped to the ground. Blood began to spray out of him as he spasmed, his wings thumping as more blood spurted out of them where they had been shorn. Gradually, Nyxal's cries of agony died away to silence, as did the warrior himself.

Hear-fan stood watching Saudett intently. "You killed my son. You will bear me another."

Saudett's eyes widened in horror as the pleading words flew from her lips, "No, please, no. My Lord, I—"

"First, you will learn your place, caged in my home's deepest, darkest hole." He snapped his fingers, and two hulks entered the tent and crudely took her away after dislodging the legs of the corpse of Nyxal from the chain.

Saudett watched as Hear-fan Skaad stood like a statue brooding within the tent. He vanished from sight as the curtains closed behind her. She was carried, screaming in terror, to the Wayfarer's Gate under the darkening shadows of navy-black clouds.

CHAPTER FORTY

PREPARE

Simon looked out at the shining beauty of the sparkling sea. The gentle waves washed against the white sands of the beach. Palm trees swayed, and a coconut fell. A ship with a bright red sail lumbered by in the distance. He breathed in the salty air and then returned to the gathering of people on the beach behind him. It was an odd gathering of nearly three thousand in all. The council mages, the Gamma and the Theta, had bolstered their forces with their own personal guards and acolytes of magic. A mixture of Hasieran, Vouri, and Shepherd's Eye comprised nearly a thousand heads of their troops.

I pray to Hettra that at least they will be loyal to me.

Anora, Kiana, and Zahir stood at the head of the nomadic peoples of Hasiera. Brena, flanked by Baal and Edvard, stood before the Vouri. Captain Cad Dermont had finally shown up with his few hundred Shepherd's Eye soldiers. The Theta, Cygne Caladrius, and the Gamma, Lila Parakeet, waited patiently in front of their superior numbers.

Here I am, leading this rag-tag group of misfits into a war against an all-powerful being of doom. Simon looked past the gathered people to the island where they had emerged from the Wayfarer's Gate. There was nothing else on the island. No civilisation. There were other islands within sight but not within easy swimming distance. They had gathered a hasty amount of supplies for the voyage. Luckily, the magi had been overprepared on that front. Not to mention, they currently had a direct supply line through the Wayfarers Gate to Aurulan. The gates were configured to one another and would stay that way until they decided to attack the Skaad Lân. The enemy would be unable to use the portals while they were active.

The Alpha had met them at the base of his tower. All three thousand men and women had poured through a mystical crack of light in the very fabric of the air and found themselves standing in the woods beside the Forest Gate, as it had come to be called. From there, they entered that Gate to find themselves on this island. Simon was still amazed that it had taken less than an hour to travel thousands of miles across the Earste Lân.

He shook himself from his thoughts and took a breath to compose himself. Then, he strengthened his voice with *Gebod*. "I hope you all enjoy coconut milk and fish because we will be here awhile."

Laughter rippled through the men and women.

"We need to build a camp here and protect this Gate. Then..." he paused, shading his eyes as he turned to look out over the sea. "We need a Skrull-damned boat."

EPILOGUE

Hata awoke and felt warm, soft skin against her arm, leg, and side. She strained to open her eyes in the dim light and painfully turned her head to see Raine snuggled up against her. The woman's gentle breath caused her chest to rise and fall asleep. She wore nothing but her under wraps and a few bandages. It was as if Raine's touch could ease the pain and make everything all right again. Hata was grateful for Raine's presence and the comfort that she provided.

Then, the memories flooded back. *Teras's thunder, what in—Saudett was here.* Hata remembered the silhouette of the winged man and then Saudett's appearance over her. *Not Raine. What happened?* Hata tried to move but was too weak to do so. Wrapped nearly from head to toe in bandages with the round healing discs of malachite beneath them.

Raine stirred at her side and quietly murmured, "Are you awake?"

"I am."

Raine's eyes opened sleepily, and her hazel gaze found Hata's. Raine's face colored slightly, and she smiled with genuine affection.

All other thoughts fled as Hata was suddenly struck by how beautiful Raine was. *Gods, I want to kiss her.*

As if reading her mind, Raine propped herself on her arm and leaned over Hata.

Hata closed her eyes and let herself enjoy Raine's essence as their lips tenderly caressed. Hata let all other thoughts fade as she focused on the woman she loved. The war, the enemy, the pain, Saudett, and even thoughts of her parents melted away as she kissed Raine Stormfall, Queen of the Himin-dvergar.

Their lips parted, and Hata whispered with all her love and devotion, "I love you, my Queen."

"I love you, my Sunstone," Raine murmured as she leaned in again.

REVIEWS

Thanks for reading!

As an independent or self-published author, marketing and promoting my business is ultimately out of my pocket. One of the most incredible things a reader can do to help with this is to leave a review. This will help other readers become interested in buying my books and give me more visibility in the marketplace.

If you liked **The Wayfarers War**, please leave me a review on the store where you purchased the book.

EARLY ACCESS

If you wish to support me further and are interested in reading the next book in the series before anyone else, consider subscribing to me at ReamStories. You can read the first chapter of the next book for FREE by following me on REAM or subscribe for access to the entire book or weekly release.

Thank you for your support,

Nicolin Odel

THE SUNSTONE SAGA

About the Author

Nicolin lives in the Greater Toronto Area with his wife and two daughters, writing books, gaming, drinking beer, gardening, or shoveling snow.

For more information:

www.nicolinodel.com

Email – nicolin.odel@nicolinodel.com

www.ingramcontent.com/pod-product-compliance
Lightning Source LLC
Chambersburg PA
CBHW061809190726

48289CB00007B/2133